Caught in the Act

Also by Kim Law

The Davenports

Caught on Camera

Sugar Springs

Sugar Springs

Sweet Nothings

Sprinkles on Top

Turtle Island Novels

Ex on the Beach

Hot Buttered Yum

Two Turtle Island Doves (A Novella)

Caught in the Act

KIM LAW

Ⓜ Montlake
Romance

Published by Montlake Romance, Seattle

www.apub.com

Amazon, the Amazon logo, and Montlake are trademarks of Amazon.com, Inc., or its affiliates.

ISBN-13: 9781477821220
ISBN-10: 1477821228

Cover design by becker&mayer! LLC

Library of Congress Control Number: 2014913870

Printed in the United States of America

To Paula Jenkins. Thanks for the title!
I miss seeing your happiness every day.

CHAPTER ONE

*H*ANDS DOWN, THAT WAS THE BEST ASS SHE'D EVER SEEN. It was even better at fifteen times magnification.

Catherine Davenport Carlton leaned over the kitchen sink, resting her elbows on the faucet handles to steady her arms, and gripped the binoculars a little tighter. She bit down on her lower lip as she watched. The jogger was heading in the opposite direction—exactly as he'd done the last two mornings—and if recent events were any indicator, he'd be heading back up the beach and passing by her rental within the hour.

Cute Butt rounded the bend in the distance and disappeared from sight, and Cat straightened from peering through the window like a stalker. She pursed her lips as she thought about how she'd spent her mornings since she'd arrived in Maine. She really should stop ogling her neighbor.

But then again, maybe she should just get up the nerve and cross their backyards to introduce herself. Then she could ogle up close.

She grinned at the picture that brought to mind. What was an escape from reality without a summer tryst thrown in to take her mind off things?

Shaking her head at her unladylike thoughts, she dumped berries and protein powder into the blender and topped it off with yogurt and flaxseed. Her one true ability as a "cook" was a healthy breakfast smoothie—which, combined with daily yoga, barely kept the width of her hips in check. Then she went back to thinking about her neighbor.

She couldn't have an affair. Even if she wasn't in the last place she'd ever consider having a fling, it had been over four years since she'd been naked with a man. Nineteen years since she'd been naked with anyone *other* than her late husband. She wouldn't know what to do with her neighbor if she caught him.

Of course . . . it *was* supposed to be just like riding a bike.

And she *was* there alone for three more weeks before her kids would show up.

She turned off the blender and grabbed a glass, reminding herself that she wasn't that adventurous. Not these days. Maybe she had been nineteen years ago when she'd seen that *other* naked man. Only, with him at fifteen, he hadn't exactly been a man. They'd both been only kids—but she *had* been willing to take a few risks back then.

Which had turned out like shit.

She sighed.

Her teenage tryst was the reason she'd chosen Maine as her getaway destination. Or rather, what had happened *because* of Brody was the reason. It was time to find closure. To figure out a way to forgive herself.

But she was also here for an escape. From her job as well as from her kids.

Her kids were great. Truly. They were her life. She loved them more than she could have ever imagined possible. But she'd been a single mother for four years now, and she needed a break.

And then there was her job.

She closed her eyes and rubbed a finger back and forth across her temple. Running her family's foundation wasn't easy. She was good at it, yes. Actually, great at it. She'd perfected the art of showcasing herself and her family in only the best light years ago. But she'd grown antsy over the past months. She wanted . . . *more*. Or maybe she wanted less.

A family legacy started by her great-great-grandfather, the Davenport Foundation served many organizations in the Atlanta area, as well as all of Georgia, and Cat had been director for the last five years. Only this year had she hired someone to share the load with her. But what she was finding was, the more the other woman did, the less Cat wanted to do. Yet Cat was a Davenport. Maybe it was no longer her legal name, but it would always be who she was.

How could she be any less?

And did she want to?

These were questions she hoped her time in Maine would answer. Not to mention, she now had to wrap her head around just who her family really was. They were supposed to be the revered Davenports. Upstanding, moral greatness representing the United States in one way or another for over a century.

They did no wrong.

Only . . . they had. A lot.

Her own secret flashed brightly in her mind. She'd believed for almost nineteen years that she was the only Davenport to risk tarnishing the name.

The flame of anger that had been churning inside her since her recent conversation with her brother grew brighter. Given the truth about her family that she now knew, her mother could have lessened her guilt all those years ago. All it would have taken was a few simple words.

Yet she hadn't done it.

The reality was, she'd only made Cat feel more guilty.

Cat peeked out the kitchen window again at the still-quiet stretch of beach running past her rental, grateful for her in-laws. They'd been able to fly to Atlanta a few days earlier than planned so she could go ahead and get away. They were all staying at Cat's house now, but the kids had Disney World to look forward to, then another week at their grandparents' Florida condo before returning home, and eventually up here to Maine. It was time to introduce them to the town the Davenports had once called home.

This wouldn't be a one-time-only trip, either. She intended to resume her long-ago ritual of summer breaks on coastal Maine. Becca and Tyler deserved that.

And she deserved to move on from the past.

Of course, they all had to survive her mother's and father's pasts first—which she hoped stayed buried.

She rinsed out the blender as she thought about what the next few months might bring.

Her mother was running for reelection for her Senate seat in the fall, and her opponent's family was known for slinging mud. Congressman Harrison was looking for dirt. And it seemed he had his pick to choose from.

Lies, secrets, and illegitimate brothers. All his for the taking.

All he had to do was find them.

Cat ground her teeth together as she grabbed her smoothie and cell phone and headed to the deck, remembering at the last minute to take the binoculars as well. Her kids would be calling soon to wish her a good morning.

And then her neighbor would be making his way back down the beach.

Since family values had been blown out of the water, she figured she might as well embrace the new peeping-tom side of herself. Why worry about maintaining high morals when no one else around her did?

———   ———

Twenty minutes later, as Cat sat at a bistro-size table on the overlarge deck, her eyes glued to the blue-gray waves beyond the sand, her cell finally rang. She took the last sip of her smoothie and reached for the phone.

It would be Becca. At seven years old, Becca was the oldest and was very similar to her mother in that she took pleasure in making sure things got done. She and Tyler were supposed to call every morning after they got up. Thus, Becca would wear her grandmother out until that happened.

Cat relaxed into her chair as she answered. She'd rarely been apart from her kids, and though she would enjoy the extended time away, she couldn't help the sudden feeling of being alone in the world as she sat there, eleven hundred miles from everyone who meant anything to her.

"Hello, sweet girl," she answered, making sure she emoted nothing but happiness.

"Hey, Shortie," her brother's deep voice said into her ear.

Cat jolted upright at JP's words. She was still mad at him for keeping her in the dark about the family secrets. He'd been trying to reach her for days but she'd ignored his calls. "What are you doing calling me from my house?" she asked.

"I had to. It was the only way to get you on the phone." When she said nothing, he added, "Come on, Cat. You have to talk to me."

No she didn't. He'd lied to her for months. It infuriated her.

Of all her family members, JP was the one she was closest to. She'd thought they'd had a bond. He was *not* supposed to keep things from her.

Especially things that could potentially drag their whole family into a scandal.

But most importantly, he was not supposed to keep things from her.

"Don't hang up," JP said, clearly sensing that she might do just that. "I needed to make sure you're all right." His voice took on a brotherly concern that she knew well, which only irritated her more. "I dropped a lot on you the other day," he added. "Are you okay?"

"Of course I'm okay," she snapped. "I just don't want to talk to you. I'd think not returning your calls would have sent that message. Now put my daughter on the phone."

"I will as soon as we finish. Plus, they're eating right now. I made them French toast."

Oh . . . her stomach growled, even though it was full of fruit and flaxseed. JP's French toast was the best.

"I'm sure their grandmother would have made them breakfast," she muttered. Though JP's food was still ten times better than anything Colette Carlton was likely to make. JP had once hired a celebrity chef to train him.

"Of course she would have, but I wanted to see them before they left town. Plus, Becca bribed me into cooking."

Cat could picture her blonde-haired, blue-eyed daughter doing just that, and another pang of loneliness engulfed her. Unlike the middle-child tendency to always try to smooth things over that Cat couldn't seem to shake, her daughter often took another tack. That of bribery to get what she wanted.

"What did she do?" Cat asked, her tone easing, but only because she was thinking of her child. "Threaten to tell your new wife that you like to play with dolls when she's not around?"

JP chuckled, assuring her that Vega already knew all his secrets, and the happy sound of his voice softened Cat's heart. Her brother had been through a lot in his life, and even though she was mad at him, it didn't lessen her love.

Nor her gratitude.

He'd been the perfect uncle over the years, making sure both of her kids had a father figure in their lives after her husband, Joe, hadn't returned home from Afghanistan. It had meant more to her than she would ever be able to express.

Which only added to her frustration now.

She managed the foundation. She managed *both* her mother and JP—in one form or another. She cleaned up the family messes. Why in the hell was she suddenly relegated to a need-to-know basis?

The slight made her want to say *screw it* to both of them and go do her own thing.

And that was the real issue.

She was a mother, a sister, a daughter, a Davenport. She would someday be the final caretaker for her in-laws. But she couldn't remember the last time she'd simply been Cat.

She caught herself straightening her spine as if someone might see her and think she wasn't prepared for whatever was thrown her way. Of course she was prepared. She was always prepared.

"I also called because I wanted to tell you about today's headline." JP spoke softly, as if trying not to be heard. His tone yanked Cat's mind out of her seething, and a pinch started in the dead center of her shoulder blades.

"What's happened now?" she asked. She closed her eyes and pictured herself relaxing, the stress easing from her body.

The fact that the Harrisons had begun snooping into Davenport business had been the impetus for JP to come clean about what he'd learned last summer. He hadn't wanted Cat to be caught unaware, he'd said. Therefore she'd learned that their older brother, Bennett, was not a biological Davenport.

And that they also had an illegitimate younger brother who *was* a Davenport.

Then there was the whole payoff thing both her parents had been involved in with the mother of the eight-year-old. And oh, by the way, JP was now funding the kid's private education.

Cat could not understand how any of that had happened. This was not who they were!

"The tabloids ran a story today," JP began, and a dull pounding started just behind her left temple. She squinted against the pain. "They suggested that Mom got the Senate appointment last year because of her relationship with Governor Chandler."

"She did not!" Cat argued. There was no way her mother had slept her way into the Senate, no matter what family scandals she might have kept hidden. "Did they happen to have any facts to back it up?"

She was already running scenarios through her head of things they could do to bring the right kind of focus back to their mom's campaign. She'd make some calls, check into regional billboards showcasing the good her mom had already done during her short time in office. A TV spot wouldn't hurt, either.

"Of course not," JP answered. "They only pointed out the close relationship Governor Chandler has had with all of us over the years. And not-so-subtly hinted that it was a lot more than friendship with Mom."

They *were* all good friends. More so over the last eight years since their dad had died.

And yes, the governor *did* have a crush on their mother. That had been clear to the siblings for a while now. But it had never become more than that. Despite everything else, Emma Davenport prided herself on her abilities. She'd worked long and hard to see her family succeed in politics—always her husband's support, keeping the name first and foremost in the community, and at times, probably being more of an elected official than her husband had been. No way would she stoop to sleeping her way to the top.

She'd simply been the best person for the job, and Chandler had known that.

That wouldn't matter to the Harrisons, of course. They'd use whatever they could find, whether facts or lies.

Cat sighed into the phone and once again slumped back in the chair. "I hate this, JP. I'm sick at how nasty the next few months could get. I hate knowing that I have to be even more careful with everything I say, and anybody I say it to." She stared out at the ocean and let the sound of the waves penetrate her mind. "Sometimes it's enough to make me want to live in a place like this with Becca and Tyler. One where we can just *be*."

Her kids would love it there. They would start and end every day on the beach. In between those hours, they'd be normal kids with normal lives.

"They're going to have the best time when they get up there,"

JP said. He and Vega would be bringing them up later in the month. "They'll be begging you to take them back every year."

"I'm not talking about a summer trip, brother," she said drily.

She cut her words off and closed her eyes again. She didn't mean it, of course. Her job was with the foundation. Her commitment to her family. She couldn't just run away.

But oh, how she often wished she had more choices in her life.

JP was quiet for several seconds before hesitantly asking, "Are you serious?"

Yes!

"Of course not," she answered.

She opened her eyes and focused on the clear blue sky. It was going to be another beautiful Maine day. Inside her chest, she ached. But for what, she didn't really know.

"Just ignore me," she said. "I'm still upset about all the lies. About you keeping everything from me. And about all that our parents were up to over the years." That thudding in her temple increased.

"I know, and I am sorry," JP apologized. "I should have told you last summer when Lexi first came to me about Dad being the father of her son. But I knew you and Dad were close, Cat. I hated the thought of tarnishing that for you. Since Lexi has no interest in Daniel's lineage coming out, it felt like I didn't have to." JP's serious tone made a sad smile lift the corners of Cat's lips.

She had been close with her father. As the only girl, she'd once been the apple of his eye.

And yes, learning he'd been unfaithful with a young girl working on his presidential campaign had damaged her memory of him. But it wasn't as if she'd ever thought him perfect. He'd been a driven man. She'd known that all her life.

"You most definitely should have told me when Mom confessed that Dad wasn't Bennett's father," she chastised, refusing to let him off the hook. Their mother had come clean with that juicy morsel last summer as well. Only, she hadn't shared *who* the father was. That would be for Bennett to worry about, if he was so inclined. She and JP had their hands full with all the other issues. "Have you heard from Bennett?" she asked.

"Nothing," JP confirmed. "I've got calls in to several people, but haven't been able to find out anything about where he's stationed. If he's gotten my messages, he's either where he can't return the call, or he's choosing not to."

She'd bet on the latter.

Bennett was career army. He'd barely come back home since he'd left at eighteen. She couldn't help but worry about him, though. More than usual. According to their mother, he wasn't aware that his father was anyone but the man he'd grown up with. However, Cat had realized as a kid that Bennett had been treated differently. She'd simply had no idea why.

He'd publicly been the honored oldest son of Jackson Parker Davenport Sr. Pride had shone from every pore of her father's being. Yet at home, her father had barely had anything to do with him. It hadn't been blatant, as he'd often had little time for JP either, but Cat had spent years watching this play out. She'd never mentioned it to Bennett, but she knew he couldn't have missed it.

This difference had likely led to him choosing to spend the last twenty years of his life *away* from his family instead of making sure to see them when he was stateside.

But if the truth of his parentage managed to get out before they were able to tell him in person, she could only imagine that would hurt him worse. Learning the news would be bad enough. Learning it from the tabloids?

Unforgiveable.

"I'll try to reach him, too," she told JP. "Maybe if he gets a message from both of us he'll realize it's not simply a request to check in. And I'll work on something to take the focus off Mom and the governor."

"No need," JP said. "She's putting out a press release Monday detailing a bill she'll be presenting to Congress. It'll get the attention back where it needs to be."

Her mother always had a backup. She may have only stepped into the limelight the previous year, but she was a born politician.

A moving shape came into view far down the beach and Cat smiled. She couldn't help it. It was the highlight of her day. What was a little vacation without secret fantasies involving a hot stranger?

If only she had the guts to see if she could make it more.

She picked up the binoculars and put them to her eyes.

"Here comes Becca," JP said in her ear.

Before he could hand the phone to her daughter, Cat spoke his name.

"Yes?" he answered.

"Don't do it again." She didn't have to say what *it* was. *Don't keep me in the dark.* "I deserve better."

"I won't. And yes, you do."

Brody Hollister pulled his T-shirt over his head as he continued running toward his beach house and mopped at his sweaty brow. Before he could stop himself, he let his gaze travel beyond his house to the one on the far side of it.

It was a large home. Close to twice the size of his—though his wasn't small. With an even larger front yard. That's what had attracted Brody to the area. The houses not only sat on one of the few sandy beaches along the rocky coastline, but they were, for the most part, secluded from the road. Large pines filled both yards, while gates remained closed at the ends of the driveways.

Not that he needed the privacy himself, but having it was nice.

There were other houses in the area, spaced out farther down the beach, but these were the only two that sat side by side. They'd been built together several years ago, his once being the guesthouse for the original owners of the bigger home. Those owners rarely spent time there these days, instead renting out their remaining property pretty much year-round.

A celebrity showing up for the summer wasn't out of the question, usually with a passel of kids or extended family. But this year's guest had shocked him.

It had gone to a single woman.

Who, yes, was a celebrity in her own right. Her family name made her one. But she'd been the last person he would have expected to find next door.

Catherine Davenport Carlton had shown up a few days earlier, and if rumors were to be believed, hadn't left the inside of the house for more than groceries since she'd arrived. She had ventured out to her deck, of course. He'd seen that one firsthand.

According to those same rumors, she was here for the month. But what he really wanted to know was why she'd landed in the beachfront rental next door to him instead of at the Davenport compound farther down the coast.

Everyone in the small town was abuzz about that very fact themselves.

Having a Davenport around wasn't all that unusual. The family had originated from Dyersport, after all. They'd owned their home and several pieces of land in the county for more than a century. Not to mention, they were a far-reaching bunch.

There were cousins, uncles, aunts, grandparents. Many of them had been involved in US politics in one way or another for decades. Several of them came to town on a regular basis for vacations and getaways.

But never did they stay in a rental on the beach.

Yet there she sat, blonde hair shining on the back deck, looking for all the world as if she belonged there. He watched her as he continued to jog in her direction. She had one hand to her ear as if talking on a phone. Her other was raised to her eyes, her face turned in his direction.

She'd been out there each morning since she'd arrived. Sitting at the little glass-topped table, leaned back in the chair, but with her back straight and one leg crossed over the other.

Pretending she wasn't watching him.

She wore what he thought of as her "Davenport air." He saw it anytime she got captured on television or in the papers. She never had a hair out of place or appeared to be anything but important and influential. Just like every other member of her family. It made his stomach clench each time he witnessed it. All that fakeness was too much. He preferred things simple and straightforward.

That's why he lived on the beach. He had his job, his hobbies, and he had his town. He didn't need what Cat brought to the party—even if finding out she was next door had stirred up something he hadn't felt in years. Mostly curiosity. But there was more to it than that. Something that kept him watching her as carefully as she was watching him.

He wondered if she recognized him. Did she know who lived next door?

But then, how could she not? It was likely the reason she'd rented the house.

And not, he suspected, due to their past. Not because of some long-lost need to have a conversation he might have once yearned for. They'd been teenagers, for heaven's sake. Kids. It had meant nothing to either of them.

No. She was there because she'd discovered who his brother was. Why else would she have binoculars?

Though how she'd pulled that off, he had no idea. No one knew who his brother was.

He wiped his brow once more, annoyed at the thought of her renting the house to spy on him. Did she think he wouldn't figure out what she was up to?

She wouldn't find anything useful; that was for sure. He rarely spoke to his brother, hadn't seen him in person in years, and *never* spoke to his "father." He had zero information that could be of value to a Davenport.

Cat lowered the phone and clasped both hands in her lap, taking on that air he so despised. He'd once thought she was different than that. Different than every other politician he'd ever known. No matter who her family was.

She turned to face the ocean as he neared, and he had the urge to make a right and confront her. He wanted to ask why she'd quit taking his calls all those years ago. Why hadn't she come back the next summer as they'd each promised? What in the hell had changed from one week to the next?

But then, he supposed he knew.

He'd seen pictures of her and Joseph Carlton in a DC paper the following summer. The man had gone on to become her husband, while Brody had deduced that the DC trip had been the lowest point of his life.

And not because of Cat.

He passed by her house without so much as a glance in her direction. He had five miles to get in before he began the day ahead of him, and he didn't miss workouts.

Being distracted by a woman who was up to no good was not an option.

CHAPTER TWO

CAT LET OFF THE BRAKES OF THE HONDA SEDAN AND MADE the turn from the narrow side road onto Main. It was Monday morning. She'd spent the remainder of the weekend alternately staring at her neighbor, thinking about how people had flings all the time, and taking late evening walks on the beach.

And continuing to shake her head at the depth of her family's secrets.

Her mother had called both Saturday and Sunday, but Cat had let the calls go to voice mail. Her mother could be a little much sometimes, and Cat hadn't been ready to talk to her yet.

She wasn't sure when she'd be ready.

She opened the sunroof of the car to let in fresh air but was careful not to open it too far so as not to mess up her hair. She had a good impression to make that morning. Not just for herself, but for her whole family.

After talking to JP on Saturday morning and then looking up the offending tabloids online, she'd decided that her mother's planned press release could use a bit more oomph. She'd talked to her brother again yesterday, and the two of them had agreed to make a generous donation to the Dyersport Museum and Historical Center.

There was a Davenport collection on display there that she'd been sending family memorabilia to for years. She intended to spend the morning enjoying the exhibits before talking to the proprietor about making a monetary donation. She also had an AP reporter out of Portland scheduled to show up later in the day for pictures. The article should run nationally.

She did worry that a donation might bring attention to her being in the area, but was hopeful they could keep the focus on the good the Davenports were doing and not on the fact that one of them just happened to be in Dyersport.

The people of the town knew she was there, of course. The few times she'd left the house she'd caught more than one person eyeing her as if excited to see what she might do next. But it was a laid-back little place. They weren't into following her every move just because of who she was. And if Cat were to bet, she'd say they weren't into running to the tabloids to report she'd been seen buying strawberries at the supermarket, either.

At least, it hadn't happened so far.

Not that the paparazzi were a huge concern for her in Atlanta, either. That was mostly her brother's issue, though less now that he was married. He was the epitome of hot, and until last year he'd been expected to follow in their father's political footsteps. His refusal to accept the Senate seat left vacant by their cousin's unexpected death had given their mother the opportunity to finally step forward.

However, paparazzi following *her* or not, the world never stopped watching. That meant Cat was always careful with everything she said and did.

She drove along Main Street, taking in the quaint storefronts lining the edges of the sidewalks, each building painted a different color. Yellow, orange, pink, green, blue, lavender. It was charming and added a nice sense of comfort. Dyersport was a calm, lovely place to spend a few weeks. She was glad she'd come. Even if everything she saw did make her think of her last summer here.

Her first-born daughter would have graduated high school last month had she lived.

Not that Cat would have been around to witness it. She'd made the painful decision to give her daughter up. That fact still weighed heavy on her heart. She should have done better for her. At times, she'd wondered if Annabelle had died of a broken heart because she'd believed her mother hadn't wanted her.

Which was ridiculous; Cat knew that. Annabelle had been born sick. Cat's mother had found out months later that the baby hadn't made it. While Cat had been clueless that her little girl had been struggling to live.

Alive or not, Cat had been unable to forgive herself for walking away from her daughter.

She hadn't had a choice; she understood that. She'd been sixteen and her father had been running for reelection to the House. He hadn't needed a pregnant teen on the campaign trail.

But giving her baby up had destroyed Cat's spirit. It had changed her.

Given the chance for a redo, she'd often wondered if she would make the same decisions a second time. Was that really the type of person she was? Or had she merely let circumstances convince her otherwise?

Possibly her guilt had as much to do with Brody as anything. She'd never told him. She'd tried. But she could have tried harder. He'd been even younger than she was, and no doubt as ill-prepared for parenthood as she. But still . . .

Telling him was one decision she most definitely would do differently the second time around.

He'd been from New Hampshire, here that summer attending a program at St. Mary's College when they'd met and become fast friends. Nights of hanging out at beach parties had turned into more. She'd given him her heart.

They'd had a glorious last day together that had ended with them making love. Then they'd gone their separate ways.

Promises had been made. They'd talk, keep in touch. They'd return the next summer.

But little of that had happened.

There had been a few phone calls. Great calls. Calls she'd anxiously waited for.

And then nothing.

Cat couldn't help but believe his life was better *not* knowing he had a kid who'd died, though. That was a pain she wouldn't wish upon anyone.

She pulled her head back out of the past and realized she was being watched. She smiled and waved at the residents dotted along the sidewalks. Some appeared to be owners opening up shop, others out for a morning walk. All with an easygoing sense about them. All seemingly blissfully happy. It made her once again think about how Becca and Tyler would love this town. She was anxious to get them up here.

Though she was just as anxious to enjoy her remaining free time as a single woman.

Which once again made her think of summer flings and getting naked with strangers.

She mentally rolled her eyes at the thought. She couldn't allow her hormones to get the best of her. The risk of dragging her kids into the middle of something like that wasn't worth it.

Heck, the risk of dragging *herself* into something like that wasn't worth it.

With her luck, it would make the front page of the national news. *Cat Carlton finally dates again.*

She sighed. She couldn't let that happen. This was a trip about remaining *under* the radar.

Instead of driving straight through the square and taking the direct route to the museum, she turned beside a florist's shop and headed down a street where she could see additional stores lining both sides of the road. She'd looked up a bakery before heading out, having decided to arrive at the museum bearing tasty treats. It seemed a good way to start her introduction off right.

Several minutes later, as she slid back behind the wheel of her car with an armful of white boxes, she breathed in a lungful of sweet bread and salty air and reached out to close her door. When she did, a sign in a window across the street caught her attention. Sea Mist Playhouse.

Dyersport had a community theater? Her pulse sped up. She hadn't been in a local theater in years. She'd loved being in the drama club in high school. She'd even been somewhat of a star.

If only in her mind.

She pulled the keys from the ignition and hurried across the asphalt to the entrance of the building to find a small sign stating that opening night for the next play would be this Friday.

Too late to audition.

She took a quick step back, almost falling in her haste, shocked that the thought had entered her mind. She wouldn't want to audition even if there was time. She hadn't done anything like that in years.

But she could come back and see the play. That would be fun.

Hurrying to her car, she pulled out of her parking spot feeling more lighthearted than she had in a long time, and made the turn onto Main. That lightheartedness allowed her to answer her phone when it rang. It was her mother.

"Catherine." Her mother breathed the word out as if Cat had been missing for weeks.

"Hi, Mom. I'm just heading to the museum." JP had filled their mother in on their plans. "Do you have your press release ready to go today?"

"I'm fine, yes. It's set to go out within the hour. But are you okay? It's not like you to not take my calls. I've been worried sick."

No, it wasn't like her. Normally she immediately jumped when her mother called, but this *was* her vacation. The way she saw it, she could ignore phone calls while on vacation if she wanted to. Especially when the subject matter wasn't something she was anxious to discuss.

She chewed on the inside of her lip as she thought about how to best answer her mother. No, she was not okay. Each of her parents had had a kid with someone else. They'd paid off her dad's mistress. She wasn't happy about any of it.

But she didn't want to say all that. "I've been better," she finally conceded.

"I know it's a shock to learn. I wanted to tell you before."

"You did?" Then why hadn't she? That had bothered her, too. JP had found out, and still, her mother had kept it from her.

"It's just," her mother hedged, "there was no need to worry you. Nothing changes. We're still the same people we were."

Which was part of the problem. Cat was now confused as to who her parents were. Certainly not the people she'd always believed them to be.

"It doesn't make a lot of sense to me, Mom. None of it. And then, you wrote a check to that girl? A *big* check."

"I had to. I did it for her son."

The girl in question had been a seventeen-year-old volunteer at her dad's campaign headquarters. And Cat kept finding herself questioning the validity of her mother's explanation. Had it really been for the child?

Or to keep the underage girl quiet?

"Everything I've done is for the good of the family," her mother said. "I've always had nothing but the best of intentions. You know that. You know I'll do whatever it takes to maintain our high integrity."

Like hiding her own pregnant teenage daughter. "It's just a lot to take in," Cat said.

"I know. But surely you can understand. We all do what we have to do."

The passive-aggressive barb was directed at her. Cat had allowed herself to go "abroad" for the school year; she'd told no one she was pregnant—including the rest of her family—then she'd given her baby to another woman.

She'd had to.

If she hadn't, her father's political career could have been cut short. She'd loved her father, and it would have destroyed him in more ways than one.

Only . . . she'd lived with regrets since, and she wasn't so sure her mother had ever regretted anything. At least she'd never said as much to Cat.

Cat braked at a stoplight, seeing the museum several blocks ahead, and thought about that morning's call from her brother. It pained her that she was questioning her mother's words at this point, but she found she couldn't help it. "You *didn't* actually sleep with Governor Chandler, right?" she asked.

"What? Of course not." Her mom came across as highly affronted. "How could you even think that?"

"I don't think it. Not really. I just . . ." She just didn't know what to think anymore.

"Well, of course I didn't," her mother soothed. "You know better than that. Douglas and I are merely friends. Exactly as he is with you and your brother. Now tell me about this house you're renting up there." Her mother easily changed gears. "Is it safe? I'd prefer you were at the family compound."

"I'm perfectly fine where I am, Mom. You can barely see my rental from the road." She'd reserved the house months ago when she'd first decided to spend the summer there. She wanted to be a normal person for a few weeks. Not "a Davenport." So the beach house had become a must. "Plus," she added, "I'm not JP. No one cares what I do."

"Well, that doesn't keep me from worrying."

"I know." She wheeled one-handed to a stop in front of the historic building. "And thank you for worrying. But I need to go now. I just pulled up at the museum."

"Okay, but be careful at that house. Anything could happen out there."

"Anything could happen anywhere, Mom. I'll talk to you later."

She grabbed the boxes off her passenger seat and stepped from the car, pushing aside the remaining unease about her mother. Things happened. People made mistakes. She was as aware of that as anyone.

So okay, her parents had made mistakes, too. She supposed they were allowed. She just never would have imagined it.

She glanced down at herself before going in the museum. White cotton eyelet skirt, coral polka-dot sleeveless top, and cute wedge sandals to match. She looked fun and hip, yet professional. Perfect. Time to make an impression.

The front door of the building creaked slightly as she pushed it open, and soft music hit her ears. Dark, glossy wood surrounded her on the floors and four feet up the walls, before heading up along the staircase to the second floor. She glanced around and found a woman, probably thirty years her senior, smiling softly at her from behind a reception desk.

"Welcome to the Dyersport Museum and Historical Center," the lady said, her voice cheery and polite, and sounding like it was just barely able to contain a secret she wanted desperately to share. Her hair was pulled back into a sedate bun at the base of her neck, and she wore a long dress that looked like something out of another century.

It was the same costume that had been used twenty years ago. Cat had volunteered there one day a week before she'd stopped coming up with her cousins for the summers.

"Thank you," Cat greeted her. She gave a polite nod. "I'm Catherine Davenport Carlton. My family has a collection on exhibit here. I thought I'd stop by and see it."

"Of course. I know who you are, Ms. Carlton. Welcome." The woman waved a hand, motioning her closer. "It's a pleasure to have you here. I'd heard you were in town."

Cat nodded. She'd assumed word had gotten around. She held up the boxes in her hands. "I brought doughnuts."

"Ah. From Lily's Bakery." The woman patted her stomach, which was not flat by any means. "I started there this morning myself." Her eyes glowed as she took in the boxes, as if someone had plopped a cake piled high with frosting down right in front of her and told her it was all for her. She gave Cat a wink. "But that was over an hour ago."

Cat laughed. She already liked this woman.

"My name is Louisa. Let's put those in the break room, then we'll find Janet. She's the owner. I'm sure she'll be thrilled to show you around."

"Sounds perfect, Louisa. Thank you so much."

As Cat trailed behind the other woman, she took in everything her gaze could seek out. From the outside, the museum looked smaller than it really was. Inside there were hallways and rooms stretched out in every direction. She peeked into the rooms as they passed, running her gaze over centuries worth of treasures she couldn't wait to explore. She wasn't a history fanatic, but when it came to the country's story, she found most everything about it intriguing.

Louisa led her to a small break room in the back of the building, and then grinning, took out a glazed doughnut for herself. She held it on a napkin, and Cat could tell she was fighting the urge to dig in.

"Please," Cat encouraged. "Go ahead. That batch just came out of the fryer."

"I know," Louisa whimpered. "I can tell from the smell."

Before Cat could say anything else, Louisa chomped into the sugary treat and let out an unladylike moan. Cat couldn't help but laugh at the sight of pure bliss on the woman's face.

In fact, it looked so sinful that she found herself plucking out a doughnut as well. She normally stuck to a sensible diet since extra carbs threatened to do their best to make her wider, but heck, she was on vacation. Wasn't the old saying that calories didn't count when on vacation?

That was the story she was going with.

She bit into the pastry and her eyes went wide, locking on to the older woman's. Louisa laughed gleefully. The doughnut was pure sin. Her hips were most definitely going to have issues after spending an entire month here.

Both women collapsed into laughter as they shoved their mouths full of the delicious treat. "Had I known what those would taste like," Cat began when she had her mouth empty once again, "I might not have bought them. I can't imagine how I'll exist without one every day."

"Tell me about it." Louisa took one last, longing look at the open box before closing the lid and shaking her head. She patted her rounded figure. "Good thing there's plenty of room in this dress. I can tell you, it's already about three-quarters full of Lily's doughnuts, as it is. Just wait until you try the Boston cream–filled ones."

Cat groaned at the thought. She might have to add running to her morning yoga routine simply to continue fitting into the clothes she'd brought with her. And nothing got her running unless something with big claws was chasing her.

But then, maybe if she ran with a certain hot body and cute butt . . .

Nah. She'd do better to watch from the deck . . . then welcome him back with a shower.

And suddenly her body temperature shot up again. Dang, she really had to stop thinking about that man.

But it's been four years! her body protested.

Yeah, and she wasn't the type for a hot, torrid affair.

Unfortunately.

She was, instead, a sensible, responsible mother.

A Davenport.

They rinsed the glaze from their fingers, and Louisa led the way out of the small room.

"Janet McMillan is our owner," Louisa began, speaking with her hands as well as her mouth. "She was with our group of students earlier, welcoming them for the summer program, but they should be in with our resident historian now. He's a doctor of history at the college here in town but always takes time to teach a weekly class with the students during the summer. Not much for chitchat," Louisa muttered under her breath, "but sure is a looker."

She fanned her face as if having a heat stroke before resuming her monologue about the different programs offered for the children. They continued through the maze of hallways, Louisa's hands swishing back and forth with her words. When she got to the back wall, she turned right, but sounds from the room on their left caught Cat's attention.

She glanced in to find a man with his back to her, short dark hair haphazardly spiked in a way that didn't look intentional, addressing a roomful of enthralled five- or six-year-olds. Cat stopped, stunned. She'd never seen kids of that age sit so quietly. Certainly not her own kids. And especially not for a history lesson.

Glancing at the teacher, she watched as he interacted with the children. He addressed each personally when they raised their small hands, taking the time to make sure they felt special, and making a game out of everything he was teaching them.

He was good.

A sweet little girl with dark curls and big brown eyes raised her hand and gave a shy smile when he looked her way. Instead of simply asking what her question was, the teacher—she had to assume this was the doctor of history that Louisa had mentioned—squatted to address the little girl.

As his jeans molded to his crouched form, Cat made a strangled noise in the back of her throat. *That ass!*

She would recognize that rear anywhere. Hadn't she been watching it for days?

She turned to go, bumping into Louisa—who'd somehow suddenly gone quiet and was standing right next to her. Her eyes were focused on the exact thing Cat had been watching. Cat blushed when the older woman gave her a knowing smile. Apparently age didn't keep a woman from enjoying a man's backside when such a fine specimen presented itself.

Cat couldn't help it. She turned back to the view.

"What can I do for you, Amy?" the man asked the little girl, his smooth, deep voice sending a round of shivers through Cat's body. She wanted to get to know this man.

For the next three weeks.

The girl pointed directly at Cat. "There's a woman here," she said in a loud whisper.

Ah, crud.

Cat whirled around again, intent on leaving, but Louisa remained in her way. Instead of stepping back, Louisa gave a polite, almost demure smile and nodded toward the room behind Cat.

"Mrs. Catherine Carlton." Louisa's voice took on the same I've-got-a-secret tone it had welcomed Cat into the building with. "Please let me introduce you to Dr. Hollister."

Cat froze. She felt her expression go flat as she stared at Louisa. She had to be joking. But then, how would the other woman know the name Hollister would mean anything to her? Cat swallowed.

The entire back of her body tingled as if someone had run a roller of sharp tacks over it. It couldn't possibly be him. Not after all this time. In this same town?

He wasn't even from here.

With dread settling low in her stomach, she slowly turned. Her gaze caught at his waist first. He was trim, and from the tight gray T-shirt tucked into his jeans, she could see that he was all muscle. She forced her eyes higher as saliva disappeared from her mouth. It couldn't be Brody.

Her breath stopped when her eyes hit the dark-stubbled jaw. She did not want to look any farther.

Because, no. She did not want to be standing there lusting after Brody Hollister.

Three more inches and a long rush of air escaped her. Those eyes. She could never forget the eyes of the man she'd given her virginity to. Even if they had aged almost twenty years.

Vibrant green irises stared back at her from behind trendy black frames as if not at all surprised to see her. But then, he lived there. He probably *wasn't* surprised to see her. In fact, he'd probably been aware that she'd been in town for days.

Living right next door to him.

Hot anger suddenly shot through her. The man could have at least walked the thirty feet to her door and said hello.

She pressed her lips together as she seared him with her gaze.

"Brody," she finally said, her voice tight. "It's been a while."

CHAPTER THREE

*W*ELL THAT ANSWERED ONE QUESTION, BRODY thought. The woman had had no clue whom she'd been staring at for the last five mornings. The shock in her eyes was not faked. Nor was the undisguised lack of excitement at finding him standing in front of her.

All of this left the question of exactly why she'd been watching him if she hadn't known who he was. It also suggested that she didn't know who his brother was, after all.

It was almost too hard to believe.

The daughter of his biological father's nemesis showed up next door, gawked at him through binoculars every morning, and she had no ulterior motive?

He didn't buy it. She had to be faking.

He took in her glass-blue eyes and the pink tint high on her cheeks. She was a darned good actress if she hadn't known.

"I . . . uh . . ." Louisa's stumbling words caught his attention. She was looking back and forth between them, confusion marring her face. "I guess you two know each other?" she finally asked.

Brody's gaze met Cat's. They nodded simultaneously.

"We know each other," he said. "Though it's been a long time."

Cat nodded again, the anger he'd seen flash across her face softening back into surprise. "Long time," she muttered.

And then her gaze skittered away.

Her lack of eye contact intrigued him, and he took the moment to study her appearance. Her makeup was just right: applied with a light hand but enough to come across as professional. Her hair, with its wide band perfectly matching her top and shoes, didn't have a single flyaway strand.

And her stance screamed that she was important—only not so much as to not fit in with the locals. She wore her Davenport air, and from everything he'd seen over the last two decades, she should be standing there with a high level of confidence.

However, she was still focusing on anything other than him.

And then he got it. She hadn't been spying on him for the last five days. She'd been ogling.

Him.

This brought a broad grin to his face. It had been nineteen years since he'd seen her. And yeah, he knew that people checked him out. He took care of himself. According to gossip at the college, he was a "hottie." But to have Cat think so. After all this time. The very idea sent a rush of hot pleasure through his body.

And he could see it on her face when she peeked up at him once more. Her chin tilted stubbornly in the air. Catherine Davenport had just figured out that the guy she had the hots for was the very boy who'd once fumbled his way into her panties.

And she lived right next door to him.

The summer suddenly looked a whole lot brighter.

"Mr. Hollister," a high-pitched voice said at his side. A small hand yanked on his belt loop, and in the next instant, multiple hands yanked on multiple belt loops, with additional "Mr. Hollisters" thrown in.

Brody looked down. He was surrounded by every kid who'd been sitting perfectly quiet only two minutes earlier. Not that he couldn't handle them when they weren't sitting quietly, they'd just caught him off guard. It would be only a matter of getting everyone calmed back down, and things would be fine.

He pried Amy's tiny hand off his jeans while ignoring Cat still standing in the doorway. "What can I do for you, Amy?"

"Can the woman stay?" the girl asked.

"Yeah!" Fourteen other kids shouted the word in unison and began bouncing up and down, almost as one entity. "Let the woman stay," they chanted. "Let the woman stay."

A soft chime sounded overhead, and Louisa mumbled something about the front door. She was gone before Brody could ask for help.

Amy tugged on his belt loop again. "Mr. Hollister."

"Yes, Amy?" Once again, he pried small fingers from the denim.

"I need to pee."

Oh geez.

Brody looked around, panicked, feeling suddenly out of control. He did not want to ask Cat for help. There was a certainty in him that if he let her in, even a millimeter, she would quickly become more than a pretty neighbor to secretly fixate on.

He shoved the thought from his mind. She may be next door, and he may still want her—no matter how they'd ended—but it didn't mean he had to act on it. Even if one glance at her in close proximity had him thinking that he wanted to peel that innocent-looking white skirt from her body and see what she looked like in a teeny-tiny pair of bikinis.

It had nothing to do with her personally. It had simply been a while.

And men had needs.

"How about we all make a bathroom run?" he suggested. He stood tall and swept his gaze over the children. "Line up." He motioned with his arms, each drawing out a line the kids should step to. "Boys on one side, girls on the other."

Cat entered the room.

She reached out a hand for Amy's. "I'll take the girls."

"There's no need," Brody started. He grabbed Amy's hand before Cat could. "I can handle it."

Sculpted blonde eyebrows rose before him. "So can I."

She stared at him, and it was as if nineteen years slipped away into nothing. Something had happened that summer that he'd never been able to replicate with another woman. Not even the one he'd been engaged to.

And it seemed to be happening again whether he liked it or not.

All of a sudden, he felt like the geeky teenager he'd once been. She'd been so out of his league. A Davenport. A year older. She'd had a license, for Christ's sake.

Yet she'd been drawn to him, too. She'd become his best friend during those weeks. He would have followed her anywhere.

Fine. He silently relented. He narrowed his eyes at her as he released Amy's hand. *But I didn't ask for your help.*

Shocker.

He'd been proud even then. No father, a single, struggling mother. He'd needed to be on top of his game for the scholarships he sought.

Cat had needed to be pristine for her family's reputation.

All of that had disappeared on their last day together.

Cat pasted on her fake, public smile now and proceeded to ignore him. She glowed down at the line of waiting girls. Each of them tittered in front of her as if in the presence of a princess. "Let's make it a game," she suggested in a secretive voice. "I'll be the mama duck, and each of you are my ducklings. That means you have to hold on to your duckling sister in front of you." She showed them how with one arm outstretched toward Amy's shoulder. "And stay in a single-file line."

The girls solemnly nodded and then assembled behind their leader, each with one hand on the girl in front of her. As they filed out of the room, the occasional soft *quack* could be heard coming from the hallway. Brody couldn't help but smile.

When the last one disappeared out the door, he realized that he stood in the middle of five silent boys. All of them—including him—had fallen under Cat's spell and were now staring awestruck in the direction she'd gone, tongues practically lolling out of their mouths.

Terrific. Nothing had changed. She had a way about her.

He looked down at Dylan, the oldest of the boys, who had lifted his head and was studying Brody intently. A quizzical expression was etched on the boy's face.

"She's pretty," Dylan said innocently.

Brody nodded. "Yes, she is." She had only gotten prettier since he'd last seen her.

"I like her," the boy stated.

It didn't take long to figure that out about Cat. Everyone liked her. Dread settled in Brody's gut. He may have been only fifteen before, but she'd broken his heart in two.

I like her, too.

─────────── ───────────

"And . . . action."

Brody watched the scene act out on the stage in front of him while listening to Clyde Reynolds, the director, give suggestions and make adjustments as needed. At the same time, Brody took notes. Everything was coming together exactly as he'd envisioned. Only a couple of points to discuss with Clyde and they'd be good to go.

This year's lead actress was the best they'd ever had.

He could almost feel success closing in on him. It would be the tenth year he'd written a play for the small theater, and though last year's production had made a lot of noise in the press—all the way down to Boston—he'd still not managed to get attention from anyone in New York.

This year, though. This year, after many e-mails and calls, and still a few more e-mails, he'd finally gotten a commitment from a producer. The man would be up, himself, on opening night. Which was only two days away.

This could be it. Finally, he might see one of his plays adapted for Broadway. The thought was enough to bring him to his feet.

"Cut!" the director yelled.

The cast broke for a much-needed break, and Brody's mother took the side steps, heading straight for him. She had a bit part, as she always did, and she loved it. She grinned from ear to ear. Though she still lived in the same New Hampshire town she'd grown up in, still taught political science at the community college there, she always made time for Brody's plays. She tried out every year. She enjoyed being in them as much as he enjoyed seeing her there.

"This one is good," she said as she reached his side. She grabbed his hand and squeezed. "I can feel it. You'll get it this year."

His mom, his biggest supporter. Brody shot her a wry look. "You say that every year."

"And I mean it every year. But this one . . ." She broke off, looking around the small, dimly lit space. Her pride shone bright. "This one is different, Brody. The humor is so much more sophisticated than before. And that lead actress is phenomenal. Maybe when they offer you a deal they'll offer her one, as well."

The humor had always been his sticking point. As a history professor, it wasn't far-fetched to say he'd been called dry a time or two in his life. But that hadn't stopped him. He'd wanted to write screenplays since he'd been a kid. And he wanted to write funny ones.

He actually had been writing them for as long as he could remember, only no one had known about them until ten years ago. Except for Cat. But he doubted she remembered the dog-eared copy of his first attempt.

But ten years ago, when he'd gone home after a long day at his Georgetown teaching position, determined to set a wedding date with his then-fiancée, his life had changed on the spot. Instead of looking forward to a wedding, he'd packed his bags and moved out. At the end of the semester he'd headed north for the last time. He hadn't belonged in DC. Too many people in the town were only looking for an angle. How best to use each and every person they met. That's a lesson he should have learned when he was sixteen.

The job here at St. Mary's had practically been handed to him. Having graduated from the small, prestigious school at the top of his class, they'd eagerly welcomed him on board. Next thing he'd known, he'd swallowed his pride and had approached the head of the theater department. He'd wanted to know how much work he had ahead of him to become a viable playwright.

The following summer, he'd convinced the local playhouse to put on one of his plays. He'd wowed them with uniqueness and sophistication, while at the same time keeping it family friendly for the entire community to enjoy. Clyde had been coming back to him ever since.

They would love for him to write more than one play a year, but he didn't want it as a career. Teaching was his career. But he did intend to fulfill his dream. He would someday see one of his plays on Broadway. There was no reason he couldn't do both.

And his mother was right. All the pieces were lining up for this one to be it.

"So . . ." his mother said. She leaned back in the chair she'd settled into, going for nonchalant, but Brody knew her well. She had something on her mind. He lowered into the seat beside her.

He knew exactly what she was about to bring up. And he knew why.

Cat.

"About Catherine Carlton being back in town," his mother finally finished.

"Drop it, Mom." His tone was clear. This was not a topic she needed to worry about.

She gave him an unconcerned shrug. "I can't."

"You can. Just close your mouth and say nothing more."

"Brody, you have to talk about it. You haven't seen her in years.

And you were so crazy in love with that girl. You came home walking on air that summer."

"I was a teenager. I'd just had sex for the first time in my life." He tossed that bit of info out for shock value, hoping to back her off. "Of course I was crazy in love with her."

The shock didn't seem to work. Apparently his mother had figured that one out years ago.

"But you were so—"

"Mom." He turned to her, taking in her graying hair and the lines that had begun appearing more defined around her eyes over the last few years. He loved his mother, but this was none of her business. "It was a long time ago. Yes, I was crazy about her. She was a bright light for a nerdy, awkward guy like me. She made my summer special. But we were kids. And we clearly weren't right for each other. Hell, it was less than a month before she found someone else."

He still remembered every word when her mother had answered the phone and told him that Cat didn't wish to speak with him anymore. She'd moved on. He'd been informed it was time for him to do the same.

His mother's green eyes, a couple of shades darker than his own, stared back at him. He didn't waver from her look, certain she would break first. But as the two of them sat glaring at each other, he realized that what he was seeing wasn't her simply trying to get her way and force him into talking about Cat. There was something else in there as well. And damned if it didn't look suspiciously like guilt.

He blinked, breaking the connection.

"I have to tell you something, Brody." She spoke quietly.

His jaw tightened. What had she done?

"Great play this year, Dr. Hollister," one of the production crew said as he passed by. He carried replacement lamps for the two spotlights they'd been having trouble with.

"Thanks, Tom."

"Should be a good one."

Brody watched as Tom positioned a ladder beneath the lights. He very much hoped it would be a good one. He also found himself wishing Cat would come see it. Which was utter foolishness. He shouldn't even be thinking about Cat.

But even though he hadn't seen her out on her deck the last two mornings—or anywhere else, for that matter—he'd been doing pretty much *nothing* but thinking of her. First she'd butted her way into his classroom at the museum the other day, and then she'd burrowed herself into his mind.

And now he apparently wanted her to come to his play.

Ludicrous.

He turned back to his mother and crossed his arms over his chest. "Whatever it is you have to tell me, Mom . . ." He shook his head as his words died out. He didn't want to know. But he couldn't find the words to tell her not to say it.

Because when it came right down to it, he did want to know.

He and Cat had been friends. He hadn't imagined that. They'd met his first week in town and had spent nearly every evening together. There had been a spot on the beach where locals liked to hang out. Somehow he'd gotten invited, and before he knew what was happening, he'd found himself in the middle of a gaggle of Davenports.

Of course, he hadn't known at the time that he was Congressman Arthur Harrison's illegitimate son. Had he known, he most certainly wouldn't have told anyone.

But he also might have considered keeping his distance.

Because . . . a Harrison and a Davenport together? Not a good idea. The political rivalry between the two families had been well under way by that point. A tug-of-war that continued today.

But no one in Dyersport had known he was the bastard son of a Harrison—including him, until the following year—so he'd stayed a part of the group. He'd told Cat more about himself that summer than he'd ever told anyone.

He closed his eyes now and thought about the night they'd snuck away and gone skinny dipping. They'd both darn near frozen to death, but he would do it again in an instant. She'd had a life in her that brought something out in him. She'd made him want to be somebody.

The last week they'd been in Maine together had meant the most, though. She'd told him she loved him.

They were too young to fall in love. But damned if he hadn't felt it, too. And then she'd given herself to him. That night remained one of the best of his life.

So yeah, he did want to know whatever his mother had to say. It wouldn't change anything, but he was a sucker for being kicked in the nuts when it came to Cat.

He sighed and ran a hand through his hair. "Okay, fine," he growled out. "What is it?"

His mother opened her mouth, but then closed it as if unsure how to begin. The director yelled that they'd start again in five minutes. Brody shot her an impatient look.

She sighed. "You know that all I've ever wanted for you is to find someone to make you happy, right?"

He narrowed his eyes. Surely she didn't think that Cat at sixteen had been the person he was supposed to end up with. "I'm aware of that, Mom. What does that have to do with Cat?"

She shrugged. "I've watched you over the years. You don't let people in."

No, he didn't. They didn't need to be in.

"And, well," she continued. She licked her lips nervously. "She's in the news occasionally. Sometimes just her family, but there might be a mention of her, *specifically*, in the papers. Maybe on the TV."

"Where are you going with this?"

"You watch her. I've seen you watch her. Since you were a kid."

He didn't watch her that much. Plus, being in Maine, there

wasn't that much to see. "I like to stay up on current events," he stated evenly. "It goes with my profession."

"I know." She nodded and patted him on the knee. "But I've often wondered if I shouldn't have . . ." She trailed off and just looked at him, apology in her eyes.

"Shouldn't have what, Mom?"

Another shrug. "Her mother called the house a few weeks after you got home."

That surprised him, but somehow it didn't shock him. "Her mother called you? Or was she calling me?"

"No." She shook her head and glanced down at her hands. "She was calling me."

After ten seconds of silence he prodded, "And?"

She let out a small breath, her shoulders sagging along with it. "She made it clear that you weren't the boy for her daughter."

"I could have told you that," he mumbled. Anger lit inside him. Cat's mother had had no business sticking her nose in their lives.

"She also knew who your father was."

His mouth dropped open. *No one* knew that. Well, his ex had eventually found out, but that had been years later. "How?" he asked carefully.

"I met her once," she said. "When I worked at the Capitol." His mother had worked for his biological grandfather when he'd been a senator. That's how she and Arthur had hooked up.

"And?" he prodded.

She shook her head, his same questions reflected back at him. "I have no idea. I don't even know if she remembered me from back then. But Brody, *she knew*. And she was not happy at the thought of a Harrison courting her daughter."

"I'm not a Harrison," he growled in a low whisper.

"I know," his mom soothed. "But . . ." She shrugged. "You are. And that made her furious. There was more than one veiled threat in the conversation."

Brody stood, his chair tumbling over behind him. "What kind of threat?" His voice rose, and he saw several people stop what they were doing and look his way. He ignored them.

"Nothing physical." His mother waved the words off and motioned for him to sit back down. He remained standing. "Just insinuating that she could make things difficult." She lowered her voice. "Not getting into the right schools, that kind of thing. It seemed a bit much when *you* didn't even know who your father was—and I was the last person who would tell anyone—but given all she was saying, I tended to agree. You weren't the person for her daughter."

"So . . . what? You agreed that I wasn't the boy for her princess?"

That wasn't fair. The Davenports may be political royalty, but Cat had done nothing that summer to act as if she thought she deserved special treatment. If she'd felt that way, she would never have talked to him in the first place.

Instead, she'd been totally down-to-earth. The complete opposite of what he'd expected.

The complete opposite of what she was today. She was most definitely a full-fledged card-carrying member of her family now.

He began pacing across the concrete floor.

His mother peeked up at him as he passed in front of her. "I agreed that you weren't the boy for her daughter. And then . . ." Her voice tightened. "When *she* called . . . I never told you about it."

Brody went still. "When who called? Cat?" He stopped directly in front of her. "Cat called the house? *After* her mother told me she'd found somebody else?"

She nodded. "Twice. Once a few days after her mother called. She asked for you to call her back." His mom swallowed. "The other time was months later. I . . ." She shook her head as she paused and wet her lips. "She asked again for you to call her. Said she just needed to talk to you one time. But I couldn't figure why she'd be calling. Not after all that time. You'd moved on. I didn't want you to get your hopes up again. And frankly, Brody, I couldn't see you being involved with a Davenport as a good thing, either. Not given who your father is."

"So you didn't pass along the second message either."

Unblinking eyes stared back at him. "And I told her not to call again."

Brody took it all in. Cat's mother had intervened, and then *his* mother had. While both he and Cat had been reaching out to each other.

His heart thudded so hard he could swear anyone could see it pounding through his shirt. He didn't know why it mattered at this point, but to know Cat hadn't just forgotten him, that she'd been thinking about him, too. That meant something.

That meant he hadn't been the only one to feel it. Whatever *it* had been.

Simply a connection?

Love?

Love was what they'd both called it.

He shook his head. People didn't know what love was at that age. Not the lasting kind. It had been lust.

Nevertheless, it had broken his heart when it ended.

And now he found out that Cat hadn't even been the one to end it.

Well, shit. Life sometimes handed you crap.

He pointed at his mom. "You shouldn't have done that. I deserved to know what was going on."

She nodded. Sorrow filled her eyes. "I just wanted to protect you."

He knew that. He may have been *able* to handle the truth, but she'd still been his mom. And he'd still been only fifteen. Of course she would have done her best to protect him.

It was simple. He and Cat had been too young. He hadn't needed to risk the threats her mom had made, not to mention, it would have benefitted no one if Emma Davenport had gone a step further and decided to exploit his true parentage. Especially when he hadn't even known about it himself.

So yes, it *had* been for the best. Going their separate ways, he and Cat had had the world in front of them. She more so than him, but he couldn't complain. He liked his life. He'd done well.

He was just tired of being alone.

That thought caught him out of the blue, but it was true. He was tired of going home alone. Of not having someone to confide in. Even his ex-fiancée had been someone to talk to. He'd wanted that in his life. A wife, kids. There was regret there. Not for losing Devan. He was lucky not to have married her. She'd used him.

She'd had a goal and she'd made it happen. Just one more huge lesson about not getting mixed up with politics.

Yet there was regret nonetheless. He'd wanted so much more.

He looked at his mom, at the weariness coloring her eyes. He didn't want her to hurt because of this. It was history. No sense crying over spilled milk.

"It's okay, Mom." He sat beside her and reached for her hand. "Her mother was right." It galled him to say that because the woman had overstepped her bounds by making veiled threats. "We weren't right for each other. But I do appreciate you telling me now."

She was silent for a moment before asking, "So there's still something there?"

"What?" He jerked back. "No. There's nothing there. I've barely spoken to her."

"But she's staying next door to you."

"How do you even know that? You live an hour from here."

She shook her head. "I didn't even have to come into town to find that out. I got a call last week when she arrived. Apparently she's big news up here."

Geez. People needed to mind their own business. Leave the girl alone. She was barely leaving her house, so it was clear she'd come for solitude.

"Fine," he said. "Whatever. People are talking about her. But don't add to it, Mom. Give her privacy. And no, there is nothing between her and me."

"Not even old feelings?"

He studied his mother. No way in hell he would tell his mother that he'd thought about Cat more than once an hour since she'd arrived practically on his doorstep. And at least three times an hour since he'd seen her at the museum.

"Not even old feelings," he said.

Her mouth softened into a smile. "Good," she whispered. "Because this time *I* would be the mother telling *you* that you don't need that in your life. You don't need the trouble of being mixed up with a Davenport, no matter how good a person she might be. Not given the campaign your brother is currently running against her mother."

Brody just barely managed to hold in a grunt of disgust at the thought of how his brother, Thomas, and Arthur Harrison ran campaigns. He'd watched from afar plenty of times over the years to know the drill. He still couldn't believe he shared their blood.

"Don't I know it," he confirmed.

CHAPTER FOUR

*T*HE BREEZE FROM THE OCEAN LIFTED CAT'S HAIR AWAY FROM her neck Wednesday evening as she wandered along the pebbled sand at the edge of the water. The sun was dipping below the horizon, and everything had turned to long shades of blues and pinks. She carried a large, bushy flower in her hand, and every once in a while the wind whipped one of the small, white petals away, sending it floating through the air. Each time this happened, Cat stopped walking and watched until it drifted out of sight.

Her heart was aching.

She'd come out about an hour earlier, and the farther she went, the more her steps had slowed. Not because of the long walk she'd have back to her cottage. In fact, she looked forward to it. Even in the dark, with the nip in the air. She was able to think here. About the past. The future.

About Brody.

She touched the blossom to her cheek.

She was able to see reality for what it had been.

She'd been a very young girl making a very big decision. Cat knew her daughter would have had a far better life with her adoptive mother than she ever could have with Cat as a teenage mom. Or with Cat and Brody—if that could have somehow happened. And yes, she'd known that for years. But here, it somehow made more sense.

Patricia Weathers had been a good woman. A college friend of Cat's mother and an OB-GYN working in San Francisco, Patricia had taken Cat in during her pregnancy. Her understanding and compassion had helped assuage Cat's guilt about giving up her baby.

As the months wore on, Cat continuing to worry over the decisions she'd made and the future of her daughter, she'd begun to see that Patricia cared about Annabelle, too. Even before the baby had been born. Thus, when Patricia made the suggestion that *she* be Annabelle's mother, Cat had known it was the right thing to do.

It would be a closed adoption. And Cat would never see her daughter again.

That was the way it had to be. They couldn't have a Davenport out in the wild. Neither Cat nor her unborn child would be able to live their lives without the story continuously making the rounds—not without criticism for decisions made, and interruptions to her daughter's life.

But it had still broken Cat's heart.

She'd loved her daughter. She'd wanted the very best for her.

Annabelle would have been an adult now. She would have been a lovely woman, and Cat would have been proud of however she'd turned out.

So it was time to let go.

She stopped walking and closed her eyes as the cool, salty breeze brushed over her skin. She'd seen Annabelle for only a few seconds before she'd been whisked away. And then Cat had cried for months.

Annabelle still showed up in her dreams occasionally. Some nights she had blonde hair like Cat's, but more often, she was a brunette. Nine times out of ten her eyes were green. The exact shade of Brody's. And always, she smiled upon seeing Cat.

Possibly, Cat could have moved on easier if she'd been able to make the decision to give her up alongside Brody. That's a regret she'd lived with for years. She should have tried harder to contact him. But he'd stopped calling.

They'd declared their love, said good-bye, and she'd never seen him again.

Until now.

Nineteen years ago, he'd been unsure of himself. Smart and funny and sweet and kind. Such a good guy. But so unsure. He'd been brainy and thin and hadn't felt as if he fit in.

But now he volunteered his time to kids. He had a doctorate and taught history at the college. And from the Internet searches she'd performed over the last couple of days, he was a well-respected, well-honored person of the community.

And he was hot.

Steaming.

And he jogged on the beach every morning.

Not that she'd been outside watching him lately. After realizing who he was, she'd been too embarrassed to be on the deck at the same time he was jogging. She feared he'd figure out she wasn't just out there enjoying the arrival of the new day.

That didn't mean she hadn't stood at her window and enjoyed the view, though. A girl did deserve *some* fun.

Plus, she'd confined herself to the house until the news about the donation to the museum had died down. It had been released to the larger publications, but she'd wanted to maintain her privacy as much as possible. At least as long as she could. So she'd stayed in.

When her kids came up later in the month, her brother and sister-in-law coming along with them, there would be no hiding then. At that time, she'd move over to the Davenport home.

But for now, this time was hers.

Which stupidly meant she still wanted to cross the yard to her neighbor's house.

She opened her eyes and started moving again. What was the worst that could happen? He'd say no? It's not like she'd lose anything. That particular well had been dry for four years. Going another summer running on empty wouldn't kill her.

She walked a few more minutes before realizing she'd reached the spot she'd been working up the courage to visit all week. It was where she'd hung out that summer nineteen years ago. There had been anywhere from ten to thirty people here on any given night. With bonfires, parties, dancing. Drinking.

They'd told ghost stories and real stories. They'd just been a group of innocent kids—most of them here for the summer with limited parental supervision—having the time of their lives.

And not far from the spot she now stood was where she and Brody had shared their last night. They'd found an old gazebo on one of their many walks, and the two of them had sat there for hours talking, knowing they would be separating the next day. Knowing they wouldn't see each other again until the next summer.

Just before daylight they'd made love.

It had been clumsy, neither of them having any idea what they were doing, but it had been one of the sweetest things she'd ever experienced. They were memories she'd hold for life.

She continued making her way across the beach as she recalled the tender feelings of those eight weeks with Brody. She had loved him. As much as a sixteen-year-old could. He'd been her first love. She'd fallen for the slightly geeky, shy boy because she'd seen the beauty inside him. He'd loved his mother, he'd loved learning new things. And he'd loved her. She'd wanted it to last forever.

She wasn't that girl anymore, though. She'd married a terrific man who'd given her two beautiful children before he'd been killed in a friendly fire incident. Her life was good. It couldn't be better.

Only, Brody was here again. And so was she.

The instant she'd realized who he was, all the old feelings had resurfaced. He'd been standing in the middle of those kids at the museum with a wild look on his face, as if horrified at the mere potential of things getting out of control. And he'd suddenly reminded her of the unsure teen she'd once known, who'd been worried that none of her friends would like him.

She'd *had* to step in and help. Even if he hadn't needed her. She'd also wanted an excuse to be near him.

When she'd returned from the bathroom with the girls, she'd hung out for only a few minutes before Janet, the museum owner, had located her. Since Cat had been there on business, she'd left without another word.

But she wanted that word. She wanted a lot more.

She wanted to know how he was and what else he'd been doing that hadn't been depicted in the local archives.

And she wanted to know if he ever thought about her.

She rounded a dune to where the once falling-down gazebo had been, and there in its place stood Brody. He wore cargo shorts and another fitted T-shirt, and had both hands tucked into his pockets. He was watching her.

"Evening, Cat." His low words almost disappeared in the wind before she heard them. God, he looked good.

His hair was unkempt, a few dark tufts standing up as if he'd been running his fingers through it, and dark, precisely trimmed stubble covered his jaw. The whiskers made him seem daring and untamed.

It made him look wild. Like he knew exactly what to do with a woman these days. Not at all like the uncertain boy she'd known.

Of course, his vintage wayfarer glasses reminded her that behind all that strength and sinewy muscle was a brain. She'd once teased him about his IQ. He hadn't registered as a genius, but she'd never met anyone as smart as him.

She took several steps toward him, meeting his gaze. "Brody," she said, unsure what else to say.

His returning look reached inside her. It made her heart stop for just a second.

She blinked to break the connection and glanced away, back out at the sea. Her breath stuck in her throat, and she forced it out as normally as she could. It was growing dark around them, but she could still make out everything about him. At the same time, she wished the sun was around so it wouldn't feel so secluded. She wasn't sure being alone with Brody was a good idea when she'd done nothing but think about him for the last three days.

Even more than that, if she counted her reason for coming here.

"I saw you leave your house earlier," he finally said. She felt him step closer. He didn't touch her as they stood side by side, both facing the water.

"Yeah?" She plucked a petal off the blossom she carried. "I've been coming out for walks in the evenings."

Trying to get up the courage to come here.

"I know. I've been watching you. You've quit sitting on the deck in the mornings."

She glanced at him. A small smile lifted the edges of his mouth and she couldn't help but linger on the curve. Yep, he knew she'd been out there watching him.

She sighed. At least he didn't know about the binoculars.

"It's good to see you again, Brody," she finally said. Because it was. Really good.

He nodded. "I would have to agree. Though I must admit I'm not so sure what to say to you. I'd like to know how you've been, what you've been up to. But I've seen a lot of it in the news over the years." He paused before saying sincerely, "I'm sorry about your husband."

A knot formed in her throat. "Thank you," she whispered.

She still missed Joe. He'd been a good man. A good husband. But she'd eventually had to force herself to move on. She wasn't sure she could say she'd done the same thing with Brody, though. Before this week, she would have sworn she'd gotten over him years ago.

But since seeing him? She'd been obsessed. It was disturbing.

She buried her nose in the hydrangea bloom. It didn't have a potent smell, but she liked the feel of the soft petals against her skin. It reminded her of lace.

The low sound of a boat horn sounded far off in the distance.

"So," Brody said. He shuffled his feet in the sand. "How *have* you been?"

She laughed lightly and looked back at him. He was about six inches taller than she was; his head tilted down as he watched her, and he was giving her a crooked smile. He was comfortable to be around. She relaxed. "I've been good. Really. I'm in Atlanta running the family foundation, two kids, no pets—*yet*—and a mother who still drives me a little insane. But you probably—"

"Know all that," he finished. "Yeah, I know the outer stuff. But how about *you*? Have you been good? Are you happy?"

Cat stared at him, trying to remember the last time someone had asked if she was happy. She was content, yes. And yeah, she was happy. She was a mother of two great kids. But that was the coating. And Brody was asking about the inside. The middle. He wanted to know if she was enjoying every moment of her life.

She nodded. Of course she was happy. But the words that came out surprised her. "I could stand to liven my life up a bit."

He laughed, the sound catching her as off guard as her words had. It was rich and sexy, and rolled out of him in a way that had her leaning just a little closer. She wanted to live in that laugh.

"Well, you've just brightened mine up." He chuckled some more. "Honesty. I always loved that about you."

She gulped and looked down at the flower again. Maybe she had been honest—a long time ago. But if she were really honest now, she'd tell him they were standing in the spot where they'd once made a baby.

Instead, she held up the flower, ready to get out of there before the memories tempted her to do or say more than she was ready for. "Not complete honesty," she said. "I stole this from the bush outside your deck."

"I know." He winked. "I watched you do it."

Heat swept over her. She would have sworn he hadn't been

home when she'd snuck over to get the flower. Clearly her stalker skills needed some work.

He reached out and cupped the large bloom in his hand and her heart squeezed tight. "These were my grandmother's favorite flowers," he said. "Annabelle hydrangeas. She named my mother after them."

It was hard to force enough air through her throat to speak. She nodded. "I remember."

It was the reason she'd named their daughter Annabelle.

A look crossed Brody's face as if he were shocked that she remembered something he'd once told her. She reached out her hand and touched his. It was warm. And she wondered what Patricia had changed Annabelle's name to after the adoption. What name her daughter had died with.

"It was a great summer, Brody. I remember many things about it. I'm just sorry . . ."

"I am, too," he replied when she couldn't find the words to express all that she was sorry for. He studied her in the waning light, and she felt another chink form in her armor. She had no protection around him. Just like the first time, it simply felt right to be with him.

She took a small step back and looked away. Stooping, she placed the hydrangea on the sand behind them, trying to force herself to say good-bye to their daughter. But she found she couldn't do it. She couldn't let go.

Guilt shredded her. She should have told Brody about Annabelle.

"Want to walk back to the house with me?" she asked as she rose. Her voice was impressively steady.

Brody pinned her with his gaze before sliding it to the flower she'd placed on the ground. "You brought that all the way out here?" his words sounded odd in his throat. "To put in this spot?"

She looked at him in the shadows. No words would come out. She nodded.

He studied her for another moment, no doubt seeing far more than she wanted him to, but she knew he couldn't see the truth. He couldn't see the reason she'd needed to be in this very spot.

"What has you so sad?" he asked. His gentle tone almost did her in.

"Nothing." She shook her head. She couldn't tell him. "I'm fine."

She turned and started back the way she'd come, hoping he would follow. He did.

"Then why the long face?" He matched his pace to her shorter legs. "And the holing up in your house all week?"

A warm sizzle began in her and she shot him a sidelong glance. "Have you been spying on me, Brody Hollister?"

"Yes," he answered the instant her words stopped. His voice was strong and solid. She liked that. He leaned in a bit, bumping his arm against hers. "I have been spying on you," he whispered. The back of her neck tingled.

She let out a nervous laugh.

"I've been trying to figure out why you're here, actually." His tone went back to serious.

She raised a brow. He was honest, too. She'd forgotten he would say or do whatever crossed his mind.

"But at least I haven't been using binoculars," he teased.

Her feet tripped over some magically appearing rock, or maybe a stick—surely it hadn't been mere sand—and Brody reached out a hand to steady her. He managed to keep her from face-planting at his feet.

When she regained her balance, he kept his hand around her elbow.

Probably he was afraid she would fall in the dark again.

Wouldn't surprise her if she did. Especially if he kept flirting with her. Wait . . . he was flirting with her?

She glanced at him. He raised his brows.

Her chest squeezed.

She was pretty sure he was flirting with her.

But she still didn't want to admit she'd been staring at him through binoculars.

Instead, she changed the subject. They talked about mundane things on the walk back. Both laughing at times. Occasionally one of them bringing up something that had happened during their summer together. It was nice remembering.

They'd been so young. Being with him now wasn't as uncomfortable as she'd thought it might be, because they both realized that. Life had turned out the way it was supposed to. He'd seemingly met all the goals he'd set out for himself. He was brilliant and successful. He had a good life.

And she'd . . . well, she'd done what she'd been born to do. Be a Davenport.

She made a face at the thought.

"What was that for?" Brody asked.

"What?" They'd reached the bottom of the steps to her deck and turned to face each other. There were small solar lights dotting the perimeter of the deck railing, which lit the space enough that they could see each other.

His hand had dropped from her arm at some point on the walk back, but he lifted it now and smoothed the pad of his index finger across her forehead. "You're scowling."

She scowled again. "No, I'm not."

He hiked an eyebrow.

She sighed. "Okay, fine. I'm just thinking about how things didn't quite turn out the way I'd once imagined."

His hand lowered and cupped hers. "How so?" he asked.

It was hard to remember what she'd been thinking when his fingers slid lightly over the center of her palm.

"Well," she stammered. She licked her lips. "What have I done, exactly?" It was a question she'd been thinking about a lot this week.

"From what I can tell, you've done a lot. You *do* a lot. I follow the news religiously, and I regularly see something that has your mark on it. Additionally, I'm sure you're a great mother—as I can't see how you wouldn't be. You arrange for your family's foundation to help out many people and organizations. You—"

"Don't do anything out of the ordinary," she said, the exasperation inside her coming out through her words. "I don't ever color outside the lines."

His fingers stilled on her skin. "And you want to color outside the lines?"

She didn't even have to think about it. *Yes!*

She wanted to push the boundaries. To be more than who she was.

She wanted to be *her* at sixteen.

The person she'd been *before* she'd gotten pregnant. Because after . . . things had been different. In one move, she could have single-handedly destroyed her family's reputation. All because she'd gone and followed her heart instead of logic.

The decision to be with Brody that night had changed her permanently. It had solidified the life she'd been born to live.

But did that mean she never got a break?

"I want to do something that no one sees coming," she whispered quietly.

He released her then, studying her carefully for a few seconds before turning to peer out toward the waves. His jaw was strong and solid, and she found herself wanting to reach over and touch it. To feel his whiskers against her fingers. She didn't, though. She simply stood there, the sound of the waves making their way ever closer to her deck, the lights from the railing casting their shadows together in a haphazard way across the sand.

Finally, Brody faced her. He hooked a thumb over his shoulder and gave her a teasing grin. "You once went skinny dipping up here. I don't think anyone would see that coming."

She snorted with laughter. "I'm thirty-five years old now. I know better. I already froze my rear off out there once. That was enough to last a lifetime."

But the thought of skinny dipping with the grown man standing in front of her did have appeal. Not that he'd offered to go in with her.

"Tell you what," she said before he could read her mind. For some reason, she felt as if her feelings were plastered across her face tonight. "How about I start by suggesting we be friends while I'm here? Be someone I can hang out with. That would be different. I haven't had a person in my life who wasn't family—or looking for an in with my family—in a long time."

His stance didn't change, but he went still.

"Unless you don't want to," she hurriedly added. Good grief, how embarrassing. She'd just had one of the more enjoyable hours she could remember, and he'd apparently been feeling—

"I would love it," he said. His tone was full of sincerity, and her heart did a little squeeze-jump thing. "I could use a friend myself."

At the look on his solemn face, she wanted to hug him close.

"I can't see how that's coloring outside the lines, though," he pointed out, bringing the teasing back out. "I'm a college history professor. I'm not exactly risqué."

She thought about the past and of how adamantly her mother had insisted Cat have nothing to do with Brody. He *was* risqué. At least in *her* world.

She gave him a wide smile. "My mother wouldn't approve."

His returning grin heated her from the inside out. "Far be it from me to keep a girl from rebelling against her own mother."

The joy she felt at having Brody in her life once again was like sunshine coming out after a late-summer storm. It appeared quickly, bright and strong. She'd never been able to talk to anyone like she could him. Not even her late husband. Which probably should make her feel more guilty than it did. There had been something special between her and Brody. More than he knew, but even without the pregnancy, it had always been there.

Given their easy conversation of the night, it appeared it still was.

Maybe they would simply spend a few weeks hanging out, or . . .

She studied him as he stood in front of her, his eyes mostly hidden in the shadows, but the curve of his mouth saying all she needed to know. He did something to her. She wasn't looking for a relationship. Who had time for that with two kids and a foundation to run? But she couldn't say that she would object to a fling if the opportunity presented itself.

Either way, her summer was looking up.

She smiled up at him, letting it once again grow wide across her face. She felt lighter than she had in years.

"There's a play opening at the community theater Friday night," he said in a rush. "How about going with me?" He paused before adding, "As my friend."

She nodded, no hesitation. "I saw that when I drove by the theater the other day. I would love to go with you."

A gust of wind picked up her hair and tossed it in front of her eyes, and as she reached to swipe it back, she noticed the massive blooms of the hydrangeas in his yard. They swayed as if dancing in the wind. Then something occurred to her.

"If you were in the house when I picked the flower," she began, trying to figure out the answer to her question before she asked it, "how is it that you were . . ." she paused and motioned back toward the way they'd come, not wanting to say *in our spot*, ". . . already out there before me?"

His features did a quick change, and she would swear embarrassment shone back at her before the line of his mouth tightened in a grimace. "I drove out there," he confessed.

Her lips parted. "And yet you walked all the way back with me?"

One shoulder lifted under his T-shirt. The man filled out his clothes nicely. "A pretty girl asks me to take a stroll on a moonlit

55

beach, I'm going to say yes every time." His voice gentled as he said the words, and though it was hard to tell for certain, she would lay money down that he'd shifted his gaze to her mouth. Did he want to kiss her?

Because hell yes, *she* wanted to kiss *him*.

At one point in her life, she'd been the kind of girl who'd gone for whatever had struck her fancy. It was time to channel that girl.

Inching up on the balls of her feet, she caught her bottom lip between her teeth. She desperately hoped she didn't do this wrong. It had been a really long time since she'd had a first kiss.

Brody's eyebrows shot up at her movement, and then his hand touched her. Lightly.

His hot palm grazed the skin of her arm, and a shiver danced across her shoulders. She sucked in a breath. Then she inched higher.

And then her cell phone rang.

They froze. Both leaning in within breathing distance of each other. Both wanting what the other was offering.

"Ignore it," she begged. *Oh please, ignore it. Just kiss me.*

Brody gave a little nod as the phone stopped ringing. He moved closer.

And it rang again.

"Oh, for crying out loud," she muttered, dropping back on her heels.

Brody chuckled. It was late and she'd already talked to her kids tonight, but possibly one of them needed something.

"Let me make sure it isn't my . . ." She didn't say "kids," instead waving the word away. What a way to ruin the moment, to bring your children into the mix.

She dug into her back pocket for her phone, shaking her head at the timing. Was this some kind of message from the universe? That she needed to keep her priorities straight?

And what? The universe didn't think Brody Hollister was a priority?

Too bad.

Screw the universe. She wanted sex.

What she saw on the lit screen, though, made her grind her teeth together. It was her brother. Geez, the guy needed to give her a break. She was on vacation. She did not need her family calling all week to make sure she wasn't still upset.

Planting a tight smile on her face, she sent the call to voice mail and shoved the phone back into her pocket. Then she peered up at Brody.

"Problem?" he asked.

"No. Just my annoying brother."

He nodded again, but then glanced over her shoulder toward the road. A heavy pause hung in the air. "I should probably go get my car."

Her spirits sank. He wasn't going to kiss her.

Probably for the best. No need risking making this uncomfortable.

She nodded just as her cell went off again, this time signaling that she'd received a text. With a growl, Cat pulled out the phone and jabbed at the screen.

The message that came up froze her. It was from JP.

`The tabloids know there was a mistress.`

CHAPTER FIVE

*T*HE NEXT AFTERNOON, CAT STOOD IN THE MIDST OF reporters and Dyersport city officials, smiling and shaking hands, doing whatever it took to make sure they knew she was there for the right reason.

In reality, she was standing in the middle of a plot of land owned by her family for exactly the wrong reason. To take the focus off the paparazzi having a field day in Atlanta. Her father's mistress from nine years ago had yet to be identified, but an ex-campaign manager had been unearthed, stating that he'd witnessed Jackson Davenport Sr., more than once, canoodling up to an underage volunteer.

Pictures had been posted, but they'd been fuzzy.

But canoodling with an underage volunteer was exactly what her father had done. Though the girl *had* been eighteen when she'd had his baby.

None of it, however, meant that Cat or her family would lie down and declare the Harrisons the winner. They had an image to uphold—a political lineage—and she would do her best to help maintain it.

Even if it did interrupt her vacation to do so.

At least it hadn't ended it. That had been her first thought. She would be needed at home.

After saying a quick good night to Brody the night before, she'd gone inside the house and immediately returned JP's call. She'd had her laptop open and was looking up flight schedules before he'd answered.

But her brother had calmed her down. He'd reminded her that this was the first time she'd had to herself in years, and that he and their mother could handle things in Atlanta.

They *had* come up with an alternative plan for her, though.

Which was why she stood in front of reporters today.

She, her mother, and JP had decided to dedicate a piece of land to the city for a multipurpose park. Given that Dyersport held decades of Davenport history, it would look good to give back. The only drawback for her was that her location would be publicized to the world. So much for her quiet little trip away.

But still, this was their way of life. Thinking she could maintain her privacy for the full month had been a pipe dream, and she'd known it. No one in her family went anywhere for very long without being found out.

The bigger issue was that they had exactly twenty-two days to get the park functional.

And that there were more secrets in danger of being exposed.

Her father had experienced a huge lapse in judgment in getting involved with Lexi Dougard, yes. But he'd made an even bigger one in getting her pregnant. And Cat's mother had stood by him. She'd *known* about the seventeen-year-old. About the kid. She'd written out the million-dollar check.

Thankfully, nothing about the money or the child had been discovered.

Yet.

Thus they needed to draw the attention north.

The hope was that the rest of the world would somehow forget that there was a woman out there whom her father—Mr. High Morals and Family Values—had cheated on her mother with, while also helping to deflect many of the sordid questions the media was now firing at her mother.

Cat nodded a greeting as yet another reporter joined the group, and silently expounded on the last thought to run through her head. Her father had cheated on her mother after over three decades of a seemingly perfect marriage.

With a teenager.

How did something like that happen?

Other than the fact that power went to a person's head, she could come up with no possible explanation. And now she worried that same power would change her mother as well. Maybe it already had.

Emma Davenport hadn't exactly been mother of the year as Cat and her brothers were growing up, but she'd been a good mom. They'd never wanted for anything other than a bit more time with their parents. But all Davenports understood that family came first. And the family was politics.

Her dad had been involved at the federal level for sixteen years before he'd run for president. If he hadn't lost his battle with cancer before the election, Cat was certain he would have won. He was that good. So was her mother.

The fact was, the country needed the wisdom and experience that her family brought.

So she'd stand before the crowd, today, and she'd donate the park. And she'd be gracious as she did it. Even if she did feel a little dishonest in her motives.

She understood the need, but for the first time in her many years of representing her family, her actions weren't sitting quite right with her. Maybe it was simply because she knew she'd prefer to be on her deck at that very moment, enjoying the blue skies and the afternoon sun. And thinking about that almost kiss from the night before.

Actually, that almost kiss would have probably turned into a real kiss.

And then they might have—

A low rumble cut off her thoughts, and she looked away from the crowd to watch a two-door, dark red car roll up behind the row of vehicles parked along the side of the road. The car had wide white stripes down the hood and a white convertible top, and it growled, low and dangerous, like a savage animal ready to pounce.

She knew little about cars, but if she were to guess, she'd say it was a sixties or seventies model. Maybe a Chevy? A Ford? Heck, she didn't know. But it was drop-dead sexy. And it made her think devilish thoughts about what she'd wanted to do with Brody last night.

When Brody himself uncoiled from behind the wheel, dark sunglasses in place, her heart rate took off as if it planned to meet him at the car and dance him into the backseat.

Brody drove a hot, sexy machine like that? She almost purred at the thought.

But what was he doing here?

"Ah," the mayor hummed at her side. "Clyde must have sent Dr. Hollister in his place."

"Clyde?" she asked, not taking her eyes off Brody. "The owner of the playhouse?" Clyde Reynolds had been invited to the press conference to ensure that all members of the community who would have a stake in the new park were included.

Part of their plan was to build a community amphitheater for open-air plays. That's why they had only twenty-two days to get the park ready. The last run of the play would be held on day twenty-three. Right here.

Cat eyed Brody as he shrugged a blazer on over dark jeans and a light blue oxford shirt, and set off across the lawn in a lazy stroll.

"Does Dr. Hollister have something to do with the theater?" she asked absentmindedly.

Brody hadn't looked anywhere but toward the small group of people she was standing with since he'd stepped from the car, and though she couldn't see behind his glasses, she was almost positive that he had his gaze set on her.

Was he thinking about almost kissing her the night before?

About their friendly "date" coming up the next night?

Or maybe he was replaying their walk along the ocean.

All three of those things—as well as knowing he would be outside running on the beach—had been the impetus for getting Cat out of bed that morning with a happy attitude, no matter the mess her parents had made of all their lives.

Or the fact that she was in charge of cleaning it up.

In charge or not, she wouldn't be doing all the work. She'd already hired a project manager for the job. The woman would be arriving later that day to get started.

"He sure does," the mayor said, reminding Cat that she'd asked a question. She dragged her gaze away from Brody and glanced at the mayor, forcing a polite expression back to her face as he stretched out his hand to greet Brody. "He writes the best plays that Dyersport has ever seen."

Cat's smile faltered as her brain stuttered over the mayor's words. She looked back at Brody.

He what?

——— ———

Brody watched Cat as shock passed across her face. There was one secret out of the bag.

Not that he'd been planning to keep it from her—or that he would have been able to. His name was listed on the program. But he would have loved to get her honest feedback before she found out he was the playwright.

He flicked his gaze over the rest of her now, taking in her attire and noting that she was dressed for her Davenport role today. Slim, yellow tailored skirt with a perfectly ironed white short-sleeved button-up tucked into the waistband. Her blonde hair was pulled up behind her head, and she even had on tiny glasses. Dark, wire-rimmed frames that made him think naughty teacher instead of the dignified professional he assumed she was going for.

He'd seen pictures of her in glasses before. He liked it.

"Dr. Hollister." She held out her hand, her tone polite. He looked at it before closing his fingers around hers. Did she not realize that everyone knew they were living beside each other? Of course they would be friendlier than "Dr. Hollister" and "Ms. Carlton" at this point.

Her hand was soft in his.

"Cat." He dipped his head with the word. He wouldn't tell them that she'd been the first girl he'd ever seen naked, but he also wouldn't act as if they'd never met. "I heard you were out here," he added, releasing her hand. "Something about a land donation?"

Clyde had only given him the barest of details. Land for a park was being donated, the city wanted it opened for closing night of the play. Clyde had been unable to come out himself when he'd gotten the last-minute call, but had caught Brody as he'd been leaving the college for the day. Brody had one summer class and kept morning office hours three days a week.

At first he'd been thrilled at the news. There would be another venue for the local acting community. And Dyersport could always use another park.

Then Clyde had mentioned the Davenports, and all the pieces had clicked into place.

Brody had seen the news that morning. Her family was in the spotlight at the moment, and not for a good reason. Of course, he assumed his "family" was behind it.

A secret Davenport mistress that had been hidden for nearly nine years? No doubt someone had helped that along at this opportune moment.

Or made it up.

Until he'd arrived, he'd assumed a fifty-fifty chance of the rumor being false. But Cat had quite the crowd assembled here. Her family was clearly intending to make some noise.

Which told him that Daddy Davenport *had* been the bad boy the news was making him out to be.

And, of course, Cat was going along with whatever her family needed her to do.

As she picked up a conversation with the mayor, city planner, and several other dignitaries about her plans for the park, Brody stepped to her side, inching closer until he was just slightly behind her, and waited until she stopped talking long enough to take a breath. When she did, he whispered, "Not coloring outside the lines today, are you, Cat?"

Her crystal-clear gaze shot immediately to his. She didn't like having the obvious pointed out to her. Or maybe she didn't like the role she was playing?

He gave her an evil grin. "Such a rule follower."

Why he was teasing her, he didn't know. Other than the fact that he'd almost forgotten who she was the night before. He'd been about to kiss her.

And he'd intended to take her to bed.

Luckily, she'd gotten a call and he'd had a moment to pull his brain back out of his pants. This was Cat. They did *not* need to be anything more than buddies.

For his sanity, but also for her peace of mind. A Davenport and a Harrison?

That would go over like a sinking ship.

Not that anyone would know, but still. If his brother or father were to find out—

The sound of a camera clicking caught his attention and he shifted his gaze from Cat's perturbed expression to the nearest reporter. There was a lens focused directly on them.

Well, shit.

Arthur and Thomas Harrison would most definitely be watching the papers to see how the next round played out with the Davenports, and Brody did *not* want them to see him with Cat. It was none of their business whom he associated with.

He glanced at her as she suddenly smiled brightly and shifted her focus back to the crowd, no doubt aware of the cameras as well. His gaze clung to her lips as she talked.

And it was no one's business whom he kissed.

Or didn't kiss.

But he still stepped back out of the shot. This was her show.

"I'm sorry your friend canceled." Cat's soft words registered as the lights went up in the theater. "It was a terrific play."

Brody looked to his side, where she stood smiling hesitantly up at him, her hair once again swept up and behind her head, but this time into a looser, sexier knot. It made her look years younger than she was. Everyone was on their feet clapping, the actors were taking their final bow. He forced the tension in his jaw to relax.

"No big deal," he said, trying hard not to let his irritation seep into his voice. And it hadn't been a friend who'd canceled, but the producer he'd been working on since January. Though Cat didn't realize that. "But thanks."

At this point, he had no doubt Cat was lying through her teeth about the play. Nothing about it had been terrific. Everything that could have possibly gone wrong had.

At the last minute, the producer—actually, the *assistant* to the producer's *assistant*—had e-mailed, saying Mr. Searcy was sorry that he wouldn't be able to make it tonight after all. Then there had been the emergency call from Clyde. Their lead actress would be in tonight's play, but she'd just found out about a family emergency back home. In Iowa. A sickness that would keep her out the remainder of the summer.

And they didn't have a backup.

Of course, with the girl worrying about what she'd find when she got home, and frustrated that there was no flight out until the next day, the actress's mind had been on everything but the play.

Then his mom had caught sight of him sitting in the crowd with Cat and had missed her cue. She had eight lines in the whole damned play, and she'd missed her cue. Twice.

He felt his jaw clench again, and this time left it that way. What a night.

"Thank you for inviting me," Cat said. He could hear the note of trepidation in her voice. She had no clue what to say to make it better.

He didn't either.

"I'm sorry I wasn't able to pick you up," he said. Yet one more thing that had gone wrong. His mother's car wouldn't start so he'd had to make the hour drive to her house to get her, only to arrive and find that her neighbor had just finished fixing it.

The alternator had gone out.

"It's not like this was a date or anything." Cat laughed lightly, which only set him more on edge. She bit her lip as she watched him.

No, it wasn't a date.

She'd been perfectly "friendly" all evening. Clearly, since going up on her toes the other night—her mouth inching toward his—she'd had second thoughts. As had he. And third thoughts. And fourth thoughts.

He should not kiss her. He knew that.

Yet when he'd seen her walk into the playhouse tonight wearing a sundress covered in bright red cherries, along with her sexy, strappy heels, he'd wanted to rush to her side and finish what they'd started.

He'd wanted it to be a date.

She reached up and touched his hair, smoothing her fingers across it, then a shocked expression popped onto her face. "I'm sorry." She snatched her hand back. "It was standing up. You kept running your hands through it tonight."

Brody caught her hand in his as she flushed with embarrassment.

"You must have been nervous," she whispered.

He nodded. He couldn't take his eyes off her. "Yeah. Silly, huh?"

"Not silly." The cool blue of her gaze heated. "It means a lot to you. I remember the play you wrote that summer. What was it called? *Much Ado about Dyersport*?" Her light laughter pinged through his body, hitting all the hot spots. "You had it bound, but the thing was falling apart; you'd carried it around and worked on it so much."

Her words started a buzz inside him. She remembered his play? "It was the first one I'd ever written."

"I know." Her free hand landed on top of his. "I was so impressed. I'd never known anyone who'd written a play before."

The actors began mingling with the crowd, and he caught sight of several people handing out bouquets. Opening night was always exciting. His mother reappeared on the far side of the room and headed their way.

"I think you were just easily impressed," he muttered as he turned her hands loose. He didn't want his mother to interrupt, yet he knew there was no way of getting out of it. Plus, he had flowers for her.

Cat shifted around in front of him then, catching his full attention as she tilted her head back to stare up at him. Her lips parted slightly and he couldn't help but take in the red lipstick that perfectly matched the cherries in her dress. Her bare throat arched and he found himself wondering if her skin was as soft as he remembered it.

He was amazed that he remembered what she felt like. But he did.

Every last inch of her.

She studied him carefully, her eyes hiding her thoughts, and he wanted to wrap his arms around her and drag her off backstage.

This friendship-only thing was not going to last.

"I apparently still am," she finally murmured. Her gaze dipped for a brief second to his mouth, and his dick twitched in his pants. Friends shouldn't look at friends like that.

"Can I take you home tonight?" he asked, his voice coming out scratchier than he'd like, but hell, Cat was staring at him as if she wanted him for a midnight snack.

"But my car—"

"Will be fine here. We'll get it tomorrow. I want to take you for a ride in my car."

Didn't that sound naughty? *Come here little girl, I have some candy for you.*

"I'll put the top down," he coaxed.

Surprise lit her features. "Oh," she breathed. "Your car. The red one."

"The Chevelle," he said drily. Good Lord. It wasn't "the red one." He shook his head, somewhat offended. "It's a 1970 Chevelle SS. It's the first car I ever owned," he added. "The actual car I owned, not one like it. I managed to find it last year and paid a hefty price to have it restored."

Cat snickered. "Touchy about your car, Brody?"

"He's touchy about a good many things." His mother joined them. She smiled widely at him before looking from him to Cat. "Don't you want to introduce us, dear?"

"No," he said. "Not really."

But Cat turned and gave his mother a warm hug. "You were so good up there, Ms. Hollister. What a pleasure to meet you."

His mother made eye contact with him over Cat's head. Her look seemed to be saying *What the hell? Is she blind?*

He returned the look. *Yeah, you stunk.*

His mother frowned at him.

Cat pulled back and Brody retrieved the bouquets of roses he'd stashed under his seat. He held one out for his mother. "Undeserving this time, Mom, but here you go."

"What do you mean, undeserving?" Cat squawked like any good mother would. "She was terrific."

"She had eight lines and she missed her cue both times."

"I was caught off guard," his mother stated. "I didn't realize you'd be here with a date."

"Oh." Cat brushed the words off and slipped her arm through his mother's. "We aren't on a date. We're just neighbors." She grinned broadly at Brody. The look came across a little too bright. "Friends."

His mother stared at her. Cat was several inches shorter, but with the heels, they were almost the same height. His heart squeezed at the sight of the two of them standing arm in arm. At fifteen, he'd wanted to introduce her to his mom. He'd thought they had the kind of love that lasted forever.

Funny how things turned out.

"Annabelle Hollister," he finally said, clearing his throat and inclining his head toward his mother, "I'd like you to meet Ms. Catherine Davenport Carlton."

Cat beamed and squeezed his mother's arm tighter. She really seemed to be having a great time tonight. "Please," she said. "Call me Cat. I only get called Catherine when I'm in trouble with my mother or when the media wants to make me out to be more important than I am."

His mother's eyes widened slightly. "Cat it is, then. And aren't you just the cutest?"

"*Mom.*" Good grief. "Please."

His mother made a face. "Women love compliments, Brody. Even if it is by an old woman instead of a young man."

She shot him a look he found hard to interpret. If he wasn't mistaken, he would swear she was giving him the go-ahead with Cat. As if he needed her permission. Yet it had been only two days ago that she'd been warning him off.

Cat's power to turn a person's head apparently wasn't restricted to boys and men. She could also wind mothers around her little finger.

"Cat stole a bloom out of my yard the other night," he told his mother, at a loss for what else to say, but finding himself shocked at "tattling" on his neighbor. But she knocked him off balance. "One of the ones you're named after."

At the mention of the hydrangea, Cat's relaxed expression tightened and she put a couple of inches between her and his mother. It was barely noticeable, yet he seemed to be unable *not* to notice everything about her.

"Is that right?" his mother asked. "They do look great in a vase, don't they? I have several bushes of them at my house, too. I cut them and bring them in all the time."

Cat didn't say anything. Likely because she hadn't cut the bloom to put in a vase. But he wasn't about to tell his mother it was now christening the exact location where their teenage selves had once thought they'd found forever.

The look on Cat's face made it clear she wouldn't be admitting that, either.

"Come on, Mom." Brody reached out an arm to her, slipping her hand over his elbow. "Go with me to give the other roses to Kristi." Kristi was the lead in the play. "This is her only night to perform."

"What?" Cat lifted her gaze from where it had fallen to the second bundle of roses he held. "Why? She's perfect for the part."

"An emergency." And yes, she was perfect for the part. But then . . . it wasn't as if he could get an interested party anywhere within three hundred miles of the place, anyway. "We've had to cancel the show for the next two nights, hoping to get someone else up to speed to replace her. But I've stressed over this all afternoon; no more about it tonight. Right now I'm taking you both over to talk to Kristi," he said, then pointed a finger at Cat, "and then I'm going to show you what my 'red car' can do."

CHAPTER SIX

CAT LAUGHED OUT LOUD, HER FACE LIFTED TOWARD THE clear night sky, as she and Brody drove down the highway in his pride and joy. His car purred and vibrated beneath her, adding to the excitement of the ride. When they'd walked out of the playhouse earlier, amid claps on the back and congratulatory handshakes on another play well written, he'd stopped before opening the car door and looked her up and down with a deadpan expression. She'd accused him of wanting her to take her shoes off before letting her inside. He'd shut her up by picking her up and plunking her down in her seat.

"I can always vacuum the floor mats tomorrow," he'd teased, leaning into the car with her.

She'd grinned up at him, letting him buckle her in, while feeling like a teenager going out on her first date. Thankfully, no one was at home waiting for her return.

She'd been afraid he'd simply take her home. Or give her a quick pass through town and *then* take her home. But instead he'd snaked through back roads for a while before heading out to Highway 1, where he'd been pushing the speed limit ever since.

She had her hands at the back of her head now, holding her hair out of her face and trying to maintain some sort of order to the messy bun she'd spent way too much time perfecting earlier that evening. But the bun couldn't be contained. Wildly blowing tendrils continued to escape and whip around in front of her face.

"I'm freezing over here!" she shouted into the wind as they sliced through the damp night air. It wasn't cold out, exactly, but fifties in June—with the top down and her in a sundress—was not quite what she was used to in Atlanta.

"Such a Southerner," Brody teased. He glanced at her. His left hand was on the steering wheel and the right was casually fidgeting with a plastic water bottle held against the side of the vinyl seat. He flashed his white teeth at her and her belly quivered. He was so handsome in his charcoal suit that her mouth watered every time she looked at him.

"Want me to pull over and put the top up?" he asked. "We can roll up the windows and turn on the heat."

She could barely see his eyes through the lenses of his glasses, with only the lights from the dash as a backdrop, but she shivered as he looked at her. It felt like he was mentally undressing her, which heated her right back up.

She shook her head. "Not on your life."

Giving up on her hair, she pulled the remaining pins out. So much for the stylish look. Driving with the top down was more about freedom and fun anyway. She might as well go with it.

She sank her fingers into the depths of her hair and shook it free, and the bottle in Brody's hand crackled with a pop.

"Where were the glasses tonight?" he asked. He'd turned his gaze back to the road ahead, but leaned closer to talk above the roar of the wind.

"You mean the ones I had on yesterday?"

At his nod, she patted her clutch. "I have them, but I wear my contacts most of the time. The glasses only come out for special occasions."

He shot her a quick glance. "Like when you want to appear all professional?"

"Exactly. Most of the time I don't look my age, and though most people would be glad of that, it isn't always a good thing. The glasses help."

"I like them," he said.

She studied his profile. "Because you're stuck with a pair yourself, so you think everyone should wear them?"

"No." He straightened and put both hands on the wheel at ten and two. "Because you look naughty in them instead of professional."

She got a lungful of cold air and realized her mouth was hanging open. She had no reply to that. She'd never been told she looked naughty in her glasses.

The car began to slow.

"Where are we going now?" she asked, ignoring his comment. It was exhilarating, just getting in the car and going wherever he took her. Not her norm, but she'd always trusted Brody. Seems that hadn't changed.

"There's a spot up ahead I want to show you."

The road grew darker and added curves, and she could tell they were heading back toward the ocean. "Awfully secretive, Mr. Hollister. Keeping me in suspense for a particular reason?"

His body language took on a more serious tone.

"What?" she asked, the word barely slipping out. The cool air swept over her upper chest, where the sweetheart neckline of her dress started, and she shivered. At least the dress had sleeves. Otherwise she'd be a Popsicle by now.

"Nothing." Brody shook his head. "Just thinking about secrets."

She didn't want to think about secrets. She had too many.

And she was having to cover up even more. Another phone call had come from her mother earlier that day. Apparently they were continuing to defend their father's honor. They didn't believe he'd done anything wrong. No affair. It was a fabrication. Of course, no one would come right out and say that in front of a camera in case they got caught in a lie later on, but it was the impression Cat was to give if questioned.

When questioned. Because someone *would* ask her about it.

Thankfully, yesterday's press conference had remained primarily focused on the park, but there was no way that would last. Not with all the tabloids and even some national papers now picking up the story.

In the next instant, a flash of light caught her attention and she held her breath. They were driving out to a lighthouse.

"You remembered," she said softly. She'd once told him that she and her dad had both shared a fondness for the nautical buildings. When she'd been six, they'd taken a father-daughter trip along the coast, where they'd visited as many lighthouses as they could fit into a five-day span.

"Absolutely," he said. "Just like you remembered that I'd written a play."

She chuckled. "I did remember that. In fact, it had a big impact on me."

Brody pulled off the road into a gravel lot and parked so they were facing both the lighthouse and the ocean. He turned off the car and all went dark. Stars covered the sky. The sound of waves crashing into the rocks fifty yards away hit her ears, and she inhaled a deep breath, catching the sweet scent of the lilac bushes along the walkway to the lighthouse.

It was gorgeous there. And they were the only two people in sight.

Brody shrugged out of his suit jacket and held it out for her, and she leaned forward, letting him slip it over her shoulders.

"Thank you," she murmured. She snuggled into the pristine white bucket seat, the heat from his jacket wrapping around her.

"You're welcome. I should have thought of it before." He slipped low into his seat and faced forward. His dark hair was a stark contrast against the back of his seat, and his hand once again began to fidget with the plastic bottle. He tapped it against his thigh. "Tell me how my once-pitiful excuse for a play could have had a big impact on you," he said.

The sounds of the night woke up around them as they sat there, both quiet, while she silently replayed the year after she'd met him. It had been a rough time for her, and coming out of the pregnancy hadn't been easy. In fact, she'd been on antidepressants for several months.

But when she'd returned home and had gotten back into her regular school the following fall, she'd known she had to do something to get her mind elsewhere or her grief would have eaten her alive. So she'd joined the drama club. It had felt good to pretend to be someone other than Catherine Davenport for a while.

She unbuckled her seat belt and turned to face him. When he mimicked her actions, shifting one thigh onto the seat between them, she spoke softly into the dark. "I saw how passionate you were about that play, and I wanted something like that in my life. So I joined the drama club."

His eyebrows rose. "You were an actress?"

She shrugged. "I was in high school plays. My junior and senior year." And she'd loved every minute of it. "My teacher said I was a natural."

Her parents had rarely had time to come to her performances, but that hadn't stopped her. She'd found her own passion, and she'd given it everything she had.

Brody put the water bottle in between the seats and reached for one of her hands. "That explains the look I saw tonight."

"What look?"

He leaned closer and his voice lowered. "The one where you were almost salivating as you watched the hot mess that was happening up on stage."

"It was not a hot mess," she protested. "Yeah, it could have been a little smoother in a few places, but it was good." She paused, feeling the heavy thud of her heart against her chest as Brody slid his fingers between hers. "And I don't think I was salivating," she finished softly.

It almost felt like he was putting the moves on her.

And she was pretty sure she liked it.

He nodded and gave her a smile so small she leaned even closer, as if hoping to catch it with her lips. "You were salivating," he whispered. "You were having a blast. It was almost as if you wanted to find those crayons right then and say to hell with those lines."

She closed her eyes and bit her lip at his words. She *had* wanted to color outside the lines tonight. She'd sat on the edge of her seat for most of the night, memories of her high school days bombarding her. At times she'd almost felt as if she'd been the one up on stage.

"I *was* having a blast," she admitted, opening her eyes. There were only inches separating them. "It's been a long time since I've been to a community theater. But my enjoyment wasn't just from watching the play. It was from knowing that you wrote it. That you never lost that desire." She eyed him in the dark. "You *were* going to tell me yourself if the mayor hadn't outed you, weren't you?"

She'd been floored when she'd learned that Brody still wrote plays.

"Of course." He brought his free hand up and stroked the back of one finger down her cheek. Tiny sparks were left in its wake. "I couldn't have kept it from you even if I wanted to. My name is on the program. But I would have liked for you to see it without knowing first," he told her. "To give me an *honest* opinion afterward."

"I gave you one."

"No, you didn't." He shook his head. "It stunk." He dropped his hand to their joined ones and let out a little sigh as he looked out toward the sea. "This whole evening did. Kristi couldn't concentrate, poor girl, and then the—"

He stopped talking abruptly and pulled his hands away, turning his body to align with the windshield. An emotional barrier slammed between them.

"What?" Cat prodded. "What else happened?"

She reached through the barrier and touched the hand that held the water bottle—which he'd picked back up and had started tapping against his leg again. She trapped his fingers beneath hers. "You can talk to me. Tell me what's bothering you."

A light breeze floated through the car and made the hair framing her face dance.

He pulled his hand free from hers, but he didn't pull away. His voice came out low and gravelly. Almost as if he were in pain. "The 'friend' who didn't show tonight was a producer. Ben Searcy. From Broadway. I'd been working to get him up here for months. Now I'm back to square one. Then again, given the many hiccups in tonight's performance, maybe it's best he didn't see it."

Wow. She hadn't realized it meant that much to him.

"So you want to sell to Broadway? That's great," she enthused. "We just have to get someone else to come up. I can make some calls. Maybe—"

"No. Don't make calls on my behalf."

"There's nothing wrong with letting someone help." He'd been like that, even as a teen. Stubborn and prideful.

"Maybe there's nothing wrong with it for some people," he stated, his voice solid and sure. "But not for me. I take care of myself."

"You make it sound as if you've always been alone or something."

He gave her a sardonic look.

"That's not true," she insisted. "You have your mother." She paused as it occurred to her that she knew nothing about his father. She couldn't remember him ever saying the first thing about the man. Maybe he'd never had anything to do with Brody. "Your mother is so proud of you," Cat told him, at a loss for what else to say. "It was written all over her face tonight. She would do anything in the world for you."

The beam from the lighthouse flashed over Brody and she thought she saw anger, but the light swung on around and she wasn't sure what it had been. This evening was not turning out how she'd expected. It was supposed to be about fun.

Finally Brody looked away. "You're right, she would do anything in the world for me. Same as your mother, I suppose."

That sounded like an accusation. "What do you mean?"

When he didn't answer, she focused on the light flashing out over the water. It was a lonely place to be at night. No one was around, only the lapping waves and the seeking light. But it felt right to be sitting there with him.

He pushed open his car door. "Let's go for a walk," he suggested.

"Brody." When he turned back, she held out one foot. "I'm wearing heels, and we're parked in gravel. I'll twist an ankle if I try to walk in the dark."

He let out a groan and circled the car to her door. Before she could guess his intent, he bent at the waist and scooped her up.

"What do you think you're doing?" she squeaked.

"I'm carrying you to the sidewalk." The words came out as though "of course" he was carrying her to the sidewalk.

"What's wrong with the car all of a sudden?"

He stared down at her, and she caught her breath. The strength of him was clear when he looked at her like that. Even though it was so dark she could barely make out his features. He was a man on a mission, and he was going to get what he wanted.

She only wished she knew what that mission was.

"You ask a lot of questions, you know that?" With his words, he headed to the sidewalk. Cat scowled at him from her inferior position.

"And you're a bit of a bully," she grumbled.

A grin softened his jaw. "Got to get what I want somehow."

She could feel her pulse pounding in her throat. "And what do you want?" she whispered. The words came out far more suggestive than she'd intended.

His head angled down to her again, right as the light landed on his features, and she shuddered in his arms. It wasn't anger on his face now. And she had a pretty clear idea of what he wanted.

"I want you to be my new lead," he answered.

Her eyes rounded. "In what?"

She felt his gaze stray to her mouth. "In the play. What else?"

In his bed, maybe?

And then his words sank in. She wiggled in his arms, ready to get down. "I can't be in your play." The words practically screeched out of her.

"Why not?"

Two more long strides and he put her on the sidewalk that led to the lighthouse.

"Because I'm not an actress," she said. Was he crazy?

But oh, the mere idea stirred something inside her. She *wanted* to be up on that stage. The suggestion lit a fire inside her, and she could almost feel herself coming to life. As if she'd been lying dormant for years.

Plus, this was her vacation. Why couldn't she do what she wanted on her vacation?

Because she was a Davenport, that was why. And because the world was always watching.

The fuse fizzled out.

Brody grabbed her hand and tugged her along behind him as he headed for the benches she could just barely make out up ahead. "You are an actress. I see it all the time."

She tugged on his hand but he didn't relent. "What are you talking about?"

"I saw it yesterday at the park. I see it anytime you're in the news. You act on behalf of your family all the time."

A groan slipped out before she could catch it. "Do not bring up my family tonight," she warned him. "I'm supposed to be enjoying myself here. The first time to myself I've had in years. I don't want to spend the evening talking about museum donations or building parks."

"Or about what your father did before he died?" The slash of Brody's mouth was hard.

"Especially not about that."

"Then why do you do it?"

They emerged from behind the lighthouse into the clearing and stopped. There were three garden benches positioned in a half circle, facing out over the ocean, and bushes, dripping with flowers, lining the walk all around them. She let Brody push her down onto one of the benches. He followed to sit beside her, his hard thigh pressed against hers, and it warmed that entire side of her.

She shot him a questioning look as she repositioned his jacket around her shoulders. It was almost as cold out here, closer to the ocean, as it had been driving down the highway. "Why do I do what?"

"Have the press conferences." He stretched his arm out behind her on the bench. "Cover for them."

"Because it's my job." That sounded lame. She lifted a shoulder, giving him an I-don't-have-an-option kind of shrug. "You probably can't understand it, but I have to. It's my family. Plus, things are kind of rough right now. The Harrisons are intent on making us look bad. They'll do anything to stir up trouble before the election."

Brody went quiet. She watched him, catching a small tic along his jawline and wondering what he was thinking so seriously about.

After a long moment, he finally spoke. There was no animation in his voice. "I do understand, actually. And I think you do have a choice."

She started to protest, but he captured her hand again. The rightness of it stopped her.

"Didn't you say only two nights ago that you want to do the unexpected?"

"But I won't just ignore my family."

"Why not?"

She stared at him. He had no clue. "Because of who we are, Brody. I won't simply pretend I'm not a part of them just because I want some time to myself."

"Even if you're doing things you don't want to do?"

"I never said I didn't want to do them," she protested. "I love my family. I love my *mother*. Of course I want to be there for them."

"But you also want to be bold." His gaze held hers. "Color outside the lines."

"I—"

"Try out for the play," he urged. "Do what you want to do."

The moment was too heavy, but his words were also making sense. She shook her head. She wasn't that person.

"You were bold the other night," he told her. "You were going to kiss me."

She gulped. "I was."

"If your phone hadn't rung, I think you would have."

She nodded again. She most definitely would have.

"Why?"

Who asked a girl why she wanted to kiss him? She glared at him.

"Why, Cat? Were you just curious after all these years? We were kids back then. I'm sure a lot has changed."

She *had* been curious, but that hadn't been why she'd gone up on her toes. "Not exactly," she murmured.

His thumb stroked a heated circle on the back of her hand. "Bored?"

She shook her head. It hadn't been boredom, either.

"I would have kissed you back, you know?"

"I know." She lifted her other hand from where it rested in her lap and put it over both of theirs. "I was counting on it." Her forward words sent a streak of excitement racing through her.

His pulse picked up beneath her fingers as his hand clenched hers.

"I was going to take you to bed after you kissed me," he told her.

She gulped as the tension between them increased.

"Why?" she asked, the word almost taunting. She didn't know where it had come from, but she could feel that boldness coming on again. Same as it had the other night on her deck.

One side of his mouth twitched up. "Because I wanted you."

"Because you were curious?"

He shook his head. "Nope."

"Because you were bored?"

"Oh hell, no."

"Then why?" she prodded.

He tugged and she leaned closer, then he released her only long enough to cup her face in his palms. He put his mouth inches from hers. "Because you're sexy as hell and I haven't been able to think of anything but you since you drove up in your boring little four-door sedan."

She gave him a sardonic twist of her lips. "It's a rental."

His head dipped closer, and her heart thudded against her chest. "You don't drive a sedan in Atlanta?" he whispered. The words seemed to scrape slowly down her body.

Why in the world were they talking about her car?

She wet her lips, wishing he would close the distance. She wanted his mouth on hers. "I drive an SUV." Her voice became breathless. "A Volvo."

His lips grazed over her then. Barely. And she moaned when he stopped.

"No wonder you came looking for me," he said.

She edged her chin forward, reaching for more, but he inched back.

He put enough space between them that she could see his eyes once again. "Why were you going to kiss me the other night, Cat?"

She blinked, the action feeling as if it were in slow motion. She'd started to kiss him the other night because she'd wanted to do what was *not* expected of her.

She reached for his glasses instead of answering, and pulled them from his face. Then she went up on one knee. Her arms closed around his neck, and she whispered in as sexy a voice as she could dig out, "Because I wanted to."

CHAPTER SEVEN

Cat's mouth closed over Brody's so fast it caught him off guard. Even though he'd been goading her into it.

He slid his arms around her, pulling her tight against his body, and his coat slipped from her shoulders. Both of his hands went immediately to her back. It had been far too long since she'd been in his arms, and he wanted to make sure she didn't get away too soon.

She felt—tasted—sinful.

He'd pushed her to see if he could bring back the boldness she'd exhibited on her deck, and apparently it had worked. He liked this side of her.

Hot lips devoured his. Then she closed gently around his tongue and sucked him inside her mouth. He was left without a drop of blood in his head.

"Cat," he whispered when he could get in a quick breath. He strained with the effort to not stretch her out on the bench beneath them. One hand slid into her hair and he tightened his fingers around a handful of silk.

"What?" She sounded frustrated, and he wanted to laugh at the giddiness of it.

Of them kissing. Right there, in the middle of the night. With the wind whipping around them.

This was exactly what they should be doing.

Her arms looped tighter around his neck and her breasts pressed high on his chest, and he lost every last thought he had in his head.

"Surely you don't want to talk *more*," she whispered urgently into his ear.

He shuddered at the feel of her hot breath. Hell no, he didn't want to talk more. But he paused . . . something felt off.

Oh yeah.

Fuck.

He was a Harrison.

Could he do this when he had no intention of telling her the truth about his father?

And he most certainly had no intention of telling her. The one time he'd gone down that path it had backfired in a spectacular way.

But how much of a dick would sleeping with her, without telling her the truth, make him?

There was also the issue of knowing that her mother had come between them before. It wasn't relevant to the here and now, but he suspected Cat would appreciate being made aware of the fact.

"Brody," Cat moaned into his neck. "Are you going to kiss me or not?"

She pressed into him with undisguised desire and he said to hell with it. He was going to be a dick. It was his life. If he couldn't kiss who he wanted, when he wanted, what was the point?

He tightened his fist in Cat's hair and pulled just enough to tilt her head back. She stared up at him. The light circling above them glowed over her face, showing her heavy eyelids and parted lips. Short, hot breaths bathed him. God, she was beautiful.

"That was a hell of a start," he murmured. "Especially since it's been such a long time since we've tried this. But I think we can do even better."

He angled his head then, and swept his tongue deep inside her.

Her response was a full-body-shaking moan, and he almost cried out loud at the pleasure that coursed through him.

———————   ———————

Cat shuddered as Brody's hands explored her body. They roamed with intent and purpose. Like a man who knew what he was looking for. His mouth was no less demanding. He plundered and pillaged, leaving her panting for more, then quickly headed off in the direction of her ear.

He was not kissing her as though this was merely going to be a kiss down memory lane. No. She squeezed her eyes shut as his teeth nipped at her earlobe, and her nipples tried their best to bust free of her bra. Brody was kissing her as if he intended to soon strip her of her clothes.

And she was going to let him.

She arched her neck as he made his way over the sensitive spot below her ear, and her whole body trembled at the mastery of his touch. In seconds, he'd brought places on her body to life that hadn't been awake in years. She gripped him to her, silently begging him not to stop. She wanted this. And she wanted more.

It may be uncouth to go to bed with someone so fast, but it wasn't as if she was a kid anymore. She had limited time before her children showed up. Limited time to try new things.

See something you like, go for it.

Made perfect sense to her.

As long as she kept it out of the news.

She gulped for air as his mouth hit the dip at the base of her neck. Only two minutes ago, she'd been freezing, thinking they were on the back side of crazy to be sitting out in the cold, and now she was hot enough to toss her clothes and christen the bench.

But really, she was thirty-five. Women of her age didn't have sex on public benches. Even if they *were* there all alone.

She pictured the convertible waiting for them in the parking lot and almost giggled.

That she could do. The backseat of Brody's car? Heck yeah. She'd never had sex in the backseat of a car before. Who better to do it with than the boy she'd lost her virginity to?

She dug her fingers into Brody's hair as he traveled farther down her body. His whiskers skimmed the more sensitive skin above the neckline of her dress, and every hotspot in her burned feral. She literally vibrated in his arms. For someone who hadn't had a man touch her in years, this was not healthy.

"Brody." She pulled back. She couldn't catch her breath enough to say more. She was not going to think about her actions; she was just going to go with it. She wanted that fling.

When he looked up, she was struck by the raw passion in his features, and she couldn't help but wonder if he looked at every woman he kissed like that. She gulped.

It was potent stuff.

And it added a drop of fear to what they were doing.

This was just sex, right?

She bit down on her bottom lip.

He seemed to realize that neither of them were speaking, only staring at each other as they attempted to catch their breaths. Then he reached down to the ground and picked up his suit jacket. He slipped it around her shoulders.

"I'm not cold," she told him.

His movements stalled, both hands at her shoulders. "No?"

She shook her head. "That's not why I stopped."

"Then why did you?"

She couldn't hide the smile. "Because I just had the craziest idea that involves you, me . . . and the backseat of your car."

His face went momentarily blank, and then his eyes widened. He shot a frantic look toward the parking lot.

"You want to do it in my car?" he croaked out.

Sheesh, he didn't have to sound repulsed by the thought. It

wasn't like they'd get it *that* dirty. She gave a hesitant nod. "It seemed like a fun idea."

"It's . . ." he started. Then he snapped his mouth shut.

The look on his face was priceless. Boys and their toys. But really . . . she was offering sex.

"Brody?" she asked carefully.

"Yes." He nodded. Then he nodded again, his movements more vigorous. "Yes," he repeated. He stood and thrust a hand out to her. "My car."

She leaned back. Her fingers gripped the lapels of his jacket and tugged it closed around her. She stared up at him in the dark as reality began to seep in. Damn, but she wished he hadn't had that pause. "You're right," she forced herself to say. This was best. "We shouldn't."

"No. We should." The horror-stricken look this time seemed to come at the realization that he'd royally screwed up. "Really," he insisted. He reached for her again. "You just caught me off guard."

But the blood rushing through her had slowed. She'd begun to think.

Did she really want to do it in the backseat of a car? In public?

Where anyone could show up and catch them.

Suddenly she pictured the two of them plastered across CNN, her dress bunched at her waist. Her children watching the news.

Brody's glasses were clenched in her hand, so she shoved them out to him. "Here."

Damn. She'd really wanted that sex.

He took the glasses at the same time his shoulders slumped. "I just totally blew that, didn't I?" he mumbled, and she couldn't help but see the teenager he'd once been. Bless his heart, but he was too cute.

"It's probably best we don't anyway," she admitted, though it pained her to say so. She stood and they turned as one for the sidewalk. "We just lost sight of things for a moment."

"I was just an idiot," he lamented. "How about we go back to my place—"

"No." Her word silenced his.

He let out a heavy sigh, and together they walked side by side. When they could see the parking lot, she looked over at him. His hair was standing on end again, but this time she fought the urge to brush it down.

"Hanging out is good," she told him. "We should just do that. Or maybe . . ." She shrugged, not feeling the half smile she tried to give him. "I don't know. Maybe not even that."

"No." The word shot out of him. He stopped and turned to her. "Maybe we don't do this," he said, waving a finger back and forth between them. "Though I'm not sure *not* doing this is the best idea either. But say we don't." He tilted her face up to his. As he looked at her, his features softened, and his thumb slid along her jaw. "I'm not just going to disappear, Cat. I live next door to you. I like talking to you. I like . . ."

He went silent, and she held her breath. "What?" she whispered. "You like . . . what?"

With a shake of his head, he blew out a breath. "You," he said, emotion filling the word. He kissed the tip of her nose. "I like *you*, Cat Davenport. Just like before. We just . . ." He shook his head instead of finishing, and glanced off in the distance.

But she understood what he was saying. They just *got* each other.

They fit.

She nodded. "Okay," she agreed. She didn't want to push him away. Not so soon after finding him again. The thought of not having him to talk to over the next few weeks was distressful. Even more so than witnessing his reaction to the idea of sweaty sex in his classic car.

Though funny now—*kind of*—his reaction had stung.

"I'm sorry," he apologized, as if aware she was thinking about that moment. The words came out a mix of sincerity and frustration, and once again, his gaze locked on hers.

"Me too."

But really, this was better. No complications. No risk of the media catching wind that there was anything more between them than being neighbors.

And no chance of someone plastering a "relationship" in the news.

She did not need her children hearing something like that.

"But don't write me off just yet," Brody teased. He grabbed her hand and squeezed. "You kind of woke something up in me back there."

He turned to the car before waiting for her to reply, and she smiled secretly to herself. She'd kind of woken something up in herself, too. The heady need to not simply have sex, but to have hours on end of sweaty, calorie-burning, needing-more-than-protein-and-flaxseed-the-next-morning copulation.

She needed orgasms.

And she needed them to come at the touch of a man's hands.

But reality was reality. And in the real world, she was a mother. Not to mention, part of a family whom the entire world was watching. None of that was going to change.

They reached the gravel of the parking lot, but before she could take a step forward, Brody scooped her up.

"I can walk," she complained, even though she knew it was an empty statement.

"And I can carry you," he told her.

So she shut up and let him carry her.

Her heart did break a little as they crossed the parking lot, though. Not because of what they didn't do, but because of what they'd lost so long ago. She would have liked the opportunity back then to find out what would've happened if nothing had changed. If she could have come back the next summer.

She would have loved to know how far they could have gone. First loves were special like that.

But that was ancient history. The past was the past.

He got to the car, but instead of putting her down, he studied his backseat, his mouth pursed as if in deep thought. Finally, he shifted his gaze back to hers. "We still could?" he offered hopefully.

She laughed and shook her head, suddenly feeling more upbeat than she had in ages. Even if she did still want a long night of doing things a responsible single mother shouldn't do.

She dropped her head to his shoulder.

"We're good, Brody. Really. And it was good to get this out of the way. It was bound to happen sooner or later."

If she were being honest, what had happened there tonight had been as much about the past as anything.

But she wanted to live in the present.

And in the present, she wanted to have fun. She lifted her head from his shoulder, her thought surprising her. "I just made a decision," she said.

"About?" There was optimism in his voice, and one more glance shot toward his backseat.

The smile on her face felt as if it might have physically reached her ears as she giggled at his antics. "What time are auditions tomorrow?" she asked.

His attention swung back to her. "Why?"

A bubble of unguarded happiness began taking hold, and she gave him an easy shrug. "Because I want to try out for your play."

CHAPTER EIGHT

$\mathcal{M}$R. HOLLISTER?" AMY'S SMALL HAND REACHED HIGH IN the air Monday morning as Brody tried hard to concentrate on the task at hand. He was teaching about US landmarks that day. At least trying to. He'd started with the monuments found in the country's capital, but so far had only gotten through the Washington Monument.

The hour had also been disrupted so the whole class could go to the bathroom—twice—and upon each return, it had taken more than ten minutes to get everyone back under control. Then there was the fact that he'd spent the better part of the class time glancing toward the doorway. As if Cat would show up the way she had the week before.

"What can I do for you, Amy?" Brody stooped to the rambunctious little girl and made sure his voice remained calm. Surely he could pull off patience for five more minutes. Normally he loved teaching these classes at the museum, but today he'd wanted to be anywhere but here. He wanted to be with Cat.

"Why didn't the lady come back today?"

Because he'd been an idiot when she'd suggested sex in his car?

He loosened his tense jaw and smiled at the child. "It's not her class, honey. That was just a special day."

"I like special days," she told him with great sincerity.

He did too. He hadn't had one since Friday.

Though he and Cat had agreed that nothing would change between them, he'd barely seen her since dropping her back at the theater Friday night. She'd wanted to go ahead and get her car, so he'd followed her home. First, though, he'd tried to apologize. Again.

She'd brushed him off. *No big deal.* But really, how could it not be a big deal? She'd offered and he'd balked.

Because of a car!

He wanted to bang his head against the wall, to erase the memory of her face when he'd realized what she'd been suggesting. Could he get any more geeky? He would have thought he'd long outgrown that by now.

Apparently not when it came to Cat.

At least she had gone ahead and tried out for the play the next morning. And she'd made it. She had amazing talent.

The director had asked him to sit in on the readings since they had to make a decision on the spot. Only two other actresses, ones who were already in the play, had shown up, but after they'd watched Cat's audition—along with the fact that they'd been awed by Cat herself . . . *and* everyone was excited about the thought of a Davenport being lead in the play—both actresses had declared they were more than content with the parts they had.

One of them had been chosen as an understudy, though. Just in case. No need to risk going through that again.

The whole situation could have gotten dicey given that Cat was a newbie. Brody and Clyde had worried the other two women might feel a bit of seniority, having been there for all the rehearsals. But thankfully, it hadn't gone down that way. And Cat was simply brilliant on stage.

After the auditions, he'd been ushered out of the theater. The director had no time for distractions, he'd said. So Brody had neither seen nor spoken to Cat since.

He had watched for her during his jogs, though.

But nothing.

No Cat. No chance to apologize again. No way to fix things. What else could he have said, anyway?

And now she was probably mired with learning her lines and stage marks with the rest of the cast. Who knew when she'd have time to resurface?

He glanced at the doorway, certain someone was watching him, and found Louisa standing there. She gave him a closed-mouth curve of her lips before disappearing on her merry way.

"Mr. Hollister?" This time it was Dylan.

A sigh escaped before he could stop it. It simply was not a good morning. "What is it?" he asked.

"Can we go? I saw my grandparents pull up outside."

Brody looked at the young boy and then at his watch. Two minutes were all they had left.

"Yes." He nodded. *Please, go.*

Fifteen miniature people disappeared in an instant, and Brody was left standing alone, staring out the floor-to-ceiling window of the historic building, wondering what he was going to do about Cat. That kiss had knocked his socks off, and now they were just going to forget about it?

He didn't think he could.

He wanted more kisses. He wanted Cat.

Louisa popped back by the room with a doughnut in hand. "Class was kind of disorganized today, huh?"

He made a face at her. "It was an off day for me."

"Maybe you were thinking about something else." She paused and took a bite of the deep-fried goodness before speaking around the food. "Or someone else."

Brody shoved his monument pictures into his briefcase and looked at her. He had no clue what she was talking about. "Explanation?"

He liked Louisa. She'd been around since well before he'd first volunteered at the museum. But sometimes she drove him crazy with her cryptic sentences.

She held out the doughnut. What was left of it. "Want one?"

"No." He wanted to get out of there and come up with a reason to knock on Cat's door.

"Cat brought them."

His shoulders went tight. "Cat was here?" he asked. "I didn't see her."

Louisa laughed loud enough to be heard out on the street. "Guess she didn't come to see you, Doctor." She held the last bite of the doughnut up in the air. "She came to bring doughnuts."

He must have made a face because she only laughed some more.

"Said she was just being nice."

"She didn't stick around, then?" He asked the question casually, trying not to show that he hoped she was still somewhere in the building. But he knew he wasn't fooling Louisa. His tail was practically wagging.

Louisa winked. "She intended to come back and say hi, but then she saw the newspaper and left."

The *Dyersport Gazette* was a daily paper, one that he read religiously. After his morning jog, he typically started the day by reading it with his breakfast. Delivery had been late that morning, so he had yet to see it.

"What would be in the paper to make her run off?"

Of course, with her family, he supposed it could be any number of things.

His cell rang before Louisa could answer, and he pulled it from his pocket. He stared at it as if not understanding the number on the screen. Louisa waggled her fingers in the air in a "good-bye" move and was gone before he could decide whether to answer the phone or not.

The number continued staring at him. It was his brother. Thomas never called.

Brody phoned him a couple of times a year. He had some masochistic idea that they were bound by blood, thus should have a "relationship," even if their true connection remained hidden from the public. But never in the eighteen years that he'd known Thomas had Brody gotten the same overture pointed in his direction. It made him wonder if something had happened to Arthur.

Brody hadn't seen the man in years. He had no intention of *ever* seeing him again, dead or alive.

But why else would Thomas be calling?

A tiny hope flared to life that Thomas finally wanted to put out an effort at being brothers, but Brody squashed it with the increasing lump growing in his throat. Thomas couldn't put out that effort. The media might then discover he had an illegitimate brother he'd known about for years. And that could be damning to his political career.

Curious, Brody put his cell to his ear.

"Is everything okay?" he greeted his brother curtly.

Hearty laughter came through the earpiece. "Sure, sure. Why wouldn't it be? I just wanted to talk to my older brother. It's been too long."

Brody closed his eyes. His brother sounded just like their father. Including the forced joviality.

"It has been a while," Brody agreed. He grabbed his case and left the room. "How are things?"

"Things are good. Never better. Looking great for the election this year."

Rarely was a conversation held between the two without politics being involved. Therefore, rarely was a conversation held. It bothered Brody more than it should. Just once he'd like his brother to ask about his life. To wish him well in his endeavors. Normal family conversation topics.

But Brody lived in the real world. Most of the time. Thomas was only about himself.

Yet, stupidly, Brody kept hoping for something different.

He passed the break room and glanced in to see the box of doughnuts sitting on the table. He grabbed one.

"Glad things are going well," Brody replied noncommittally. "I'm happy for you." Honestly, he couldn't care less. He shoved a bite of a cream-filled chocolate glazed in his mouth.

"Speaking of which . . ." Thomas started.

Here it came. Whatever Thomas had called for, Brody was about to find out.

"Saw you in the paper today."

Brody stopped in the middle of the hallway, the bite of doughnut suddenly refusing to go down. It was as if his heart shoved hard against his chest wall, desperate to get out. There was only one reason Thomas would have called at this moment in time because he'd seen Brody in a newspaper.

"What paper?" Brody asked calmly.

Irritation colored his view. Who had taken a picture of him and Cat? And when?

"Today's *Dyersport Gazette*. You're looking quite chummy with one Catherine Davenport."

"It's Carlton, actually," he muttered. Thank goodness it was just the local paper. No one would think twice about the two of them being photographed together in Dyersport. This was simply a situation of Thomas seeing something he thought he could use.

"Since when do you get the *Gazette*?" Brody asked. And how had he gotten it so soon?

Brody wanted to see that paper. He backtracked to the break room, saw no sign of it, then peeked into every doorway he passed on his way to the front, checking horizontal surfaces as he went. No paper anywhere.

Several patrons of the museum glanced at him, though, as if they thought he were slightly insane. No doubt he had an alarmed look on his face. He needed to know what Thomas was talking about.

Another chuckle came through the phone. Fake. "I subscribed online when I realized your lady friend was in town trying to build up support for her mother."

"She's not my lady friend." Brody stepped into the lobby of the building, and the minute his gaze landed on Louisa smiling serenely behind the reception desk, she innocently batted her eyelashes at him. "And what support do you mean?" he asked Thomas.

He could play pretend as well as his brother.

"Well," Thomas drew the word out. "There was that mighty large donation she and her brother made to the Dyersport museum last week. That hit all the big papers, as I'm sure they intended. Right after word got out that Emma Davenport had slept her way into office."

A muscle twitched in Brody's left eye.

"Then there was the park donation. Two big moves in one week. This one right after Cat's daddy's extracurriculars were exposed. Seems suspicious, wouldn't you say?"

"I wouldn't know."

After checking every seat and table in the lobby, he shot Louisa a glare as if it were all her fault. Her smile intensified. Then she lifted an arm and passed the newspaper over her desk.

He gave her a frown.

"So what's the deal between you two?" Thomas asked. "You talk her into being in your play? Or was that her idea?"

Brody's pulse almost returned to normal. This was about the play? He'd been afraid someone had been out at the lighthouse.

And then his heart rate kicked up again when he looked at the paper. On the front page was a color picture of him holding Cat high in his arms, her grinning wildly up at him, as he was about to deposit her into his car.

What had incited him to pick her up in a parking lot full of people, he had no idea. Other than she was tiny and cute and every single time he looked at her he wanted to touch her.

He eyed the caption under the picture, then did a quick scan over the details of the story. Nothing other than a mention that they'd been spotted sitting together and looked chummy. And of course, the article was about her being the new lead in his play. That was big news here. Most likely big enough it would get picked up by larger publications as well. He wondered if Cat had thought of that when she'd made the decision to do it.

The bite of doughnut he'd swallowed earlier now seemed intent on coming back up as his next thought hit.

Had she done it intentionally?

It would be the good kind of publicity to draw more attention away from her mother.

The sour feeling inside him intensified. He didn't want to believe she was that way, but he saw it every time she stepped outside the house. She was a Davenport through and through. And she always represented her family well.

Bringing her into the play may have been his idea, but she didn't do a single thing without thinking about the consequences.

Except maybe try to have sex with him in the backseat of his car.

"I hear the paper rattling," Thomas said into his ear, reminding him that his brother was still on the phone. "I take it you hadn't seen it yet?"

"It didn't get delivered on time this morning," Brody muttered as he finished the article. A reporter had been at the theater over the weekend, and Cat had impressed.

Brody had a momentary thought, wondering if he could use this notoriety himself. Maybe knowing a Davenport was in his play would get a producer up there to take a look. He still had the play out with a top-name agent. He should probably shoot the man an e-mail, pointing out the new lead of the show. That had to say something about the quality.

It felt dirty, but then, that seemed to be the game everyone else was playing.

"I understand she's your neighbor," Thomas informed him. "That's convenient."

"How do you mean?" And how did he know that? Brody handed the paper back to Louisa and stepped from the building. He was ready to end the conversation. It was going nowhere.

"Neighbor with a Davenport? Come on, man, surely you can help me out here."

Brody paused on the front porch. "In what way?" Had his brother just asked him to use Cat on his behalf?

"Looks like you're already friendly with her. Do some digging, is all I'm saying."

"Don't even—"

"This election is important, Brody. I'm not asking for anything illegal."

"But unethical doesn't bother you?"

"I never suggested lying." Thomas went into his politician's voice.

"You're not asking me not to, either." It hadn't been said, but Brody knew his brother would love a fat, juicy story, even if it was made up.

"Does she know who you are?" Thomas suddenly asked.

"She knows my name."

"Your real one?"

"My real one is Hollister. It's on my birth certificate."

"So she doesn't know?" The interest in Thomas's voice sickened Brody.

It surprised Brody to find that the reason for the call hurt. It shouldn't. After all this time, Thomas remained the same. No big surprises there. But Brody had wanted them to mean something to each other. He'd wanted to have a brother.

Hell, he'd even taken the teaching job at Georgetown hoping for the chance to form a relationship—while still not exposing to the world that they were related, of course.

Nothing about Georgetown had worked out as Brody had planned.

Nothing about brotherhood had either.

"Listen," he began. It had been almost two decades that he'd been trying to grow a relationship with Thomas. Maybe it was time to give up childish notions and accept that the two of them would never be close. Sadly, the idea bothered him as much as knowing why Thomas had called. "I've got to run. It's been good talking to you."

There was a pause, then Thomas followed with, "It's been good talking to you, too." The sincerity in his voice actually sounded real. "Think about it, will you?" Thomas tacked on, ruining any remaining positive thoughts Brody had about his sibling. Thomas was a politician to the core. He always would be.

"Sorry, man. Can't do it. And you know that." They'd had enough conversations over the years about Brody's thoughts on the secrets and backstabbing that so often showed up in politics. He was not on board with that kind of duplicity, and never would be.

They hung up and Brody stared at his phone. He wanted to call Cat.

Only, if he called her, what was he supposed to say?

Hey, nice article in the paper? Are you in the play only for the publicity?

Oh, and by the way, my brother—Thomas Harrison—wants me to find some dirt on you. Got any?

And one last thing . . . about Friday night . . . can I have a do-over?

He shook his head and shoved the phone back into his pocket. She would be at the playhouse later that evening, ready to make her debut. He would see her then.

The hum of the crowd built up a slow energy inside Cat. It was scary, but also exciting. It was downright thrilling, actually.

She paced backstage, crossing from side to side before taking a quick peek out at the crowd. There were so many people in attendance tonight. That newspaper article had apparently brought them out. It looked like all of Dyersport was trying to pack themselves into the small theater.

All but Brody Hollister, apparently.

She hadn't seen him all day. Or all weekend, for that matter. Other than a brief conversation Saturday morning when she'd shown up to try out for the part. But that's as it should have been. She'd had lines to learn, rehearsals to attend. Then countless more hours of practice in the privacy of her own cottage.

Her nerves were strung tight at the thought of stepping onstage.

Good thing she hadn't had time to think about Brody.

She snorted at the very idea. Somehow, Brody had still managed to creep into her mind. So much so that she'd gone by the museum that morning to see him.

She dropped off doughnuts for Louisa, planning to pop into Brody's class. Keep it casual. Show that all was cool between them—even though he *hadn't* jumped at the chance to sleep with her the other night.

But then she'd caught sight of the paper, and she'd been mortified. Being on the front page in the arms of a man was not what she would call flying under the radar.

Of course, trying out for lead in a play wasn't exactly flying quietly, either. She hadn't really thought that one through very well. She also hadn't taken into account the effort required to prepare for a three-act play in the span of one short weekend. She'd be lucky to get through tonight without looking like an utter fool.

Or making Brody look like one.

But she could salvage this; she was certain. It wasn't as if she hadn't been tasked with worse in her life. She simply had to do a good enough job to ensure that anything else written up showcased both her and the play in the best possible light. Maybe she could turn on the charm, even if she flubbed her way through parts of the play.

Reversing positions, she moved to the narrow back hall, her sights set on the far door. There was fresh air beyond the barrier, and she suddenly needed it. As she squeezed past the other actors in the hallway, she sternly told herself that she had this. She would wow them tonight.

But the reality was, she had no idea if she had this at all.

In fact, she was pretty sure she didn't.

Her cell buzzed as she reached the door, and she saw that it was a text from her mother. Terrific. She'd spoken to her mom the day before, excitedly telling her about the play, but Emma Davenport had not been impressed. In fact, she'd thought it was "silly." So Cat had ignored the many calls that had come in from her that afternoon. She had too many nerves as it was, and she didn't need her mother getting in her head and adding to them.

However, receiving a text from her mom was odd. It typically took an act of Congress to get Emma Davenport to punch out a message.

Cat was intrigued.

She stepped out the back door and swiped the phone to bring up the message.

Call me.

Well, that put it bluntly. And only because Cat was looking to take her mind off her nerves—even if that meant an argument with her mother—she pushed the call button.

"Catherine." The call was answered with a single word.

"Hello, Mother. The play is just about to start. Did you need something?"

"I *need* to know why I'm looking at a picture of you in Brody Hollister's arms."

Cat stood up straighter. "What?"

"I have a copy of the *Post* in front of me, and there in full color, is you in *his* arms. What is going on up there?"

The picture made the *Washington Post*? Lovely. She'd just wanted to have a little fun, not make national news.

"It's his play," she explained. Clearly it had been a mistake answering the text. This was not the argument she'd expected. "He wrote it."

"Then you need to bow out of it."

"Excuse me?"

"Tell them thanks, but no thanks. Bow. Out."

Cat stared at the phone. Had her mother lost her mind? Cat wasn't a teenager anymore. She was a grown woman. With two kids and a house. She was a widow, for crying out loud.

Her mother didn't get to tell her what to do.

And if Cat wanted to be in Brody Hollister's arms, then she would be in Brody Hollister's arms.

Though she *would* prefer to keep it out of the papers.

"I'm going to have to say no to this one, Mom." She knew that would be a new concept for her mother, but it felt strangely empowering to say it. In fact, it made her a little giddy.

Maybe it was simply that her nerves were still on the edge, and giddiness was an aftereffect.

"I'm not joking around, Catherine." Her mother used her stern voice. "You can't get messed up with him again."

"First, I wasn't messed up with him before. We *hooked* up, yes. And things happened."

"Things that I had to help you fix."

Cat clenched her jaw. "Yes. Things that you had to help me fix."

"Then I don't see what the problem is."

Cat's nerves took a backseat to her blood pressure. She didn't need her mother reminding her of her past actions. They weren't anything she would ever forget.

But she did need her mother to move on. This wasn't nineteen years ago.

"And *I* don't see what the problem is," Cat stressed. "That happened almost twenty years ago. I was a teenager. But I'm an adult now. I don't need you worrying about my private life."

"Well, someone needs to. You don't want your past coming out. Not to him."

Anger colored Cat's view. "Were you planning to tell him?"

"Of course not."

"Then what's the issue?"

"I'm just saying—"

"Looks like I need to run," she interrupted. She wasn't doing this. She simply wasn't in the mood. "We'll talk later, Mom."

"I'm only thinking of you," her mother tossed in before Cat could hang up.

Cat closed her eyes. It was a tired expression. One she found that she didn't particularly care to hear anymore. "Then how about you *don't* think of me so much?" She paused for only a second before adding, "And do not throw my past in my face, Mom. Never again. I'm well aware of what happened."

"Catherine—"

"Brody and I are friends. Deal with it."

She hung up, realizing that her hands were shaking. But at least her nerves had calmed.

What was her mother so upset about?

Cat shook her head as she stood there facing the back parking lot. She pulled in several gulps of cool air, letting her gaze hang on the waning light as she tried desperately to refocus on the play. Her mother always bore a tendency to go off about the oddest things, but really, Cat talking to a man she'd befriended years ago wasn't the end of the world. Even though they had become more than friends and she had left him out of a very important decision.

It didn't mean they couldn't be grown-ups now.

Especially because Brody wasn't even aware of Cat's deception.

She lifted her phone again, needing to calm the anger now, and decided to pull up the good-luck text that had come in from JP earlier. There was also an obviously high-pitched squealing, shouting text from her sister-in-law. *They* were excited for her. Rereading the messages now would help reset her mind, but the e-mail indicator caught her attention first. A new e-mail had come in.

When she opened it, she discovered it was from Bennett, her older brother, and she sucked in a breath. This was the first time he'd responded to any of the messages she and JP had been trying to get to him over the last two weeks.

She opened it cautiously.

Break a leg, Sis. I remember you being quite the drama queen when you were a kid. Too bad I can't be there to see it in person. I would like to.

An unexpected tear appeared in the corner of her eye, and she dabbed a finger at it to keep from messing up her stage makeup. How had Bennett known about the play? She wouldn't think the news would make it to him—wherever he was.

She loved that he thought enough to contact her, though. She just wished he'd reach out in person so she could tell him about their father. Or in his case, the lack thereof.

She hit Reply and typed in a thank-you, then tacked on:

Please call me. I really need to talk to you. It's important.

When she stepped back inside the building, the first thing she saw was Brody. He was leaning casually against the wall, flowers at his side, a blank expression on his face.

She let out a slow breath. She'd missed him the last few days.

"You're late," she chastised.

He held up the huge bouquet of yellow roses. "I had a stop to make."

"You brought me roses." The gesture softened her insides.

Her phone rang before he replied. It was her kids this time. Her heart thudded. They'd been so excited for her when she'd told them about the play.

"I have to take this." She held up the phone.

Brody gave a nod. His eyes studied her, but the blank expression didn't change.

"Mom!" Becca squealed the instant Cat answered.

Both nerves and anger disappeared that fast. Her kids always made it better. "Hey, Becca. What are you doing, sweetheart? Did you have a good day at the beach?"

They'd worn their grandparents out at Disney World the previous week and had moved into the Carltons' condo the day before. The next few days would be all about seeing how much sun they could soak up and how much sand they could track inside. Cat had offered to pay their part-time nanny to go with them to help her in-laws, but Colette and Francis would have none of it. They'd wanted this time with their grandkids to themselves.

It helped Cat not to miss them so much, knowing they were having such a great time.

"That's not why I called, Mom. This is your big day. Are you excited?"

"I am. I feel like a star."

"You are a star, Mom." Becca's words gushed out of her. "And I'll bet you're *beautiful* in your costume."

Her daughter was the one who should be onstage. *She* was the drama queen.

Cat could hear someone talking in the background before Becca returned to the conversation. "Grandma says it's time for you to take the stage," she explained in a somewhat calmer voice, as if she were working hard to force control, "so I'm hanging up now. But I just wanted to say I love you, Mom."

Another tear appeared and stuck in Cat's fake lashes. "I love you too, sweetheart."

She got off the phone, a smile lingering on her face, and once again took in Brody.

"Your kids?"

She nodded, a lump in her throat. "My daughter. Becca's excited for me."

Then she reached for the flowers and buried her nose in their scent. Gratitude suddenly engulfed her, making her chest feel too small to hold it all in. For her kids. They were the best part of her life. And for the chance to be in this play. It gave her an excitement unlike any she'd had in years.

But also for Brody. It was nice to have him around again.

He stepped in front of her then, blocking out visibility to anyone else standing in the vicinity, and slipped her hand in his. "Any chance you've forgiven me yet?" he asked quietly.

She swallowed. "For what?"

But she knew for what. And it was cruel to make him say it. He'd already apologized Friday night on the way back to her car. He felt bad about putting the sanctity of his car above sex with her.

He didn't reply now. He merely angled his head at her and gave her a look.

She fought the smile but lost, so she pulled in another deep whiff of the flowers. But when she peered back up, she sensed a heartfelt concern coming from him. He really did feel bad.

"I forgave you the other night," she told him.

"No you didn't." His words sent a shiver down her spine. "You pretended to, but you were offended."

She opened her mouth to speak, but he interrupted with, "Acceptance is not forgiveness."

The director called out that they were live in five, so Cat made a quick decision. If Brody wanted to bring it up again, then fine, she wouldn't let him off the hook so easily. She'd tried to play nice, to be polite. But if he wanted to hear the truth, she'd tell him. She leaned in and spoke softly. "I offered you sex, Brody Hollister. Free sex. No strings. And you had to *think about it*. Because of a car!"

A deep red brushed his neck and cheeks. "I'm an idiot. Make the offer again. I swear I won't make the same mistake twice."

She eyed him shrewdly. "In the car?" Dang, he did bring out the boldness in her.

"Wherever you want."

He seemed sincere. And a little desperate. It almost made her smile.

And then something occurred to her. "You have a blanket in your car now, don't you?"

The flush deepened, and she had her answer.

"Oh, my God." She made a face at him. "You're unbelievable." She thrust the roses at him. "Hold these for me. I have a play to get through."

She turned and headed to the stage, only then realizing she'd lost the anxiety that had been tying her up in knots all day. Well, most of it.

She also realized something else.

If Brody pushed much more, she was going to say yes.

To his car, his house, her house, or the danged beach.

Wherever she could get him.

Only, out of the reach of nosy photographers.

CHAPTER NINE

$\mathcal{T}$HE CROWD ROARED AS BRODY SAT IN THE AUDIENCE cringing at what Cat was doing to his play. She had changed so many of his lines he was no longer sure what was his and what wasn't.

To be fair, he didn't think she'd changed them so much as forgotten them. He'd seen her go deer-in-headlights about half-way through the first act, and the next thing he knew she'd come out with a line he'd never thought of. The guy sitting next to him had almost fallen out of his seat with laughter.

And not because he'd thought she'd messed up.

The guy had loved it. Everyone seemed to be loving it. Most of the time. Occasionally something fell flat, but overall, Cat Carlton was the funniest person Brody had ever seen. And bless the rest of the cast, they'd gone along with it, never once break-ing character.

He glanced around at the crowd as the second act continued to play out in front of them. Everyone was on the edge of their seats with anticipation, eagerly waiting to see what she would do next. Hell, he was, too.

And though every time she messed up one of his lines it was like ripping a Band-Aid off a particularly hairy body part, the response from those around him made it clear that he wasn't yet ready for prime time. He had more work to do.

Which stunk.

But it was a heck of a lot better to know that *before* he got a producer up here.

Of course, he *had* e-mailed the playwright agent that very afternoon, causally slipping in that they'd secured a Davenport to play the lead. That would teach him to try to use something other than his own hard work for personal gain. Now he'd have to redo the play, asking the agent to take another look later on.

"She's fantastic. I didn't know she could act." He heard the words from a couple of rows behind him. Several people agreed. In fact, he'd heard the words over and over throughout the last hour and a half.

And she was. Not to mention glowing.

Another line was changed and the crowd once again roared. He gave in and pulled out the small notepad he kept stashed in his coat pocket. Might as well write down some of the one-liners as she was coming up with them. He'd be an idiot not to use them.

He only hoped she could remember what he'd been too stubborn to write down before.

Fifteen minutes later, as the final scene came to an end and the actors took their bows, the crowd surged to their feet. There were several reporters in the group, all either with a camera or a photographer by their side. And they were not merely local people. In fact, he'd caught more than one of their credentials stating they were from Boston.

In one small move, Cat had gotten more people interested in one of his plays than he'd managed to accomplish in ten years of trying. It was sobering.

As she stepped to the edge of the small stage, instantly being surrounded by audience members seeking to meet her, her gaze sought him out. The blue of her eyes was bold and hot. And though she periodically glanced away to accept congratulations, her eyes kept returning to his. The action sent his pulse skyrocketing and his feet moving in her direction. His mother caught him before he reached Cat.

"I can't believe how good she is." She raised her voice to be heard over the noise, and squeezed his arm, darn near bouncing in place. "This is it, Brody. This is really it. You're totally going to get noticed."

He looked down at her. The radiance on his mother's face matched that on Cat's. "You do know that half of that wasn't even my work?"

She motioned with her hand as if batting away a gnat. "So you'll change it. Big deal."

Yeah, big deal. Only, he liked to do things on his own. Seemed that was about to take a flying leap, though. Because yes, he was definitely changing it. Cat had turned an ordinary play into a gold mine, and he would not be too foolhardy to admit it.

And then Cat was standing two feet in front of him.

Her grin spread wide as he looked at her. "That. Was. Amazing!" She shouted.

In the next instant she lunged at him, and his breath caught. Her mouth had landed on his.

Her arms twined tight around his neck, his around the small of her back, and he scooped her up so that her feet dangled several inches off the floor. It wasn't a passionate kiss, more of a release of excitement, but it was hot nonetheless.

And he couldn't get enough.

When she leaned back, her smile still in place, he forced himself to put her on her feet. And not to kiss her again. Because hey, they were in the middle of a crowd of cameras. Instead, he grabbed her roses and handed them over.

"I can't believe you don't do this professionally," he told her.

The glow from her somehow managed to hike up another notch. "I can't believe I haven't done this since I was eighteen. What a high!"

She hugged him once more, this time turning her mouth to his ear. "I'm so sorry I messed it up."

He pulled back. "What?"

Was she kidding him?

But before he could tell her she had messed up nothing, Brody's mother captured her in a tight hug, then the two of them were swept off to join the others greeting the crowd as they filed out of the small auditorium.

Brody watched her go, jealous at all the other people now on the receiving end of her glow, and worrying over what she'd just said. Did she really think that what she'd done up on that stage had harmed the play?

He hung around the auditorium as everyone dispersed, accepting his own congratulations and pats on the back, and eventually making his way over to Clyde.

The two men took one look at each other and nodded.

"You'll be making changes?" Clyde asked.

"First thing tomorrow morning."

Clyde gave another nod. "Then I'll bring everyone in early for a quick run-through before we go live."

The heavy smell of flowers filled the kitchen as Cat dug through the cabinets to find yet another vase. She'd not only come home with two dozen yellow roses from Brody, but three other people she didn't know had given her roses as well. She'd been loaded down with them.

Brody had stuck around only long enough to help her to her car, carrying the majority of the flowers for her, but then he'd disappeared. He'd given her a quick hug and muttered something about seeing her at the house.

She plunked the last dozen into the oversized glass she'd pulled from one of the cabinets, then stood, hands on her hips, and turned in a circle. She didn't *see* him at the house.

Not that he'd said he would see her *tonight*. She'd just hoped he would.

Actually, she'd hoped he would invite himself over. Especially after that kiss she'd laid on him at the theater. She hadn't meant to do that—still couldn't believe she'd done it in the middle of all those people—but as the play had ended, she'd been so amped that all she could think about was finding Brody.

Then all she could think about was being in his arms.

So she'd put herself there.

And she'd kissed him.

Which had not been one of her smarter moves. Especially since they'd already made the papers once that day. But she had to do something with all that energy built up inside her. And when a hot, studly professor looked at her as if *he* wanted nothing more than for her to be in his arms?

Well, a girl could only hold back so much.

She'd wanted to invite him over, but the look in his eyes as he'd loaded the flowers in her car had warned her away. It had almost been as if he was upset with her. Maybe because she'd botched so much of his play?

But she hadn't meant to. She'd forgotten her lines! She'd had to improvise.

The crowd had seemed okay with it, though. Most of the time. But still, she should have rehearsed more. It wasn't like her to slip up in public, and she didn't particularly care for it. She'd work extra hard tomorrow to make sure the same thing didn't happen again.

If only Brody would show up so she could explain.

She sank into a chair at the kitchen table, sitting in the midst of three bunches of the flowers, and sighed. Her foot bounced up and down on the floor as she opened her laptop. Her kids would be hours asleep, but maybe JP or Vega would be online and she could video chat with them. Or possibly she'd gotten an e-mail asking how the night had gone. Anything would be better than sitting there alone.

When she got the laptop booted up, no one seemed to be around.

She checked her cell. No texts, no missed calls. Not even another message from her mother.

Ugh. She couldn't just sit there. She was too hyped on adrenaline.

Making up her mind, she grabbed her cell and a small flashlight and headed for the back door. It was well after ten and heavy darkness outside, but she refused to sit inside bouncing off the walls. She would go for a walk on the beach. The fresh air would help. Hopefully.

Only, when she stepped out her back door, there was Brody at the base of her stairs.

He'd changed out of the suit he'd worn to the theater and into heavily washed jeans and a dark green pullover. His feet were bare, his glasses were nowhere to be found, and his hair once again stood on end. One hand was on the railing, while the other held a bottle of champagne and two glasses.

She blew out a breath.

Thank goodness he hadn't left her alone tonight.

He looked up the stairs, his expression unreadable in the shadows, and held up the hand carrying the champagne. "Want to celebrate?"

"You bet I do."

He took the three steps up to the deck, but before a single drop was poured, set everything on the small table and reached for her. She slipped into his arms.

His mouth settled over hers and she poured every ounce of energy she had into the kiss. Electricity sizzled through her body, seeming to shoot out through the tips of her toes. She licked his bottom lip. He groaned into her mouth.

Then she smiled against his lips.

In the next instant, he reversed their positions and lifted her to the narrow railing. This put her at a better height, but she had to hold on to his shoulders to ensure she didn't tip over and fall to the ground.

When he stepped between her thighs, she quit worrying about falling. She simply hung on and let him have his way.

Neither of them said anything as she tugged upward on his shirt, and he went to work on the row of buttons running down her chest. His shirt hit the deck flooring, then he pushed hers from her shoulders. It slipped down her arms and silently disappeared into the dark behind her.

She did have the momentary thought that they were out on the deck and there were solar lights glowing all around them. However, the lights only added to the ambience.

If anyone happened to be watching from a distance, it would look only like two people making out. As opposed to the fact he was currently tugging at the fabric of her skirt, trying to get it below the cheeks of her butt. She held tight around his neck and let him lift her just enough to pull the skirt free. Then he plopped her back down. She sat on the deck railing in her matching hot-pink demicup bra and bikini panty set. They'd been a birthday present she'd bought for herself earlier that year. Just in case this ever happened again.

Heat from Brody's bare chest taunted her, and she slid a hand over him. He was hot and solid and taut. Everywhere. She wet her lips, thinking about putting her mouth to him, but wanted to explore with her hands first. He was like a clay-sculpted model put out in the sun just long enough to bake to perfection.

She'd never realized daily jogging could do that to a body.

The thought made her suck in her own gut. She didn't look bad, but she had birthed three babies over the years. There was no doubt her offerings weren't nearly as chiseled as what she was getting in return.

Too bad.

She bit her lip to keep from leaning forward to kiss his skin, and dragged a finger down the middle of his stomach. It slipped right between his six-pack, and her insides quivered. They were about to do naughty, naughty things.

And then she realized that she was the only one actively participating.

"Brody?" She held her breath. Surely he hadn't changed his mind.

He still had his pants on, but there was a bit of distance between their bodies now, and he'd stopped all movements. He hadn't protested as she'd explored him, but his hands had not taken their own path over her.

"What?" His voice held a sharp edge.

"You okay? You . . . uhhh . . . *stopped.*"

"I haven't stopped." He brushed the backs of his fingers over her cheek. "I'm simply watching *you* as you touch *me*. It's hot as hell."

"Oh," she breathed out. Her lips were dry again. His gaze zeroed in on her mouth as her tongue darted out to her bottom lip. "So you don't want to quit?"

He chuckled softly, and it felt like what they were doing took on a new degree of danger. "I might die if we quit." His voice was so raw that a shiver wracked her body.

She left her hand on his abdomen but spread her fingers wide, pressing her palm flat to his skin. The feel of his pulse pumping so close to the surface had her closing her eyes. She felt suddenly shy. It had been a long time since she'd done this.

"I think I'd rather you touch me at the same time," she whispered. She hated the note of insecurity in her voice.

She opened her eyes and caught a question in his. He was asking if this was what she wanted.

She nodded. She did. She was just nervous.

Then he took a half step forward and pressed against her once again. His legs were hard and solid against the softer skin of her inner thighs, but his jeans were butter soft. He placed a hand at her waist, gripping her securely, and dropped his other hand to the top of her thigh. His fingertips skated lightly over the surface. She shivered. And then he kissed her.

This kiss wasn't quite like their first one. It still said that he knew what he was doing, and that included ridding her of her clothes. But it also said he was going to take his time doing it. He savored her. He took small tastes of her lips, the space between her eyes, her forehead. Then he nibbled the spot directly behind her ear.

An uneven sigh dragged from between her lips.

His mouth edged under her jawline and headed toward her chin, urging her head back as he went, so that she tilted her face up to the black sky. When he reached the spot just under her chin, he slipped an inch lower and held her there, her neck arched back, her eyes closed, feeling everything he was doing to her.

As he kept his mouth right at that spot, his heated breaths washing over her, his fingers suddenly touched her just below her belly button. She sucked in a sharp breath at the contact. He'd essentially blinded her by keeping her face tilted away from what he was doing. It heightened her sense of touch.

"Shhh," he whispered against her, soothing her with his words as his fingers swished back and forth where they lingered against her stomach.

Then they dipped lower. This time sliding along the lace of her panties.

She whimpered. Her nipples reached for him. They ached. She wanted to lean into him. To force him to touch her breasts.

But she didn't move for fear he would stop something else he was doing. She would have to trust him to do things right.

His mouth nipped very softly just off center of her throat and then his fingertips slid under the lace and slipped easily between her thighs. She gasped and arched her back. Her chest pushed forward, and if his other hand hadn't still been holding her at the waist, she would have tumbled backward into the dark.

"Brody," she begged.

"Shhh." His fingers swept softly over her. "Just feel."

"I am feeling, but it's—" She stopped talking, panting instead when he rubbed back and forth over the most sensitive, swollen part of her. Oh God, she couldn't remember anything ever feeling so good. Her whole body tensed as if readying to take flight.

"Brody," she whispered again, this time more urgently. "I'm not going to be able to . . ." She sucked in a sharp breath at a movement below. "It's been four years," she moaned out.

His hand stilled. "Since . . . you've been with a man?" he guessed.

She tried to nod, but he still had her head pinned back. "My husband," she murmured. "I have kids. I can't . . . not easy to . . . date," she finished.

He eased slightly away from her but left his hand where it was. She lifted her head until she was once again looking at him through the night.

"Not four years since you've had an orgasm. Surely?" He said it as a question.

A hoarse laugh came from the back of her throat. "No," she assured him. "But it's been a while for that, too. I've been busy."

He watched her steadily, then his thumb swished over her once more and she shivered in his hands. "So what you're telling me is that you're going to come really fast?"

She nodded, embarrassed.

"Sweetheart." He leaned in and put his mouth to her ear. His lips brushed over her as he spoke, and goose bumps lit down the side of her neck. "That's nothing at all to worry about. In fact, it's the best thing I've heard all day."

When his words stopped, his fingers started.

She said nothing else, deciding to simply go with it. But she did tighten her arms around his neck and press into his chest. The feel of his hard muscles soothed her aching breasts, but only temporarily. He shifted back to her lips and kissed her, covering her mouth with his and smothering the moans she made each time his fingers made a faster, tighter circle.

Her hips were tense, and she felt as if she would jump out of her own skin at any minute.

Finally, with a pulsing press of his thumb right into her core, she slipped over the edge of control. She groaned and thrust against his hand. And then she shot off into her happy place. She rode the wave, shaking and begging, almost crying at the pure pleasure coursing through her.

It lasted for what seemed a very long time, yet ended way the hell too soon.

As the contractions dissolved, she went limp in his arms, thankful once again for the hand at her waist. She tilted forward and put her forehead to his bare chest. Then she smiled lazily at the vibrations of his soft laugh.

"Don't make fun of me," she groaned. "It's been way too long since a man has touched me."

"Sweetheart," he whispered. His head was resting on hers, his cheek lying against the top of her hair, and his arms now wrapped around her back. "I would never make fun of something like that. I might try to make it happen again, but making fun of it, never."

She nuzzled her cheek against his warm chest before lifting her face to his. "Thanks for coming over tonight. I appreciate the help getting rid of some of my adrenaline."

He gripped her behind both knees to wrap her legs around his hips and scooped her up in his arms. "As long as you don't think we're finished."

He turned for the house, reaching for the champagne and glasses at the last minute, and she laughed languidly at his words. She was too relaxed to do more than hang on.

"I seem to be your prisoner at the moment," she said. "Do with me what you will."

CHAPTER TEN

$\mathcal{B}$RODY LOOKED DOWN AT CAT AS SHE CLUNG TO HIM, AND wondered what she would think if he told her he wanted to lock her away in his house for the next two weeks, just to see if there was a chance he could get her out of his system.

He feared there wasn't, but he would man up and give it his best shot.

Because if he was calculating right, they had just about two weeks. And that was all.

From what he'd overheard at the playhouse tonight, her children would be arriving in exactly thirteen days. Which meant he had no time at all to waste.

He stepped inside her back door, and before he could ask, she pointed to an open door on the far side of the room. He headed that way. Once he reached the room and could see the precisely made bed inside, he glanced down at her before stepping across the threshold. "You're okay with this?"

He'd honestly meant to have a conversation when he'd first come over. Talk about the pros and cons of an affair. Make sure it was what both of them wanted. But then he'd seen her through the glass of the back door, her eyes a little too wide, her face still flushed from the excitement of the evening, and he'd known he couldn't wait.

He wanted her. And he hadn't wanted to waste another minute making it happen.

Thankfully, she seemed to be on the same page. But now that he had a small moment of sanity, it was the polite thing to do, he supposed, to make sure he wasn't taking advantage.

She lifted her head slowly, as if it were too heavy for her body, and locked her blue eyes on his. "I'm wrapped around you like Christmas paper, Brody Hollister. Do you really think I don't want to do this?"

He smiled, and the trickle of blood that remained in his brain headed south.

When they reached the bed, he set the champagne and glasses on a side table and deposited her in the middle of the mattress. At his nudge, she lay back. Then he feasted on the sight of her. Her blonde hair tousled around her face, her eyes glazed, and some of the pinkest underthings he'd ever seen.

His gaze roamed over her curves, anxious to start exploring with his hands. He made it down her legs, all the way to her toes. Then he headed back in the other direction.

By the time he got to her chest, it was heaving beneath the tiny scraps of pink.

"You might have been wrapped around me like Christmas paper," he pointed out, innate understanding settling in that though this was as casual as any other encounter he'd had in the last ten years, it was worlds apart, "but *you're* the present."

He took a moment to uncork the champagne—going slow and a little clumsy because he could feel her watching him—then poured them each a glass before settling down on the edge of the bed. She shifted her position, lifting to one elbow.

"You did *amazing* tonight." He clinked his glass to hers. Liquid splashed over the rim. "Congratulations."

They each took a sip, her eyes locked on his, then her finger slipped inside the waistband of his jeans and she pronounced, "You need to take off your pants."

Champagne burned up his nose as he spat out his laughter.

"Woman," he said, shaking his head. "I never know what you're going to say." He put his champagne flute on the nightstand and stood, starting on his pants while she rolled to her side and watched. "One minute you seem so sweet, maybe a little shy. And the next, I wouldn't be surprised to find you with a whip in your hand, ordering me to do you bidding."

Her eyes eagerly watched his movements as he pushed his jeans to the floor. When they returned to his face, they glinted with mischief. "Whips are an option?" she asked.

"No." He laughed. He climbed into bed and slid a palm up her leg. "Whips are not an option."

"Awww," she murmured, pouting. "How sad."

She was the sexiest damned thing he'd ever seen.

She rose to her knees then, and pushed *him* to the bed. He still wore his boxer briefs, but she had the look of someone about to shed him of that particular piece of cotton. She straddled him, and his dick surged, trying to reach up for her, but she stayed on her knees.

She took another sip of champagne, eyeing him steadily as she did, before tilting her glass over his chest. The liquid dribbled over his skin, and he sucked in a breath at the coldness, quickly letting it burst free as her mouth followed the champagne down.

Her lips were hot as they moved over him. She licked at the liquid, she licked at him, she left nothing unexplored. He reached for her hips and pulled her down, wanting to feel her against him. Dying to get inside her.

The instant they connected—with two layers of underwear still between them—her ass bounced back up in the air and she shot him a dirty look.

"Don't try to hurry things along here."

He growled. "Just because you've had yours . . ."

"Hey," she began, "that was your doing. Now shut up and relax. This isn't going to hurt at all."

And it didn't. Though this time her teeth did come into play. She nipped and sucked and generally drove him stupid. And then she inched down his body until she was sitting astride his knees. He caught the gleam in her eyes as she stared at the flagpole in his underwear.

"You do know what's in there, right?" he teased. He loved teasing her.

"Mess with me, Hollister," she warned, though the heat in her voice was not a real threat, "and I'll leave it in there."

He reached for her. "Come here. You've had your fun. It's my turn."

She shook her head and pulled back out of his reach. "I'm not finished." Then she gripped his underwear and tugged, and he was free.

Brody watched as she looked at him. Her eyes glittered and her lips parted. His mouth went dry. Slowly, her small hand closed around him and Cat stroked him so gently he damn near screamed at the frustration. He forced his hips to remain still, letting her take her time, but it required every last ounce of control not to pump against the feel of her.

Several agonizing seconds later, he gave up. He was no super-hero.

"That's enough," he gritted out. He flipped her so he was the one on top, and then he stared down at all of her gorgeousness. He needed to be inside her. They could play games later.

Within seconds, he had his briefs on the floor and was reaching for her bra.

"Wait." Her hands clasped around his wrists.

He stilled. His breathing was ragged. "What's wrong?"

Embarrassment colored her features, reminding him of when she'd told him outside that she hadn't been with anyone since her husband. "I just thought about . . ." She paused and gave him a pained grimace. "I don't look like I did the last time you saw me."

He drew back at her words. She was worried about her looks?

"Stretch marks?" He'd already noticed a few on her stomach. They hadn't seemed to bother her.

"And not as . . . buoyant," she added.

The way she said it make him grin like a fool. "Good thing we're not in the water, then."

"Brody, I'm serious. I've had children. I'm not a teenager anymore."

"Damn straight you're not."

"But—"

"No buts." He leaned forward and touched his mouth to hers, and then he whispered, "You're beautiful, Kitty Cat." He winked when she made a face at his use of the old nickname. "Inside and out." He kissed her again, lingering this time, and slid his hand down to cup around her rear. "But definitely *out*," he finished with a quick squeeze.

His words made her snicker. Which had been his intent.

"I'm just saying—"

He raised his brows and she cut off her words.

She stared at him for a few seconds before rolling her eyes and huffing out a breath. "Fine," she muttered. "But don't say I didn't warn you."

She reached behind her and unfastened her bra, but an evil gleam showed up in her eyes before she removed it. Slowly, she brought her hands back around to her front. Her bra was undone but stayed firmly in place.

"You're teasing me now?" he asked.

"I might be."

He nodded, liking where this was going. "As long as you understand that I'm going to make you pay for that."

She stared up at him, her blue eyes the color of marbles, daring him to strip her of her remaining clothes. Daring him to make her pay for her misbehavior. But damned if he didn't catch one more glimpse of nerves.

It really worried her what he'd think of her body. Which did something to him. She'd been his first. She'd been innocent and untouched. And he was about to have her again.

That was special.

She was special.

And hell if that rationale didn't terrify him. Because she was only a summer fling.

Pushing the thought from his mind, he shut up his brain and reached for her bra.

———————   ———————

Cat held her breath as Brody bared her to him and took his time looking his fill. Her nervousness had caught her off guard. She'd been focused so much on being away from her life, on being more than just a mother. More than a Davenport. But she hadn't thought about the fact that Brody had been the first boy to see her naked. He'd seen her unblemished. Unflawed. And he'd seen her almost twenty years younger!

But from the look on his face now, her worries were for naught.

His jaw tensed as his hand cupped her right breast. Her nipple puckered at his touch.

And Cat wished for all she was worth that she hadn't voiced her concern. It had slowed things down too much. Made the moment softer. She didn't want slow. Not tonight. Nor did she want soft.

She wanted all-out, balls-to-the-wall sex.

The green in Brody's eyes deepened then, and she held her breath, certain he was about to say something profound. She prepared herself to appear moved at whatever proclamation he came out with, when really, all she wanted was his mouth back on her body.

His fingers tightened on her breast, the light squeeze seeming to reach through her body and show up between her legs. Then he gave a careful nod and opened his mouth. "You're right," he said solemnly. "The buoyancy is gone."

Laughter burst from her, joining with his, and the soft, slow moment disappeared.

He brought his other hand to her body, and suddenly he was everywhere. His hands stroked. Caressed. They gripped and squeezed. They found every hidden spot on her body, while at the same time his mouth sought out the same locations. And his tongue . . .

Oh, God. She sucked in a harsh breath as his tongue met places no tongue had met in way too long a time.

His *tongue* was her salvation.

Somewhere in the mix, her panties disappeared and he had her right on the edge again. She was ready for another release.

And just like that, he pulled away. She convulsed at the loss, her breath sticking in her throat as he braced himself over her, not touching her, but staring down in fascination. There was a bead of sweat clinging to his forehead, just at the hairline, and she wanted to reach up and swipe it with her finger. She was too weak to lift her arm.

He continued watching her for a few more seconds, then did a quick push up and came down. The only thing that landed anywhere was his mouth. On her breast.

She surged up as heat exploded, but too soon he lifted away. She made a gargling noise in the back of her throat.

He did it again.

Once more. Only, that time catching her other breast, and she couldn't help it, she whimpered. "Enough, Brody." He was destroying her. Her arms lay limp at her sides. "Enough," she whispered.

Humor flashed through his eyes. "But I have to make you pay."

"I've paid," she begged. "I swear, I've paid. I'm about to die here."

He laughed at her words, giving her a quick kiss. "You are so fantastic."

Then he rolled to the side of the bed and grabbed his jeans from the floor. He put a condom on and was back on top of her in an instant, easing himself between her legs.

It was a little odd, being spread by someone other than her late husband.

But not odd in a bad way. She was ready for this.

She lifted her hips, seeking Brody out. He gave a small nod and then he inched inside her. She held her breath. He was large. She'd seen that earlier when she'd gripped him in her hands.

Larger than he'd been at fifteen, and most definitely larger than her husband. Joe had been a good man and a good father, but he hadn't exactly been Hercules in the bedroom.

Brody, though, he might be deserving of such a nickname.

Once he was fully in, he raked his gaze over her, and she knew one thing for certain. The games were over.

He meant business now.

CHAPTER ELEVEN

CAT FELL TO THE BED COVERED IN SWEAT, WITH A SMILE ON her face so big she worried it might crack the corners of her mouth. It was the next morning, sometime right before sunrise, and she and Brody had just had another really excellent round of sex.

"*Ohmygod.*" Her breaths came out short and hard. She'd gotten more exercise in the past eight hours than she had in the last ten years of her life. "You have certainly learned a few things in the last two decades."

A muffled chuckle came from the pillow on the other side of the bed before a heavy arm slid across the space and captured her. It hooked around her waist and pulled her to his side. Brody lay on his stomach, his face buried in the down pillow that now smelled of sex.

Everything smelled of sex. They'd been up the majority of the night. And dang, but she was going to be sore today.

"Surely you can't go again," she questioned halfheartedly. "I didn't know anyone had that kind of stamina."

Brody rolled to his side and lazily propped his head on his hand. Early gray light from outside had crept into the room, and she could see that he seemed as satisfied—and exhausted—as she.

"I know you make a living stroking people's egos to get money out of them," he began as he tugged her even closer, this time burying his nose against the side of her neck. "But did anyone ever tell you how really great you are at it?"

She snickered. "Are you suggesting I'm merely saying what you want to hear, Dr. Hollister?"

"I'm suggesting that it's been a hell of a long time since I've been able to go four times in one night. *Something* you're doing is making it happen."

It felt like she was surrounded by a glowing bubble of happiness. She hadn't had so much fun in years. She paused, realizing the truth of it. "Don't take this as me trying to taunt you into seeing if you're man enough to go for five, but I haven't had a night like that in . . ." She lifted a shoulder in a shrug. "Forever."

He growled at her before returning his face to her neck. "I like snuggling with you," he murmured against her body. "You're soft and comfy."

She snorted. "I'm soft because I don't do crazy-ass things like jog every single day of my life."

"I don't jog for my body," he said. He rolled to his back and threw an arm over his forehead with a grunt. "Which reminds me, I need to get up and get out there." He looked at her. "I jog for my brain."

She laughed. "You think your brain has a six-pack going?"

"No, smart-ass. Exercise and watching what you eat keeps your brain healthy."

"Well, I do like your brain."

He pinched her ass and winked. "The six-pack is merely a bonus."

She would have to agree. It was a bonus. She ran her hand up his middle as he lay there, and licked her lips when the sheet over his groin stirred. "My, my, Dr. Hollister. I think you might be more man than I thought."

"It's reflex," he groaned out. "Trust me, I couldn't make it happen even if you did that thing you did again."

She grinned. She had done a thing. She'd surprised herself at how quickly the skill had come back to her. "Are you sure? I could give it a shot." She inched her fingers closer to the rising sheet.

His stomach chose that moment to protest in hunger, and they both burst out laughing.

"I guess that answers my next question," she said. "I was going to ask if you were hungry."

"Starving."

"I can make you a smoothie. Flaxseed and fruit. Would that be good for your brain?"

He shot her a horrified glare. "Is that the pink thing you drink out on the deck in the mornings? Not that you've been out on the deck in a while," he grumbled the last sentence.

A blush stole over her. "I couldn't go back out there. You caught me watching you. You called me out on it the other night on the beach. I had to stop."

"Too bad. I discovered that I liked being watched."

"Then you should have been gentleman enough not to point out that you were on to me. Let me be a dirty voyeur, and you be Mister Studly Running Man, preening at the woman who can't get enough. That way we could have both been happy."

He caught her hand in his. "I'm pretty happy as it is." He ran a finger down her arm. "How about you? Any regrets?"

She shook her head. "None." How could she have regrets after a night like last night?

"We should have talked about it first. That was my intent when I came over. Make sure we're both thinking the same thing."

"That we both wanted sex?" she teased. She threw back the covers and climbed from the bed. "I'm starving. If I had eggs I'd offer to scramble you some, but all I have are the ingredients for smoothies and a few frozen dinners. I'm not much of a cook."

Brody followed her up. She shrugged into a short robe as he pulled on his jeans. "I'll run to my house and bring back eggs," he offered. "I'm not drinking my breakfast."

"Suit yourself. But you don't know what you'll be missing."

133

He grabbed her by the wrist when she headed for the door and swung her back around. "Just sex, right?" he asked.

His words shouldn't bother her. Of course it was just sex. That's what she'd called it herself. But still . . . did he have to sound so casual about it? She gave him the nod he was expecting. "I was thinking we'd call it friends with benefits."

He studied her for a moment. She could see a pulse beating steadily in his neck. "For how long?" he asked.

She hadn't really thought about how long. Well, she had. She couldn't be running around naked with the man after her kids got there. But it wasn't like she'd put a date to it or anything.

"My kids will be up here the Sunday after next."

"Then we have today, plus eleven more days."

She nodded. "Twelve days."

His eyes were solemn and steady as he watched her, and she couldn't help but wonder what was going on in his head. Finally he said, "We have a lot to do in the next twelve days."

His tone sounded like more than "just sex," and she was just about to ask him what he meant when he pulled her close and slid his hand down to palm her rear. He fitted her against his newly formed semi-erection. "*A lot.*"

Ah. He *was* just talking about sex. Good. Because that's all it could be.

"I do have one request," she added. At his look she continued, "Can we keep this just between us?"

"Meaning what?" He released her. "You don't want me to take out an ad announcing that I'm sleeping with a Davenport? Could make me popular."

She whacked him on the arm. "That's not what I'm saying. But no, don't take out an ad either."

"Then what are you saying?"

"I'm saying, let's confine this to our houses. No PDAs. No one else's business what we're doing."

"Don't grab your ass in public. No Frenching in front of little old ladies. Got it. Can I ask why?"

"Do you *have* to ask why?" She knew he wasn't blind. He had to realize how things were for her.

"I'd like to understand."

She blew out a breath of frustration. "I'm a public figure, Brody. Not in the way my mother is, but I'm a part of things. I'm right there in the middle of my family. Always. People watch me. People *judge* me simply because of who I am."

"And you don't want them to know . . . what? That you're sleeping with *me*? Or that you're sleeping with anybody?"

"That I'm sleeping with anybody." She licked her lips, as nerves had made her mouth go dry. Brody didn't look especially pleased with the direction the conversation had taken. "I'm a mother of two small kids. I don't run around having flings. I don't want to be portrayed in the news that way, potentially confusing my own children. Plus, I'm here on vacation. To relax. And though you wouldn't know it by me now being in the play—*and donating a freaking park*—I actually came up here hoping to remain under the radar. I don't want to give anyone anything to talk about. There's enough talk about my family already."

His eyes had taken on a darker hue, nearing the color of seaweed washed ashore. "You don't want anyone using *you* to benefit *them*?"

"Exactly." Thank goodness he understood.

He gave a nod. "I can respect that. Yeah, we'll keep it between us."

"Just sex," she reiterated. Though she wasn't sure why she felt it needed to be said again.

"Just sex," he agreed. A tiny muscle twitched in his jaw.

She gave a forced smile. She hadn't meant to bring the mood down. "Thank you," she said softly.

"My pleasure."

His gaze made her nervous, as if he could see too much, so she turned and headed to the kitchen to fix her smoothie. As she went about pulling strawberries and mangoes from the freezer, Brody remained silent behind her. Scooping out the correct portions, she did her best to act normal, trying not to guess at what he might be thinking. Or if her request had bothered him as much as it appeared to.

He was so silent, her nerves ratcheted up once again, and she was just about to ask if they should just forget the whole thing when she turned to dump the ingredients into the blender.

That's when she found him standing at her kitchen window. Holding her binoculars.

One side of his mouth slowly turned up. "I thought you quit."

Embarrassment laughed out of her, but she refused to care. Yeah, she'd still been watching him jog every morning. And she'd enjoyed every second of it.

She was also tired of always having to worry about what others thought. Maybe some—most—parts of her life had to be that way, but this part didn't. Might as well own it. "Actually, I merely decided to be a bit more discreet," she pointed out in an upper-class tone. "So sue me. You have a cute ass."

She plucked the binoculars from his hand and put them back on her windowsill. Then she returned the fruit to her freezer. Screw a healthy breakfast.

"And now," she began, "your punishment for calling me out on my bad habits, *yet again*, will be twofold. First, you must feed me breakfast." She held up a finger as if to stop him from speaking. "At *your* house. You aren't messing up dishes that I'll have to clean up. I want eggs," she added, "oh . . . with *cheese*. I love eggs with cheese. And a biscuit." She looked at him with imploring eyes. "Please tell me you have biscuits at your house?"

The slash of his mouth turned dangerous. "I also have jelly. It'll taste good licked off you."

She swayed on her feet at the thought of Brody licking her

clean of jelly. Then she groaned, thinking about her genetic pre-disposition to wider-than-she'd-like hips, no matter how many three-legged dogs she did every morning. "My behind is not going to approve of any of this."

His fingers trailed the outline of her hips. "Then let me worry about your behind. I happen to like it."

She blushed. No one had complimented her backside in years.

"What else?" he asked. His hands remained at her hips.

"For breakfast?"

"For punishment," he clarified. He tugged, closing the distance between them, and the nakedness of his chest rubbed against the silk covering hers. Her nipples went on red alert. And then his hands gripped both sides of the material and tugged.

Next thing she knew, a breast was being supported by his palm, and his mouth was heading her way.

Cat's pulse leaped as Brody's tongue laved over her turgid flesh. The stubble on his jaw scratched at her skin, and she dug her hands into his hair, pulling him close. She arched her chest upward. She wanted more. She wanted it all.

"Brody," she groaned, already forgetting the need for breakfast.

"What else?" he repeated. He slid his hands behind her and cupped her bottom, shifting his mouth to her other breast.

"Uh . . ." She tried to think. What else had she been intending to say?

Then he fitted his denim-clad erection to her midsection and hiked her legs around his waist. He pressed into her.

Pinning her against the countertop, his body was hard against her soft places, and she focused her eyes to watch him toy with her breasts. Finally, she remembered part two of his punishment. She wet her lips.

"I want you to do *this* until I've had enough," she breathed out.

His eyes lifted to hers. They went dark, and he popped her nipple from between his lips and sought out her mouth. It wasn't a gentle kiss. It was greedy and hungry, and she met him stroke for stroke.

When he pulled back, they were both breathless. Her lips felt raw from the assault, but she was ready to go again.

"Lady." The word came out as a low growl. "I'll do *this* until you beg me to stop."

Before she could guess his intent, he scooped her up and headed out her back door.

"Brody!" she screeched as he bounced down her deck steps. "My boobs are showing!"

She caught a glimpse of her discarded shirt from the night before, lying haphazardly in the sand, as she reached for the edges of her robe. Somehow, her actions only made things worse. One entire side of the silk slipped between her and Brody, and he clamped their bodies tight, exposing her to the rising sun and the dew-filled morning.

There was no one around to see her, but that didn't keep the zip of excitement at bay. She hadn't been naked in public since the last time she'd been with Brody. It was heady stuff. Even though it was highly irresponsible, and she *had* just laid out all the reasons why they had to be careful.

"Brody," she pleaded. "I'm practically naked. Anyone could see me."

"I know." His words dropped lower, making him sound even more animalistic. Making her barely care about her state of undress. "But we're still at our houses," he said hotly. "So this is not a public display of affection. Only a little coloring outside the lines."

He lifted her higher in his arms and the other side of her robe slithered away. She was completely exposed.

And she didn't care.

———————   ———————

A couple of hours later, Brody came within sight of his house and his feet kicked into a higher gear. Sand sprayed up behind him.

After making love to Cat in his own bed, then feeding her break-fast—which had included licking strawberry jelly off places straw-berry jelly had likely never been—he'd taken a quick shower and headed out for his run. He would have to get to work on his play soon, if he was going to get it to Clyde in time to rehearse with the cast before tonight's performance. But he needed to clear his mind of Cat first.

Like that was possible. Throughout the miles, she had been front and center in his mind.

The night before had been incredible. The morning even more so.

But the clock was ticking on their time together, and that bothered him. He could already tell that twelve days wouldn't be enough. He would prefer the whole summer. Or more. But he was nothing if not pragmatic.

She had kids. She had a life.

He was merely a blip.

Which he was okay with. Being a blip worked for him. Even keeping it a secret wasn't so bad. It grated on his nerves, but he could see her point. Plus, it meant Thomas wouldn't get the opportunity to dissect them, looking for something he could use.

But damn, it would be hard to walk away without a back-ward glance this time. At least this parting would be of their own doing, though, and not from someone else's manipulations.

Thinking of her mother made him wonder if he should tell Cat the role Emma had played in their past. If it was him, he'd want to know. But then, he didn't live his life devoted to a name. And Cat most assuredly did. He wasn't sure she'd want the reality of deal-ing with the truth about her mother. Not for a two-week fling.

A twelve-day fling.

Damn. He already knew he was going to miss her and they were only on day one.

His house grew larger as he continued up the beach, and he let his gaze settle on Cat's place. He'd dragged her out of there so fast that morning that they hadn't even locked up. Given who she was, that hadn't been an intelligent move. Yes, there was a security gate at the end of her driveway, but that was there to keep sightseers from being too nosy. It was not true protection. And it wouldn't stop anyone from parking at the road and walking straight into her yard if they wanted to.

Given the number of cameras attached to strangers he'd seen around town lately, he suspected there were plenty of people around who would like to do just that.

The only positive was that he hadn't actually seen any of them near their houses. Apparently the locals were keeping their mouths shut on Cat's whereabouts. They liked her being a part of Dyersport and they were used to the Davenports coming and going every so often, so they were being protective of her. For now. But there was limited time on that holding steady. Cat was a public figure. And she was now in the local play. That alone would lead to talking. Which could lead to revealing her rental location, whether intentional or not.

He *had* stopped by her house before heading out for his jog, though. He'd closed it up, grabbed her cell and keys, and dropped them off at his house. But he hadn't bothered to pick her up any clothes. He liked the idea of keeping her naked and to himself for a few more hours. He'd eventually have to head to the college. He had class on Tuesdays and Thursdays. But for now, his feet ran a little faster because of what awaited him at home.

Two minutes later, he entered his house to find Cat pacing in front of the bookshelves lining his family room wall. Her eyes were closed and her lips moved, light whispers coming from her as she ran through her lines. Her fingers fidgeted in front of her.

He didn't interrupt, instead taking in the three stacks of books piled neatly on one end of his coffee table. Those books had previously been scattered over the couch, several having been on the floor. Similar piles of newspapers stood on the opposite end of the table. He hadn't realized there had been that many papers in here. Normally he took them to the recycle bin before they piled up that high. His glasses were perched in the dead center on top of the papers.

This room was where he spent most evenings, either reading or grading papers. Or catching up on national news. He could—and did—use the Internet for news, but he still loved to hold newsprint in his hand. And he loved the time spent simply sitting by himself and reading the paper.

He didn't worry too much about tidying up when it came to his books because he was always pulling one down to look something up. His office at the college was the same way. But it was kind of cute the way she'd cleaned up after him.

And she looked cute right in the middle of it all.

Except she now had clothes on. He frowned.

He must have made a noise, because she stopped walking and lifted her lashes. Clear, blue eyes the color of a Maine sky on a low-humidity day stared back at him.

"You have on clothes," he accused.

She glanced down at the sundress, which covered her but did leave her pretty shoulders bare. "I couldn't very well sit around naked all day."

"Why not?" he yanked his sweaty T-shirt over his head.

"Because . . . I . . ." she stammered as her gaze traveled south. He smiled.

"You what?" He wiped the shirt across his brow and purposely tightened his abs. He'd discovered her fascination with his abs the night before, and he wanted to do everything he could to help her out with that.

She licked her lips and her eyes went soft, and damned if she didn't swoon while standing right there in the middle of his books. He wasn't sure he'd ever actually had a woman swoon for him before. He liked it.

When she said nothing else, only gave him a heated look that suggested he could scoop her up and carry her off to his bed right that very minute, he made the bold decision to change the subject. Yes, he wanted to carry her off to his bed. And yes, he intended to. But first he needed to talk about what she'd done to his play. He had to get to work on the changes or he wouldn't be able to get them over to Clyde for that afternoon's rehearsal.

"Running through your lines?" He nudged his chin in the direction of the couch, where her copy of the play lay open on one of the cushions.

"Don't you think I should?" She laughed drily. The sound did not come out as humor. "Did you see how many times I messed up last night?"

"You call that messing up?"

"Well, you certainly didn't hear me saying *your* words up on that stage, did you?"

"No." He shook his head and tossed his shirt on a chair. Then he crossed the room to her. "I heard something far superior."

She made a face at him. "You're just trying to make me feel better. I should have . . ." Her jaw tightened with her frustration. "I can't believe I forgot so many lines."

And he couldn't believe she was upset when she'd had the entire crowd sucked into every single word she'd said. "It was your first time," he coaxed. He reached for her hands, bringing them to his chest. "You'd also only had three days to rehearse."

"And I should have been perfect."

Her thumbs slipped from his grasp to rub back and forth across his chest, and his heartbeat sped up. He knew of more places she could rub. "Why?" he asked, forcing himself back to her statement. He had to keep his mind out of the gutter or the play wouldn't get redone at all that day.

At her questioning look, he reluctantly pulled her hands from his chest and held them at her sides. He couldn't concentrate with her touching him.

"Everyone knows you stepped into the play cold," he

explained. "Anyone else would have missed lines, too. Though I'm guessing they wouldn't have recovered quite so well."

She rolled her eyes at him.

"Why be so hard on yourself?" he asked. "Perfection on day one rarely happens. You saw what happened on Friday night, during the play's first performance. There were a number of hiccups and the cast had been rehearsing for weeks. You guys had a couple of days."

"Perfection for me *always* happens," she stated matter-of-factly.

Really?

That shouldn't surprise him so much given who her family was. "Does it have to?" he asked quietly.

"Yes."

There was no hesitation in her answer, and no wavering in the determination on her face. She was one hundred percent serious. She expected to be perfect. All the time. And, he suspected, she probably *was expected* to be perfect.

He studied her, imagining what it must have been like growing up a Davenport. He'd lucked out when his mother had moved from DC back to New Hampshire, effectively eradicating both her and him from the Harrison name. Hearing Cat's "yes" made him feel bad for her. It made him wish he could have been there for her when they'd been teens. That he'd already been grown and could have shown her another kind of life.

Instead, he'd had growing left to do himself.

He'd also had his own eradication to enact.

And Cat had . . . gone on to marry a man her family had no doubt approved of.

He squeezed her hands in his and kissed her on the forehead, refusing to let retired jealousy of Joseph Carlton resurface. They couldn't go back in time, but maybe in the coming days he could show her a glimpse of another way to live. It wouldn't change who she was at her core; he understood that. She would always be a Davenport. Always about the family name first.

And he would never be that way.

He hated that she'd asked him to keep their relationship behind closed doors, and he didn't want to make things hard on her, but that was not his modus operandi. Maybe even within her rules, though, he could give her a small taste of something else. He hoped so. He wanted to do that much for her while she was there.

"Help me fix it," he suggested now.

She eyed him cautiously. "Fix what?"

"The play." He nodded toward the open copy on the couch. "Let's make it better."

Her eyes went wide with shock. "I don't know anything about writing plays."

"Honey, you rewrote half the thing last night."

"But I was just winging it."

"Ouch." He pressed his hand to his heart and hung his head. "I slaved over those pages for months, and you just *winged it* and had the crowd roaring. Sweetheart." He paused and pulled her close to kiss her on the forehead once more. This time he let his lips linger. "You may not know anything about writing plays, but you're a born actress. And you completely shine in front of a room full of people."

She pulled back and stared up at him for several long seconds, seeming to take in his words as if she hadn't heard him the first time. Finally, she gave a slow up-and-down move of her head. "I did have them laughing pretty good, didn't I?"

"You did."

She eyed him once more, her gaze flicking over his features as if in deep analysis. "And you really want me to help?"

Lord help him, yes. He wanted her to help. He nodded.

"Hmmm," she mused. "This must be a new thing for you."

He was confused. "What must be a new thing for me?"

A hint of a smile finally found her lips. "Asking for help."

Though she was laughing at his expense, he suddenly felt ten times lighter. Yeah, asking for help was a new thing. And surprisingly, it didn't taste nearly as bad as he'd expected.

He twined his fingers through hers. "You're quite the smart-ass, aren't you?"

She shrugged. "I can be."

"Just so happens that I like a little smart-ass now and then," he said. Then he released her hands, and with one of his, knocked over one of her perfectly aligned stacks of books. "I also like my books the way I had them."

She gasped. Her gaze took in the mess, and he could tell that she wanted to pick them up.

"Leave them," he dared her. "Perfection is boring." Then he knocked over another stack.

She seemed to get his meaning, because she turned from the books and propped her hands on her hips. She was a half foot shorter than him, yet he would swear that she was looking down her nose at him.

"I'll have you know that I am not boring," she proclaimed. She glanced back down at the scattered books. "But I'm also not a slob."

"Neither am I." He toppled the third stack.

"Brody!" She huffed out a breath as if he'd just done a terrible injustice to her. "Really. There's no sense in—" She cut off her own words when she caught herself bending over to right the books.

She quickly straightened, leveling a first-class glare his way when he laughed at her.

"Really, Brody. The way you had those kids in line at the museum the other day, I'd have expected more from you. Far less . . . *clutter*."

She could be such a snob. "My books aren't clutter, babe. I know exactly where each and every one of them is." He peered down at the floor, rubbing his fingers over his jaw as he contemplated. Then he lifted his head and retracted his statement. "Or I did know where they were. Before you messed them up."

It was funny the way her nostrils flared at him. He merely grinned back at her.

"You did not know where everything was," she argued half-heartedly.

"Sure I did. I have a system."

"There's no system here. You're simply a slob."

"Yet the rest of my house is clean."

He had an excellent point, and he knew it. He even saw when she registered it. The rest of his house was orderly, if not in pristine condition. She quit glaring at him long enough to look around at the open space of the rooms, where there was little more than the necessities lying about. It made him suddenly nervous, her scrutinizing him in that way. It had been a long time since he'd brought a woman to his house, and he'd never brought one over who mattered.

Finally, Cat turned back to him. "It's just your books. Why?"

"I like to read. I get lost in it sometimes."

She shook her head as if disgusted with him, but the crinkle at the corners of her eyes gave her away. "You are such a nerd," she muttered.

"Yeah." He shot her a wicked look and brought one of her palms to his mouth. "But if I remember correctly, that was one of the things you once liked best about me."

She lowered her gaze to the spot where he touched her hand. "I was," she confirmed, her eyes remaining on his mouth, "quite fond of your brain. It was fun when you went all cerebral on me."

He worked his lips to her inner wrist. "And it was cute watching you hang on my every word when I did."

She actually flushed at that.

"Damn, Cat." He scooped her against him. "I've missed you and I didn't even know it."

Her head bobbed up and down. "I've missed you, too."

He kissed her then. Because, honestly, he should have kissed her when he'd walked into the house. And because she looked so soft and kissable, and he couldn't wait any longer.

But mostly he kissed her because he'd missed her. For nineteen long years he'd wished she was in his arms. "Come take a shower with me," he urged. After his run, he needed a second shower. And he wanted his hands on her while he took it.

Her eyelids were hooded. "I've already showered."

"Then help me wash my back."

She peered up through her lashes, the look a mix of heated lust and wanton woman, and he whimpered like a baby. Good Lord, he'd loved this woman once. Even in his hormone-fueled teenage mind, he'd known what they'd had was special. He couldn't imagine having years to spend with mornings exactly like this one. Him finding her here, mixed in with his things. Her looking at him like that.

Every day, her being his.

"Help me with my back?" he whispered against her neck as he kissed the spot he'd found last night that she liked so much.

"Yes," she breathed out. The single word was one of the hottest things he'd ever heard.

He nodded, and he suddenly knew that these twelve days had the potential of ending very badly. He could fall in love with her again. Whether he believed in love anymore or not, he somehow suspected that she could change the playing field on him. Because this was Cat. And because she'd had him wrapped around her little finger since the first day they'd met.

CHAPTER TWELVE

CAT PULLED TO THE SIDE OF THE ROAD OF THE SOON-TO-BE park and turned off the ignition. Then she sat in the sedan, thinking about how the morning had gone. And the night before.

And then the morning again. In the shower.

In a word, spectacular. The man was a giver, and he knew what he was doing.

Her body ached in places that hadn't seen action in years, and her spirits seemed to be permanently up. That was all Brody. He made her body sing and her mind laugh. He made life more fun.

He also made taking off her clothes something she wanted to do again. Many times.

After he'd pulled her limp but sated body from the shower that morning, they'd begun working through his play. They'd started with her dialogue, but had ended up making changes for several other characters as well.

In the end, Brody had seemed pleased with the result.

She had, too, only now she had even more lines to learn.

She'd suggested that he try getting Ben Searcy up again, but Brody had declined. It frustrated her, because she wanted to see him get everything he desired. And the play was really good. If she didn't think he would get angry about it, she'd call the producer herself. See what she could do.

But she knew better. Brody was proud. He wanted to do things himself.

She couldn't blame him, she supposed. Knowing your accomplishments were your own was empowering. But when she could make one call and potentially get the man to head north, it was a hard pill to swallow to have to sit on her hands.

After their call-don't-call conversation, Brody had headed off for his class with plans to drop off the revised script to Clyde on the way, and Cat had returned to her house to continue running through the changes—where she'd ended up ignoring yet more calls from her mother. She was determined to pull off a much better performance that night. Which would be easier if she were still back at the house practicing now, but she couldn't avoid the park any longer.

Sharon, the project manager she'd flown up from Atlanta, had been on the job for six days, and though she'd kept Cat up to date through daily calls and e-mails, Cat knew she needed to make an appearance. It was part of the expectations when making a family donation such as this. Plus, they had only two and a half weeks left to get the park in a usable state. There was no time for even the tiniest slipup. It was best to check out the progress herself on a semiregular basis.

As she climbed from her "boring little sedan"—as Brody would call it—she noted the small clump of people standing in the shade of a tree. Reporters.

Lovely.

But it wasn't as if she could ignore them. She was news up here.

Between the park donation and construction, and now being in the play, there would likely be cameras showing up more and more. Which was why she'd pushed Brody to keep their affair behind closed doors. She knew the media would be looking for anything that would make a juicy story. She didn't want to be the one in her family to give it to them.

She only hoped they didn't start staking out her beach rental.

It was a fairly private place, but not as much as the Davenport home. And she wasn't ready to go there yet. She grinned to herself as she thought about the reason why.

Yeah, she was selfish like that.

But she couldn't help it. She wanted every last one of those twelve days before she completely returned to her reality.

Up ahead, a bulldozer was clearing out a large space, with another piece of machinery scraping a path around the perimeter. A team of people worked on the amphitheater, which amazingly was already a structure. Sharon had clearly been producing her typical magic. The two of them had worked together in the past, and Cat had known Sharon could be counted on to get the job done.

Cat saw the other woman about one hundred yards off and gave her a wave.

"Mrs. Carlton," Sharon shouted as she hurried in Cat's direction a few minutes later. She had one hand on her hard hat to keep it from jostling off. "Good morning. We've been busy here. Let me give you a tour."

"Hi, Sharon," Cat greeted the other woman as she reached her side, reminding her to call her Cat. They went through this every time. Then they picked up a protective hat for Cat and headed toward the work being done.

As they walked through the site, Cat noticed the reporters push away from the tree. They didn't get in the construction zone, but they did meander in her direction.

"Have they been out here before today?" she asked, motioning to the group of three men and one woman. She knew there had been reports of the occasional out-of-town reporter milling about, hoping to catch her in town. Most likely wanting to grill her about her father's supposed mistress. The story was still national news. And the media *still* had no sufficient answers.

"Usually just one or two," Sharon said. "The local ones. Today must be special."

"And you didn't tell them I was coming?" Cat asked with hesitation. She didn't think Sharon would do that, but it felt like someone had. Then she thought of Thomas Harrison. Her brother had told her that morning that there was now an ad running on the local stations back home. Unsurprisingly, Thomas Harrison was trying to devalue the once strong reputation of the Davenports.

As if he needed to run an ad to do that. Spilling their dirt was effective enough.

But she didn't know how he would have known she was coming out here.

Was he having her followed?

But that made little sense. What did he think following her would accomplish?

"Of course I didn't," Sharon said. "They just showed up, all of them about the same time, as if they'd gotten a memo."

With Sharon's words, Cat suddenly knew precisely who had tipped them off. It hadn't been Thomas Harrison.

It had been her mother.

JP had promised to update their mother after he and Cat got off the phone that morning. Her mother, therefore, would have known that she'd be at the park today.

And her mother would want the world to see her "doing good work."

Because after the last week and a half of rumors and made-up half truths showing up in the papers every day, Senator Emma Davenport needed some good face time. Even if it was her daughter's face to do it.

"Right here is where the toddler area will be." Sharon raised her voice to be heard over the machinery as they stood to the edge of the plot of land where the bulldozer was working. "We've got volunteers lined up to come out first thing Monday to construct the toddler playground, and then we'll start on the main play area. Those parts should be delivered by Wednesday."

As they'd discussed over the phone, there would be two areas with playground equipment, a knee-deep water feature, a sand volleyball court, and a soccer field. Eventually there would be tennis courts and an outside exercise track, but that would be phase two. The walking path would be created at this point but wouldn't be paved until later. The most important thing at the moment was to have the basics up and functional for opening day.

"I'm impressed, Sharon. Brilliant work, as always."

"It's a pleasure to work for you again," Sharon stated more formally than Cat would have liked. "And I want to say thank you for giving me the opportunity. To work with the Davenports is always a dream."

Cat fought not to let her smile slip. This was the problem with doing business as a Davenport. Everyone always felt the need to suck up. She liked Sharon. The woman was her age, had a couple of kids of her own, and worked hard for everything she'd gotten. Cat could see the two of them being friends.

If only Sharon could see that Cat was just a regular person, too.

A cute older couple whom Cat had seen around town stopped by. They were both about five feet tall and had been strolling around the perimeter of the area holding hands. Cat couldn't help but smile. *These two* were normal people. Actually, everyone up here seemed to be normal. She liked it.

"This is a wonderful thing your family is doing, Ms. Carlton," the woman said. She stuck out her hand. "I'm Delle McCann. This is my husband, Ray."

"Nice to meet you." Cat shook both their hands. "And please, call me Cat."

"Thank you," Delle said. "Our grandson met you at the museum last week." Delle's blue eyes were sharp with humor. "Something about you taking the girls in the class to the restroom."

"Yes," Cat said. "I happened to be in the building when the need arose. I helped out."

"That's what Dylan said. I think he developed a small crush that day."

Cat laughed lightly.

"I've heard good things about you," Delle added sincerely. "We saw you out here and wanted to stop by and say hello. Introduce ourselves and thank you for the park."

"I'm so glad you did, Delle. I hope you and your husband will attend the opening of the amphitheater." Cat shifted her gaze to Ray McCann. "It'll be the last night of the play that's currently running at the Sea Mist.

"We know it," Ray spoke up. "Good job there, too. We saw you perform last night."

"Did you?" Cat felt her face heat. Though she'd had a blast being on stage, it was nerve-wracking to think about people watching her, possibly knowing how badly she'd messed up.

"And we wouldn't miss the opening of the park," both husband and wife assured her. "Nor would Dylan." Delle winked, and then the couple went on their way. Cat turned back to Sharon, a happy grin on her face, and was met with the reporters.

"Mrs. Carlton, Frank Billings from the *Boston News*."

Cat's smile tightened, and she smoothed a hand over her hair. She nodded at Sharon's questioning look, letting her know it was okay to head back to the job. Cat could handle this.

"Can you tell us about that kiss you planted on local man Brody Hollister at the end of the play last night?"

Cat paused in surprise. Well, that surely wasn't what her mother had intended with the reporters. But that kiss had hit the papers. She'd seen it herself before she'd left Brody's house that morning.

Nothing could be done about it now, though. So she went into action, turning on the charm. "Adrenaline, Mr. Billings." She gave a teasing wink. "Were you at the play? It was fantastic. Mr. Hollister wrote brilliance, and I got to act it out. I was riding quite a high afterward."

"So you know him?"

"We've been friends for years." Which was only a white lie.

But at the interest that gleamed in the female reporter's eyes, Cat realized what she'd done. Shit, she was losing focus. Never give them more than they ask for. Public face 101. She knew better. Only tell them what she wanted them to know.

And they did not need to know that she'd known Brody before.

Not that they'd find anything if they looked into her past. Patricia would never tell anything about the pregnancy or Annabelle.

And Cat's name hadn't gone near a birth certificate.

"I wasn't at the play last night," Mr. Billings continued, "but if I come tonight, will you lay an adrenaline kiss on me?"

The question was met with laughs all around.

"Are you and Mr. Hollister in a relationship?" This came from the woman.

Cat made direct eye contact with her. "No, ma'am. He's a good guy, but I have kids to raise." She motioned behind her, hoping to get them back on topic. "And a park to build."

"Where are your kids?"

She gave a tight smile. "No worries, my children are fine. They're enjoying time with their grandparents."

"There's a rumor that you and Brody Hollister have been spending a lot of time together. Are you more than friends?"

"And your name is . . . ?" Cat asked.

"Trenton," the reporter filled in. "Claire Trenton from the *Dyersport Gazette*."

Cat made sure to keep her posture casual. She could handle these types of questions all day. "It's a small town, Miss Trenton. Mr. Hollister and I work together in the play. We pass on the street. That's all there is to it."

"What about your father's mistress? Have you met her?" Mr. Billings decided to play hardball. Which, no doubt, was why they were there. "Word is she's younger than you."

"Do you know her name?" Claire Trenton pushed.

Cat held her ground. She did not show nerves, and she did not show fear. She showed solidarity with her family. "We miss our father terribly, Mr. Billings. As I'm sure you can understand. These rumors are an ugly thing. It's a shame he's not here to defend himself."

"Story is she was on his presidential campaign."

Yep. They had the story right.

Her phone rang, and every pair of eyes shifted to her hand.

Her first emotion was relief. She hated this part of her job, and a phone call could excuse her from it. She didn't lie to people, but she sure as heck skirted the truth. And she didn't like thinking deep down that was the type of person she was.

Her second emotion was giddy-filled hope. Was it Brody?

She glanced at the screen and her stomach did a flip-flop. It was Brody.

A quick smile appeared before she could control it. She flattened it and held up the phone. "Excuse me. Duty calls."

She turned her back to the small gathering and put the phone to her ear.

"Tell me I'll see you tonight." Brody's "sexy voice" was sexy as hell, and he used it the instant she answered the phone. She wanted to return the favor, but kept her tone even and polite instead.

"I do believe that could be taken care of at the play this evening."

"Oh, Miss Davenport is on the phone, I see. Well then, Miss Davenport. Will I see you *after* the play tonight?" Brody insisted.

God, she wanted to be with him right then. She wondered if he had a closet in his office at the college. Could she sneak in? Have an afternoon quickie with his students wandering about?

She moved away from the reporters and let her smile return. "Don't you sound a little desperate," she teased. She'd glanced back to make sure no one had followed her. They hadn't, but they were watching. "I do believe we're still at twelve days, correct?"

"Actually, it's eleven and a half now."

She giggled. "Right. Eleven and a half. But my thinking is that *after* the play constitutes part of that eleven and a half."

"Me too," he quickly agreed. "Just wanted to make sure you hadn't changed your mind."

"After that shower this morning?" Her voice rose slightly and she reined it back in. "Why in the world would you think I might change my mind after that?"

"Mmmm . . ." He purred into the phone, and Cat's knees went weak. "I had a really good time taking that shower this morning." Brody paused, and she wondered if he was thinking about when he'd been on his knees in the shower or when she had. "I had a good time last night, too," he added.

She nodded. "A really good time."

One more peek over her shoulder, and she saw that the gap between her and the reporters was closing. She stood straighter. "I do need to run," she said. "There are . . . people here."

"Ah. The media. Probably because we made the paper again today for that kiss you laid on me."

Embarrassment rushed through her. She still couldn't believe she'd been the one to do that. "They asked me about it." She spoke quietly.

"There? Today?"

"Yeah."

"What did you tell them? That you kissed me a hell of a lot more later?" He waited a breath before adding, his voice deepening, "Did you tell them that I kissed you, too? And where all I kissed you?"

Just that quick, she was once again heated to boiling. "I really do have to go."

His laugh flowed over her, and she closed her eyes as she visualized it wrapping tightly around her. "You do that, Miss Davenport. Put your public face back on. Wouldn't want to be caught living your own life, would you?"

They said their good-byes, and she stared at her phone for an extra moment. What had he meant, exactly? She lived her own life.

Her phone rang again. This time it was her mother.

Oh.

That's what he'd meant.

Her life was never really her own. Her mother would be calling to see how the visit to the park had gone—while no doubt also chastising her over kissing Brody.

And if she didn't answer, the phone would just keep ringing.

She stepped father away from the crowd and answered once again.

CHAPTER THIRTEEN

THE SWISH OF THE SLIDING DOOR SOUNDED BEHIND CAT AS she sat on the top step of Brody's deck Friday morning, huddled inside the handmade blanket she'd grabbed off the back of his couch. Unable to sleep, she'd been out there for over an hour. Though the sun still had a ways to go before making an appearance, everything was beginning to turn gray.

She peeked over her shoulder to find Brody's dark silhouette against the glass of the door. His hair stood on end, and he wore a dark T-shirt and low-hanging jogging pants. His feet were bare. The vision made her shiver. He was mostly shadows, but she knew every detail of his body, as well as how strong that body was. And how caring the man was that went with it.

This had been both a wonderful and a rough week for her. Brody was a great lover. He was a great guy.

Her heart thudded as she thought about the rough part of the week. This was temporary.

"What are you doing out here?" His voice was heavy with sleep.

She held up her cell phone. The face of it was dark. "Reading the news."

And thinking about life. And Brody.

And their daughter.

He studied her quietly. Probably guessing that she had a lot more on her mind than current headlines. "Anything new?"

She shook her head. "Not really. Ratings for both Mom and Thomas Harrison are taking a beating. Mom for all the bad press, and Harrison for his part in digging up the bad press. But other than that, things seem to be calming down. Barely a mention of Dad's mistress today." She glanced back at the phone, pushing the button to bring the screen to life, but not bothering to load the news app. "There's backlash from some football coach down in Texas that's taking front page this morning. He got caught recruiting high school players when he wasn't supposed to."

She was rambling. Because her growing feelings for Brody made her nervous.

He padded across the deck, lowering himself to the empty space on the step beside her and handing over his cup of coffee.

"Thanks," she murmured. She buried her nose in the top of the mug as she took a sip.

"When I woke to find you not in bed with me, I thought you'd gone home."

"Nope." She dropped the phone to her lap and cupped the coffee with both hands. She'd gotten chilled from sitting out there for so long. "Just wanted some fresh air."

He eyed her again before shifting his attention to her phone. "Anything else of note?"

"An article out of Boston about the play," she said. "It's a good write-up."

Though Tuesday night had once again been rough as she and several others had stumbled a few times on the changed script, the last two nights had been near flawless. On everyone's part. She'd been pushing Brody to contact the producer once again.

"You should call him," she stated now.

"Maybe."

The wind brushed over her, and she tugged the blanket tighter around her. The T-shirt of his that she'd grabbed before coming out didn't do much to keep her warm underneath the blanket. "You're not going to, are you? Afraid to take the help my name might bring?"

"I didn't say I wouldn't call. I said maybe."

"But you're not going to," she pushed.

"I like earning my own way, Cat. You know that. I like accomplishing things on my own. Not tossing around someone else's name, as if that suddenly makes my work more worthwhile."

"You have issues." She sipped at the coffee. "And too much pride. In the play or not, my name could open doors for you, but beyond that, you deserve this. The play is good. It has nothing to do with me being in it. There's nothing wrong with taking help when it's offered."

"Except I don't believe in using people for my personal gain."

"It's not using me if I tell you to do it." The man could be so exasperating.

"Yeah." He nodded. His tone had turned surly. "Sure. Maybe I will then."

She didn't think so. Picking up her phone, she passed it over. "Do it now."

Dark eyes bored into her. "The sun isn't even up yet."

"Umm-hmmm. *That's* the problem." She didn't know why she was trying to pick a fight, but she suspected if she kept at it, he'd go a round or two with her. He seemed to be right on the edge, just like her.

He took the coffee back and downed a large gulp. After wiping off his mouth, he stared out at the ocean. The lap of the waves was more soothing than the moment felt. "What else?"

She brought up the news app and began scrolling, but his hand closed over hers.

"What else are you doing out *here*?"

"Oh."

He took her phone from her and slid it across the deck. One foot farther and it would have tumbled into the hydrangeas. As she watched it, she thought about what else. Her chest ached with all her thoughts.

"What else" was this whole week. It was supposed to just be about sex, only it seemed to have shifted when she hadn't been looking. They hadn't talked about the past or their lives between then and now. They'd been keeping it strictly an easy affair. Like they'd agreed to.

Only, last night they'd sat up in bed together watching a documentary about early politics in the United States. They'd debated opinions, and they'd laughed and teased each other good-naturedly. Then they'd kissed good night before snuggling together, his arm wrapped securely around her.

There was also the easy drive along the coast they'd taken Wednesday afternoon.

And the mornings here at his house. She'd stayed over every night that week, rising when he did to run through her yoga routine while he went for his jog, then having breakfast together when he returned. Very domestic. Very natural.

Very much feeling like more than sex.

Only, she couldn't let it continue. It had nowhere it could go because she'd never told him about Annabelle.

But she didn't know how to stop it.

Or if she wanted to.

She ran her eyes over his features now, noting that his whiskers were scratchier than usual that morning. Then she remembered he hadn't shaved yesterday because she'd interrupted his morning routine with a last-minute quickie before he'd headed off to class.

They'd been getting ready in the bathroom together each day, and she'd grown aware that he never veered from his routine. For some reason, she'd wanted to see if she could shake things up. She'd succeeded.

"I've had a good time with you this week," she said quietly. She could sit and look at him for hours.

He lifted a brow. "Had? Our time isn't over, babe. We have nine days left."

"Yeah."

He traced the pad of his thumb across the apple of her cheek, and she closed her eyes at the touch. He could be so gentle with her. So much like something she wanted in her life.

"Why so sad?" he asked.

"I'm not sad."

"Right. And I haven't found my books stacked on my coffee table every single day this week."

She smiled at that, and opened her eyes. The books had been an ongoing theme between them. When he wasn't looking, she'd straighten up the room. He'd knock the books over right in front of her the instant he saw them. If he caught her trying to pick them up again, he'd scatter them even more.

There was no reason for the mess, as far as she could see, but it was growing on her. It was so much a part of Brody that it simply felt right to be in his house that way. Yesterday she'd gone so far as to stack the books only because she liked the look on his face when he first saw it.

She ignored his barb now, as well as his question. "You going into the office this morning?"

"I need to. No class, but I have posted office hours."

She wrapped her arms around her legs and propped her chin on her knees. The moment was strained.

"You going back out to the park?" he asked.

She'd said last night that she needed to make another appearance today. "I should."

"But?"

She blew out a breath and turned her head so her cheek rested on her knee and she was looking at him. She'd been out at the park the last three days. "But shaking hands and showing how wonderful my family is is the last thing I feel like doing today."

"Then don't do it."

It wasn't that simple. She shook her head. He wouldn't understand. And she shouldn't have admitted her feelings out loud.

"Cat." The way he said her name, she knew he intended to push the issue. He'd given her grief a few times this week after she'd talked to her mom or her brother on the phone. He accused her of letting her family invade her vacation. "You don't *have* to go out there," he said now.

"Let it go, Brody. Because yes, I do."

"Why?"

She looked out toward the ocean again. She was mentally drained. Not simply from whatever this was growing between her and Brody, but from the familial requirements that were always hanging just over her head. She was weary of it all. It hadn't been so bad before all of the scandals. But now? It felt like her sense of right and wrong were warring with her sense of family duty. It was taking its toll on her.

"The Harrisons are ruthless," she offered. "You know that. And you know they won't stop. I need to make an appearance."

"For your mother?"

"For my family."

She felt him staring at her. Could sense his anger lying just below the surface. And she could understand his frustrations. He lived his life exactly as he wanted. But that didn't mean she got to do the same. "Let's not fight," she said. She waggled her brows suggestively at him. "We still have nine days."

Neither her words nor actions made him smile. But he did scoot closer. One arm came around her, and the heat from his body permeated the blanket. They sat there like that, both lost in their own thoughts for several minutes, and for the first time in years she felt normal. Like a woman simply being held by a man. They were sitting in the dark, the romance of the ocean lulling them into intimacy, with not a soul anywhere around. And she found she desperately wanted to confess her sins.

She wanted to make Brody understand how much she'd loved their daughter.

And she wanted to apologize for not giving him the opportunity to do the same.

"Have lunch with me today," he tossed out. "I'll leave the school by noon. And I don't mean here at the house. Let me take you out. A real date. We'll end it at Lily's. I'll buy you the doughnut of your choice for dessert."

That would be a Boston cream filled. Louisa had been right. They were killer.

But he wanted to go out in public with her as a couple. They'd talked about that.

She studied him. Daylight was just beginning to peek up out of the water, and he looked so cute with his mussed hair and his geeky little glasses. Moments like this made her wish her life was different.

"You know I can't do that," she finally said.

"Actually, I don't know any such thing. Why can't you, exactly?"

"I told you. I don't need the publicity. I don't *want* the publicity." And she didn't want to listen to her mother. She'd just gotten her mom calmed down over the kiss picture that had shown up earlier in the week. A lunch date would only get her started again.

"Afraid you'll be disinherited if seen with a nobody like me?"

She chuckled and rested her head on his shoulder. "You know that's not it."

He picked up her hand, holding it in his, before putting it to his mouth and kissing each finger one at a time. The move was gentle, but it was also loaded with meaning. It said that he was having some of the same thoughts she'd been fighting with herself.

Was this more?

Could this be more?

"Are you trying to romance me, Dr. Hollister?"

He looked her in the eyes then. The day had grown a couple of shades lighter, and she could make out every thought on his face. It was scary to see that he was as confused as she. "And if I am?" he asked.

She turned away because there was a sudden pressure at the back of her eyes. She did not want to sit out there and cry for him.

But he didn't let her escape. His hand touched her chin and brought her back to him.

"What would be so bad if I am?" he whispered.

"It's complicated."

He nodded as if he understood. Then he put his lips to hers. The kiss was gentle, and it took her breath away. It explored her mouth slowly, showing her how well he knew her. He knew how to make her respond and what would pull a moan out of her.

And he knew exactly when to stop to keep it from going too far.

"Complications are merely the road bumps of life," he told her. "In the end, you still reach your final destination." He tucked a strand of hair behind her ear, his eyes warm and inviting. "The only question is, which destination do you want to choose?"

His words hurt her heart. Because in that moment, she wanted to choose him. She wanted to step away from her life, to not have made her decisions in the past—to not have *had* to make them—and she wanted to choose Brody.

But she couldn't. She'd messed up too much.

"You don't understand."

His jaw hardened just a fraction, but he kept his words easy. "Then explain it to me."

She closed her eyes once again as the picture of a tiny baby girl formed in her head. How could she explain that to him?

"You can't let her control every aspect of your life, Cat."

Her eyes popped back open. "What do you mean?" He didn't know about Annabelle?

"Your mother. You're here on vacation, but you're letting her control you."

"I'm having the vacation of my life," she argued. And she was. She'd found him again.

"So your idea of your perfect getaway is to do your family's bidding?" Before she could respond, he added, "Letting her control your every waking hour?"

He was starting to piss her off. He didn't get it. He'd never been in her shoes. This was what her life was. It had always been her life. She wasn't sure she'd ever had an option in the matter. It just *was*.

"Live a little," he coaxed when she didn't immediately respond. "Go out with me."

She shook her head. She had to make him stop this before she caved. "We're just sex, remember? That doesn't entail dates."

His eyes turned hard. As she knew they would. It made her feel guilty.

"Don't be mad." It was her turn to coax now. "It's just easier if I give them nothing else to talk about. That's all. It has nothing to do with you."

"Oh, I'm aware it has nothing to do with me. It's all about the Davenport name. I get that. I've known it all along."

They fell silent once again, both staring out at the ocean, watching the sky turn from gray to pale blue to pink, the sun just barely hidden below the edge of the ocean. It was a beautiful morning, and she was with a man she cared about. And she would soon have to go home and put these memories aside.

It sucked.

"Will you tell me about your husband?" he asked.

She jerked her gaze to Brody's. The request shocked her. He still had the hardness of anger, but he was trying to hide it.

"I know you met him not long after you and I were together," he continued.

She nodded. He wanted to know about her life since they'd last seen each other. And damn it, she wanted to know about his. Because this wasn't just sex, no matter what she'd said.

"He and I actually met as kids," she started slowly. "He lived in DC year-round. We would hang out when my parents brought us to town. When I was ten, Mom and Dad bought a house there and we began staying through the school year. Joe and I became good friends."

"You didn't date, then? Before?"

"Before *our* summer?" She shook her head. "No. I expected we would eventually date, but it wasn't pressing, you know? I had things to do, he had things to do. His family was very much like mine. We attended dinners and events together. Although his parents were considerably more laid-back than mine. But the summer I came home—" She broke off, having almost said the summer she came home from having Annabelle. She tucked her hair behind her ear and cleared her throat. "The summer after *us*," she said instead, "I'd been away. At boarding school." She told the lie easily. It was one she'd repeated to her friends back then. Even to her brothers. "When I came home that summer, it seemed like time."

"You didn't want to come back up here?"

She shook her head. She couldn't have come up here. "I thought we were over," she whispered.

He nodded as if he understood. "I came up just to make sure."

"You were here the next summer?" She hadn't expected that. *He'd* been the one to quit calling *her*. Why would he have come back?

"Only for a few days," he admitted. "I had my license by then." He shrugged. "There were a few other things I needed to do, but I had to make sure you hadn't come back first."

She didn't understand. If he'd changed his mind about them months before, why would he have bothered looking for her again?

"What happened next?" he asked before she could form the question. "I saw a picture of you two that summer. I knew you were dating."

"How did you see us?"

"In a DC paper."

"You got a DC paper? When you were sixteen?"

He looked away from her then, his profile solid and firm, and she wanted to reach over and caress it. "I've always been into history," he explained. He didn't meet her eyes. "I've read newspapers from all over the world my whole life."

She'd forgotten that he'd always been that way, but yeah, even at fifteen, he'd routinely mentioned some story or another that he'd read in a paper.

"I also saw your wedding photo a few years later," he admitted.

Surprise kept her from speaking.

"I was engaged at the time," he added casually.

She sat up straighter, the blanket slipping from her shoulders. "Was? What happened?"

"The *marriage* itself didn't happen," he explained. "I had a teaching position at Georgetown back then. I came home one day and we had a fight. She chose to . . . go a *different* path than marriage. I chose to come here."

Cat stared at him. The story sounded simple, but he still wasn't making eye contact. There was more to it.

"How did you meet?"

"In school. She was from Bar Harbor. She went to St. Mary's like me."

"And then you moved to DC?"

"She had an interest in politics." He grew quiet before nodding. "And I had a bit of an interest at the time, myself."

"Yet you didn't go into politics?"

"My interests changed."

Again, she could tell there were things left unsaid. She studied him, trying to figure out how to get him to open up, but the set of his jaw indicated that wouldn't be happening.

So she switched gears. "Any other serious relationships?"

He shook his head.

"Kids?" She didn't know why she hadn't thought about that before. He could have kids tucked away somewhere.

Again with the head shake. This time there seemed to be sadness with the movement, and she couldn't help but picture him with a small, pink bundle in his arms. Then she pictured him with fifteen kids hanging on his every word at the museum.

"You would make a great dad," she said softly.

His mouth twitched as he peeked at her out of the corner of his eye. "My mom says the same thing. It wasn't meant to be, I suppose."

Guilt turned her gaze back to the ocean.

After a couple more minutes of silence, she pulled herself away from her memories and swallowed past the burn now lining her throat. "So you lived in DC for a while. When did you move up here?"

"The semester after the engagement ended. The college had a position open, and I'd made a good impression while attending. Plus, I like the ocean. I had nice memories of being here." He flicked his gaze at her. "Of one particular summer here. So I bought a house. I had some money saved up. I chose the beach so I could sit out on my deck and watch the sun rise with a beautiful woman if I wanted to."

His words made her tuck herself in closer to him. It was a good way to start the day.

"What was your degree in?" she asked.

He picked up her hand. "A double major in history and psychology."

She watched as he traced her fingers with his thumb. "I went to an all-girls school," she told him.

169

"I know."

His movements on her hand were hypnotic, but somehow she dragged her gaze up to his. "You seem to know a lot about me."

He nodded. "I also know that you spent a couple years in the peace corps. I don't remember where."

She eyed him thoughtfully. Had he been keeping tabs on her?

"I like to read the news," he explained defensively. "I told you. And the Davenports have always had a penchant for making the news."

That was true. Even when she didn't want to. But her parents had played up her joining the corps to help showcase what a caring, nurturing family they were. She had no doubt the story would have run in several of the papers Brody read.

At the feel of his lips brushing over her hair, she swallowed around the lump in her throat. Them being together was so easy.

"Guyana," she said. "I spent twenty-seven months there." She hadn't wanted to head directly off to college the minute she'd graduated high school. She'd needed to get away. Needed time to mentally recover from giving her baby away.

Her mother had protested, of course. Cat should be with the family, with her dad's campaign. Blah, blah, blah. But Cat had used the family against her mother that time. How great would it look for a Davenport to give back by joining the peace corps? Of course, then her mother had gotten the story run worldwide.

Joe had been at West Point by then, so they'd dated long-distance. By the time she'd come home, she'd been almost ready to deal with her life again.

Or at least she'd been better equipped to fake it. Some things never completely went away.

"Tell me about being over there," Brody urged.

As if he could sense what those twenty-seven months had meant to her, he encouraged her to talk about them. She told him about working with the kids, learning their language, and even about bathing in a creek.

"A Davenport bathed in a creek?" he asked. He still had his arm around her, and his palm now stroked up and down her bare arm. Steady winds washed over them as the soothing waters lapped closer to his deck. The aroma of salt clung heavily in the air and the sun became a bright ball of light making them squint into the day.

"There were no cameras around during those times," she pointed out. "And yeah, it was either bathe in the creek or go dirty."

"I would've liked to have seen that."

"Me dirty?" she glanced up at him.

He dropped a kiss on her nose. "You in the middle of all those kids. In the middle of a third world country. You being dirty and disheveled. Just being . . . real."

She nodded. She knew what he meant. And she had been.

There had been no headlines to make, no butts to be covered.

It had been all about the people of Guyana. The time spent with them had helped to heal her broken spirit.

It was one of the best times of her life.

"Since we're unburdening ourselves of secrets," he began after a couple of minutes of silence, but didn't continue until she looked up at him. "I have one for you."

Her entire body tensed as it went on alert.

"What?" she asked cautiously. She tried to pull out of his grasp but he didn't allow it. He kept her tucked close, his arm tight around her.

"I found out something interesting last week," he said. There was a grimace on his face.

It couldn't be that bad if he'd just found it out. "What is it?"

He swallowed, and her nervousness remained high.

"Your mother once called my mother."

Cat's jaw loosened. She could think of no reason her mother would have to call Annabelle Hollister. Ever. "I don't understand."

"She called the house after she'd already told me that you'd moved on."

She was missing something. "What do you mean moved on?"

"Found someone else. As in, *another guy*."

"Back then? But I hadn't," she muttered. "Not until the next . . ." A dark cloud suddenly seemed to loom overhead as answers began to form. Her heart raced. "When did she tell you that?"

"About three weeks after we left Maine."

"But—" She clamped her mouth shut. The missing puzzle piece had finally clicked into place, and anger spread quickly throughout her body. Her mother had been the reason Brody had stopped calling. Why had that never occurred to her?

From the day Cat had come home and announced she'd met the boy she wanted to someday marry, her mother had been against the idea of Brody. She'd gone so far a week later as to forbid Cat from talking to him again. Cat hadn't stopped.

Of course her mother would have figured out another way to end it. Didn't her mother always do "whatever it took"?

"And you believed her?" she asked. That hurt as well.

"I'd called several times and you were out." His fingers tightened on her arm. "She can be convincing."

A cracked laugh escaped Cat. Couldn't they all? It was a talent her family had.

Not only had she and her mother kept the pregnancy from her brothers, but from her own father as well. The one person Cat had felt safest with in the world.

She'd never once gotten to cry on her father's shoulder because she'd given up her baby.

Because her baby had died and she hadn't been there for her.

"Why did my mother call yours?" She pulled out of his arms now, and crossed hers over her chest. "And does it have anything to do with you not returning *my* calls?"

When he'd quit calling her, she'd finally given up and tried him. Twice. The first time, his mother had said she'd pass along the message, but Cat had known Brody wouldn't be calling. She'd heard it in the tone of Annabelle Hollister's voice.

The second time had been months later. Annabelle had told her not to call again.

"She wanted to make sure my mom understood that I was not to talk to you again," Brody confirmed. "Ever."

Yep.

Cat should have known.

"Sometimes I could hate my mother," she whispered quietly. She hadn't meant to say it out loud. In fact, she hadn't realized she'd been thinking it at all. Or ever thought it.

But she did, and she had.

Her mother ran her household with an iron fist, and it had always been that way. She still ran her family that way. But Cat had resented it more than once in her lifetime. She just hadn't allowed herself to admit it.

Emma Davenport had acted like their family was damned near perfect, and she expected them all to behave that way. But the last few weeks, Cat had seen the Davenports were a long way from perfection.

Cat wasn't the only one who had potentially brought shame to their good name.

"Anything else?" she asked.

He eyed her. The wind whipped across them as if as angry as she. And she could tell that there *was* something else. She saw it in his eyes.

But he shook his head no.

"What is it?" she demanded. Fear burned inside her. Did she even want to know?

Did she even know who her mother was?

Again, he shook his head in a negative motion. "I could hate her, too," he told her. Meaning her mother. Because she'd ended them before they'd been able to figure it out on their own.

"Why did you call me months later?" Brody suddenly prodded.

She couldn't tell him the truth. She'd been seven months pregnant and terrified she was making a mistake. She'd wanted him to come rescue her from her life.

"I was just thinking about you that day," she finally said. "It'd been a while."

"Yeah." He held his hand out to her and she put hers in it. "I missed you, too," he said.

Not allowing the anger to completely overwhelm her, Cat sat there, her hand in Brody's, and watched the rhythm of the rolling water. Her mother had made sure Brody wouldn't find out about the pregnancy. She'd had a hand in things from the moment Cat had peed on a stick. And no one was going to get in Emma Davenport's way.

The sun climbed higher. It was going to be a beautiful day.

Cat didn't feel so beautiful. She should have guessed what had been going on.

She should have known better.

"You okay?" Brody asked.

She nodded. "I take it your mother just told you about this?"

"Last Wednesday. She saw that you were back in town and came clean. Apparently the guilt of not passing along your messages had eaten at her over time."

"Must be nice to have a mother with a conscience." Cat smirked. She couldn't blame Annabelle Hollister for her part in things. The woman hadn't known about the baby.

Brody chuckled lightly and tugged on Cat's hand. "Come on. Let's get you inside. You have to be freezing out here." His voice dropped lower. "But you do look really good in my T-shirt."

She smiled then. It was forced, but the small act made her feel better. She liked wearing Brody's shirt. And she liked having mornings like this with him—though she could do without discovering past lies. "If we go in, will you warm me up?" she taunted.

"Absolutely." His arm slid around her once again, and he lifted her face to his. The concern and understanding on his features eased her anger. But just a fraction. Her mother had wronged both of them. Yeah, Cat should have pushed harder. It was her life; had been her baby. But she'd been only a kid. A kid who should have been able to trust her mother to do the right thing.

"Thanks for telling me." She didn't have to like the facts. However, she was glad to know them.

Brody smoothed his fingers over her face then, as if committing her to memory. "I should have told you Tuesday morning. After . . ."

She shrugged. "Maybe." He probably *should* have told her after they'd first gotten together. But then, they were supposed to be just sex. "But we all have reasons why we do things."

Once again, a shadow passed through his eyes and she wondered what else he hadn't told her. But then, maybe some secrets were best left undiscovered.

The last thing she wanted to worry about right then was what her mother had or had not done in the past. Or what *she* had done. This was now. This was them. And she only had nine more days to live in this particular moment.

She touched her mouth to his, and this time, *she* kissed *him*. She wanted to show him that she knew him, too. Only, she didn't pull back when she reached the tipping point. She pushed harder.

His hands came up to hold the back of her head, and he took over. He lapped at her mouth as if he'd never tasted anything quite so savory, then he angled his head and plunged deep inside.

She moaned.

The next moment, she was in his lap. Straddling him, with the blanket no longer around her. It had also become apparent that she hadn't pulled on underwear along with his T-shirt.

"Cat," he breathed her name against her neck as his hands smoothed over her body. He touched her as if he'd never explored such treasures. "You do something to me, lady. Something crazy."

She nodded. He did something to her, too.

Then he kissed her again, and she put everything else in her life out of her mind.

It was a shock when he abruptly pulled away a few minutes later, but it took her only a couple of seconds to realize why. Her phone was ringing.

"It's probably my kids." She thunked her forehead against his, their ragged breaths mingling.

"That's what I was thinking. But they're early this morning."

He was right. The sun had just come up. Her kids should still be asleep.

Worry settled in as she slid from Brody's lap and moved to get the phone from where he'd slid it across the deck. But when she picked it up, she saw that it wasn't Becca calling, but JP. "It's not the kids," she said. She didn't answer it. She didn't want her morning to be interrupted just yet.

When it quit ringing, she muted the sound, but a text came in before she could put the phone away and return to Brody.

`Call as soon as you can. It's important.`

It was from JP.

Then she saw that another call had come in that neither of them had heard. That one had been from Bennett.

"Oh, no," she whispered. She pressed her fingers to her mouth. The phone signaled that yet another text had arrived.

`Catherine, call home. Your brother and I need to speak with you immediately.`

She felt sick to her stomach as she read her mother's words.

Had the Harrisons somehow figured it out? That Bennett wasn't biologically a Davenport? But how would they know that? How would anyone but her mother and the man who'd gotten her pregnant possibly know that?

"Everything okay?" Brody came up behind her.

She shook her head. "I think something has happened."

"Your kids?" he asked immediately. The stricken look on his face comforted her.

"No." Her hands began to shake. "I don't think so. It was JP."

"But you talk to him every morning, too."

She had been that week. She swallowed and looked toward the back door, wondering if the news had already broken nationally. "My mother also sent a text," she added softly.

She didn't mention Bennett's missed call, or what she suspected the problem actually was. Poor Bennett. She hadn't wanted him to find out this way.

"I need to turn on the news." She moved toward the door as if in a trance. Her legs felt twice as heavy as usual, and as if they no longer bent at the knees. "I don't have a good feeling about this," she mumbled, talking only to herself.

Brody gripped her by the elbow and led her into the house. She neither wanted to turn on the television nor to call either of her brothers back. She wanted to return to the deck with Brody. She wasn't ready for more intrusions on their time.

And if this was the problem she thought it was, it would be a *major* intrusion.

So big, she'd have to go home.

No matter how angry she might be with her mother, if her brother's lack of paternity had come out, Cat couldn't ignore the scandal that would ensue—or how it would hurt her brother. Her mother would be finished for her run for reelection, but that didn't mean they wouldn't have major cleanup to do. The whole family would be all hands on deck.

Brody pushed her down to the couch as she brought up JP's number. He grabbed the remote to turn on the television, and a well-known anchor for one of the major news stations filled the screen. In the background was a picture of Cat's late father.

Her last bit of hope fizzled out.

The phone rang in her ear as the picture on the screen changed to a woman and young boy dashing from a car into a well-kept house, and Cat gasped. All the blood drained from her face. This wasn't about Bennett after all.

JP answered the call, and at the same time Brody must have heard whatever the reporter had said on the television. He turned to her, his jaw slack.

She spoke to both men at the same time. "They found out about Dad's other kid."

CHAPTER FOURTEEN

$\mathcal{B}$RODY PACED FROM HIS KITCHEN TO THE LIVING ROOM, while keeping an eye on Cat. With her announcement, she'd lost the color in her face, and it had yet to come back. Additionally, there were now cars lining the street out front. Someone had revealed where she was living.

Of course, the reporters were watching *her* rental, not *his* house. And his blinds were now closed. They didn't know to point their cameras thirty feet to the left.

After Cat had finished talking with her brother, her phone had immediately chimed again. She was perched stoically on the couch now, talking in monotones to her mother. Brody listened in, feeling like a spy. Cat didn't know his connection to Thomas. If she did, she would not be so open in her conversations in front of him.

He currently had a front-row view to the plans being laid out on the Davenport side of this race, and if he were the wrong kind of person, he could use that to his brother's benefit.

He knew Thomas would be keeping a close watch on every last move right now. And he knew Thomas would be calling again. In fact, he already had. Brody hadn't answered.

Thomas was calling only for information, and Brody had no information to share.

"Of course they did this," Cat said into the phone. "We already covered that." She rose and moved to the front door, where she carefully peeked out the side window, and Brody couldn't help but take in her trim legs coming out from under his Stonehenge Rocks T-shirt. He liked her being comfortable enough to wear his clothes.

"I had nothing to do with it." Her voice rose, one hand flitting in the air as she paced back and forth in his foyer. "Who would I tell? Why would I tell anyone?"

She listened, and Brody wondered if her mother was explaining to her at that very moment exactly who *he* was. Because in Emma Davenport's eyes, he was the enemy. Especially with this kind of news. There was an illegitimate Davenport son. That was explosive.

He really should tell Cat who he was.

He'd actually considered it for one brief moment outside. If she'd said yes to going out in public with him, he'd sworn to himself that he would tell her. They couldn't be more than they were if she didn't know his background. And he wanted to be more than they were. No matter that she *had* thrown their just-sex rule in his face. The way he saw it, that had been her way of fighting her own feelings.

So he'd fought back by pushing forward. He wanted to know all about her. He wanted her to know about him.

He *wanted* to see if they could go somewhere other than to bed.

But there remained the issue of her family standing between them. The importance of the Davenport name was a viable living entity in Cat's world, and it probably always would be.

Which would never allow them to coexist.

Brody would have to be first in a woman's life or he wouldn't be in it at all.

Cat blew out a breath. "Fine. I'll be ready."

She hung up and began punching out a message on her phone. She didn't even look up at him. "JP is readying his jet to come and get me," she informed him. "I'll have to get back over to my place without those vultures out on the street catching me. Do you have a hoodie I can borrow?"

Brody stared at her. "You're leaving?"

Of course she was leaving. Her mother had spoken, thus Cat would be getting on that plane. No thoughts about him. Him and her. Or the fact that she was the lead in his damned play.

Cat shot him a quick look. "They're setting up a press conference for this afternoon. That barely gives me enough time to get there and get changed."

"What about the play?"

It finally appeared as if something other than her precious family had crossed her mind. "Ah, crap," she muttered. "Brody—"

"You're really going to do that to me?" He cut in. "To everyone?"

"This is my job."

"It's your family." He hid his hurt with anger.

"Exactly." The word signified that he should understand. And he did understand. Politics and saving face would always come first with people like her.

"You have a commitment here," he stated bluntly. "But hey, you're a Davenport. That trumps everything doesn't it?"

"Don't be like that."

"How am I supposed to be? Nothing will ever be more important for you than your precious name. No matter who it hurts. No matter how much it might have hurt *you* in the past."

"You mean what you told me outside? About my mother breaking us up."

"Does that not bother you at all?"

"Of course it bothers me," she suddenly yelled. "I'm furious with her. And you can bet I'll let her know it. But there's not a hell of a lot I can do about it at this very moment, is there? And it just so happens, something a bit more important than what my mother did nineteen years ago has come up. I kind of need to deal with that first."

They stared at each other, both furious, both breathing hard, and Brody beginning to wonder if it would've been better if she'd never come back. It would've hurt less.

"Please, Brody," she began. The level of her voice lowered, but he could tell she was still riled. "I can't be in the play now anyway, can't you see? The press would hound the theater. Is that what you want? They'll hound *me* when I so much as step outside."

"Life must be rough for you."

She turned angry eyes to his. "You're not being fair. I'll come back. I just need to be there for this. This one night. To show a united front."

"Right. I'm the one not being fair." He moved to his front closet to pull a hoodie from a hanger, and tossed it to her. "I thought you were on vacation, Cat. I thought you had more backbone than this."

Her shoulders dropped. "Can you ever really be on vacation from your family? What if *your* mother needed *you*?"

Cat had a point, but his mother would never ask him to ignore his obligations and leave a group of people hanging. And certainly not to protect her reputation.

He raked Cat over from head to toe. Ten minutes ago she'd looked to him like a woman he could consider risking everything for. He'd been ready to do anything to try to win her over. Even break his own rules about playing political games in public. She might be someone he could do that for—on occasion, and for good reason, of course. And he'd even believed he stood a chance.

But now, the only thing he saw standing before him was a Davenport.

Before he could think too hard about the heaviness in his

chest at the thought of Cat going back to Atlanta—possibly never seeing her in the flesh again—his phone rang.

Thomas.

Shit. His brother would likely just keep calling. He was persistent when it came to politics. His doggedness had won him more than one race over the years. However, Brody had no desire to talk to him. He didn't want to be used.

He also didn't want to risk saying anything that could inadvertently hurt Cat.

Not that it mattered. Hell, she already had one foot out the door anyway.

He wouldn't stand there and continue arguing with her, though. She clearly wouldn't be changing her mind, thus more confrontation would only lead to him saying things he didn't really mean. She said she would come back. That didn't fix the fact that she was walking away to begin with. Leaving the play. Leaving him.

But it stupidly did something to his heart. Something *he* needed to fix.

Maybe talking to Thomas would help harden his heart.

He held up his still-ringing phone. "Don't forget to let Clyde know you're bailing."

And then he very purposefully stepped out the back door and closed it soundly behind him.

"I assume she's there with you?" Thomas oozed his special brand of charm the instant Brody answered the phone.

"What do you want?"

Thomas laughed the laugh of someone who knew he'd just won the grand prize. "I want you to tell me what's going on. Mama Davenport ready to pull out yet?"

The entire situation made Brody sick. The games that went into running for office were beyond his tolerance.

"How did you even find this to leak it?" Brody bit out. Her dad had been dead for years. It had clearly been a closely guarded secret.

"Hey, there's no proof it came from me. Not that I won't pounce on it. It's the best thing I've heard in . . . well . . . in a decade," he finished, his final words said in such a purposeful manner as to put an itch between Brody's shoulders.

"What happened a decade ago?" Brody asked carefully.

Thomas didn't hesitate. "Your fiancée dumped you."

A chill traced Brody's spine. "And this made you happy?"

Brody had taken the job at Georgetown to be close to his brother. To form a relationship. They'd pretended to be friends over the years, meeting up a few times. But if they'd done it too often, the fear was that their actions might look suspicious. Yet Brody had always wanted more.

Thomas had been enrolled at the college at the time, and seeing each other in passing had made it possible to begin that relationship. His ex-fiancée, Devan, had gotten herself involved as well. Strategically, though unbeknownst to Brody at the time.

"She wasn't right for you," Thomas pointed out.

"How would you know?"

"Because she dumped you for Dad."

Irritation squeezed like thick fingers around Brody's neck. She'd dumped him to *work* for his father. Which still pissed him off. Brody had come home one afternoon, having decided to press her to set a wedding date. They'd been engaged for a couple of years at that point, and she'd sidestepped the conversation each time he'd brought it up.

Only, on that day, when he'd pushed, she'd pushed back. Said she'd have to clear the time off with her new boss. Once Brody had learned her new boss was his father, he'd given her an ultimatum.

Brody might want to build a relationship with his brother, but he wouldn't live with Arthur Harrison in his life. Ever.

Devan hadn't even needed time to think about it.

"She used you since day one," Thomas added. Which was true. After the breakup, Brody had realized that she'd only gotten serious about him after realizing he was "friends" with Thomas Harrison. The up-and-coming son of Senator Arthur Harrison.

Eighteen months after their engagement, after Brody had finally shared with his future wife who his father was, Devan had conned him into attending a fund-raising dinner for the express purpose of meeting Arthur. Brody had not been pleased to find himself standing in the middle of a crowd, pretending he and Arthur were longtime acquaintances, and being forced to introduce his fiancée.

And now?

Now Devan was press secretary for the White House. She'd gotten exactly what she'd gone after. Another step up the career ladder.

"You didn't need someone like that." Thomas's words lost their charm and took on a seriousness Brody couldn't remember ever hearing. "She was only out for herself."

Brody suddenly recalled a rumor he'd heard not long after he'd moved to Dyersport. He hadn't wanted to believe the rumor then.

He still didn't.

However . . .

"You slept with her," he stated. He didn't need an answer. Thomas didn't bother to give one.

Which was fine. Deep down, Brody had known all along. And he hadn't been surprised. He supposed he'd never asked about it because then he could go on blindly pretending they shared nothing more than DNA.

"She came on to me," Thomas explained.

Brody made a noise of disgust.

"You guys were over. I knew that. I also knew what she was up to. She had the job with Dad, but she wanted more. She *wanted* to be in the family."

"Then why didn't she marry you?"

A bark of laughter echoed through the phone. "Are you kidding me? I didn't want to marry her. She was using me." He could almost see Thomas shrug. "So I used her. I wanted to make sure that if *you* happened to have second thoughts, you'd see the type of woman she was and steer clear."

Thomas was saying that he'd slept with Brody's fiancée to protect him? Bullshit.

He'd slept with Devan because he was just like their father. He'd wanted to prove that he could. Because people like that did things for the pure power of it.

"She was livid to find out she'd barked up the wrong tree yet again," Thomas told him.

Brody did get some slight satisfaction from that. "Yet she's made her way to where she wanted to be," he pointed out. "She always wanted the White House."

"She also slept with many people to get herself there."

Disgust had Brody moving to the railing. He let the wood press into his lower stomach as he leaned over the edging, wanting to vomit up the fact that he'd ever cared about someone who'd cared so little for him. She'd been conniving from the start. And he'd been a blind sap to ever think it was love.

Then it occurred to him what else Thomas was saying. Brody stood up straight.

"She slept with Arthur?" he asked.

"Still does from what I gather. An occasional thing."

"But didn't he remarry last year?" To some woman who was less than half his age, if Brody remembered correctly.

"Marriage has never kept our father's pants zipped," Thomas pointed out.

"What about you?" he asked.

"What about me?"

"Do you have a problem keeping it in your pants?" Thomas had gotten married two years before. Brody had been invited to the wedding. He hadn't gone.

"My marriage is very happy," Thomas stated.

Brody noticed his brother didn't say monogamous. He simply couldn't imagine living that kind of lifestyle. "I need to go," he said abruptly. No possible good could come from this conversation.

"Can you at least tell me—"

"No." He had no idea what Thomas intended to ask. But no, he wouldn't tell his brother anything. Ever. "And don't ask me to again."

"Okay." Thomas accepted defeat. "But the latest gossip wasn't the only reason I called. I wanted to check on you."

"Why?"

"You once told me about her," Thomas said, his words coming out cautiously. "The summer we first met."

Brody closed his eyes and tilted his face up to the sky. He *had* told Thomas about Cat. He'd been staying at the Harrison house in DC for a few weeks, having just learned who his father was—and still believing it mattered—when he'd seen the paper with the picture of Cat and Joseph Carlton in it. Thomas had caught him staring at the photo as if wanting the man to step out of the picture so Brody could rip his throat from his body.

"You were in love with her."

"Lust," Brody corrected. "We were kids."

"You're not kids now."

He gripped the railing in his hand, taking note of two additional vehicles pulling up behind the line of cars already parked at the road. He could barely make them out through the trees, but they were there. All lining up, waiting to pounce. "What's your point?"

"You back with her?"

Brody shot a glance at his back door as it opened. Cat stepped out dressed in jeans, tennis shoes, and his hoodie. It completely covered her blonde hair and hung to midthigh. Her gaze landed on him.

Did she want him to tell her it was okay for her to go?

He wouldn't do it. It was not okay for her to run back to Atlanta just because her mother told her to. There was more to life than living it for someone else.

He turned his back to her and closed his eyes against the sound of her feet heading down his deck stairs.

"I wouldn't call it 'back,'" he finally muttered into the phone.

At four o'clock that afternoon, Brody was sitting in his cramped office at St. Mary's, the small television that was attached to the wall in the corner tuned to a national news station. He was still steaming from his argument with Cat.

He couldn't believe she'd walked out.

He couldn't believe he'd thought she might change.

But she had left. And she hadn't changed.

An hour after she'd crossed their yards, he'd watched her car back out of her garage. She'd still been wearing his hoodie. And every single vehicle parked on the street had pulled out after her.

Irritation with himself had him muting the TV in his office. He needed to put her out of his mind. Probably he should have left the school hours ago. Found something else to do. Maybe someone else to do. He certainly didn't need to continue sitting there, waiting to see what Cat's family planned to say. Or to see Cat standing there with them.

He needed to accept that the two of them were over.

Because if she came back . . . and if he took her back . . . it truly would be just for the sex.

He picked up his cell phone and scrolled through his contacts. He needed to call Clyde. Make sure Cat hadn't forgotten to let him know she was gone. Laura would have to step into the lead role tonight, which meant Laura's role would now be left empty.

He and Clyde had talked about that potential, and Clyde's wife was a possible backup. The woman usually took part in the plays but had decided to sit this one out. She'd wanted to spend the summer at the beach with the grandkids instead of at the playhouse with her husband. But she *was* the director's wife. She'd step in during their time of need.

Brody only hoped that Laura was ready for her new role. Because this poor play had stood about all the ups and downs it could take.

Such as his latest rejection. He'd sent an updated copy to his dream agent earlier in the week, but it had failed to impress. The man had passed.

Additionally, there had been no further word from Ben Searcy. No matter what Cat had said, Brody hadn't wanted to use her name to entice the man up here. Looked like that had been a wise decision, given that she'd left town.

He gritted his teeth.

When the full-screen view of the reporter pulled away to allow a picture to appear in the top corner of the television, Brody turned the volume back up. Cameras were positioned in front of a stately front porch where a podium and microphone were set up. The on-air reporter was making small talk about the Davenport home as she waited for the press conference to begin.

He found Clyde's number and hit the button to make the call.

"And joining us from Portland, Maine . . ."

Brody whipped his gaze back to the television. Cat was on the screen now, her public face in place as she nodded politely to the camera. She was in another inset box, this one in the lower corner.

"She's still in Maine," he muttered.

"Hello?" Clyde said on the other end of the phone. "Brody? Who's still in Maine?"

Brody realized his call had connected. "I'm sorry. I'll, uh . . ."— he couldn't take his eyes off the TV—"call you back."

"Oh-kay." Clyde sounded as confused as Brody felt, but Brody didn't give himself time to worry about it. He disconnected and once again grabbed the remote.

At the noticeably higher volume, the department receptionist leaned back in her desk chair and stared into his office. Her head was tilted down so she could see over her bifocals, and she wore a seriously perturbed expression. He got up and shut the door.

Then he walked backward to his desk, never taking his eyes off the TV.

Emma and JP Davenport stepped out onto the porch, followed immediately by JP's wife. The screen switched so the Davenports filled the space. Cat remained in her own box.

She wasn't with them.

Brody's heart raced as he wondered what that might mean.

He couldn't take his eyes off her. She had on a green dress that complemented her blonde hair flawlessly, and she looked softer than he'd ever seen her. She still wore her Davenport air, but she somehow seemed more like the girl he'd known nineteen years ago. Not the daughter of Senator Emma Davenport.

She looked more solid in herself. As if she finally had a foot stuck firmly outside those lines that gave her so much trouble, instead of both being planted directly within her mother's reach.

The three in Atlanta stood quietly as cameras in the audience flashed, then the crowd hushed. Emma Davenport stepped to the podium. "Good afternoon, ladies and gentlemen. And thank you all for being here. We'll make this brief. There have been allegations about my late husband that have been brought forward in the past week, and it pains me to say that unfortunately, we now believe some of these allegations to be true. Jackson Senior *was* involved in a brief relationship during his last campaign. He was riddled with cancer, and it was very poor judgment on his part, but that did not change the stalwart man that he was. The man who did decades of good for this country."

Brody tuned her out. He didn't care to hear her words, because that's all they were. Words. What he was interested in was Cat. And knowing why she was in Maine.

She looked amazing.

"Since we've learned of the child," Emma said, her voice droning into his brain once again, "we've done everything for him and his mother that we can. My son has set up a trust for the boy's education."

"It's lies."

Brody jerked his gaze to the door. Cat stood there. In the same green dress she wore on TV.

"What's lies?" he asked. He could barely speak from the adrenaline roaring through him.

"Everything she's saying."

Of course it was. He could have told her that much. He rose from his seat but stayed behind his desk.

Cat glanced at the receptionist—who was, no doubt, leaning an ear in their direction—then quietly closed the door. They stood looking at each other from across the room.

"Not about the school," she continued. "JP *is* paying for that. The kid has severe dyslexia. JP suffered from the same so he understands the need for specialized tutors and the right schools. I would have helped, myself, if he'd bothered to tell me about Daniel when he first found out."

"When did he find out?"

"Last year." She moved farther into the room, a tiny scowl creasing the spot between her eyes as she edged a heeled foot around a pile of books on his floor. "Actually, *JP* found out last year. My mother has known about Daniel since before my dad died."

Brody was floored by both the pronouncement and the fact

that Cat was sharing it with him. "Your mother knew the woman was pregnant?"

"Girl. Woman." Cat nodded. "Whatever you want to call her."

Oh God, he couldn't be hearing this. He was the enemy.

Only he wasn't.

He was Cat's lover.

He was the man who wanted to be a whole lot more than a lover.

"When did *you* find out?" he asked.

She reached the spot directly in front of his desk and her solid gaze landed on his. "Right before I came to Maine."

He was beginning to understand why she was staying in a rental house instead of the family home. She may not be ready to admit it, but she was distancing herself. She was trying to break free.

His chest burst with renewed hope.

"She also wrote a fat check," Cat added. "Eight years ago. With the instructions that Lexi was to stay quiet. Forever."

"Ah, shit."

"Right." She smirked. "Just wait until that one comes out."

"Hopefully it won't."

Her eyes held pain. "I'm not sure I even care if it does."

That was a change. And he wasn't sure he believed her. But she *was* here. That had to mean something.

The voice on the TV changed to Cat's, and Brody shifted his gaze to watch her make her statement. She was saying all the right words, but he knew her better now. Whereas before he would have thought she believed everything she was spouting, he now saw deeper. He saw that she was hurting inside. She hadn't wanted to say those things. She didn't believe them.

"Why are you here, Cat?" He could feel his pulse pounding in his neck.

"I prerecorded my statement earlier in Portland. That way I didn't have to be at the station live."

He nodded. Not the question he was asking. "Why are you *here*? In Maine. Why did you change your mind about going home?"

"Oh," she whispered. She looked away then, her eyes seeming to focus on something that wasn't in the room, before they cleared and returned to him. She pulled her shoulders back. "I couldn't do it," she stated bluntly. "I got back to the house, and everything you'd told me out on the deck kept running through my head. Yeah, it was in the past, but that's who my mother is. That's who she's always been. And, I suppose, that's who I thought I was. Do whatever it takes to protect the family."

"You don't think that now?"

"I think I don't *want* to be that person. Not to the extent of hurting people, lying to them. I'm not sure who I am anymore, but I don't want decisions made solely due to public opinion to be what my kids witness for the rest of their lives. It's not what I want them doing themselves. Plus, I didn't want to go home. I'm on vacation. And I have a play I have to be in tonight."

He circled his desk and gathered her in his arms. "I am so proud of you."

"Me too."

He kissed her then, hoping it would be okay, because he couldn't wait any longer. He hadn't lost her. Not yet. And maybe he wouldn't have to. He *would* tell her who his father was, though. The air needed to be cleared between them before they could figure out what came next.

But not today.

Not when she'd already been through so much. He just wanted to hold her right now.

"Thank you for coming here," he murmured as they separated. "To the school."

He brushed a hand over her hair and kissed her forehead. What he left unsaid was that by showing up at the college, people would have seen her on campus. Probably had witnessed her entering the history building. They could put two and two together.

He kissed her again. They wouldn't stay a secret much longer. He hoped she was prepared for that.

"I was worried I'd have a hard time finding you," she said into his neck. She'd snuggled tight up against him. Right where he liked her to be. "But then I saw your red car in the parking lot."

He sighed. "You kill me with that. It is so much more than a red car."

"Maybe." She kissed him on the cheek. "But I'll bet the backseat has never been appropriately broken in."

CHAPTER FIFTEEN

THE BACKSEAT HAD NOW BEEN BROKEN IN.

Cat blew out a breath of air as she pushed off Brody's chest and sat up, resting her shoulders against the back of his front seats. She stared down at the man between her thighs. He sat bare assed on the uncovered seat, breathing as if he'd just run a marathon.

But it wasn't a marathon he'd participated in.

Unless there were competitions for quickies.

She grinned at him as she leaned forward and planted one last scorching kiss on his mouth. Their chests were slick with sweat as she rubbed against him. This whole backseat thing had been an excellent idea.

"Your garage isn't quite the romantic location I'd envisioned for this," she pointed out.

He chuckled tiredly as his eyes took a slow sweep over her body. "My garage was the only safe place we had."

Safe from the paparazzi. Yes, she would have to agree. They'd been relentless tonight.

She and Brody were sealed up tight in the small space, sitting in the dark with the top of the car down. They'd left the key in the ignition, adjusting it so the dash provided faint illumination over the space, and if she were to be honest, it was actually kind of romantic.

The instant Brody had turned off the engine, they'd crawled like horny teenagers into the backseat. She'd teased him with the idea all afternoon, and apparently had won him over, no matter how much "abuse" his precious car might take.

They'd stripped articles of clothing from their bodies as they'd fought their way back, and Brody had barely gotten his pants off before Cat pushed him down and climbed on top.

She blew out another breath. "It was fun, though."

"Oh yeah."

He dropped his head to the seat back, and she gave one more tiny grind against his lap. His fingers squeezed her hips, but nothing else moved.

"You've drained me, Kitty Cat," he mumbled. He lifted a finger to outline one side of the glasses he'd talked her into wearing for him, then let his hand drop limply by his side. She thought he might fall asleep sitting right there in the stale night air of his garage. "The entire day has," he added.

She couldn't argue that point.

The entire day had been exhausting. First was their morning argument. Lots of mental anguish had been expended on both their parts, followed by make-up hugs and kisses at the school—which had *not* led to a secret closet rendezvous, unfortunately. The receptionist had been a wee bit too nosy.

On the heels of making out at the school had been dinner, then the play. Where they'd stood arm in arm afterward, as she'd greeted the crowd.

Of course, the play had once again been a disaster.

Not because of the acting. No one had missed any lines. But because of the paparazzi that had been camped outside. They'd been loud and obnoxious, and some of them had even managed to sneak inside before the last act had completed. They'd been bold. So much so that it had not only created a fire hazard in the small building, but it had taken Cat and Brody an extra forty-five minutes simply to extricate themselves after the show.

It was not good for business, as no person in their right mind would want to be subjected to the craziness of the media circus that had been experienced that night.

Between questions about her father, she and Brody had also taken plenty about themselves. It had become obvious to anyone looking that they were now a couple. Prior to the play, they'd ridden all over town, the top down on his car, as if blatantly declaring a relationship.

Yep. She was full-fledged out in public with her man. And she was okay with that.

She'd talked to the Carltons before leaving the house that morning, filling them in on the latest information to hit the news, and asking them not to let the kids watch anything other than cartoons on the television. She didn't need Becca and Tyler hearing stories about their grandfather before she got a chance to have a talk with them about it. Which also meant they wouldn't catch any pictures of her and Brody that might show up before she got a chance to explain that, either.

Assuming there would be something left to explain by the time they got up here.

She still had to tell him about their daughter.

That had been the other major decision to come from her reckoning that morning. As she'd paced every room of her rental, trying to decide how she wanted to go forward in her life, what she'd concluded was, it was *her* life. And she should get to live it her way.

Not only was she tired of jumping through family hoops, but she had a wrong to right. She should have tried harder to tell Brody about her pregnancy.

If not at the time, at least when she'd found out that Annabelle had died.

Or when she'd first seen him again here in Dyersport.

She'd had so many options. So many times she'd failed.

She'd behaved like her mother. Turning a blind eye to what was right. What kept her family "innocent" of any wrongdoing. Because they *had* done Brody wrong.

As she'd sat on his deck before sunrise that morning, she'd known they could be more. She cared about him. How much she cared was too scary to think about at the moment, but she'd like the opportunity to *see* what it was. To determine how much.

In her house later—after she'd unsuccessfully been able to get Bennett back on the phone and had sent her mother a text simply stating, "I'm not coming, I'll record from Portland"— she'd allowed herself to think about Brody. And she'd known that to truly have the chance she wanted, she had to share their daughter with him.

The more she'd thought about her mother's phone call to Annabelle Hollister all those years ago, the more Cat realized she'd behaved like her mother far too much in her life. Her mother had crossed the line by stepping between them when she'd known there was a baby at stake.

Cat had crossed that same line by not trying harder to tell Brody the truth.

She'd been carrying his baby. He'd had a right to know.

It was as simple as that.

And now she had to pay for her past.

Brody's breathing deepened to a steady rhythm, and she caressed his cheek with her fingers. Her big, strong man was asleep in the middle of the backseat of his prized Chevelle after having hot, sweaty sex. Without putting a blanket down first.

It was the sexiest thing she'd ever seen.

She reached to the front of the car and turned the key in the ignition, sending them into darkness. Then she removed her glasses and snuggled in against him. Her arms went around his waist, and she laid her ear over his heart. Then she, too, tumbled toward sleep.

A single ray of sunlight landed on Brody's closed eyelids the next morning, forcing him to crack open one eye and look around. That's when he realized that he wasn't in his bed.

He was in his car.

With Cat sprawled out across his chest. Completely naked, but still, he was in the backseat of his car.

He shook his head in wonder. The woman had talked him into desecrating his one true love. But then, he couldn't think of anything else he would rather have been doing last night. Especially after the way she'd shown up at his office, then stuck by his side the rest of the day.

She'd come back to town a changed woman. It had been quite the turn-on.

He opened his eyes wider now, blinking the sleep away, and noticed that the beam of sunlight had slipped in around the edge of the blinds attached to the high, narrow windows. It gave the entire garage a dusty hue, but enough light that he could take in his surroundings.

There were clothes everywhere.

His shirt was slung over the side of the driver's-side door, her panties dangled from his rearview mirror, and there was . . . he did a double take as he stared at the wadded-up tissue perched carefully on the edge of the seat beside him. He didn't even want to think about what that might have been used for. Or the fact it was touching his car.

He dropped his head back and stared at the ceiling. If the sunlight hadn't woken him, the cramps in his back surely would have. Geez, he was too old to sleep in the backseat of a car.

Last night had been insane. He'd never experienced anything like the madness that had descended on the tiny theater, and honestly, he would be okay going through the rest of his life never experiencing it again. He was not a fan of the utter madness.

But if he wanted to be with Cat . . .

He glanced down at her, still sleeping on his chest, her blonde hair splayed out everywhere.

If he wanted to be with Cat, the media would be a part of it. At least occasionally. And it would not be something he could set limits on. Not the kind of limits he would be able to enforce. He'd have to be okay with that.

For Cat.

For them.

He closed his eyes again. If that's what it took, he'd do it. Assuming she could get past the Harrison name. And that was still a big assumption on his part. She might have taken a nice first step to independence the day before, but one step did not wipe away a lifetime of training. He simply had to convince her that a name he'd never had anything to do with would not hurt her family.

Emma Davenport could continue hating Thomas Harrison for years to come. Brody being a Harrison wouldn't matter. Because no one needed to know. And hopefully mortification that her daughter was with a Harrison would be enough to keep Emma Davenport's mouth shut on the matter.

Cat stirred against his lap, and as she wiggled, his lower body stirred right along with her. God, he couldn't get enough of this woman. When he opened his eyes this time, a pair of gorgeous blues stared back at him. She yawned behind her hand and shot him a sexy half smile.

Her breasts were naked, her hair had that I've-been-loved-well tangle, and she looked as if she might be up for a good-morning round as well. It took everything he had not to dig out another condom.

"Morning," she muttered.

He winked at her as his heart whispered things he wasn't quite ready to hear. He had to pull the reins on his emotions fast if the two of them didn't stand a chance.

"What have I let you do to my car, Kitty Cat?" He had to tell her about Arthur.

"Don't complain. You enjoyed every minute of it," she said around another yawn.

He slid his hands to her bare rear and squeezed. "I did. Though I'm not sure I can unbend enough to climb out of here."

"Tell me about it. I feel like a pretzel."

He chuckled and leaned forward, searching out her mouth. He slid both hands into her hair and closed his mouth over hers. She was warm and pliant, and she gave as good as she took. It was the kind of kiss he could stand to wake up to every day.

When they separated, she let out a shaky breath and flopped back to his chest as if she'd used up every last ounce of energy she had. One hand inched upward until it reached his jaw, where she simply touched his cheek.

He captured her hand in his. This was perfect. Except for being in the garage.

"What are you thinking so hard about?" she asked.

He tucked his chin in and looked down at her. Where did he start? With the fact that he might just want to keep her? Forever?

Or jump right into the harder issue? That being his Harrison blood.

"You." He went with option three.

She pushed herself up off his chest. "What about me?" Her eyes remained squinted with sleep.

"You're tough," he told her.

"How so?"

"You lost your husband," he began, "your dad. You've been through some rough times."

She nodded. "There wasn't any other choice."

Brody twined their fingers together. "I know you were close with your dad."

"Yeah. Which makes all of this even harder." She let out a soft laugh that turned into a sad sigh. "I wish he was here so I could ask him what happened. What went so terribly wrong that he would cheat on my mother after all that time? With a seventeen-year-old."

Brody rubbed his thumb over the back of her hand. "You think you'd like the answer?"

A bleak look met his and she shook her head. "I'm not naive. But sometimes I wish I was. Dad was a driven man. Like Mom. Driven people enjoy the power that often comes with hard work." She shrugged. "And power isn't always used for good."

Brody hurt for her. That abuse of power was the reason he kept his paternity secret.

"Life sucks sometimes," Cat said wistfully. She once again tucked herself against him, one finger moving in tiny circles on his chest.

"It does," he agreed.

And sometimes it was pretty darned good. He tilted her chin up. "This is more than sex, Cat. You know that, right?"

She silently nodded.

"I'm not exactly sure *what* it is. And we don't have to define it yet. But if we're going to do this, you have to be on the same page as me. It's more than sex."

He was surprised at the lack of hesitation in her eyes.

"I agree. It's more. And we both probably knew that before we started. And no, I don't know what it is either. But I want to find out. It could be something good."

It was as if the garage no longer existed and he was staring directly at the sun. The day was glorious. This was going to be okay.

"I have a brother," he blurted out.

He held his breath as shock ricocheted through her eyes.

"That's who I was talking to on the deck yesterday morning. He called because he was . . . *worried* about me." Which wasn't a complete lie, but he would work up to the true reason for the call. "He knew you were up here. That I once loved you." Brody tightened his fingers around her thighs as she simply watched him, not saying a word, and fear began to fill him. It kept him from immediately sharing Thomas's name. "He'd been watching the news," Brody explained as if she wouldn't understand why Thomas might have been worried.

"You never told me you had a brother." She finally spoke. It came out as a question, but also as if it hurt that he hadn't shared that information before.

"I didn't know about him then. He's two years younger than me. I met him and my father, both, when I was sixteen."

"So he's not your mother's son?"

No, he's Arthur Harrison's.

Brody held his breath instead of speaking. That had been it, the perfect opportunity.

And he hadn't been able to do it.

How in the hell was he supposed to tell Cat that he was the son of the family trying to destroy hers while he had her naked in his lap? He'd planned this poorly.

"Let's put our clothes on," he suggested. His words seemed to let her know that his father was a difficult topic. Off the table for the moment. She nodded and climbed out of the car.

"Tell me about your brother, then. Are you close?"

"No," he said wryly. He reached for his pants. "I once wanted to be, but he's . . ." He paused, trying to figure out how best to describe it. He lifted his hips to pull up his pants and watched Cat as she stepped into her panties. "He's not like me," he finally said.

"How so?"

In every way that mattered. "We want different things."

"And that makes it wrong?"

With a first and last name he could explain why it made it wrong. But he was a coward.

He hoisted himself to the side panel of the car and swung his feet over. "It makes it *difficult.*"

She grew quiet, as if contemplating what "difficult" might mean. She had her tiny scrap of a bra on now, and the car stood between them. He wanted her back in his arms.

When she spoke again, all that came out was a soft, "Hmmm."

He shoved his arms through his shirtsleeves. "What?"

"I guess that means you weren't out there talking to a reporter yesterday morning."

He paused. "That's not what you really thought?"

Because if it was, they had even more issues than he'd believed.

She gave an apologetic shrug. "Not really. But with everything coming out lately, I get nervous. Especially when people leave the room to keep me from hearing."

"I left the room because I was mad at you." And to keep her from hearing.

"I know. Circumstances just have a way of making me question things I'd otherwise trust."

"And you trust in us?" He stopped all movements to watch her closely.

Blue eyes carefully studied his from the other side of the car. The look lasted longer than he would have liked given that particular question, but in the end she gave a small nod. He blew out a breath of relief.

"I trust in us," she stated.

"Good. Don't question us. We're good."

"I know. That's why I didn't go home yesterday."

Her soft words placed a large lump in his chest.

"Cat. I have to tell you something."

She nodded encouragingly.

"My brother . . . he's—"

The phone inside her pursed chimed loudly in the quiet garage, and Brody groaned with frustration. Good God, the number of times they'd been interrupted by her family was ridiculous. He gripped the side of the car. "Ignore it," he pleaded.

"I—"

"They can wait. I need to tell you something. Something important."

"Okay." Her eyes darted to the small purse lying on the front seat of the car. "I thought it might be my kids," she mumbled.

Damn. She was right, it could be her kids.

And he didn't want to be that person.

He stood straight and waved a hand at her purse. "See if it's your kids," he conceded.

She hesitantly dug into her bag, and he sagged in exhaustion. Unburdening himself was not an easy task.

The instant her eyes locked on the screen, Brody knew their conversation would have to wait. She had an *ohmygod* look about her. "Who is it?"

"My brother."

He scowled. Her brother was not an *ohmygod* thing. He'd called her every day this week.

"My *older* brother," she stressed.

Ah.

She'd explained that she and JP had been trying to get in touch with their older brother for a while. She hadn't told him why, but he'd sensed she had a good reason.

Probably more secrets.

Which he did not want to know about.

He held up his car keys and motioned for her to take her seminude body into his house. "I'll go for doughnuts," he said. They'd have to put off *their* talk until he got back.

CHAPTER SIXTEEN

*B*ENNETT," CAT SAID IN A RUSH AS THE CALL CONNECTED.
"Squirt," Bennett teased.

Emotion flooded her. Finally, she'd reached her brother. "You are one hard person to contact. I called you back yesterday but it went straight to voice mail."

"Yeah, sorry. I got pulled into some things. Thought I'd try again this morning before the same happens again. I take it what's going on in the news is why you've wanted to talk to me?" her brother drawled out. For someone who'd lived the past twenty years outside of Georgia, he certainly still sounded like a Southern boy.

"Not quite," she stalled.

"You mean there's more?"

She sank into a chair at the kitchen table. "Where are you? Can you take a few days' leave? Catch a flight to the States?"

"I'm in the States."

"Then come up here. I'm in Maine."

"Hon. I know where you are. You've been on the news almost as much as our mother." He chuckled lightly, the sound easy and familiar. His laugh had a way of taking her back to her teenage years. He'd teased her mercilessly as a kid. Always poking at her. Laughing when he got her riled up.

She missed him.

"So you're an actress now?" She could hear the smile in his voice.

She blushed. "No. I'm just having some fun. I was in the drama club in high school."

"I remember." He'd been away in the army by then, but they'd kept in close contact those first few years. "You were pretty good, if I recall the stories correctly. Sounds like you still are."

"I'm not bad," she admitted. And then she remembered why he'd called. "But that's not why I need to talk to you. The press is ruthless lately. All over the place, looking for a story."

"Doesn't appear they have to look very hard." Bennett's tone turned somber. "Sounds like Dad had some issues. How long have you known about this?"

"A couple weeks," she said. "JP found out last summer."

"And Thomas Harrison is the one getting the pleasure of sharing it with the world." His tone was dry.

"You know him?"

"I've met him. Along with his father."

"I take it you didn't care for them?"

There was an odd pause before Bennett answered. "Arthur's a piece of work, that's for sure. Thomas is a replica. The way they're running this campaign doesn't surprise me. What about the kid?"

"Daniel?" she asked.

"Is that his name? No one has said."

"Yeah. Daniel." She couldn't help but imagine Lexi alone, scared, and pregnant at the age of seventeen. With hush money as her only comfort. "His mother's name is Lexi Dougard. She was seventeen when she volunteered on Dad's campaign. From what JP says, she's gone off the grid now. She never wanted Daniel to be exposed as a Davenport, and she doesn't intend to come up for air anytime soon."

"Can't say as I blame her," Bennett muttered.

They both fell silent, each in their own thoughts, and Cat pictured Daniel in her mind. JP had shown her a picture when he'd told her about him. Dark hair, vibrant blue eyes. The child looked like a Davenport. He looked like JP.

She ached with the thought that she had a brother out there she didn't know. May never know. All because her father and mother had hidden him from the world.

"What in the hell was Dad thinking?" Bennett spoke once again.

"I know. It's a mess. Our parents . . ." She closed her eyes as she thought about her own secrets. She wasn't one to judge. "They've done some things, that's for sure. And I'm terrified the Harrisons won't stop." She paused again. She didn't want to have to tell him over the phone. "There's more, Bennett."

"Something big?"

"Yes." The word shook.

"And, what? It involves me? Or do you just want me there to stand by Mom?"

It broke her heart to think about telling her own brother that he was actually her half brother. "Come see me," she pleaded. She rattled off the address of her rental. "It involves you."

"Can't you just tell me over the phone, Squirt?"

"I want to see you. It's been years. Tyler doesn't even know you."

"Is he there with you?"

"The kids will be up next weekend. Vega is flying to Florida to get them tomorrow, then they'll stay with her and JP in Atlanta for the week. We'd *all* love to see you."

She pictured Bennett pacing in whatever room he was calling from. He'd paced as a kid any time he'd had a decision to make. Big or small, it hadn't mattered. He'd paced over joining the army. He'd paced over which girl to take to senior prom. The memories made Cat smile.

"And you won't tell me what this big secret is unless I come there?"

"I'd rather not," she hedged.

A sigh sounded through the phone. "I'm not making promises, Cat. I'll try." The heaviness of his voice worried her. "But it'll take some time."

She heard people in the background, and Bennett said something, but not into the phone. When he returned, he was all business. "I've got to go."

And just like that, her spirits sank. She wanted more time with her brother.

"Please try," she begged. "I miss you."

"I miss you too, Squirt."

Cat sat there all by herself after the phone was silent, thinking about how few times she'd seen her brother since he'd left home at eighteen. And wondering if there was a hidden reason for that. Could he already have an idea about his paternity? Surely not. But he was the oldest. It was possible he knew even more secrets than she and JP did.

Nothing would surprise her at this point.

She put the phone down, realizing that Brody had taken off with her purse still in the car, so she rose from the table and headed for his shower. He would be back soon. With doughnuts.

She wanted to be ready to appropriately thank him when he returned.

Twenty minutes later, Cat dropped onto the couch in Brody's family room, once again taking in the disarray of books and papers. She'd hopped into the shower before pulling on one of his button-downs, and now sat waiting for her kids to call.

And trying to decide if she should clean up the room.

She settled on no.

There was no need to stress over something so insignificant as scattered books. Instead, she'd be totally frivolous. She grabbed a bottle of polish she'd brought over earlier in the week and propped her bare feet on the coffee table. She even kicked a book onto the floor that was in her way.

It was more of a gentle slide and tip off the side of the table, but she had used her foot. The delighted feeling the action produced made her laugh out loud. Brody was rubbing off on her.

She'd just started on her right foot when her cell rang. Her kids. The best part of her day.

"Hey, sweet girl."

Tyler giggled on the other end of the phone. "We tricked you! I called you today."

Cat laughed. "I hear that. Did you dial the phone yourself or did your sister do it?"

Tyler chortled this time. His full-belly laugh making her happy. "Becca did it for me," he announced amid more giggles.

"Hi, Mom," Becca spoke up. "I'm on grandma's other phone so we can talk to you together."

"Perfect," Cat purred. "The best two people in the world, talking to me at the same time."

Cat could picture both kids preening with the praise.

They settled into their normal morning routine. Tyler mostly making noises as he "zoomed" whatever toy he had in his hand, and Becca rattling nonstop about their plans for the day. It would be their last full day in Florida, so it needed to be special.

"Grandma says we can't go to the 'quarium today like we planned," Becca informed her as if stating something of high importance, "so she's gonna take us to the park."

Irritation ate at Cat. Not because her in-laws wouldn't be taking the kids to the aquarium, but because they *couldn't*. Cat had discussed the plans with the Carltons the day before. The three of them had decided something a little less public might be wiser.

But it pissed her off that her kids had to miss their trip to the aquarium with their grandparents because Cat's father had cheated on her mother with a volunteer. That was exactly the kind of thing she didn't want to infiltrate her kids' lives.

"The park will be fun," Cat said. She made sure she sounded excited.

"But we did the park already." This came from Tyler. His sad little voice broke her heart.

"I'll bet you're looking forward to spending time with Uncle JP and Aunt Vega." Change subjects. That would help.

"I am," Becca chimed in. "Aunt Vega's gonna buy me new shoes."

"Ugh," Tyler moaned. "Girl stuff. Me and Uncle P are gonna do somethin' for boys."

Cat laughed at her kids. She missed them so much. "And the week after that you're all coming up here to see me."

"Yes!" both kids shouted.

A beep signaled call-waiting and Cat glanced at the screen thinking it might be Brody.

It was her mother. She ignored it and continued talking. The kids told her all about the two sand castles they'd built the day before. But unfortunately, the ocean had swept them away before pictures could be taken.

Cat finished with her toes and leaned back on the couch as she listened to her kids.

Her feet remained propped on the coffee table, she had on Brody's shirt, and her man was bringing her doughnuts. What could be better than that?

Her phone beeped again.

She ignored it again.

But she did eye the television. A sense of déjà vu had suddenly come over her. Yesterday morning had started out with her phone ringing off the hook, too.

The beeping stopped, then started once again. Dread settled in her gut.

"Let me call you back, sweetheart," Cat interrupted when Becca took a breath. Cat told them both that she loved them and hung up.

Her phone rang in her hand.

"Turn on your television." Her mother didn't bother with pleasantries.

"What do you want?" Cat did not want to talk to her mother. Or do anything she said.

"The news, Catherine. Turn it on. Now."

Anger was pushed aside for the moment as recognition set in, and cold fear whipped down Cat's spine. Her mother wasn't merely commanding. Her voice was frantic. It was . . . *desperate*.

That was different.

Without further delay, Cat searched for the remote but was unable to find it. She stood in the middle of the room and turned in a full circle, her gaze hitting every surface, wondering if the blasted thing was tucked under one of the many books on the floor. That was the reason to keep a clean room. So the remote could be found when your mother was yelling at you.

"Is it on?" her mother snapped out.

"I'm looking," Cat snapped back as she gave up her search and went to her knees to fumble directly with the buttons on the television. "Which station?"

"Probably all of them." Her mother's reply was short and brittle. The anger seemed over the top.

But then Cat saw it. She sighed.

A picture of her and Brody was on the screen from last night. They'd been caught holding hands at the playhouse.

"I forgot to tell you," she said sarcastically. "Brody and I are back together."

Her mother was reacting about the way Cat had expected.

The screen changed to show more pictures. Her high in Brody's arms right before he deposited her into his car. Them kissing the first night she'd been in the play. Several others.

But none of them was what her attention zoomed in on.

The caption printed across the bottom had Cat rising to her feet.

The reporter's words seemed to run together, making Cat unable to understand anything being said, but it didn't matter. She didn't need to hear the words. The important part was staring at her from the bottom.

A Harrison and a Davenport . . . are they this century's Romeo and Juliet?

What?

She walked backward, away from the TV, until the edge of the coffee table pushed into her calf. She sank to the top. More books tumbled to the floor, along with her nail polish. Brody was a . . .

She blinked and read the caption again, forcing her eyes to go slower. To make sure she understood what she was reading.

Brody was a Harrison?

Fury began to simmer inside her. He was Congressman Thomas Harrison's brother?

How?

Her fingers clenched at her side as she tried to piece things together. The reporter was still rambling, not making a lot of sense, but the picture behind the woman changed, and suddenly Thomas Harrison's face was there. Next to it was Brody's. The air left Cat's body.

Oh, shit.

It wasn't completely obvious, but yes, she saw it. The same nose. The same chin.

She'd always thought he looked like his mother, but he'd also gotten features from his father. Features that matched his brother's.

Nausea rolled through her as she stared at the two photos. An unconscious niggling pulled at her, as if she was missing something else, and she tilted her head to study the shots more closely. But what could she be missing? What she saw was enough.

Brody was Thomas Harrison's brother.

Her hands began to shake. She'd slept with the enemy.

Another thought entered her mind. This one leaving her entire body trembling.

She'd told him about her mother writing a check to Lexi Dougard. She'd told him that they hadn't *just* found out about her father's illegitimate kid!

What had she done?

She'd had the stupid notion that if she wanted to have something real with him, she had to share who she truly was. Where she came from. And where she came from was a family who wrote million-dollar checks to keep mistresses quiet.

"Oh, God," she moaned. She was going to be sick.

"What have you told him?" Her mother clued right in on the problem.

"Nothing!"

Fuck. She wasn't about to tell her mother what she'd told him.

She closed her eyes, trying to calm down. Reminding herself that this was Brody they were talking about. He cared for her. He wanted more than sex with her.

He had not been sleeping with her to get information for his brother!

She hoped.

She'd even admitted that Lexi had been only seventeen!

"It's time to come home, Catherine," her mother stated in a monotone. "Enough is enough. Quit playing these games and get on a plane."

Cat shook her head; no words would come out. Brody was a Harrison?

"Do you hear me?"

"I hear you," Cat whispered. But she had no idea what her mother had said.

"Get away from that boy," her mother insisted. "I already fixed this problem for you once. I'm not sure I can do it again."

The harsh words registered, reminding Cat of her mother's involvement in her past.

"You shouldn't have stepped into things before," she growled out. "He told me you did."

"Oh please, Catherine. If I hadn't, you would have run off with the boy. You thought you were in love."

"I was in love!" she shouted. She rose and began to pace. Something else was bothering her, just right outside of her consciousness, but she couldn't quite connect the dots.

"You were sixteen. You didn't know what love was."

"I was pregnant, Mom. With Brody's baby."

"With a Harrison's baby," her mother spat out.

And that was it. The missing piece. "You knew."

Cat stopped walking as it all fell into place. Nineteen years ago, she'd come home from her summer vacation and told her mother about her new love.

Her mother hadn't said much at first, thinking Cat was silly and immature. But she had asked about Brody's parents. Who were they? What did they do? Cat had assured her Brody was just someone she'd met in Maine. Her mother wouldn't even know his parents.

A few weeks later, when Cat complained that Brody hadn't called her lately, her mother had had plenty to say then. Namely, *stay away from that boy.*

But how had she known? And did it even matter?

The fact was, her mother had scoured out the information. Then she'd put a plan into action. A plan she hadn't let Cat in on.

"Well, of course I knew." Her mother's words snapped out. She'd known nineteen years ago that the son of the "enemy" had gotten the daughter of the "upstanding, moral family" pregnant. That would have been reason enough to get rid of the baby.

At least in her mother's eyes.

Yet she'd gone on and on about how it would be the best thing for Cat. For the baby.

"You were never worried about *me*."

"Of course I was. You were sixteen. You couldn't—"

"I could have," Cat interrupted calmly. "*We* could have. You lied to Brody. You called his mother to make sure he didn't take my calls. You hurt me, Mom. And I didn't even know about it."

"I don't know what he's been telling you."

"He's been telling me the truth. Far more than you have."

"So you knew he was a Harrison?" her mother asked coldly.

That ripped at her. Because no. She hadn't known he was a Harrison. Brody had kept that piece of information from her. And she didn't yet know what to do about it.

"You didn't need him in your life, Catherine. You had the baby to think about."

Hurt and betrayal clogged Cat's throat. Had her mother ever done anything out of love? Or was it all for PR?

"I was only thinking about you," her mother tried again.

Tears began to flow down Cat's cheeks. Her life could have been vastly different had her mother not gotten involved. What the difference might have been, she didn't know. But it wasn't right that she'd been cheated of the chance to find out. The pain sliced her from front to back. "I'm not sure you've ever thought of anyone but you," she whispered brokenly.

"That's ridiculous. I love you. I've always loved you."

"Right." The garage door burst open and Brody stood there. His face was white, his eyes panicked, and there was a newspaper gripped tightly in his fist. "Only you love you more."

She turned her back to Brody.

"I had to protect you," her mother insisted.

"You had to protect *you*."

The two families may have been political adversaries for

decades, but Cat had never understood the absolute hatred her parents had for anyone with the Harrison name. It went too far.

"Don't send the plane," she whispered. She didn't know what would come next, but she could not go back to Atlanta and face her mother right now. Not yet. "I won't get on it."

She hung up before her mother could say anything else, her hand gripping the phone so tightly she worried it might crush under the pressure. Her breathing came out ragged. She forced herself to calm down, turn off the phone, and wipe the tears from her face. Then she faced Brody.

CHAPTER SEVENTEEN

*B*RODY REMAINED JUST INSIDE THE KITCHEN DOOR, HIS eyes carefully watching hers. Everyone had lied to her. Everyone kept things from her. And he was no different.

"You slept with me," Cat accused. "Without telling me who you were."

"I didn't know the first time." He looked as pained as she felt. "You can't blame me for that. I found out after I met you. I told you that this morning."

"You didn't tell me you were a *Harrison* this morning." Her voice rose. She felt shattered.

"I had planned to. *Before* you took that call from your brother."

Before she'd let her family come before her relationship. So it was her fault?

Which sounded about right. Her throat ached with more tears. *She* was the one with the shitty mother. The mother who'd intervened and reshaped their past. *She* was the one with the family secrets invading her life—and the grand need to constantly try to cover them up.

And *she* was the one who'd given away their baby. Oh God, she had to tell him.

But she wasn't the one whose family was dragging hers through the mud.

"What have you told them?" she bit out coldly.

Fury exploded across his face. "Told them?" He took a step forward. "What? You find out who my biological father is, so you immediately assume that *I'm* the one sharing your family's dirty laundry?"

She didn't know what to think. "I told you things." Her voice broke. She couldn't believe she'd blurted out family secrets to a Harrison. "Yesterday, in your office. Things I shouldn't have."

"And you know I would never do anything with that information."

"Do I? I didn't know you were a Harrison!"

"I'm not a Harrison!" he bellowed.

He moved across the room so that he stood directly before her. His body was tight with rage. Hers shook with each breath she took. He scrubbed a hand over his face as if trying to rein in his emotions, and blew out a harsh breath. They looked like two strangers facing off.

"You know me, Cat. You know who *we* are. I'm not one of them. I never have been."

"But you're—"

"Do not lump me into that category just because you're used to everyone in your family using people."

She gasped. "Not everyone in my family uses people," she spat out. "JP is the best person I know. Bennett has served our country for twenty years. My father—" She paused. Her father may have loved her, but he was a bad example in this situation. "We're good people," she finished defensively.

"Yet even the good ones stand behind the lies. Your family has made its nest, Cat. Maybe it's time they lie in it."

The sounds of her breaths were heavy in the room. He was her family's enemy. That kept repeating in her mind. He was one of them. She couldn't be with him. Only . . .

She didn't know who he was or what she *could* do anymore.

"Brody," she whispered. She just wanted all the problems to disappear.

"I'm not a part of them, Cat. Come on. You know that. Think about it. I'm thirty-four years old and no one has ever been made aware that Arthur Harrison is my father. Why do you suppose that is?"

She stared at him. She hadn't thought about that. But he wouldn't have kept this a secret simply to use against her family. That made no sense. "I don't know," she admitted.

"I don't talk to Arthur. Never. I met him at the age of sixteen, and my ex got me back in front of him when I was twenty-three. Twice in my lifetime. Two times too many. And I only speak to Thomas on the rare occasion. Only then because . . ." His words trailed off. He clenched his jaw and held his hands out to his sides. He looked defeated. "Because he's my brother. And I once thought that might mean something."

She wanted to believe him. What he said made sense.

She wanted to trust in her own feelings.

"But you didn't tell me." She ignored the inner voice calling her a hypocrite.

"No, I didn't. Because we were supposed to just be sex."

"It doesn't matter. I deserved to know. *Before* sleeping with you."

"Maybe. Yeah, okay," he growled. "I should have told you. Given who you are and that it could—*does*—impact your life, you had a right to know. I'm an ass. I'm sorry. I knew that going into it. But admit it, you wouldn't have come near me if you'd known. It would risk marring your perfect public image."

"That's not fair."

"But it's honest."

They glared at each other. She didn't want to continue arguing with him, yet she couldn't stop herself. "You also should have told me that my mother knew who you were."

His eyes frosted over. "She should have told you that herself."

Fed up with going in circles, Cat crossed to the front windows and peeked out. She needed time to think. To decide what

CAUGHT IN THE ACT

all this meant. To get away from the people in the many cars lining the street, just waiting for a chance to get a picture of them.

She crossed her arms over her chest as she tried to get control of her emotions. Then she thought about what Brody had previously said, and she turned back to him.

"Why *hasn't* anyone ever known who your father is?"

A muscle ticked in his jaw. "Because I hate him. I hate the way he does things, the way he uses people, and his lack of regard for others' feelings. And I do not want to be associated with that behavior."

She nodded. She could understand that. "Like you hate the way my family does things?"

"I don't care about your family one way or the other, Cat. I care about you. I hate the way you jump every time there might be something to cover up. It's not right," he said. "It's not honest. And it's not the real you. The girl I met as a teenager was the real you. You were vibrant and full of life. Willing to take a risk. You didn't stick strictly to the line drawn out for you."

She gulped. He had a point.

"The real you is the woman who walked into my office yesterday afternoon."

More tears filled her eyes. She *wanted* to be the person who'd walked into his office yesterday afternoon.

Nineteen years ago she'd been that person. But she'd followed her instincts, and the results had changed her for good. Her heart—her spirit—had been crushed. She'd put her family's reputation at risk, and she'd made a decision that still haunted her today.

Since then, she'd behaved. She'd gone to an all-girls school, had gotten degrees to help her work behind the scenes with her family. She'd dated the man her parents had picked out for her. She'd even *married* the man her parents had picked out for her.

Joe had been good for her and she'd loved him, but he had been her parents' choice.

She'd done everything right.

She'd been a perfect daughter.

And in return she'd lost her husband and ended up with a life she no longer recognized.

Fast forward to today, and damned if she didn't feel as if she'd just stepped off a cliff by repeating history. Only this time she was taking Brody down with her.

She wiped away a tear. "You've been outed. Those cameras out there aren't just looking for me anymore."

He deadpanned. "Why do you think I'm so pissed?"

"I'm sorry," she whispered.

"Don't be sorry for me," he said. "It's not me I'm worried about at the moment. I'm worried about my mother."

"Oh, no." Cat moved to his side. "Your mother. She'll be pulled into this."

"Exactly. And the only thing she ever did wrong was fall for the wrong guy. She doesn't deserve to be sucked into this mess." He tone was accusing.

"Meaning, you think my mother does?"

He shot her an incredulous look. "Seriously, Cat? Who do you think leaked it?"

"But my mother didn't—" Cat pressed a hand to her mouth. Her mother had known who Brody was all along. It hadn't occurred to her that this secret could have come from a different direction than the Harrisons.

"Yesterday the Davenports had an illegitimate son," Brody started sarcastically, "today the Harrisons do, too. Couldn't have worked out better for her, don't you think?"

"It could have been Thomas," Cat argued. "He knew we were together. He called and asked you about it yesterday."

"He actually called to get the scoop on your mother. You were merely an afterthought."

"But was I really?" she asked. "Maybe I *was* the reason he called. He wanted to ensure we were together before leaking the news."

"That makes no sense. Why would Thomas expose us? Expose me? It would harm him."

"Because he now has a long-lost brother to win him sympathy," she pointed out. It pained her that she thought so much like a politician. "One he never knew existed."

"But he did know I existed."

"Yet that part of it didn't come out."

She saw the shock in his eyes as the truth of her statement registered. The shock was followed by worry. And possibly a streak of pain.

"My mother would have used it," Cat stated flatly. "It would do far more damage to Thomas's campaign."

"Your mother probably doesn't know that we've ever talked."

"Do you believe that enough to be sure?" She didn't know why she was defending her mother on this, other than that was what came naturally to her. Also, she very much didn't trust Thomas Harrison. "This could be his doing, Brody. He's been taking a hit in the numbers right alongside my mother. What do you want to bet he contacts you now? He'd be the big guy if he extended a warm welcome to his newest family member."

Brody's cell began to ring.

"I'll pay off your mortgage if that isn't him," she said, her words as cold as stone.

Brody didn't reach for his phone. "It doesn't matter who it is."

She nodded. "I know. And I think I should go."

"None of this changes anything, Cat," Brody said.

"Do you really believe that?" She peeked out the blinds again. She had to cross their yards to get back to her place, and she knew long-lens cameras would zoom in on her the instant she stepped off Brody's deck.

All she'd wanted was a short escape from her world, and instead she got this.

"We can figure this out, Cat. We just need some time."

"I don't know if we can." She looked at him then. At his unruly hair and his unkempt whiskers. At his glasses framing his gorgeous green eyes. She also took in the books and papers scattered across the room. She missed him already. "But I'm pretty sure standing here continuing to argue isn't going to solve anything. I need time to think. We both need to figure out if this is worth it. And you need to go check on your mother."

He didn't disagree.

Without another word, she went to the garage. The clothes she'd worn the night before were still in there, as well as her purse in his car. She took her time dressing, holding his shirt to her chest and inhaling the smell of him deep into her lungs. She did not let herself get emotional when she looked at Brody's backseat. They'd taken a giant step on that seat this morning. A step she'd thought might lead to a new kind of forever.

And now it felt as if that backseat might have just been the end.

When she came back into the house, Brody was waiting by the back door. "I'll walk you to your house."

"You don't have to do that."

"Yes, I do. There are photographers hiding in your bushes. I've already called the cops."

Her jaw dropped open. She hated paparazzi. "I'll have to move out to the compound."

"I would expect so."

Her life had gotten completely out of her hands. If it wasn't for finishing the playground and still being determined to give her kids a vacation here, she would go home today.

When Brody reached to open the door, she put a hand to his arm. "I'm sorry," she said softly.

He nodded solemnly. "Me too."

CHAPTER EIGHTEEN

*T*HE PLAYHOUSE WOULD BE PACKED THAT NIGHT. IT WAS A good hour and a half before the show was set to start, but already the parking lot was full. A line of people formed at the main entrance, wrapping around two sides of the building, and there were four police officers standing guard among the crowd. Their stance was feet spread, thumbs tucked inside their utility belts, stern expressions on their faces.

Cat wanted to smile. They looked so tough. She'd seen these very officers around town several times over the last two weeks, and not once had any of them done anything but offer pleasant greetings. They looked downright lethal tonight.

She sat in the passenger seat of the dark SUV parked at the back of the building, peering out through tinted windows and dreading having to get out.

She'd personally rather be at home, with her kids curled up at her sides.

In fact, she'd made arrangements to soon do just that. The instant she'd pulled into the six-car garage of the Davenport home, she'd felt adrift. She didn't know what would happen with her and Brody at this point. She was furious with her mother and didn't see that changing anytime soon. And she desperately missed her kids.

She'd been without them for over two weeks, and that—she'd

decided—had been enough. Not to mention, she didn't want them having to deal with paparazzi without her around.

Bringing them up here wouldn't shield them, of course, but if she went back to Atlanta, the cameras would simply follow. At least for the foreseeable future.

So she'd bring her kids up early. They'd still get their trip to Maine—now to be even longer—and Cat could finish out her responsibilities with the playhouse.

And maybe she and Brody would . . . she didn't know what. They hadn't exactly broken up that morning, but they had parted ways. It was too difficult at the moment to consider anything else.

Also, he was still a Harrison.

Not that she'd let that be a deciding factor for her, but if this was truly just a fling, then maybe it was time for the fling to be over. No need to exacerbate things for only a few more days.

And if they were more than a fling?

Well, she was hoping time apart would answer that question. She would still tell him about Annabelle. Eventually. But she had to figure out "them" first. There was the saying that absence made the heart grow fonder, and she supposed they were about to put it to the test. If the test failed, then all the hoopla could go back to normal much sooner.

Vega and JP had offered to go ahead and bring Becca and Tyler up this week. They would arrive Wednesday morning, just in time for all of them to participate in the installation of the park's main play area. The kids couldn't work within the main area, but Cat's project manager had made arrangements for a kid-friendly zone so no one in the community would feel excluded. It even came with babysitters.

"Looks like a busy place," Stone Walker said from the driver's seat. Stone was a security guard out of Boston. She'd hired him and another guy that morning, along with making arrangements for one of the family's regulars out of Atlanta to travel with the kids.

Her second security guard had been left at the house while

Stone had driven Cat into town. Nothing unsafe had happened so far, but with the number of people currently in the area looking to score a great shot, she figured it was better to be safe than sorry.

"Wonder how many of them actually have any interest in seeing the play," Cat mused.

She slumped in the seat when a couple of women she recognized from around town glanced in her direction. Most everyone would be looking for the sedan she'd been driving. They hadn't yet figured out that Stone had arrived, or that he'd come with his own vehicle.

"I'd say you could read the script backward tonight and no one would notice," Stone remarked. "Or just mumble for an hour and a half."

"I suspect you're right."

Three cars over, a door swung open, and a graying head slowly emerged. It was Annabelle Hollister. Suddenly, a swarm of cameras and microphones headed her way.

"Oh, no." Cat shot up. "We've got to help her."

She had her door open and was out of the vehicle before Stone could stop her. Her appearance brought more people over and caught some of them trying to make an important decision: go after Annabelle or go after Cat.

Thankfully, Stone made everyone's decision for them.

He was a big guy. Six five, at least three hundred pounds. Though he was in his fifties, he was solid muscle. With his wraparound shades and bald head, he looked more than scary.

As he approached, people backed off. Cat hurried to Annabelle's side, wrapped her arm around the woman, and hustled them both in the back door. She left Stone to deal with the mob.

Once inside, she pulled Annabelle into a small room. The woman looked a bit shell-shocked.

"Are you okay?" Cat asked. She ran her hands over the other woman, checking Brody's mother over as if she were frail and had been attacked by starving gorillas.

Annabelle gave a nervous laugh. Her fingers flitted down her own body as if to check for herself that she remained intact. "That was quite a crowd," she finally managed.

"Insane, right?"

"And you deal with situations like this a lot?"

"No. Not a lot." Then Cat winked, hoping to lighten the mood. "Only when I hang out with big-name people."

Annabelle's green eyes lightened, and some of the shock seemed to lift.

"I'm so sorry you've gotten pulled into this mess," Cat said. She wrapped Annabelle in a hug. "You shouldn't be subjected to this madness."

"The way I see it, I've had thirty-four good years that I haven't had to deal with it. Thirty-five if you count the months I was pregnant."

"Good point," Cat allowed. "But still, this is my fault, and I feel horrible about it."

"How do you figure it's your fault? Did you sleep with Arthur Harrison, too?"

Cat jerked back. "No." Then she realized how rude she'd sounded, and held out her hands in apology. "Not that it was wrong for you, of course."

Annabelle laughed. "Of course," she agreed. "But I should have known better."

"Maybe. But if Brody and I hadn't . . . *been seen together*, none of this would have happened."

"But if you and Brody hadn't *been seen together*"—Annabelle mimicked Cat's words back to her—"then he wouldn't have gotten a peek at what he's been missing."

"Excuse me?" The change of subject caught Cat off guard.

Annabelle trained her eyes on Cat. They'd turned serious. "Forget the craziness going on outside for a moment. Forget everything else that might feel like a big deal. Brody cares about you, Cat. Surely you can see that."

Cat nodded. She hadn't expected a lecture from Brody's mom tonight. "I care about him too. I always did. But *he* shouldn't have to deal with this, either."

Annabelle snorted. "Why not? What makes you so special?"

This wasn't going at all how she'd thought. She'd just wanted to get Annabelle safely inside the building.

"I'm just saying," Annabelle added, "that I was fully aware of who Arthur Harrison was when he and I were *seen together*. I have a bit of a leg in this game as well. I played my part. And you shouldn't let any of it determine where you and Brody go from here."

Clearly Brody had been talking to his mother.

"What did he say about it?" Cat asked.

"About you?" Annabelle shook her head. "Nothing. But I'm his mom. He doesn't have to say anything. I can see it in his eyes."

Cat had seen it in his eyes, too. As he'd said good-bye to her at her house earlier that morning, he'd stood there an extra minute longer. She didn't want it to be over between them. She didn't want the madness that was going on around them. And she didn't want it to be her mother who'd done this to them.

That worried her a lot.

Talk about a line being crossed. If her mother had leaked this—and Cat very much suspected that she had—then the game had changed. Forever.

You don't hurt family to help yourself.

"Where is he?" Cat asked now. She hadn't seen Brody's car in the lot, and he wasn't there with his mother. "He should be here. You shouldn't have to deal with this by yourself."

"I sent him on an errand." Annabelle's eyes softened. "Mostly because I wanted to talk to you."

Cat arched a brow.

"I saw you in the parking lot. I was waiting for you to arrive. And I knew you'd send your big guy over to help me if those crazies out there got too close."

"You did, huh? How about I hire you your own big guy to watch out for you?"

"No need, dear." Annabelle patted her cheek. "I'm just fine. Plus, no one wants to hear what an old lady has to say."

"I think you may be wrong about that. And you aren't that old."

Annabelle glanced behind her as the back door of the building opened momentarily and the outside craziness could be heard. Stone appeared in the doorway to their room, took a quick look in, and disappeared on the other side of the wall.

"Wrong or not," Annabelle continued, "don't you worry about me. This will pass, and things will go back to normal. But I wanted to tell you something." Guilt flashed across her face. "To apologize, actually."

"For what?"

"For those two times you called the house."

Goose bumps lit down Cat's body.

"I should have told Brody about them back then. I'm sorry."

Words got stuck in Cat's throat, but she managed to push them out. "I understand my mother had something to do with that."

"Didn't mean I had to go along."

Cat swallowed. She would not let herself cry over this. Annabelle Hollister had not known that Cat had been calling about her granddaughter. "I imagine you were doing what you thought was best for your son."

The moment was quiet, though there was still madness going on around them. Doors slammed, voices could be heard from outside. Someone yelled down the hallway an instant before the sound of feet hurried away.

"I was," Annabelle agreed. "A mother has a need to protect her child, as I'm sure you're aware. You have two beautiful ones of your own. But I might have been wrong this time."

Cat couldn't say anything else. She didn't blame Brody's mother for what had happened in the past. She'd had her son's best interests at heart. No doubt Emma Davenport hadn't simply said, "Don't call." Her mother had known who Brody was. She would have used that against both him and his mother.

Cat probably would have made the same choices as Annabelle. No mother should have to choose between protecting her child from others and letting her child be loved.

She closed her eyes on a wave of grief, and for the first time in her life, she felt like her own daughter could have forgiven her for giving her up. Deep down, Cat hadn't wanted her child to be raised by Emma Davenport. And at sixteen, if Cat had kept her, she knew Emma's influence would have played a heavy hand.

Annabelle would have grown up being just like Cat.

And that wasn't what she'd wanted for her daughter.

"Don't cry, sweetheart." Brody's mother pulled her in for a tight hug. "Things happen for a reason. You two have found each other again. It's up to you this time. No one else. You get to choose your path."

Her reassurances only made it worse.

Tears overflowed from her lower lashes, and Cat let Annabelle Hollister rock her gently in her arms. It was nice. It made Cat happy for Brody that he'd had such a caring mother throughout his life. Everyone deserved that.

A quiet clearing of someone's throat sounded at the door, and Cat lifted her eyes to find Clyde standing there. He wore a grave expression, and Cat's heart broke even more. She suspected she knew what was coming next.

"I'm sorry, Ms. Carlton."

"Clyde," she interrupted. She pulled out of Annabelle's arms and wiped at her eyes. "After all this time, call me Cat."

Clyde nodded. "I'm sorry, Ms. Cat, but . . . well . . ." He looked worriedly down the narrow hallway where Cat knew other members of the crew were coming and going. Then he turned back to the small room. "Laura's up to speed now."

Meaning he wanted Laura to step in as the lead. Cat nodded her understanding. She brought too much baggage with her. "I'll get my things."

"It's not that we don't appreciate everything you've done for us—"

"I get it, Clyde. You have others to think about. The playhouse to think about. It isn't safe right now. I understand that. I saw what happened last night, and that was before this latest news broke."

Clyde nodded sadly, and Annabelle patted Cat's cheek once again.

Cat squeezed the other woman's hands. "I'm sending Stone back to help you," she said. "No arguments." She looked at Clyde. "And I'm paying for extra security here until things die down."

Sadness lay heavy inside her. She didn't want to leave, but it was for the best.

"I'm sorry, Ms. Cat. Maybe you can be in another play sometime. Next year?"

She gave him a small smile. She *had* planned to come back next summer, but now . . . she just didn't know. She'd have to see how things went with Brody.

How an overdue discussion with her mother turned out.

"Maybe," she whispered.

And then she had Stone take her home.

CHAPTER NINETEEN

THE SIZZLE OF SPINACH AND ONIONS KEPT BRODY BUSY AT the stove as his mother moved about her kitchen, pulling out forks and glasses. He hadn't wanted to leave her on her own the night before, so he'd stayed over. She'd been even more popular with the paparazzi than he had, and though she was handling it well, he'd seen the worry in her eyes.

She didn't want to talk about Arthur Harrison in public. She also didn't want other people talking about the man to her. He'd hurt her years ago, and she should be able to live the rest of her life without having to rehash it.

Brody tended to agree.

None of that had kept the questions at bay.

"So," his mother began as she placed napkins on the table, "Laura did a good job last night."

She picked up the newspaper he'd run out for earlier, as if to put it somewhere *other* than the kitchen table, but he narrowed his eyes at her. She knew better. He liked to read the paper while he ate his breakfast. She sniffed in annoyance and put the paper back down.

"Laura did do a good job," he agreed.

"It's a shame it couldn't be Cat, though."

Brody didn't reply. Instead, he stirred the vegetables and added eggs and cheese to the two skillets. He'd been shocked to discover that Clyde had asked Cat to leave, but he'd understood the man's point. With her and Brody both in the building—along with his mother—no one would be able to focus on the play. Additionally, people could get hurt. The three of them together simply brought out too many spectators, many of them aggressive.

But he'd missed Cat last night. He'd wondered how she was holding up.

And he'd hoped like hell that she hadn't gotten on a plane and gone home.

The plan had been to talk to her after the play. To make sure there hadn't been any problems out at her family's home. To make sure *she* was okay. The argument in his house hadn't been pleasant, but he also hadn't gotten the sense anything between them was final. They needed time to figure things out. Him being a Harrison wasn't a big deal to him, it wouldn't change his way of life. But Cat couldn't simply overlook it. She had things to think about.

As did he. Being with Cat would be chaotic. And he wasn't a fan of the chaos his life had taken on. They both had to consider the consequences before making the next move. As well as let the media die down. Which he hoped happened soon.

He hadn't called her. But she also hadn't called him.

"Want to talk about it?" his mother asked.

It meaning Cat, as well as it coming out that he was a Harrison.

"Not really."

He'd refused to talk about either so far. He was still trying to digest what it meant for him. He hadn't wanted that information known. Ever. But since it was, things would be different. He just wasn't sure by how much.

His house had been covered with reporters all day yesterday, as had the street outside his mother's house. He'd been followed every time he'd stepped outside. And he was pretty sure the world would get a glimpse of him buying this morning's newspaper in tomorrow's news.

Or it might already be out on the Internet now.

"Do you love her?" his mother asked.

"What?" Brody rammed the spatula into the eggs, splashing liquid over the rim of one of the skillets. "I said I don't want to talk about it."

"We're going to anyway."

"Mom." He moved the omelets from the hot burners and turned to his mother. She was dressed in a multicolored skirt to her ankles, shod in pink tennis shoes, and had a look on her face that he'd seen his whole life. She wasn't backing down from this.

"Do you love her?" she asked again. "It won't go away by ignoring it. Didn't I raise you to deal with your problems?"

She had. That's why he'd shot off at sixteen to find his father.

And returned weeks later swearing never to speak to the man again.

"You know me better than anyone," he lashed out. All of this was bringing up too many bad memories. "How about you tell me?"

She nodded serenely. "I think yes."

He stood there glaring at her. He hadn't gone there in his mind yet. He didn't want to go there.

"I don't know, Mom," he answered honestly. The air seemed to seep out of him, and he found himself wanting to talk to someone about Cat. Wanting to put his fears out there. "If I let myself love her, then what happens if she walks? That would be it for us. We won't get another chance."

"Maybe she won't walk."

He grunted. "Maybe she already has. You have to remember, she's been hardwired to be a Davenport first. I won't spend my life always coming in second."

He returned to their breakfasts while thinking about Cat and her family, and the hordes of paparazzi that came with both.

Then he thought about love. Love was a very dicey thing. On the one hand, it could provide a lifetime of happiness. His and Cat's summer nineteen years ago came to mind. It hadn't been a lifetime, but those were some supreme moments.

But on the other hand, if one person didn't love as much as the other . . .

He turned the burners off and slid the omelets onto plates, but he left his on the counter. He was suddenly not hungry.

If one person didn't love as much as the other, then the other was terminally screwed.

"Tell me what I'm supposed to do." He sat at the table and looked across the space to his mom, his hands automatically wrapping around the mug of coffee she'd set out for him.

His mother only stared back.

Because, sure, now that he'd asked for advice, she apparently had no words to give.

"Tell me about you and Arthur, then."

She choked on her eggs.

"Okay, fine," he said. "How about I do the talking?"

"What do you mean?"

"I'm sorry for what happened back then. I should never have doubted you." He should have apologized when it happened, but he'd been a kid, and he'd had his ego destroyed. "You'd always told me that my father wanted nothing to do with me, and I should have taken you at your word."

"Some things a boy has to figure out on his own."

"I guess we're morons like that."

She gave him a wink, and he let his mind drift back.

She'd never told him the name of his father, only that he knew Brody existed but chose to have nothing to do with him. Then Brody had found an old picture the summer he was sixteen. After a little digging and a lot of questions, he'd figured out that Arthur Harrison was his father. Arthur was well known in politics; he'd been a US senator at the time. He was a damned pillar of the country.

So Brody had set off to confront him.

When all had seemed to be going well—he'd suddenly had a father *and* a brother—Brody had come home to pack his things. He was moving in with Arthur.

He and his mother had argued, and it had grown nasty. He'd accused her of keeping his father from him for her own selfish gains. In the end, she'd said very little to denigrate the man, but Brody had seen the hurt on her face as she'd stepped out of his way. He could make his own decisions. He could live wherever he chose.

He'd chosen Arthur.

Which had lasted only until Brody had returned to DC earlier than Arthur had anticipated. Brody had learned the truth that day. Arthur was using him, same as he'd used Brody's mother.

So Brody had once again returned home. He and his mother had had a long-overdue conversation about his father, then they'd all returned to their pre-Brody-finding-out ways, all pretending the other didn't exist. Except Brody and Thomas *had* known about each other by that point, and Brody had cared about his younger brother. He'd always wanted a brother.

"He's not a good man," his mother told him now.

Her words pulled Brody back from the past. "Thomas?" he asked. Thinking she'd read his mind.

"Arthur." He watched long-ago pain move across her face. "I was so glad when you chose not to get involved with him."

"It was the right decision." And he'd never regretted it. Neither, apparently, had Arthur. "What do you think of Thomas?"

He'd never asked his mother for her opinion on his brother. He'd tried to have a relationship with him for years, but deep down, he'd always feared Thomas was too much like their father.

And if Brody were honest with himself, he'd admit he'd been shown that over the years. He'd just never wanted to believe it.

And now, Cat was right. Thomas was calling, wanting to come up. Wanting to get to know his brother.

Brody hadn't talked to him, but several messages had been left. The first while Brody and Cat had been arguing the day before. She'd been right. It had been Thomas calling.

"I'm afraid that's another one you're going to have to figure out on your own."

"But do you think he's like Arthur?" Brody pushed.

His mother put her fork down and looked up from her plate. Lines etched her face, and that made him sad. He wanted her to remain young and vibrant forever. "It would be a real shame if he was," she said.

Brody nodded. "Yeah."

She returned to her food, and he picked up his coffee. She tried to get him to eat something, but he wasn't in the mood. Too many things to think about. And too much worrying about Cat.

He would call her later. Not knowing what was going on with her was killing him.

His phone beeped in his pocket.

When he didn't pull it out, his mother waved her fork at him. "Check it."

"It's rude to have your phone out at the table, Mom."

"You aren't eating anyway." She waved her fork again. "Check it."

She had a good point. He pulled out his phone. "It's Cat."

His mother glanced up. "Tell her thanks for Tank."

She went back to eating, and Brody rolled his eyes. She kept calling her bodyguard Tank. His name was Stone.

He brought up the text.

How was the play? How did Laura do?

The play wasn't right without you. But it was okay.
Mom sends her thanks for her new bodyguard.

Stone had been waiting outside the playhouse at the end of the night. He was most likely sitting in Annabelle's driveway at that very moment.

She said she didn't want one, but I was worried about her. Seriously, did she get home okay?

She's fine. I'm here with her now. How are you?

He paused for just a second before sending another.

You still in Maine?

He held his breath as he waited for her reply.

I don't scare that easily. I'm finally having the downtime a vacation is supposed to be. I swam in the pool this morning. Now I'm reading a book.

Sounds good. Don't watch the news. You're not having downtime there.

Good to know. No television. No news. Got it.

He kept his eyes on the small screen as he thought about what else he wanted to say. There was so much. But he wasn't sure if this was just her checking on his mother or if this was something else. And he didn't want to push too soon.

Thank you for the security guard. He makes me feel better about Mom. I need to be at the museum in the morning and would have been worried about leaving her.

He wanted to ask if he could come see her, but that didn't play into his plan of them both taking a breather.

Let me know if you need anything else, and I'll throw some money at it. I may not be able to do much while hiding in this big house, but I can do that.

I feel like a kept man. He tacked on a smiley emoticon.

She replied with her own smiley. I'm just trying to help. I feel like this is my fault.

It's not your fault.

Okay. But let me know if you need anything.

Will do.

He wanted to answer with, "I need you," but decided against it.

But he did need her. And somehow that small exchange had sealed it. He put down the phone with a new determination.

"I'm sorry I hurt you back then," his mom said. "I should have told you when she called."

"You did what you had to, Mom. I get that. We both know Emma Davenport never would have allowed more. She'd have ruined us both. I wouldn't be where I am today if you hadn't intervened."

"And you're happy where you are today?" Her soft eyes watched him carefully, and he knew she could see all his secrets. Growing up as a single parent and only child, they'd had to rely on each other through a lot. They'd been close.

A quick yes was on his tongue, but he held it in. "I would like a bit more," he admitted.

"Then fight for her."

He suspected he would.

"And what if I win? This could become my life, Mom." He motioned to the closed blinds and the unseen paparazzi they both knew were outside the doors. "It could become yours."

"A bodyguard anytime I need to go out?" She acted as if the idea were nothing. "I could get used to that."

"I'm serious, Mom."

"I am, too." She reached across the table and grabbed his hand. "Cat's a good woman."

Overcome with unexpected emotion, he pulled his hand back and shoved his now-cold coffee aside. He grabbed the rest of his mother's omelet. "That's enough eating. Let's go out. We'll go antiquing today. We haven't done that in years."

Hitting the many antique stores along the coast had once been their one-Sunday-a-month thing. Or, it had been *her* thing. He'd gone along because he liked spending time with her. And because there were used bookstores in most of the same areas. He could shop for books while she picked out a gold-painted horse with only three feet or whatever ridiculous "antique" she happened to find.

"You really want your picture to show up in the tabloids with your mother?" she asked.

"I want to do whatever I want. That's the problem I have with all of this. I won't hide from my life. I won't pretend to be someone I'm not. For anyone. That would be a deal breaker."

His mother thought about that for a minute, then gave a firm shake of her head. She stood from the table. "Sounds like a good plan to me. Let's go. We'll take Tank with us."

"His name isn't Tank, Mom."

She shot him a wicked wink. "I know, but did you see the size of that guy?"

CHAPTER TWENTY

CAT WAITED A COUPLE MORE MINUTES TO MAKE SURE BRODY
didn't text anything else, then she picked her phone back
up. It was time. She'd put off the call to her mother too long, but
the brief conversation with Brody had bolstered her confidence.

She dialed the phone.

Her mother picked up on the first ring. "It's about time I
heard from you."

"Did you do this?" Cat asked calmly. No need beating around
the bush. Her mother intended to win that Senate seat, and
Thomas Harrison had been leading the polls.

"Don't be ridiculous, Catherine. Davenports don't do things
that way. We run a fair race."

Right. High standards and all. Because they had so many.

"Mom." Cat lost the composure in her voice. She felt battered.
Broken. And the hits had come from her own mother. "This hurt
me. A lot. I care about him."

"You can't care about him."

"I do."

Her mother tried her lie again. "I didn't do it."

"You did, and you should be woman enough to admit it."

The line went silent.

"You intervened years ago when you shouldn't have. You convinced me that worry for my life and the life of my child had been your only concern—"

"It was my concern."

"And now you've thrown me and Brody under the bus, all for the hope of a few votes."

"I have to win this seat," her mother stated with authority. "It's a Davenport seat. It has been for years."

"And it's worth your relationship with your daughter?"

"You're just being silly. This does not have to impact our relationship. I did what had to be done. Nothing looks bad on you."

Cat's nose burned with the tears that wanted to come out. Her throat ached. And she lowered her head in grief. Her mother was not the woman she'd always believed her to be.

"I'm going to tell him." Cat's words came out quiet.

"You're going to what?" Her mother's words rose an octave.

"I'm going to tell him about the baby. I should have told him back then. I should have guessed that you'd meddled with our relationship, that you were the cause of my broken heart. And I should have known you'd broken his heart right along with it. Because *you* don't have a heart, Mother. I don't know what runs through your blood, but it isn't love."

"Catherine." Her mother sounded worried for the first time.

"You never even asked me if I wanted my child. You simply called up your friend and made plans to hide me away. Then you convinced me that it was what I wanted. That it was for the best."

"It was for the best. I was thinking of you."

"And we both know my opinion on that. But you can't stop me this time."

"Why tell him after all this time?" Leave it to her mother to try anyway. "She's gone. It doesn't matter anymore."

Her mother's words made the tears fall. She spoke as if Annabelle had been nothing to her.

"I told you," Cat managed to get out. "I care about him."

"Don't do it, Catherine." There was true panic in her mother's voice now. "It won't solve anything."

"It's the right thing to do."

"He's a Harrison."

"He is not a Harrison. And even if he was, you still had no right. You, of all people, should know that a person's DNA does not make you who you are. Otherwise, who would Bennett be?"

Her mother sucked in a harsh breath.

Cat continued, "I suppose that's a question you need to answer to my brother. I couldn't care less. I'll be telling Brody the truth about that, too. Just as soon as I see him again."

"Why are you trying to ruin me?"

"I'm not trying to ruin you, Mother. You've done a good enough job of that yourself. I'm merely trying to right a few wrongs."

Cat pressed the button to end the call without saying another word. Then she pulled up a number she'd tracked down the week before.

She'd called it the day before but had gotten no answer. She didn't today, either.

She left another message on Patricia Weathers's answering machine, asking her to call at her earliest convenience. She wanted to talk to Patricia before telling Brody about Annabelle. He deserved more than an, "I don't know anything about our daughter."

Cat hadn't spoken to Patricia since the day she'd handed over her daughter and ridden to the airport with her mother. She hadn't called when she'd found out that Annabelle had died because she hadn't felt she had the right. Annabelle had been Patricia's daughter then. And Cat had known Patricia was hurting over the loss. Probably as much as Cat. So she'd remained quiet.

But there were some things she had to know. What had happened to her little girl? What made her so sick? Had she been happy, even though she'd been sick? Were there pictures that Patricia could share?

These things had haunted Cat for eighteen years, and they would haunt Brody, too. So Cat had to try. She only prayed that her questions didn't bring back too much pain for Patricia. After all, she'd lost a daughter, too.

———   ———

Cat's phone chimed immediately after she crawled into bed that night, and her heart fluttered in anticipation. She grabbed it before the light went out on the screen. It was a text from Brody.

The play was better tonight. Less paparazzi.

Good. Your mother still okay? Stone taking care of her?

Mom is great. Feels like a movie star with her security detail.

LOL. I'm glad she's having fun with it.

Seriously, I think she's got a crush. Did you have to send her such a good-looking guy?

And he's almost her age. Tell her to go for it.

Don't say that. It's my mom.

Hey, she deserves some fun. How did Laura do tonight?

She did great. She's picked up some of your habits. It's almost like watching you. Only . . . it's not.

Cat smiled at the message and pressed her phone to her heart. Brody texted again before she could. How are YOU?

She liked these quiet moments with him like this. I'm fine. I talked to my mother today.

And how did that go?

About how you'd expect. There was a bit of an argument. She chewed on her lip for a second before tapping out another message. It was her. She leaked the story. I'm so sorry.

It seemed to take forever before her phone chimed again.

I'm sorry too. You shouldn't have to deal with that.

I'll survive.

There was another small delay as she stared intently at her phone. She jumped when it chimed.

What are you doing tomorrow?

Did he want to see her? Her pulse thudded at the thought.

Helping out at the park.

There'll be paparazzi there. Be careful.

I will. I'll have my own security detail with me. He's even better looking than Stone.

Should I be jealous? You're over there all alone with another man?

She smiled at the phone, then her fingers flew over the screen.

I actually have two men with me. Both hot.

She followed up with a smiley face, then held her breath as she asked a question. What are we doing, Brody? Friends? More? Text buddies?

More. Definitely more.

Are you sure? Maybe your life could quiet back down if I'm not in the picture.

My life needs you in the picture.

Brody . . .

Cat . . .

She grinned at the phone again. She felt like a teenager. My kids will be here Wednesday. They're going to help with the park.

Good. You need your kids with you.

I do. I miss them.

She missed Brody, too, but she didn't tell him. Instead she typed out another message. Will you be at the park on Wednesday?

Do you want me at the park on Wednesday?

It's a community thing, so . . .

It is. But do YOU want me there?

She wanted him there with her now. But she knew what he was asking. The same thing she was. If he came to the park, he would meet her kids.

She nodded as she typed out her response.

Yes.

Then I'll be at the park on Wednesday. Talk to you in the morning? I could call after my run?

You're not at your mom's tonight?

I work tomorrow. And I need my jog.

You'll be photographed.

Probably. Another reason to keep up my regimen. If I'm going to be in the tabloids, I want to look good.

He followed his message with a wink.

You already look good.

You too, Kitty Cat. I'll talk to you tomorrow. Sweet dreams.

She slid deep under her covers and reread the last message. What they were doing scared her, but it felt right. They weren't playing any longer. If they got back together, they would have to deal with the real world. Together.

But possibly have something really good come out of it, too.

She curled up on her side, holding the phone to her chest and closing her eyes. She'd take it one day at a time and see what happened next.

And tomorrow, Brody would be calling.

She was ready to hear his voice again.

CHAPTER TWENTY-ONE

THE HEADLINE IN THE PAPERS MONDAY MORNING READ, "Romeo and Juliet. How well do they really know each other?"

Below it was a picture of Brody and Cat as teens. She looked so cute with her "Rachel" haircut. Brody remembered how all the girls that summer had mimicked the character from *Friends*. If it hadn't been the hair, it had been the clothes. Or both.

Such as the one-strap blue-jean overall shorts Cat had on in the picture. She'd worn a stretchy scrap of nothing underneath it, the material barely covering her breasts. It had driven him crazy every time she'd had it on.

Brody smiled at the picture. He had good memories of those times.

He picked up his phone and typed.

Great picture in the paper today.

I'm looking at it right now.

I liked that haircut.

The whole world liked that haircut. Except the woman who had it first. Did you go for your jog already?

I did. Having my breakfast right now. Have you done your yoga?

Following it up with my smoothie as we speak. I thought you were going to call me.

Brody grinned at her message. She wanted to talk to him.

Which was only fair, since he wanted to talk to her.

His fingers flew over the letters. I decided this was more fun. Sexier.

If you say so.

A knock sounded at his front door, and he rose to head that direction. So far no photographer had been so bold as to come up to his house, but if one had—

His thoughts stopped midsentence as he peeked out the window and saw who stood on his front stoop. Thomas. In a suit.

Cat's message from last night flashed in his mind. *My mom leaked the story.*

Did that mean Thomas was here because he cared? Brody doubted it.

He also suspected that every camera still barricading his place had gotten a great shot of his brother walking up to his door.

He sent Cat a quick text. Gotta run. Thomas just showed up.

Oh . . . Good luck.

He was unsure how best to approach this, but fully aware that whatever he did would be in tomorrow's headlines. Meaning he probably shouldn't drag the man out of his house and deposit him in his car.

"I'm on my way out," he said at the same time that he let Thomas in. "I have a class at the museum in thirty minutes."

"I'll go with you."

Of course he would. It would be a photo op.

Then Thomas stopped just inside the door and took Brody in. The two of them stood there, a foot separating them, eyeing each other as if unsure what to expect. What to do next. Which was exactly what Brody was feeling.

They'd never been the hugging type. They'd seen each other maybe six times in their lives. What were they supposed to do?

They continued to stare.

Thomas's eyes weren't the same color as Brody's. He'd gotten his mother's brown. But that didn't mean Brody couldn't see the family resemblance when he looked at him. In fact, the older they got, the more Brody saw it. He wanted to like that about them. They shared more than blood.

It should make him feel closer.

It didn't.

All it did was make him wonder what Thomas's angle was. Because Brody knew he had one. A Harrison always did.

This trip wasn't about getting to know Brody. It was about Thomas.

Low clouds hung over the sky Tuesday morning, turning the ocean a hazy gray. The color made it appear as if the ocean and sky bled directly into each other as Cat sat on the balcony of her bedroom, overlooking the backyard.

It really was a lovely view. Not as nice as her beach house, but pretty in a different way. She could make out the inward swoop of a nearby beach—the space along this part of the coast was more rocky than sandy—as well as a lovely overlook just beyond the beach. She'd sat on the benches there many times as a kid.

It was a place she'd like to share with Brody.

She had her untouched smoothie on the small table in front of her, as well as the *Gazette*. She hadn't made it past the front page.

Thomas Harrison and Brody had been photographed together at the museum.

Long-Lost Brothers, Found.

Her mother would be fuming. Clearly, she hadn't been thinking straight when she'd leaked the story. Brody was *Arthur's* son. Thomas "hadn't known." He could be the innocent party in this.

And if Brody didn't stop him, Thomas would milk this right into the Senate seat.

She forced herself to turn the page. There was another photo of Brody. One that normally might not make the *Dyersport Gazette*, but she couldn't blame the paper for including it.

It was him, shirtless, jogging on the beach. She picked up her phone and typed, Nice picture on page two. She smiled and slumped down in her seat.

Isn't it? I was just admiring that myself.

You look good. They got your good side.

LOL. Do I have a bad side?

No.

I miss you, Cat.

I miss you, too.

Thomas is staying here with me.

And how's that going? Brotherly?

I fear you might have been right.

No . . . my mother was the one to leak it. I'm certain.

Not the story. Using it as PR.

Oh . . . I'm sorry.

I suggested he get a hotel, but they're full.

Of paparazzi, I would imagine.

Pictures must pay well. A beachfront room for a week isn't cheap.

She changed the subject with her next text. Paper says the play is back on track. You called Searcy yet?

No.

Your stubbornness will be the death of you.

More like, YOU will be the death of me. Did I mention that I miss you?

I seem to recall something about that.

Did I mention how much?

No. You definitely did not mention how much.

Tons. Which got me to thinking . . .

Yeah? Cat held her breath as she waited, wondering what he'd been thinking.

And wondering how much she'd like it.

Her phone beeped out a reply. I could come over after
the play tonight. Miss you in person.

Her heart thundered in her chest, and another text came in before she could get her fingers to moving.

You okay with that?

She nodded. I am. Don't be followed.

Count on it.

They said good-bye, and Cat placed another call to Califor-nia. Patricia still hadn't called her back.

When there was no answer at the house, Cat used her phone to search the San Francisco area where Patricia lived. She didn't remember the name of the clinic where her mother's friend had once worked, but a few words in a search engine and the office came up.

She tapped the number and placed the call.

And, of course, got a messaging service. It was three hours earlier on the West Coast.

"I'd like to leave a message for Dr. Weathers, please."

"Yes, ma'am. But Dr. Weathers is out for the week. Can I take a message for another doctor?"

Relief filled Cat as it occurred to her that she'd been terrified Patricia was simply avoiding her calls.

"Do you know if she's in town?" Cat asked.

"I'm sorry, ma'am. Did you want to leave a message for one of our doctors?"

"I'd like to leave one for Dr. Weathers, please. In case she calls in to check her messages."

"Yes, ma'am. I'll switch you over to her voice mail."

Cat quickly left her name and number, asking Patricia to call as soon as she could. Brody was coming over tonight, and he would be meeting her kids tomorrow. She had to tell him, with or without hearing from Patricia first. Time had run out.

CHAPTER TWENTY-TWO

THE NUMBERS ON THE CLOCK CHANGED TO 12:01. IT WAS now tomorrow, and there had been no word from Brody.

No text, no call. No nothing.

Had something else happened?

She opened her balcony doors and stood in the center of the space. Her short gown whispered around her thighs as she stared out into the dark. The moon was out tonight, the clouds of the last couple of days having lifted, and the faint scent of roses from the gardens wafted through the air. It was a gorgeous night with the stars filling the sky.

Too edgy to sit, she grabbed her cell and moved to the balcony where she propped her elbows on the railing and frowned down at her phone.

It chimed in her hands.

She smiled as she quickly checked the message.

Still up?

Of course. I had reason to believe I could expect company.

Oh, you can expect company. Look down.

She glanced at her feet before realizing what he meant. Then she leaned out over the railing and peered into the yard.

And there he was. In the shadows of the pines.

Her heart quit beating.

"What are you doing down there?" she asked. "I have a front door. My security guys know to let you in."

"Thank goodness for that, because at least one of your guys is huge. I think he might have ripped off my arms if he hadn't known I was coming."

"He has instructions to rip off the arms of trespassers."

"Then thank you for sparing mine."

She laughed and leaned farther over the railing. Euphoria filled her as she tried harder to see him. She wished he wasn't standing so far in the shadows. "So if you met one of my guards, why didn't you come in through the door?"

"Because you still have people in front of your house. He caught me sneaking in from the beach."

Cat grinned. How romantic. "Seems I'm popular these days. I've been trailed everywhere this week, yet no one has been impressed with the actual work I've been doing out at the park. Nothing tabloid worthy."

"Then we'd better not let them see this."

"What?"

He moved out of the shadows, and her mouth fell open.

"What are you wearing?"

"A doublet," Brody replied. "I picked it up at the playhouse tonight."

Cat squinted as she tried to better make him out. A doublet? As in puffy sleeves and a "shirt" hanging to his hips? A brush of white waved in the air. "Is that a feather sticking out of your head?"

"Out of my hat."

"And why, exactly, are you dressed in a doublet and a feathered hat?"

His teeth flashed in the dark night as he widened his stance and propped both hands on his hips. "Because I've come for my Juliet."

"Brody," she said his name with a laugh. He was dressed as Romeo. "You're crazy. *This* is crazy. You could have been caught."

"I don't care. The only reason I *snuck* past the cameras was for you. So you didn't have to deal with more tabloid pictures in the morning. But I couldn't care less if every one of them got a shot of me like this. Coming for you."

"You're too much."

"I'm just me."

She nodded. He was. And she was so glad of that. Then she noticed something else about his costume and squinted again to better focus. "Are you wearing leggings?" she asked.

"They go with the doublet," he said drily.

"You are completely out of your mind."

He simply nodded.

She looked around, taking in her bedroom, her second-story balcony, and the shrubbery surrounding the house beneath her room. If he wanted to be romantic . . .

"Think you can make it up?" she issued the challenge.

The shrubbery rattled with his movements before she got her question out.

She laughed again. Brody had a way of making her do that. "Want me to hang something over the railing for you to grab on to?"

"Wrong story," he muttered from somewhere underneath her. He followed his words up with a grunted "Ouch," and several oaths. And then he was there. His hat had dropped from his head, but his eyes gleamed at her from between two curved posts.

He'd somehow scaled the side of her house, and he was now lifting himself the rest of the way up. He grabbed the top rail and hoisted himself over, and her knees went weak.

"Wow," she murmured.

"Don't you dare mock me," he warned.

That move had been the sexiest thing she'd ever seen. Mocking him was the last thing on her mind. She swallowed and lowered her gaze as she tried to catch her breath. Then she peeked back up. "But you're in tights," she teased.

"Leggings."

"Right." She nodded. "Because that's so much manlier."

He took a step closer. "It is romantic, though, isn't it?" His voice dropped to the level that meant he was thinking about coming out of those leggings. And helping her out of her gown.

"I can't believe you scaled my wall to see me." She glanced around at the silent night. They were on the back side of the property, so chances were slim there were any cameras pointed at them. But even if there were, she didn't care. She had Brody back. And that's the way she wanted it.

"I would scale anything for you," he said, his words turning sincere. "I missed you."

"I missed you, too."

"Three days is too long."

"Three and a half."

He gave a single nod. "Three and a half. Let's not go three and a half again."

She reached her arms out for him. "Kiss me, Brody. Now."

So he did.

With their mouths fused together, he walked her backward into her room, his hands moving to her hips and her gown bunching in his grip. Then he yanked her forward, and she found her body fitting snugly to his.

He pressed into her. Everything about him was hard, everything about her needy.

As she pushed herself even closer, he moved them to the wall and they landed with a thud. She immediately wrapped a leg around his hip, moaning into his mouth as he took the kiss deeper.

When they came up for air, he pressed his cheek against hers. His breathing was rough.

"Oh geez," he muttered. His fingers trailed over her throat. "I needed that."

She nodded. "I need more."

With a groan, he didn't say another word. He simply kissed her again. This kiss was accompanied by his hands lifting her gown over her head and his teeth scraping along the top of her shoulder. She shivered as her gown sailed through the air. It landed with a whisper on the ground behind Brody.

"Nice gown," he complimented, "but we don't need it."

He leaned back then, leering down at her in the faint light from the single bedside lamp she'd left on. "But we do need more light," he determined.

She pointed to another lamp a couple of feet away, and with a click he had it on.

His gazed raked over her, all hot and steamy, and she shivered once again. The man had a way of touching her without laying a hand on her body. Then they both went to work. She attacked his shirt while he tugged off her panties. When his chest was bare, she leaned forward and put her mouth to his heated skin.

He hissed in a breath.

She licked his nipple, enjoying the salty tang of him, and slid her hands over his six-pack.

"I'm so sorry." Brody brought her mouth back up to his. He pressed a hard kiss to her lips. "I should have told you about Thomas. About your mother knowing who I was. You should have been prepared for this."

"And I should have . . ."

She cut off her words by pressing her lips together. She had things to tell him, but she didn't want to do it tonight. Not right then. First, she just wanted to feel.

Her breasts were heavy with desire, so she pushed into him. "Later," she whispered. She cupped his cheek in her palm. "We'll talk later. Right now, just make love to me. I need you."

He nodded.

His eyes turned dark, and he kissed her again. This one was slower. It reached deeper inside her and tugged at all the parts she'd long ago locked away. It begged to be let in.

And then the kiss changed. Slow was good, but they both had too much pent-up need.

In seconds she gripped the elastic around his waist, ready to strip him bare. But she paused. She roamed her gaze down over him, taking in the black, skintight pants and the very impressive bulge coming from the front. The man knew how to fill out a pair of leggings.

As he watched her, she slid her palm over his erection. Then she squeezed. Just enough to make him groan out her name. He pulsed in her hand, and she automatically gripped him tighter.

"Please tell me there's a condom somewhere in these ridiculous clothes," she begged.

Brody's fingers slipped inside the front of the material, returning with three small packages between his fingertips. "There's a key pocket inside."

"Good to know."

She took one of the condoms and shoved the leggings down. But she changed her mind. Instead of immediately covering him with the protection, she covered him with her mouth.

The sound that ripped out of him told her she'd chosen right.

"Babe," he growled as his hands landed in her hair. "I don't think . . ."

His words cut off when her tongue stroked the full length of him. She held him in her hands, needing him inside of her, yet wanting to do this for him first. She'd missed him. And she was worried that she still might lose him. So she had to show him with her actions how much he meant to her.

She opened her mouth and sucked him in deep. This time he leaned forward and reached out for the wall.

"Shit," he muttered as she heard a sound behind her. A picture tumbled from the wall, missing her back as he swatted at the frame. It landed on the small table beside them, sending the lamp to the floor with a crash.

The light blinked out and she smiled around his erection.

He groaned again.

She continued working him with her mouth. Her hands moved to his buttocks, the muscles there tight with control.

"Cat," he begged. "You need to . . ."

She smiled again as he thumped his forehead to the wall and dropped his hands to her head. His fingers clenched in her hair.

"Baby," he whispered hoarsely.

And only because she'd missed him so much—and was apparently selfish when it came to wanting her own pleasure—she slid her mouth along his length one last time. She flicked her tongue over the head, feeling his body shake in her arms, then she pulled back just far enough to roll the condom down over him.

The instant it was in place, he had her under her arms and was dragging her body up.

He didn't stop when she was on her feet, but lifted her to her toes, holding her against the wall, and plundered her mouth with his. He dipped his head and drew a breast between his lips. Her back arched. She lifted her legs to his waist.

And he pushed inside her.

There was a second when neither of them moved as her body stretched around him. A breath slid out of both of them. Then her arms closed around his neck and his hands went to her butt.

He withdrew and quickly returned, slamming her against the wall.

Then he did it again.

Her body began to shake. She was going to be done that fast.

"I didn't like not being with you," he whispered harshly against her temple.

She nodded. Words weren't possible.

"I've worried about you. I've missed you." He kissed her possessively. "I've wanted you with me."

He trapped her with his body and tugged on her hair so he had access to her throat. He nibbled, and he pumped harder inside her. And when she was right on the edge he slipped a hand between them and buried his fingers.

And she was gone.

He continued stroking himself in and out of her body as she flew, his hands once again bracing her hips to him, but he didn't have his own orgasm. Somehow, he was stronger than that. His teeth were bared when she opened her eyes, though, and she could tell that he was hanging on by a thread.

"You good?" he asked, his words tight.

She gave a quick nod, and he separated them and pulled her to the balcony. She didn't ask questions, merely let him maneuver her however he wanted her. He put her hands on the concrete railing and positioned her hips in front of his. And then he was in her again, entering her from the back this time, and she thought for sure she would combust.

A breeze blew over them, cooling her heated skin, and pointing out that they were out in the open where anyone could see. Or hear. Their voices could carry on the wind. The danger of it only added to the excitement. She moaned.

"Shhh," Brody whispered. But he didn't stop making love to her. He kept up a steady rhythm, his hands gripping wide around her hips as he buried himself over and over.

His fingers curved into her flesh as his movements slowed and became methodical. She softly begged him to go faster, but he didn't. She writhed in his hands. He kept the pace slow. He was killing her.

"Brody," she pleaded. One hand scraped up her spine until he gripped her shoulder in his fingers. Her nipples puckered and she tingled down below.

Her breasts jostled with each of Brody's movements, and the cool air continued kissing her body. The mix of heat and sweat and the swirling breeze, the hint of flowers and the scent of the ocean, all combined in an erotic fashion. Not to mention Brody's never-ending control over her body.

The combination made her eyes lose focus.

She pressed back frantically, wanting more, grinding against him. She was desperate.

Her moves seemed to sever his need to drive her out of her mind, because his fingers clenched tightly, and he suddenly picked up speed. She could tell that she was no longer the only one out of control.

He grunted as their skin slapped together.

His strokes grew tighter, and he leaned forward so that his body covered hers. Their skin slid together. His hands reached around, seeking out her breasts.

She bit her lip when he found her, attempting to hold in the groan, but she failed. Her head hung as his fingers tugged at her flesh.

"Brody," she whispered, her need urgent.

Understanding, he slid a hand down her belly until it was between her legs. His touch did the trick yet again. As she felt the contractions build, her knees dipped. But Brody was ready for her. He caught her, holding her tight, and with one final move, he ushered them both across the finish line.

CHAPTER TWENTY-THREE

B RODY HELD HIMSELF OFF THE BED WITH HIS ELBOWS, Cat's body stretched out beneath his, open to him. Her gaze was locked to his. He slowly pumped his hips, filling her, before retreating and doing it again. His heart pounded with the depth of the moment.

Neither of them spoke. They merely felt.

They'd fallen asleep in her bed a few hours earlier. It wasn't morning yet, but dawn was breaking. Which meant their time was almost up. He didn't want to be caught sneaking out of her house. She didn't need that. Plus, her kids would be arriving soon.

He'd turned his head on his pillow a short while ago to find Cat watching him. The look in her eyes had scared and thrilled him at the same time. He hadn't been the only one lost for the last few days. He'd seen that in her. Yet fear had also been in there. As if she was still unsure about them.

He refused to accept that. They belonged together. He would find a way to make it happen.

Without a word, he'd moved over her, and he'd begun to show her what she meant to him.

He pushed the hair off her face now and dropped a kiss to her cheek. He wanted to make love to this woman every morning for the rest of his life. His mouth found hers and he held on until they were both breathless.

He slid in deep, closing his eyes as his body begged for release, and let out a tiny groan when her hands moved over his back. Her nails dug in. Not deep, but enough to know that she was gaining in speed, same as he. He shuddered in her arms. He didn't want this moment to end. When it did, they had to face reality.

They still had things to work out. Being together wouldn't be easy.

He'd shown up, and they'd made love. Then they'd moved to the bed and had reached for each other again. Afterward, she'd fallen asleep in his arms before he'd been able to say all the things on his mind.

But this morning he had to get them out.

He loved her.

He would fight for her.

But she had to be willing to do the same. Was she really ready to stand up to her mother? For good?

A small gasp hit his ears, and he felt Cat's movements shift. Opening his eyes, he showed her the depth of his emotions. His love was there. And it was hers.

Several minutes later, he rolled to his side with an exhausted but happy grunt, and brought Cat with him. With her wrapped in his arms, he kissed her damp temple and whispered, "I want to tell you about my father."

Her eyes opened.

"I need you to believe that I am not anything like them, and I never will be."

"I do believe that." She sat up, pulling the cover with her and tucking it under her arms. "I knew it the other day. I know who you are. And no, you're nothing like them." She reached out to touch his arm. "But I would love to hear what you have to say. I'd like to better understand you."

He pushed himself up, propping beside her against the headboard, but he didn't start talking immediately. He grabbed a tissue from the bedside table and took a moment to relieve himself of the condom as he let his mind return to that summer almost two decades ago. Then he stared straight ahead and blew out a heavy breath.

"Mom used to work for Arthur's dad, Thomas Franklin Harrison. He was a Georgia senator. My brother got his name from him. Mom has a poli-sci degree and worked on a congressional campaign in New Hampshire the year she graduated college. She loved it. And she was good at it. Someone on Harrison's team heard about her and was impressed. He stole her away. From what I understand, she had a promising career ahead of her. She'd established herself as a valuable commodity and had secured a position with Harrison in Washington. Her life was setting up exactly as she'd dreamed.

"But thanks to Arthur, she had to give that up. He wouldn't acknowledge a child with her, and he promised ostracism if she so much as uttered his name. He wanted her gone. If she'd stayed in DC, he assured her that her choices would be limited. He'd used her, and he was done with her.

"He did offer abortion, as I understand it, but that wasn't an option for Mom—thank goodness." He winked at the horrified expression that came to Cat's face, but kept on going. "So she told no one, and she came home. She's been teaching at the community college ever since. She's happy—and she has been for years—but it infuriates me that Arthur changed her life that way. And that he had zero remorse in doing it."

Brody wrapped an arm around Cat and held her close. "Not to mention having nothing to do with me," he added. "Mom never talked about my father. I didn't understand why at the time, but I accepted it. He was someone she'd previously worked with who had chosen not to be in my life. That was all she'd ever say about it."

"That must have been hard," Cat said. "Not to know more."

Brody nodded. "It was. I was curious. But I was also mad. Why didn't he want anything to do with me? And deep down, I wondered if it was the fault of my mom. Maybe he *had* wanted me, you know? But she'd chosen not to let him?"

Cat squeezed his hand.

"I know," he agreed with her unspoken comment. "I shouldn't have doubted her."

"You were a boy, and you had no dad. Of course you'd wonder. Any kid would."

Her support warmed him.

But she was wrong. He should have had more faith.

If he had, he and Cat may not be in the situation they were in today. He wouldn't have sought the man out.

"I found a picture when I was sixteen," he told her. "It was from the time Mom worked in DC. It was her with Arthur Harrison and another guy. Arthur Harrison was a senator in Washington by that point, and the other man was a guy my mom had known since college, Clark Trent. Clark lives in Boston and works for the New England Political Science Association. Very intelligent guy.

"I'd met him a few times in my life, and we were friends." He shrugged. "As much as you can be friends with your *mother's* friend. But we got each other. We had a lot of the same likes, and he was one of the people who encouraged me to work hard in school. He'd even offered to help with college entrance essays when the time came."

"You thought it was him?"

He nodded. "Made sense to me. And that hurt. Clark had come around my whole life. Not all the time, but consistently through the years. He'd show up to visit Mom, but he always made time for me. Yet he didn't care enough to want to be my father? *That* did not make sense."

He shrugged again as if none of it mattered now. But he'd wished so many times Clark had turned out to be his dad. "So I headed off to confront him," he stated.

A laugh rolled out of him as he remembered that day. The look on Clark's face.

"I confronted him all right." He glanced at Cat and placed a quick kiss on her upturned mouth. "He didn't seem all that surprised to see me, but he *did* manage to surprise *me*. He introduced me to his life partner." Brody shook his head in fond remembrance of that day. "Clark was most definitely not my father."

Cat made a small O with her mouth, humor in her eyes. But the humor disappeared as she somehow figured out what he had yet to say. "But he knew who was?"

Brody nodded. "Told me to go home and ask my mom. But I didn't need to. The minute he looked at the picture I'd brought with me, I got it. My real father was the other man in the photo. Arthur Harrison. At the time I found out the truth, Arthur was up-and-coming. Had a kid, married for fifteen years. He had the ideal life."

He paused long enough to let his mind really settle into that time. He'd been angry. But he'd also been hopeful. Maybe once Arthur met him in person, he'd see that they were family.

Brody felt like a chump, even today. He never should have gone to DC.

He forced a curve to his lips, but he didn't look at Cat. And his smile was stiff. "I didn't go home and ask Mom. I got back in my car, and I headed south that night. The car barely made it. It was such a piece of junk."

"The car you have now?" she asked. "You said it was the first car you'd owned, right?"

Remembering her early description of his car, his smile turned real. He ran his hand up her arm. "Yeah. The car I have now. The 'red one.'"

She grinned at his teasing, and he had to force himself not to kiss her again.

She held his heart in her hands, and she could either squeeze the life out of it or she could make him the happiest person on earth. He didn't want to give her that power, but she had it. That scared him.

He turned his attention back to the open doors beyond the foot of the bed. "I had to stop at an auto shop on the other side of New York," he said, remembering that trip and the pleading he'd done to get the service guy to cut him a break. "Took the last cent of the money in my pocket, but he got it running good enough to get me the rest of the way. When I got there, it was dark. I had no idea where to go, so I slept in my car. I showed up at Arthur's office the next day."

Cat's gaze was on him, he could feel it. But he didn't turn to her.

"By this time, my mom was frantic. I'd called her the day before and left a message but hadn't talked to her myself. I'd intentionally called when I knew she would be out. Of course, I didn't get *that* particular earful from her until I talked to her days later." And he *had* gotten an earful. Until she'd learned where he was.

"I went to Arthur's office the next morning but was stopped by his receptionist. Senator Harrison was much too busy," he mimicked the snotty woman who'd been behind the desk, "but she'd be glad to give me a signed photograph of the senator as a thanks for my support.

"Please," he ground out. He rose from her bed. "I didn't want a photograph of the man. I knew what he looked like." Brody pointed to himself. "He has my eyes. I saw it the instant I knew who he was. It infuriates me. I don't want to look like him. When I told the receptionist to let him know that Annabelle Hollister's son was there, his schedule suddenly opened up."

Cat peered up at him from the bed, her hair wild around her face and her eyes as scared as he'd felt that day. "What happened?"

"At first there was denial," he said. He grabbed the ridiculous leggings off the floor and stepped into them, realizing he stood there naked. "Claimed he didn't know what I was talking about. I presented the facts. I told him to look at my damned eyes. I told him when I was born. Seven months after my mother quit working for *his* father." He swallowed and nodded, then crossed to the open doors. The sky was growing lighter. "He relented. He believed me. But he claimed he'd never known anything about me."

"That's what you wanted to hear," Cat said when he paused.

He nodded. Guilt washed over him. His mother had built her life around him and he'd doubted her.

"Over the next few days, I met his wife and son," he continued. "I stayed at his house—as Thomas's friend. It was made clear that I was to tell no one who I was. Not yet. They had to figure out the best way to share the good news."

He turned to face Cat, anger raging. "It was bullshit. The man went for two weeks acting as if he was happy to know about me. Told me to my face that my mother had kept me from him. He made me hate her. By this time, I *wanted* him to be my father. And I was willing to shun my own mother for her part in keeping him from me."

He rammed his hands into his hair, pulling on the ends before letting go and clenching his hands into fists. "He bought me a car," he gritted out. "A brand-new Mercedes." Gullibility had never sat well with Brody. "It was a hell of a lot better than the piece of shit I was driving. I even let him get rid of the old car for me. No need for me to bother with such trivialities."

His laugh that time was harsh, and he saw Cat cringe with the sound.

"The reality was, my piece of shit was parked in Arthur's driveway. It was presenting the wrong image with his million-dollar home."

Cat nodded as if she got it. And she probably did. Her world revolved around the image she and her family presented.

"So what happened?" she asked.

"He suggested I move in. We could make it permanent."

Cat's eyes widened. He'd been an idiot to believe anything Arthur Harrison had ever said to him.

"I went home to pack my bags. Mom didn't explain things at that point, but we argued. A lot. She kissed my cheek before I left, and told me she loved me. I hurt her that day. I said ugly words to her. But I didn't let that slow me down. I hopped in the car and arrived back in DC before Arthur was expecting me. I found him in his study with his personal assistant. They were discussing the best way to present me to the public. What would win him the most support? He was a wronged man, you know? Had never even known he had another son. It was a gold mine of an opportunity."

Brody shook his head in disgust. His jaw clenched. "Then he said something which took me a few minutes to digest. He said, 'Send Annabelle another check. The first one kept her quiet for sixteen years.'"

Cat put her hands to her mouth.

He pressed his lips together before finishing. His chest swelled with his breath. "'If he's going to be my son,'" he continued, his voice breaking, "'then Annabelle can't be involved. Double the amount, and tell her she no longer has a son.'"

"He'd known about you all along," Cat whispered. She rose from the bed. Naked. But he barely registered the fact.

"Of course he'd known," he spat out. "And I was an idiot for not getting that."

"You were sixteen. You wanted your father to love you."

"I should have known better."

She reached for his hands. "He hurt you, Brody. That's on him. It's not your fault."

"I'd gotten rid of my car for this guy." The pain in his chest pissed him off. He didn't care enough to be hurt by this man any longer. "I'd worked afternoon jobs for three years to save up for that car, and I gave it away without a blink." He clenched his fingers in hers.

"You left then, right?"

"I couldn't stay."

"What about Thomas?" Cat asked.

"That was the hard part. I was suddenly an older brother. I *loved* that. As an only child, you couldn't have given me a better present."

"But you wouldn't have been able to see him after that. Not after you confronted Arthur." She sucked in a breath. "You did confront Arthur?"

"Oh, yeah." He nodded. "I let him know in no uncertain terms what a piece of trash he was. He still tried to save himself. Pointed out how much better my life would be as a Harrison. All I had to do was keep my mouth shut. No one could ever know that he'd known about me."

Brody released her hands and stooped to pick up her gown. He pulled it over her head, caressing the silky material into place, and he let himself kiss her then. He needed to feel the goodness of her on him.

When he pulled away, her eyes swam in tears. She reached up and cupped his jaw.

"I came home and asked my mother about what he'd said," he told her. "Had she taken money from him? She had. She'd used it to buy our house. Didn't want us to ever have to worry about needing a place to live. She hadn't come from money. She had a degree and a job, but unless I wanted to go to community college, the job wouldn't pay for an education."

"You didn't ask Arthur to pay for school?"

"Absolutely not. I walked out of that man's life and never looked back." His body went stiff as he thought about the only other time he'd stood in front of Arthur. The experience had made a lasting impression.

"Until my fucking ex tricked me into talking to him again," he said quietly.

He turned away, gripping the doorframe at the top and stretching his body forward. He needed to go for a run.

"What do you mean?" Cat asked behind him. Her hand landed on his bare back and he stiffened. "How did she do that?"

Brody closed his eyes and rushed the words out. "We met in college, I told you that. She had big goals, and she needed to be in Washington to achieve them. I was opposed at first, but Thomas was there. He was at Georgetown. So I got a job at the university, hoping to get some time with him and actually build a relationship."

"Had you two talked at all over the years?"

"A handful of times. After he got his license we met once a year. As friends, of course. We couldn't tell anyone we were brothers. Now that I look back, I think the idea of having a brother bothered him as much as it did Arthur."

Cat went silent. When she finally responded, Brody knew she got it. She stepped around him so that she faced him. "He was already looking down the road to politics?"

He studied her, seeing understanding. Both his father and his brother had rejected him. "Couldn't have a bastard brother in the closet."

"But it wasn't his fault."

"Didn't matter." He shook his head. "He's his father's son."

"That hurts." She said the words as if it hurt her.

He nodded. "I get it, though. It's what he grew up with. I grew up with my mother and I'm a lot like her. My values are hers." He shot her a tender look. "You grew up with your mother."

She nodded in understanding.

"I might have even figured all this out years ago. About Thomas. The signs were there, I just didn't want to see them."

"So you kept trying?"

"I kept trying." He lowered his hands to put them on her. His palms curved around her shoulders. "I wanted a brother," he told her. "In some small way, that would have made Arthur's rejection okay. If Thomas cared."

She stared up at him, and he suspected she could see the rest. He let her see it. "You still want him to love you," she said softly.

"I know he's like Arthur. I get that. Yet I can't help but hope he's not *completely* like Arthur, you know?"

She went silent as she watched him. Finally she spoke. "That's understandable. And it's okay to want that."

"It's weak."

"It's your brother."

He eyed her quietly, trying to decide if he really wanted to show her how pathetic he was. Hell, why stop now?

"My brother slept with my fiancée after we broke up," he said stoically.

Cat went silent. Her eyes narrowed into thin slits.

He told her the ugly truth about his ex.

"She wasn't aware that Thomas and I were brothers, but she did know an in into national politics when she saw one. And every single time I met up with Thomas, damned if she didn't manage to show up too."

"I hate her already."

He gave her a wink. "So one night I told her who my father was."

He tried to turn away then, but Cat didn't let him. She brought his face back to hers, and he saw the concern in her eyes. She cared about him, he could see that. As deeply as he cared about her.

Swallowing his fear, he kept going. "I don't know how I didn't see it at the time, but the gleam that came into her eyes that night, it was like a bull preparing to charge. She started in on me not long after, wanting me to go to this fund-raiser. I didn't want to go. Not that I didn't support the cause, but the word was the Harrisons were big backers."

"And you hadn't talked to Arthur since you were sixteen?"

"Hadn't laid eyes on him."

"But you went to the fund-raiser?"

"I went to the fund-raiser. For my fiancée. And the next thing I knew, she had me in front of Arthur, demanding an introduction. She was aware I wouldn't cause a scene. I was more reserved around her. Always did the right thing. I even dressed differently when I dated her." His jaw tightened with disgust. "I didn't see any of that at the time."

"She wasn't the right person for you."

His laugh was hollow. "Clearly."

"So what happened next?"

"Next . . ." He closed his eyes and went back to that night. Arthur Harrison's green gaze had turned to ice the instant it had landed on Brody. "He was 'happy to see his son's long-ago friend,'" Brody explained, as he opened his eyes and looked at Cat. "'It had been too long.'"

"He recognized you?"

"Sent his admin to my office the next day. With a check."

Her jaw dropped. "He tried to buy you off?"

"What can I say? The man likes to write a check."

"And Devan. What happened there?"

He told her the rest of the story. Devan's new job for his father. Brody's ultimatum.

Devan's choice.

"Oh, Brody. I'm so sorry."

"Don't be sorry. I think I was looking for an out, too. Didn't realize it at the time. Things weren't going well with Thomas, Devan and I were more roommates than a couple, and I was living in a town which raised my blood pressure every time I stepped outside my front door. I didn't belong there." He lifted her hand to his lips. "I belong here."

"You do seem to fit in here. People love you."

He wrapped his arms around her, wanting her in his arms, and sighed at the feel of her body pressed against his. "I love them, too," he murmured. "It's a good place." He kissed the spot between her eyebrows and asked, "What about you? You ever thought about moving away from Atlanta?"

"Me?"

The shock in her eyes pricked at his heart. He didn't let that show. "It would be easier to be out from under your mother's thumb if you weren't there," he suggested, then carefully added, "if you wanted to be out from under your mother's thumb."

If she didn't, there was nothing for them. He would have to accept that.

"I can't say that I've thought about moving," she began, "but I have hired an associate director. I've been training her to run the foundation."

That gave him hope. "Yeah?"

Exactly the type of thing he wanted to hear.

"I haven't decided to quit, but I would like to be out. I'm just not sure what else I want to do."

He opened his hands and spread them wide on her back. Then he held his breath. It was time to make his move.

"You could move to Maine?" he suggested softly. "You and your kids. You could be here with me."

CHAPTER TWENTY-FOUR

CAT'S IMMEDIATE RESPONSE WAS SILENCE.

Brody watched her. His hands still on her back, his arms wrapped around her body.

Worry crept into his eyes.

He wanted her to move there? What did that mean? Did it mean he wanted even more?

But he hadn't even met her kids. She hadn't told him about Annabelle.

Panic began to churn. She had to tell him. Now. *Before* she talked to Patricia.

"I—"

Her words cut off at the sound of feet thundering down the hallway. The feet were joined by childish squeals. She and Brody both stared at the door, then he swung back to her.

"Your kids?"

"You have to go." They spoke at the same time.

She ran and locked the door, and he went into action. His shirt was in his hands within seconds, along with an empty condom wrapper and his shoes. She looked at the balcony. Then at her closet. Then her bathroom. She couldn't make him jump off the balcony.

"Mom?" Becca shouted from somewhere down the hallway. "We're here. We left before the sun came up 'cause we was in such a hurry to see you."

"Oh, God." She couldn't let her children catch her in her bedroom with a man.

"I'll got out the balcony," he said. "It's the way I came in." He kissed her, and then he went over the balustrade.

Cat winced when she heard him land in the shrubbery.

"Mommy!" Tyler yelled, his voice panicky. Her doorknob rattled. "Where are you?"

"I'm right here, sweetheart. Just a minute."

Another set of footsteps joined her kids' in the hall as Cat hurried to close the balcony doors, doing one last sweep of the room. She crossed the plush carpet, stopping only long enough to snatch up the other two condom wrappers and throw the cover over the rumpled sheets. The fallen picture and crashed lamp would have to wait. Then she rubbed at her eyes as if she'd just woken up, and opened the door on a yawn.

"What are you guys doing here so early?" she scratched out.

"Mom!" Both kids threw themselves at her. "We missed you."

Cat chuckled. "I missed you, too."

And Brody wanted her to move there.

She stooped to take her kids in her arms.

"We couldn't wait another minute to see you," Becca exclaimed in her typical dramatic fashion. "And then we got here and we couldn't find you."

"My babies." Cat hugged them even tighter. Her chest ached at the fear of telling Brody about their daughter, while at the same time it flourished in her other children's love. She'd needed them this week.

Vega reached the kids while Cat was still holding them close. She stood slightly behind them, looking an unhealthy shade of gorgeous for such an ungodly hour of the morning.

Vega had been a model in a past life. She was five ten, had long curly hair and dark eyes to match. No matter how good Cat might look, standing next to Vega always made it clear that they weren't even on the same playing field.

But beauty aside, Vega was the best sister-in-law a woman could want.

She was also astute.

Her knowing gaze skipped past Cat to take in the room. She paused on the far wall where Cat knew the lamp was lying on the floor, before finishing her sweep. She ended by taking in Cat's tightly clenched fist.

A teasing smile lifted Vega's cheeks.

"I'm sorry." Cat grimaced. She was embarrassed at being caught. Becca took the words as meant for her.

"It's okay, Mommy. We found you now." Becca pulled out of the embrace and patted her mom's cheek with pure sweetness. Tyler merely slung an arm around Cat's neck and held on.

"We missed you lots," Tyler announced. "I don't wanna miss you that much again."

Cat laughed and pulled her kids to her once more. "I don't either," she declared. "Never, never, never."

The kids giggled, and Vega reached to take their hands. "Come on, kids. How about we wait downstairs while your mother gets cleaned up? I heard something about breakfast being cooked."

Cat shot her sister-in-law a look of thanks, but both kids immediately squeezed in tighter to their mother. At their pouty little faces, Cat couldn't make them leave. "I've got them," she said. "They can watch TV in my bed while I take a shower."

"You're sure?" Vega glanced once more into the room as if worried there might be a man hiding under the bed.

"Positive." Cat motioned with her head to the balcony doors.

Vega lifted a brow. "Impressive," she murmured. Then she shot Cat a wink and headed back down the hall. Her five-inch heels made her look like a goddess and forced Cat to glance down at herself.

She was rumpled, no doubt wore the air of someone who'd spent the night doing what she'd been doing, and her gown was too sexy to be worn in front of her kids.

She grabbed a robe and stood to the side as her children entered the room. They both chattered nonstop as if it had been three weeks since she'd *spoken* to them, instead of seen them.

In a brief second of silence, they heard her phone chirp out a notification.

"Your phone is ringing, Mommy." Tyler was so helpful.

"I know, sweetie." She kissed the top of his head, nuzzling her nose in his soft hair. "It's a text message."

Both kids climbed on her bed as she snatched up the phone.

Becca sat, feet tucked under her legs, and watched her mom expectantly. "Is it your boyfriend?"

Cat gaped, and while she stood there, unable to come up with a word to say, Becca smiled sweetly. "We saw his picture at the airport. It was on the TV. He looks pretty."

"Yuck," Tyler muttered. He'd found the remote and had the TV on. "I don't like boyfriends."

Cat glanced at the TV. "Watch cartoons," she told them. "That's all."

She grabbed fresh blankets and pillows from the closet to tuck around the kids as Becca explained to her brother that only girls got to have boyfriends. Boys had to have girlfriends.

Tyler ignored his sister and continued searching for the right cartoon.

Cat looked at her phone.

See you at the park later?

Her heart rate sped up. Brody would meet her kids today. He wanted them to move there.

Yes. And tonight . . . the beach house? We need to talk.

She wondered if he'd still feel the same after they talked.

`I'll be there.`

Cat put her phone away after Brody's confirmation and decided her shower could wait. She and her children had things to talk about. Like boyfriends.

Climbing into the bed with them, she scooted up to the headboard and finagled a kid to either side of her.

"Mom," Tyler whined. "I'm watching the turtles." Looked like his stint of missing his mother was over. It was now all about cartoons. Cat grabbed the remote and turned off the TV. Tyler groaned.

"I want to talk about something for a minute," she started.

Becca watched her earnestly, while Tyler frowned at the remote.

"That man you saw on the TV at the airport this morning. He's a friend of mine."

"The news said he was your boyfriend," Tyler informed her matter-of-factly. Becca nodded in agreement.

"Well, he is a boy. And he's my friend."

"And you kissed him," Becca said.

Cat caught a hint of worry in her daughter's eyes. "You saw a picture of me kissing him?"

Both kids nodded.

"And did that bother you?"

"I don't know anything about kisses," Tyler said. "Did it bother you?"

Cat chuckled. "No," she said. "It didn't bother me."

"Boyfriends kiss their girlfriends," Becca explained to her brother as if she fully understood the workings of the adult relationship.

"Yes, they do," Cat agreed. "And yes, Brody is my boyfriend. But he's also my friend. A good friend. I'd like you both to meet him. Would you be okay with that?"

Becca's blue eyes stared back at her. Tyler tilted his head in thought.

He was the first to speak. "Will he play ball with me?"

"I'll bet he would." Cat kissed him on the nose. "We'll ask him today."

Tyler nodded. His gaze once again sought out the remote. "Then I can meet him."

"Thank you, Tyler." Cat winked at her daughter. "How about you, kiddo? You want to meet my friend?"

"Will he like me?"

"Absolutely."

"Is he going to be our new daddy?"

Cat's breath caught. Her daughter had been four when Joe had died, and Cat suspected her memories had faded. "No, baby. You'll always have your daddy. He loved you. Just like we loved him."

"But he's not here anymore."

"That's right. And unfortunately he won't ever be here again."

Tyler was watching them now. He scooted in closer and wrapped a small arm around Cat's waist. "I don't remember my daddy," he said.

"I know, baby. You were too young."

"But *could* he be our daddy?" Becca asked timidly. "I don't know if I remember our first daddy either, and all my friends have daddies."

A lump stuck in Cat's throat. It was a good question. One she'd asked herself. And the honest answer was, she wouldn't be introducing Brody to her kids if she didn't think he could be their daddy. But she wasn't sure what to tell them.

She and Brody still had things to discuss. And there was no guarantee he would forgive her.

But if he did forgive her, if they did get past this, then Cat would have hope that he could be their daddy. He hadn't said long term that morning, but surely that's what he'd meant. Uprooting herself and her kids was a big deal. He would understand that. "I'm not sure," she finally answered Becca. "But I think our hearts are big enough that we can fit all kinds of friends inside them. Don't you?"

There was silence before Becca asked, "How big is my heart?"

Cat chuckled. She pulled her daughter to her and kissed the top of her head. "It's as big as the world, baby. As big as you want it to be."

More silence, and Cat could visualize her serious little girl weighing the pros and cons of her decision. Finally, the grip on Cat's heart released when Becca announced, "I think I'd like to meet your friend. And I think he'll like me. Because I'm going to show him my new shoes."

CHAPTER TWENTY-FIVE

*L*ATER THAT MORNING, CAT WAS STILL THINKING ABOUT Brody's suggestion as she stood with her brother and sister-in-law, greeting volunteers filing into the park. Today was the biggest day for the project so far. Sharon had lined up the majority of the townspeople to help assemble the main section of the playground. It would take a full week of hard work, but before the amphitheater opened, the playground would be ready for use.

Emma Davenport was also there, right in the middle of all of it. She'd flown up with JP, and while it had been a shock for Cat to find her mother at the house that morning, the two had so far managed to be civil. Mostly due to not speaking to each other.

But they were good at pretending, if nothing else. It was a family trademark.

Cat had gathered up her family, ushering everyone to the park, while her mother had taken care of last-minute phone calls to ensure that her helping out with the family-donated park would hit papers countrywide. She wanted everyone to know that she didn't forget where she came from—or, more precisely, where the Davenports had come from. She would prove it by pounding in the first nail at the playground.

However, the multihundred-dollar designer suit she wore implied that pounding one nail was about all she planned to do.

Cat winked at her brother as they both watched Becca entertain the crowd around them. She'd been going at it for several minutes, sharing stories, talking about any- and everything in her little-girl charming way, and Cat couldn't help but laugh. If anyone in her family should be an actor, it was her mini-me.

Becca's blonde hair and Davenport blue eyes would get her far. Added to that, she had her daddy's long legs instead of being short like her mama.

Another little girl came up, the cute little dark-eyed girl that Cat remembered from the museum, and joined in with Becca's antics. Tyler ignored them both and continued playing with the ball he'd brought with him. He had every intention of asking Brody to play ball with him. It was apparently the male test of friendship.

Cat scanned the assembled crowd, looking for the man who occupied the largest part of her mind. He'd occupied even more since he'd told her the story about his father. It was eerily reminiscent of how her parents had treated Lexi Dougard and her son—both with the payoff and acting as if he didn't exist. It made her think of Daniel, the innocent child mixed up in her family's scandals, and she wondered what lasting impact this would have on him. No doubt there would be one.

She only hoped he turned out as okay as Brody.

She also hoped she would someday get to meet him. But she would respect his mother's wishes for privacy. After all, *not* being a part of the Davenports might be the best thing for him.

She finally found Brody in the crowd, standing with his mother and Stone on one side of him and Thomas Harrison on the other. Most likely, the fact that Thomas was in town was what had brought Cat's mother up.

This was Davenport country, yet the man was taking advantage of the opportunity to win national support for himself. Emma Davenport couldn't allow that. Thomas had been photographed all over town, making it clear he was a good guy, and that he was *thrilled* to learn he had a big brother. He wanted to build a solid relationship with Brody. No matter what it took. He was even thinking of buying a vacation home in the area.

Such total bull.

Brody was right. All the games and faces were too much. People simply needed to live their lives and not try to be all things to all people. Everyone would be much happier that way.

Brody turned his head then, and his gaze landed on Cat's. He gave her a heated smile, and her heart sang a fluttery little song. She loved that man.

It was all going to be all right.

Vega snickered under her breath.

"Shut up," Cat muttered. Vega had no doubt witnessed Cat and Brody making eyes at each other. Her sister-in-law had asked about him several times throughout the morning, making it clear she was anxious to meet the man who'd so romantically left via the balcony when the kids had shown up.

"Where is he?" JP asked quietly. Of course, Vega had also told JP about Cat's indiscretions.

"Leave it alone," Cat whispered.

"I want to meet this guy," her brother said. "Make sure he's good enough for my sister."

"You want to embarrass me, and we both know it."

JP's chiseled face softened to a grin. "I don't get a lot of opportunities for that, Shortie. A guy has to take them when he can."

"There are far too many cameras out here today to take that particular opportunity, so behave yourself."

Sharon stepped to the microphone at the front of the crowd, thanking everyone for coming out. She began introducing the crew who'd been hired to oversee the project and explaining how each person would take smaller groups of people to work on different sections of the playground. She was hopeful everyone would be able to come back several times throughout the next week. It was *their* park, and she wanted them to be a part of it.

Food and drink stations would be going all week, and though it would be a lot of hard work, she was confident a good time would be had by all. She also pointed out the manned kid zone, where kids would be participating in the building of the park themselves. They would be crafting flower boxes and painting artwork that would grace the area.

Sharon had thought of it all.

In the end, this would be a place the community could be proud of. A place they'd all created.

The land might have been donated for the wrong reasons, but Cat was suddenly grateful it had happened. This was the type of stuff she enjoyed being a part of. Working to truly build something in people's lives. Not merely covering her family's butts or smiling for the media.

Their mother stepped to the section Sharon had marked off, ready for her photo opportunity as she attached the first two boards of the playground together, and Cat felt her body wind tight.

"What's going on with you two?" JP asked from the corner of his mouth. "You haven't spoken to her since we got here."

"She shouldn't have come, and she knows it."

"Is this about Hollister? Her leaking the story?"

She nodded. She and JP had talked about it over the phone. She'd filled her brother in on this being their mother's antics, but she hadn't told him about the past. Or that Cat had delivered another daughter. That was something Brody got to hear first. Then she'd share it with JP.

"I'm not saying that's not bad," he said. "It is. But your anger, it feels like more."

"Her leaking the story is only the tip of the iceberg." Cat smiled at a camera when a reporter shouted out her name, then returned to whispering to her brother. "She's been manipulating things for years. I've had enough."

JP eyed her. "More than I already know about?"

"Yes."

"Tell me."

"I will. But not yet." She looked at Brody again. He was making his way over to her.

"I'm worried about you," JP said. "You seem different."

She looked up at him then, surprised that he'd noticed. "Good different or bad different?"

He studied her before answering. "Harder," he finally said. "I'm not sure if that's good or bad."

"It's *good*," she assured him. "And I'll be fine. I needed to be different."

He nodded subtly toward Brody. "So this is real? Not just teenage memories?"

She watched the man she loved. He was currently watching her kids. She was about to introduce the three of them, and she hoped with everything she had that it would end the way she wanted.

"It's real."

"Good for you." Her brother pulled her to his side, the top of her head barely skimming his chin as he hugged her tight. He whispered in her ear, "Sorry I brought Mom. I didn't realize how bad it was."

"Don't worry about it. She would have come herself. Thomas Harrison is getting her attention, and she couldn't have that."

They both turned their sights on their mother, who was now taking selfies with several people from the crowd. Humorously, Thomas Harrison was doing the same.

"I never thought she'd sink as low as them," JP admitted.

But Cat knew better. Their mother had sunk lower.

———   ———

With more nerves than Brody knew was possible, he approached Cat where she stood with her family. Her sister-in-law gave him a once-over, nodding when she finished as if providing her approval. Cat jabbed her in the side.

"Good morning, Cat," he said. He sounded stiff. "Good to see you today." Cat's sister-in-law guffawed.

Cat punched her again.

"Morning, Brody." Cat smiled up at him. "Don't look so grim. There are lots of cameras watching us right now."

He was aware of those cameras. They'd been following him all week. He also suspected the people behind them must feel as if they'd won the lottery today. Davenports, a Harrison, and a Romeo and Juliet affair, all in the same place at the same time.

Not to mention, he was about to meet Cat's kids.

And to think, he'd once sworn he wouldn't be put in the spotlight. For anyone. But Cat was different. If the spotlight was what it took to be with her, then sign him up.

Cat introduced him to her brother and sister-in-law, and the three of them made small talk for a few minutes. While that was going on, Brody noticed that Emma Davenport kept a steely look turned their way. She wasn't pleased at all to see her family cavorting with the enemy.

Too damned bad. He wasn't pleased with her for anything.

"Are you my mommy's friend?" a perky, feminine voice asked from his left side. Brody looked down. He'd seen pictures, yet was taken aback at just how much Cat's daughter looked like her.

"I am. And I'm guessing that your name is Becca?"

The child smiled sweetly, but he was no fool. This kid already knew how to work the system, and he could feel himself falling immediately under her spell. "I'm the oldest," she announced. Then she stuck one tiny foot out for him to see. Sparkly silver-and-purple shoes winked back at him. "Do you like my new shoes?"

Vega and Cat both laughed, but Brody kept his expression serious. He admired the shoes carefully before giving the girl a heartfelt nod.

"I do. They're quite lovely."

"My Aunt Vega bought them for me. She loves shoes and I do, too."

Brody couldn't keep the smile at bay. The child was precious. But there was another one to meet, too. He turned to his other side, having sensed that Tyler had joined them as well.

He'd been right. The younger boy stood there, a baseball glove tucked under one arm and a ball in his hand. He was looking Brody up and down as if he were the man of the house, and if he said no, then it would be no.

Brody hoped he didn't say no.

Finally, Tyler made his determination. "I don't like boyfriends," he said.

Becca reached around Brody and jabbed Tyler on the arm. "Mom said not to say boyfriend," she whispered. "He's just her friend."

And he clearly had his work cut out with this one. He stooped to Tyler's level. "How about girlfriends?" he asked. "Do you like them?"

The kid's face lit up. "My friend Ben has a girlfriend. She's pretty."

"Yeah? I'll bet she is. Girlfriends are like that." He glanced up at Cat before returning his full attention to her son. "I happen to think your mom is pretty, too."

The child tilted his head back to look up at his mom. She was standing there, quiet, looking as nervous as Brody felt. Finally Tyler agreed. "She is pretty. Do you want to play ball with me?"

Brody laughed. "I would *love* to play ball with you. But first, how about I help you learn how to make something?" He motioned to the cordoned-off kids' area. "Can we do that?"

"You're working in the kid zone?" Cat asked.

"For a bit. They needed volunteers there." And he'd figured that would give him plenty of time to get to know her kids. He could tell, though, that the extra time wouldn't be a requirement.

They'd already crawled into his heart. They were a part of Cat. How could he not love that?

"You're a good guy, Brody Hollister," Cat said softly.

He gave her a wink as he rose. "And you're a good woman. I look forward to talking to you later."

He hadn't said everything he should have that morning. He wanted Cat and the kids to move there, yes. But he needed her to understand that it was more than just wanting more time with her.

He loved her.

He wanted forever with her.

It was scary as hell to think of telling her that, of opening himself up to the potential hurt, but he would not risk losing her due to fear. If she walked, it would already hurt.

"Me too," she whispered, and he caught a hint of pink on her cheeks. Probably because her brother and sister-in-law were watching the two of them with rapt attention.

He nodded a good-bye to the adults, then looked down at her kids. "Come on, workers. We have flower boxes to make. I understand flower boxes are very important for this park."

———————————   ———————————

"I liked your boyfriend," Tyler declared during dinner that night.

They were sitting around the dining room table at the Davenport home—her mother included; apparently she planned to stay until the park was finished—when Tyler blurted out his proclamation.

Becca shoved potatoes in her mouth and nodded with enthusiasm. "I showed him how good I dance in my new shoes and he liked it. So I like him, too."

"Catherine." Her mother said the name as if implying that Cat needed to control her children. Cat ignored her.

"I'm so glad to hear that," she said. She winked at Tyler. "Because he has this awesome house on the beach, and I thought we might visit him there this week." In fact, she was thinking of moving back to her beach house. Her mother wouldn't be there.

"Yes!" both kids shouted.

Emma scowled. "You're being ridiculous."

What she was being was an adult. One who didn't let her mother control her actions. She wanted her kids to have the chance to get to know Brody better. They'd be lucky if they could have him in their lives, and she intended to see if that could happen.

She'd watched him as he'd worked with them that morning, more than once witnessing a look on his face that brought her to a standstill. It was similar to one he might give her. And it filled Cat with hope. For her, for him. And for her kids.

Maybe for more kids.

When she, Becca, and Tyler began talking about building sand castles on Brody's beach, her mother literally turned up her nose. "All that will accomplish is getting the paparazzi even more stirred up. Is that what you want?"

Cat snorted. "Seriously? The paparazzi is your concern? Didn't you start this, Mother?"

"Okay." Vega stood from her seat. "How about you two munchkins help me out with dessert?"

Becca glanced between her mother and grandmother, her expression one of concern as she picked up on the tension between the two women. Grudgingly, she slid from her chair. She was a sharp kid. She could sense a storm brewing when there was one. Cat appreciated Vega's fast thinking.

"Thanks," Cat whispered to Vega.

Vega patted Cat's hand, then disappeared into the kitchen with the kids.

"Don't you dare lay into me over this." Cat rose from her own chair. Only, she didn't intend to go anywhere. She leaned over the table, her fists pressed into the linen. She was ready to have this out.

"Maybe you two should take it to another room," JP suggested. "Vega can only keep the kids in the kitchen for so long."

Neither Cat nor her mother acknowledged him.

"Mommy." Tyler came running back into the room. He had her cell phone in his hand, his arm held high. Vega rushed in after him. "Your phone is ringing again."

"Thanks, buddy." Cat calmed herself long enough to speak to her son. She took the phone, not intending to answer it, but when she glanced down, she was shocked to see the area code showing on the screen.

It was from San Francisco.

"I've got to take this."

She answered the call as she walked out of the room, hearing her mother huff out in exasperation at the same time. Her mother hated it when people answered the phone while at the dinner table.

"Cat?" a woman's voice said on the phone. "Catherine Carlton?"

It was an articulate, intelligent voice. One Cat hadn't heard in eighteen years. And it made the breath leave her body.

"Yes," Cat whispered.

"This is Patricia. I got your message." When Cat didn't say anything, Patricia added, "You said it was urgent. Are you okay? What's going on?"

Cat stepped out the front door, not caring who took her picture while she was out there, or if they happened to catch her crying while they did it. Because she suspected she was about to cry. And she wasn't going to do it in front of her mother.

"Thank you for calling me back." The words barely made it out, so she cleared her throat. "It's good to hear from you, Patricia. I hope you've been well."

She could almost hear the confusion coming through the phone. "What's the matter, Cat? I haven't heard from you in eighteen years."

"You weren't supposed to."

"I know." The words were spoken gently. As if Patricia suspected that Cat was on the verge of a breakdown and wanted to keep her calm. "But I always thought I might."

"I'm sorry I didn't call," Cat said, her voice cracking again. "When Annabelle died." She squeezed her eyes closed tight. She hadn't meant to be so blunt, but she couldn't take it back. "I didn't want to hurt you, and I don't want to now. So I'm sorry I'm calling. But I need some answers about my daughter."

Patricia had gone completely silent. Cat didn't even hear breathing.

"Patricia?"

"What are you talking about, Cat?"

"Mom told me. She said Annabelle was sick. She said you'd broken down over it."

"Sweetheart, Annabelle has been the least sick child I've ever known. And I haven't spoken with your mother in years."

"Then what happened? Why did she die?"

Again, there was silence.

A flash went off somewhere through the trees in the front yard, and Cat turned her back to the road.

"Cat," Patricia began, "Annabelle just graduated high school. The two of us are in London at the moment. This trip is her graduation present."

Cat shook her head. "No. Mom told me . . ."

She stopped speaking as a pain stabbed her in the heart and slowly began to burn downward. It felt like she was being ripped in two.

Her mother had not been unclear eighteen years ago. She'd explained that the baby had been born sick, that they'd chosen to keep that information from Cat so the pain of giving her up wouldn't be even worse, but that Annabelle had *not* made it. She'd passed away, and Patricia had been overwhelmed with grief.

Her mother had told her that.

To her face!

And Cat had believed it.

Her eyelids dipped, and she stumbled backward. She flailed out, finally catching hold of the post as the backs of her knees bumped into the concrete railing and she sat with a heavy thump. Tears streamed down her cheeks.

"No," she whispered.

More tears continued to roll.

Giving up her daughter had been bad enough, but thinking she was dead . . .

Being told that was unforgivable.

"Cat?" Patricia said softly. "I'm sorry, sweetheart. I didn't know that's what you thought."

Cat nodded. Patricia was a good person. She wouldn't be a part of this.

"Are you okay?"

Cat shook her head and swiped the back of her hand across her face. The tears wouldn't stop.

"Are you still in Maine?" Patricia asked.

"Yes."

"We're coming through New York in a couple days. Would you like to meet your daughter?"

"What?"

"Annabelle. She knows who you are. I wouldn't tell her when she was younger, but she's eighteen now."

"You told her I'm her mother?"

"Her biological mother, yes. Two months ago. She's been following things with your family these last few weeks."

"Well, that has to make a good impression."

Easy laughter reached through the phone. "She has been a bit shocked."

"Does she think I didn't want her?" Cat blurted out. Her daughter was alive. That was something she'd never expected to hear.

"She understands you were sixteen. She knows your choices were limited, Cat. I know your mother. I know your family. You made the brave decision not to bring her up in that environment when you were still trying to figure yourself out, too. I explained that to her."

Cat let out a single, sad chuckle. "I feel like I'm *still* trying to figure myself out."

"Don't we all, sweetheart? But you made a phone call to me. That's pretty big. Does that play into you figuring yourself out?"

She nodded and wiped at her face again. The tears were starting to slow. "It does." Her voice remained shaky. "I'm in love with Annabelle's father, and I never told him before. I'd planned to tell him about her tonight. Whatever I could find out. I was hoping to show him a picture."

"I see." Patricia's tone was controlled, reminding Cat of a doctor speaking with a potentially unstable patient. Which made her laugh a little. Patricia was a doctor.

And Cat *was* potentially unstable.

"Does that mean her father is the man we've been seeing in the news with you now?" Patricia prodded.

"He is. And he's a really good guy."

"I've no doubt. But he never knew about Annabelle?"

"Wait." Cat suddenly stood up. "You're calling her Annabelle. Is that because that's what I always called her? Or did you keep the name?"

"I kept it. Her name is Annabelle Meredith Weathers. I changed the middle name to be my mother's."

More tears fell.

"I didn't know why it was important to you," Patricia explained, "but you started calling our little girl Annabelle the moment you knew she was a girl. I'm guessing, now that I know Brody Hollister is her father, and that his mother's name is Annabelle, that must be the reason."

"I can't believe she's alive," Cat whispered. "I've grieved for her for so long."

"And I truly am sorry about that. If I'd known . . ."

"I know."

They each listened to the other breathe for a moment, both in their own thoughts, before Patricia said, "She *would* like to meet you, Cat. I had to force her not to barge into your life two months ago when I first told her."

"Is she happy?" Cat asked. "Has she had a good life?"

"She is happy. And I like to think I've given her a good life. Do you want to meet her? We're heading back from our vacation on Friday. We could catch a flight to Maine."

"You would do that for me?"

"I would do that for Annabelle."

Cat paced the length of the porch as she took in the large grounds and the road off in the distance, and tried to get her mind to slow enough to think. She could meet her daughter. This week. Could she bring Annabelle here? The paparazzi had slowed, but they weren't gone. They would have a field day if they found this out. "It's a bit of a madhouse here," she explained.

She didn't care about the scandal it would cause, but about how it might impact her daughter.

"Then how about we meet in Portland?"

"Brody will want to meet her, too."

"And I'm sure she'd love that."

"She has a brother and sister," Cat whispered.

"Let's take it one day at a time, okay? Right now we're thinking about Annabelle. She's always wanted to meet her parents, so that's what we'll do first. She and I will fly in Friday night, and meet with you on Saturday. Does that sound okay?"

"It sounds perfect."

"Good. Can you find a place that will be private?"

"I can."

"Okay. I'll text you later and we'll settle on a time."

Cat nodded once again. She was going to meet her daughter. In three days. "Patricia?" she said quickly, before the woman could hang up.

"Yes?"

"Thank you," Cat said sincerely. "Thank you for doing this now, and thank you for taking Annabelle back then. For giving her a good life. I never told you that before, but I could tell you would love her as much as I did. I wanted that for her."

"I do. She's my world. And I actually thank *you* every day. Now you go tell her father about her. I worry that might be a tough pill for him to swallow."

"I suspect it will be. I've made a lot of mistakes."

"But you're not making one now. This is good. We'll make it work."

Cat wiped away more tears. "I hope so."

"Do you want me to text you a picture of her?"

Cat's heart thudded. "You would do that?"

"She's a gorgeous young lady. Yes, I would love to do that. I'll send one over right now."

CHAPTER TWENTY-SIX

CAT STOOD ON THE PORCH FOR ANOTHER TEN MINUTES, doing nothing but staring at the picture Patricia had sent her. She was right. Annabelle was gorgeous. She had blonde hair like Cat, but her eyes were Brody's. In fact, Cat could see a lot of Brody in her. She'd always hoped that he'd passed along his features to her.

She was suddenly anxious to share the picture with him. She wanted him to see his daughter. But before she did that, she had to face her mother.

After scrubbing her hands over her cheeks, she pulled in a deep breath, blew it back out, and pushed the front door of the house open. Everyone was still in the dining room, though desserts had been eaten. All five of them looked up when Cat entered the room.

"You want dessert, Mommy?" Becca asked. "We saved you some cake."

Cat shook her head.

"What's wrong?" Her brother stood, reaching out a hand for her, and making her wonder how unsteady she looked.

"That was Patricia Weathers," she said. She looked straight at her mother as she spoke.

It took a second, but her mother blanched. "Catherine—"

"You lied to me, Mother. You told me she was dead."

"It was only to help you."

"Who's dead?" JP asked.

"Why, Mother?"

"I told you—"

"Vega," JP interrupted. "How about you take the kids out to play in the courtyard?"

Vega hurried to her feet, and with faces still covered in chocolate cake, Cat's kids followed her out of the room. At the sound of the back door closing, JP stepped to the end of the twelve-person table so that he stood equal distance between the two women. As if placing himself in position as referee. Cat wrapped her hands around the top rung of her chair and zeroed in on her mother.

"Let's start at the beginning," JP said. "What's going on? And who is Patricia Weathers?"

Cat calmly turned her head in her brother's direction. "Brody and I had a daughter when I was sixteen."

"What?" he gasped.

"I can explain," their mother started, but Cat didn't let her finish.

"I never told him about the pregnancy. Patricia Weathers is a college friend of our mother's. She adopted my daughter. And then Mom told me that my daughter had died."

JP went hot with anger. Cat saw his temper rise as his fists clenched and his face flushed. He may be her younger brother, but as always, his protective streak was a mile wide when it came to her.

"What the hell, Mother?" JP raged.

"If you'll just let me explain."

"I'm meeting Brody to tell him tonight," Cat said. "All of it."

"You can't." Her mother was on her feet. "Think of the scandal it will cause."

299

"Fuck the scandal it will cause." Her dinner was two seconds from coming back up. She couldn't believe this was her family. "And by the way," she continued, her body beginning to shake with her anger, "I'm done. With all of it."

"You're being overly dramatic, Catherine. You know I did it for you. You weren't coming out of your depression. I couldn't let you stay like that. It wasn't healthy." Her mother's eyes pleaded with Cat before jumping over to JP as if he might help. Mixed in with the pleading was a fair bit of desperation.

Good. Cat wanted her desperate. She wanted her doubled over in pain.

"I thought it best for you," Emma repeated, though the argument came out weak.

Cat shook her head. She didn't believe anything her mother said. She never would again. "You thought it best for *you*," she sneered. "You couldn't have an unstable kid running around. That might not look right for a Davenport."

"I was worried about you."

The real truth suddenly dawned on Cat and she stood up straighter. "You were afraid I would go after her."

Guilt was evident across Emma's face. "No."

"I might change my mind and go after my daughter. Then, what? We couldn't have an illegitimate Davenport out there, could we?" Cat accused. And then she laughed. She laughed so loud that she worried for a brief second that she'd snapped. But if she had snapped, she didn't think she'd still hurt as bad as she did. "Isn't that just perfect?" She gave her mother an eerie smile as she shook her head in disgust. "Exactly what you worked so hard to hide with me, our father turned around and did to you."

Cat glanced at her brother, who remained at the end of the table. She could see sympathy on his face. He hurt for her.

She hurt for herself.

Her whole life had been spent trying to make it up to her mother that she'd gotten pregnant as a teen. Only to find out that her mother had screwed her over all this time.

"You went too far," she said. "You don't get to be exempt from this one. I'm finished. I'll stay on for the job at the park, but after that I'm done. With my job. And with the family."

"You can't be done with the family," Emma exclaimed. "It's who you are."

"It is not who I am. And it never should have been."

"You need to leave the house, Mother," JP informed her.

"I have as much right to be here as you do, Jackson. And you shouldn't talk to me that way."

"Okay," Cat said. She pushed her chair under the table and stepped away. "Then I'll leave. I have a perfectly good rental I should be using anyway." She turned to go.

"I'm sorry, Catherine," her mother said behind her.

Cat stopped. She didn't look back, but she couldn't keep from stopping. Her mother owed her an apology, and she wanted to hear it. A real one.

"I'm sorry that you and he . . ."

Cat turned around, her face a hard mask. "Are you sorry that you hurt us?" she bit out. "That you threatened his mother if he so much as spoke to me again?"

"I did not threaten."

"No? I'll ask him. I'm guessing you did."

Cat knew she was lashing out, but she had a right to. She was wounded to her soul. "Or are you sorry that you made me give my baby away?"

"I was simply trying to do what was right."

"And what would have been so wrong with letting us deal with our own lives? We may have been kids, but you had no right. Especially after you knew I was pregnant."

"He was a Harrison."

"I'm so tired of hearing that. What's really so bad about the Harrisons? They're just people."

"There's always been a feud."

Cat shook her head. Her mother disgusted her. "That's not a good enough reason any longer."

Without another word or look back, Cat walked out of the room. Behind her, she heard JP inform their mother that she had ten minutes to get her things and be ready to leave. He'd see her to the airport. It was clear that he didn't intend to take no for an answer.

CHAPTER TWENTY-SEVEN

CAT STEPPED INSIDE THE BACK DOOR OF HER BEACH HOUSE that night, thirty minutes after the play was scheduled to end. Brody would have attended, and should be arriving at the house soon.

And then she would destroy him.

She paced to the other side of the room, her hands twisting in front of her. She'd woken beside Brody that morning, him asking her to move to Maine to be with him, and she got to wrap up the day by telling him he had a daughter. Her stomach cramped at the thought.

She turned back to the door. She needed fresh air.

Only, Brody was there.

He stepped inside, and without a word, took several long strides to her side and kissed her. The kiss was long and hard. His touch was heaven.

"I missed you." He punctuated the words with another hard press of his mouth.

When he lifted his head, Cat stared up at him, her breath in her throat. This was going to hurt him so badly.

"What a night, Kitty Cat." Brody took her hands in his, squeezing them as excitement shone from his eyes. "I know we have things to talk about." He tugged her forward and kissed her again. "Plenty of things," he stressed. "Things I should have said this morning. But first"—he paused and leaned back to look down at her—"first, I have to tell you about tonight."

"Okay." She nodded. His exuberance spread to her, momentarily easing her worries. "What happened?"

He bit his lip as if to hold back his smile, but it didn't work. "Searcy showed up."

She sucked in a breath. "The producer? What happened? How'd you get him there?"

"You." Brody smirked. "He came to see you."

"So I got to help without you actually letting me help?"

"Looks like. But I still didn't want your name getting me a look."

"I guess you told him to leave, then?" She smiled.

"No, smart-ass. I didn't tell him to leave. Instead, I found him the best seat in the house, got the man a glass of wine, then went to the back and begged everyone to give the performance of their lifetimes."

"And what happened?" Cat lost her breath at his near hysteria.

"What happened is they gave the performances of their lives. I love them. They were terrific. Searcy loved them. He loved the play. There was love all around." His giddiness made her laugh. "No promises, though." He held a finger up as if to tamp down her hope. "But he did say he'd get back to me next week."

"Oh, Brody." Cat threw herself into his arms. "I'm so happy for you. Congratulations."

"Thank you." He smacked her with another hard kiss. "But it's not sold yet. And thank your name for getting him here in the first place."

"My pleasure." She wrapped her arms around him, feeling the buzz vibrate from him. So much that she seriously considered holding off on her news for another time. She couldn't bring him down. Not after this.

"What a day," he said. He hadn't stopped smiling. "I woke up with you, I got to meet your kids—two really terrific people, by the way—and then it wrapped up with Searcy in the audience." He took her by the hand and swung her out as if dancing. "And now"—he waggled his eyebrows—"I have you again."

No way would she tell him right now.

He twirled her back into him. "And the first thing I want to do is tell you that I love you."

She quit breathing.

"I should have said it this morning." He rushed the words out. "Instead of just asking you to move here. But surely you know that already. It has to be written all over me every time I look at you."

Oh, hell. He loved her. She had to tell him now.

Even if it did ruin a perfectly good day for him.

She gulped. She hated herself in that moment.

"What?" Brody asked, clearly picking up on her stress. He kept her within the circle of his arms, but she could feel his own tension take hold.

"I love you, too," she whispered.

Happiness registered immediately on his face, but disappeared just as quickly. "Then what's wrong?"

She swallowed again, the words sticking in her throat. "But . . ."

The shadow of worry that passed over his features made her knees weak, and she lifted her hands to caress his face. "I do love you," she repeated sincerely. "I swear. Very much."

"But?" he asked carefully, his tone a shade cooler than it had been before.

They remained standing together, his arms around her waist, her hands on his face. Only, tears now streamed over her cheeks, and she could feel a wall trying to come up between them. She fought for courage, but failed. Then she stepped out of his embrace.

"We had a daughter eighteen years ago," she quietly announced.

Brody's face went blank. "We what?"

Then *he* took a step back.

"That summer," Cat said. "I got pregnant." She moved farther into the room, putting the kitchen table between them. "I went to California until she was born. Mom had a friend there. And I gave her up for adoption," she finished in a whisper.

Confusion marred Brody's face. "No." He shook his head. "You wouldn't have done that."

When she didn't say anything else, his eyes narrowed.

"You would have told me," he insisted.

"Except my mother got in the way," she reminded him. Her heart pounded wildly. "We quit calling each other. We both thought the other had moved on."

The green of his eyes began to harden.

"She's eighteen," Cat told him. Her voice broke, but she kept going, fearing if she didn't, she wouldn't get it all out. "Her birthday was April seventeenth. I found out I was pregnant a few weeks after I went home, after we'd already stopped talking."

The clench of his fists made her pause, but only for a second.

She gulped. "We conceived the last day I was here. Out on the beach."

Brody's eyes were now ice. "You think I wouldn't be aware of when we could have conceived a child? We made love *once*."

"I—"

"And then you gave her away?" he suddenly roared. "Without even telling me?"

"Mom thought it was best."

Shit. She cringed when he jerked back. That had been the complete wrong thing to say.

"Your *mother* thought it was best?" His tone turned menacing.

She had totally messed this up. "Let me explain," she pleaded.

Brody shook his head, his jaw working back and forth. Cat plowed on.

"I tried to tell you about the pregnancy," she squeaked out. "I called your house. Twice." They both knew that his mother had not passed along those messages.

"So you're blaming *my* mother now?" he asked. Revulsion was clear on his face.

Cat's shoulders sank. "No, it was . . . *damn*."

She couldn't say it was her mother's fault. Emma may have been the one who'd kept them apart, but Cat had made the final decision. She'd agreed to the adoption. She'd thought it was best for Annabelle.

"*I* thought it was best," she finally stammered. "Mom made the arrangements, and I went away until I delivered. But afterward, I fell into a depression. I was on meds for months."

"Funny," he said with a nasty smirk. "I saw you in the news that summer, smiling and happy with another guy. One you *eventually* married. You didn't look too depressed to me."

"I've always been able to fake it in the media," she whispered brokenly.

"Isn't that the truth? You're good at it, too. The perfect Davenport."

Ignoring his snide remarks, she continued her story. "I wasn't coming out of my depression, so a few months later Mom told me she'd found out that Annabelle had died. She said our baby had been born sick."

With the mention of her daughter's name, Brody froze.

His green eyes—the very eyes that looked so much like the picture on her cell phone—turned to hatred. "You named our daughter after my mother?" His words were hard.

Cat nodded. "I loved you. I wanted to—"

"Don't you dare say you loved me," he snapped. "If you'd loved me, you wouldn't have had our child without so much as telling me. You wouldn't have given her away!"

He had a point. Her actions had not been indicative of love.

But she had loved him. She *still* loved him.

"That's why I took that particular flower from your house and left it on the beach when I came back. It's an Annabelle hydrangea."

Brody simply stared at her. He didn't say anything for several long seconds. Seconds in which she could hear the waves leisurely lapping toward high tide on the other side of the deck. Seconds where she took in the laugh lines at the corners of Brody's eyes and pictured her daughter someday having those same marks of life.

Seconds where she watched his nostrils flare with each indrawn breath that he took.

She was losing him. She knew it. She'd gambled, and she'd lost. But telling him had been the right thing to do.

"How can she be eighteen if she died when she was a baby?"

"Mom lied," she admitted. He didn't look surprised.

"You sicken me." He ground the words out. His mouth twisted as if the sight of her caused his stomach to revolt, and he reached a hand behind him toward the door. "Your entire family sickens me. And you're just like them."

"She's coming here," Cat added before he could go. "Annabelle is. Her mother is bringing her. I'm meeting them in Portland on Saturday. I thought you might go, too."

Brody's hand went still on the door as a flash of hatred passed over his face.

"She knows who you are," Cat whispered. "She wants to meet us both."

He slowly shook his head. As if he were in a daze.

"I have her picture." She pulled out her phone. "Her adoptive mother sent it to me tonight. She has your eyes," she finished.

Brody didn't look at the picture. "You mean Arthur Harrison's eyes?" His words were flat.

"She's *your* daughter, Brody. Not a Harrison."

He still didn't look.

"Look at her," Cat demanded.

"How long have you known she's alive?"

"I found out tonight. I've been calling Patricia—her mother—all week. I wanted to tell you about her, but wanted to know what happened first. I wanted to be able to share something with you about our baby."

"The baby you thought was dead?"

"Yes. Only she's not." Cat hiccupped out a sob. "She's alive, Brody, and she's so beautiful. And all this time I thought she was dead."

"And all this time you never told me."

"I hadn't seen you in eighteen years."

"You saw me three weeks ago. I didn't hear a confession then."

"You had things you didn't confess either!" she shouted.

"You think this compares to me keeping my father's name from you? From someone who was just a *fling*?"

She cringed with his words, but she knew he was just trying to hurt her. "I was never a fling, and you know it. We both know it."

"Looks to me like you were never anything more." He glanced briefly at the phone she still held out, but didn't make a comment on the picture. "If you'd been more, I wouldn't just now be finding out that I have a daughter."

"I was only sixteen," she begged him to understand. "I thought I could trust my mother. I thought she was helping me."

"Yeah? And how did that work out for you?"

"Brody," she whispered. "Please."

He shook his head. Hatred shone in his eyes. There was no longer love. And no longer hope.

She'd done that to him. She'd destroyed him.

"You're not who I thought you were, Cat. Go back to your mother. I'm sure she can fix it for you."

The door slammed behind him as he left, and she wanted to run after him. But her feet wouldn't move. She'd ruined everything. It was over.

Her knees went weak and she collapsed to floor.

CHAPTER TWENTY-EIGHT

*A*ND THIS IS THE DAY WE VISITED THE CHARLES CATHE-
dral. Have you ever been there?" Annabelle glanced up,
catching Cat staring at her instead of looking at the photo, and
Cat blushed with embarrassment.

"I'm sorry," she apologized. "I'm still shocked to be here. I
can't take my eyes off you."

Her daughter nodded and put down the tablet she'd been using
to show Cat pictures of her and Patricia's trip. "I get it," Annabelle
said. "I'm shocked, too. I mean, I knew who you were. That you
were my biological mom. Mom told me that, and I've wanted to
meet you since. I knew what you looked like and that I was going
to be here with you today. But . . ." She let the words trail off as
she glanced over at her mother sitting by her side. Patricia put her
hand over Annabelle's, providing a support that Cat suspected she
never would. "I don't know." Annabelle shrugged slightly, in a bit
of a careless, teenage way. "Thinking about meeting you and actually doing it are two pretty different things, I guess."

Cat nodded. Her nerves were stretched to the breaking point.
"Yeah."

She'd thought about it a lot the last three days herself. But
walking into the small restaurant's private dining room this
morning and finding the blonde-haired, green-eyed girl standing

at the window, her arms clenched over her stomach and her back a little too straight, that had been different than Cat had imagined.

There had been no long-lost hugs. No smiles of recognition. Simply stares.

Cat and Annabelle had sized each other up, noting both the similarities and the differences, before ever saying a word. And when they did speak, it had been stilted, for the most part. This was far harder than Cat had imagined.

"It's not what I'd thought," Annabelle admitted.

Cat hoped that didn't mean Annabelle wished she hadn't come. "How so?"

"Well, I know you gave birth to me. I get that. And that's a bond and all. But . . . well, I was curious about you more than anything. Mom had explained why you'd given me up already, so I don't have those types of questions so much. But I like history. You come from a long line of history, and I come from you. So, I wanted to meet you. But, I can't really say that I feel a bond."

Her daughter was direct. The words were a jab, but Cat appreciated them for their honesty. Brody would like her. If only he'd responded to any of her messages letting him know where they would be today.

"We're really just strangers at this point," Cat began, thinking fast to come up with the right thing to say. She didn't want to lose her opportunity with Annabelle before she even got started. "And that's to be expected. We've never *really* met."

She glanced at Patricia that time, thinking about the handful of seconds she had gotten before Annabelle had been taken away. "But I would like the opportunity to get to know you better. If that's something you want. No pressure, though."

Annabelle nodded, seeming to weigh the pros and cons. She sat up straight in her seat, looked Cat in the eye when they spoke, and had a poise about her that Cat didn't run into with girls that age too often.

Patricia was to her left. She'd aged over the years, of course, but other than a few wrinkles, she looked pretty much the same as she had eighteen years ago. Very put together in her tailored black suit, her hairstyle a short, dark bob with every hair smoothed into place, and a high level of accomplishment clear in both her features and posture.

Cat found it interesting that even though Annabelle was not a biological product of Patricia's, the girl had quite a few of her mannerisms and similarities. If it wasn't for looking exactly like a combination of Brody and herself, Cat would have trouble believing this wasn't Patricia's natural-born child.

There was also a protective wall surrounding the two of them. A closeness that Cat wasn't a part of. But the fact that Annabelle was here gave her hope. Maybe she could talk to her daughter once in a while. Hear about college, get invited to a wedding someday.

Maybe she would meet grandkids in the future.

"Mom told me you thought I was dead," Annabelle suddenly fired out.

Dread hit Cat's gut. She'd worried this would come up. "I did. I struggled a lot after giving you up. Suffered some depression."

She glanced around the small space and out the windows that overlooked the water, keeping an eye out for cell phones and cameras pointed her way. She had two security guards there with her, but that didn't mean a server or outside pedestrian wouldn't try to sneak a quick video. This conversation—this whole meeting—could go viral in an instant if the wrong person figured out what was going on.

Especially given the tabloid shots of the last few days.

There had been multiple photos of her crying, both on the porch of the Davenport compound and driving away from her beach house Wednesday night. There had been shots of Brody hurrying between their houses in the dark. Then another of her mother boarding a private jet. The world seemed to know that something was going on, but they weren't sure what.

Turning back to Annabelle, Cat continued, "My mother made a judgment call. To . . ."

"Lie," Annabelle supplied.

Cat nodded in acceptance. "*Lie.* She felt it would help me to move on."

"And did it?"

"Not really." But she thought back to that time and changed her words. "Maybe. It forced me to accept that you were gone. That I couldn't change my mind and run back to California to try to take you back."

Patricia's hand once again slid over Annabelle's.

"But I wish she hadn't done it," Cat said. Her heart was heavy. Life could be so complicated. "Thinking you weren't out there in the world . . ." She shook her head, unable to explain that kind of hurt. "I'm just grateful to know that you are. Even if we'd never met, finding out that you're alive, that you've flourished into a beautiful young lady, means the world to me."

Cat turned to Patricia. "And I thank you again for sharing that information. I thank you for sharing Annabelle with me, even if this is all I ever get." She looked at her daughter. "But I would love more. And I know my kids would love to meet you. We'll take whatever you're willing to give."

She'd wanted to tell Becca and Tyler about Annabelle over the last two days, but she'd held off. If this went no further than today, it would be best not to confuse them.

But she hoped it went further than today.

Annabelle sat in front of her now, taking in Cat's words, and for the first time in the forty-five minutes since they'd been there, Cat saw a small chink in the girl's armor.

"She went home, right?" Annabelle asked. "Your mother? The tabloids had a picture of her boarding a plane Thursday morning. Mom said you two talked Wednesday night. Did she go home because of me?"

"Yes," Cat stated flatly. "She went home because of you. It's a lie I won't tolerate."

Annabelle nodded. "I don't think I'd like her."

"That's completely understandable." Cat gave the girl a tight smile. "I don't like her much myself at the moment."

The stoicism that had remained on Annabelle's face suddenly disappeared, and her shoulders relaxed.

"So why isn't my father here?" she asked.

"Because *he* doesn't like *me* very much at the moment."

"Mom told me that he didn't know."

Cat shook her head. "I messed up back then. I should have told him. It's so much easier to look back and know the right thing to do, but I can't *go* back. So no, he didn't know until Wednesday night. And I can't say that he took it well."

"He doesn't want to meet me?"

"He didn't say that. His thoughts were more on me that night. We'd hoped . . ." She didn't know what to say to her daughter about Brody. She didn't know what to think about Brody. She ached for hurting him. She ached for *missing* him. "He'd thought I was showing up for a different reason that night," she said. "And instead I told him that I'd kept you from him. He was pretty upset. But I know him well, and I can't believe that he doesn't want to meet you."

"He just didn't want to meet me with you?" Annabelle guessed.

"I would suspect that's very true."

Her daughter looked at Patricia again, before turning back to Cat. "And I'm really part Harrison and part Davenport?"

She did not sound happy about that fact.

Cat smiled. "You are. You're a unique individual, that's for sure."

"I mean, that's kind of cool," Annabelle said. "Do you realize how long the political rivalry has been going between them?" Embarrassment swept over her then. "I suppose you would," she mumbled.

Cat agreed. She was well aware of the history between the families. It had started over a century ago when two best friends had run for the same political office. Since then, each family had continuously tried to beat out the other in whatever way they could.

"Anyway," Annabelle continued, "though crazy in a cool kind of way, I'd actually prefer having no ties to either. I mean, sorry, but your family . . . well, the past few weeks have been telling. Not real high quality, if you ask me. And the Harrisons? Do you know that Arthur Harrison was instrumental in—"

"Let's not get into politics today, Annabelle," Patricia said gently. She gave Cat a warm smile. "This one has studied political history her entire life. She has a list a mile long of decisions made over the years that she doesn't agree with."

"And I have good reason. I also intend to see them reversed," Annabelle argued.

"I know you do, but maybe you can wait to share some of those opinions with Cat later on. As you get to know her better."

Cat held her breath. She so wanted to get to know her daughter better. "I would love to hear about them. And I know Brody would, too. You're quite a bit like him, in fact."

"Yeah?" Annabelle chewed on her bottom lip. "I read that he's a history professor."

"He has his doctorate. He's a highly intelligent man."

Annabelle and Patricia shared a small smile.

"What?" Cat asked.

"Annabelle plans to double major. History and political science."

Cat's heart warmed. "Your paternal grandmother is a political science teacher."

"Really?" Annabelle seemed to bloom in front of her. "The woman I'm named after?"

"Yes. She's a great person, and I know she'll want to meet you. Is there any chance you could stay a little longer?" Cat glanced at Patricia. "I think we could turn Brody around, too. I'll go see him instead of just trying to call. I'll force him to listen to me, and I'll tell him all about you. He won't be able to stay away from you."

Annabelle turned pleading eyes to her mother.

"I have to be at work Monday morning," Patricia reminded her gently. "I've been away for two weeks. I can't not go back."

"Let me stay?" Annabelle asked. "For a week. I'll come home next weekend."

"Annabelle." Patricia half sighed the word. "I can't just leave you here."

"I'm an adult now, Mom. I'll be going away to school soon."

"Not if you don't decide which school you want to attend."

Annabelle rolled her eyes and looked at Cat. "I'm accepted at Brown—I'm *committed* to Brown—but I don't know. It doesn't feel right." She turned back to her mom. "But I will be in school somewhere."

"I'm worried about the press," Patricia explained. "You look a bit like Cat. People will wonder."

"This is important to me. I want to get to know them." She looked across the table and included Cat. "Both of them."

Cat's year had been made. "I'd offer for you to stay with me—we have a big house, you could have your own space—but the house is watched around the clock. There's no way we could keep you a secret."

"That's okay," Annabelle jumped in. "I can handle it."

"I don't know, Annabelle." Patricia shook her head. "I'm not sure you want to step into that. You've watched the news over the last few weeks. You've seen how crazy it can be."

"It's okay, Mom." She clasped her hands together in her lap. "Won't I eventually be there anyway? I mean, if I really want to get to know them. More than for one week."

Cat held her breath. It sounded like her daughter might be thinking she'd be in their lives long term. She could never have hoped for such.

"But you're only eighteen," Patricia said.

"And I have a brother and sister now," Annabelle added softly. "Whom I'd kind of like to meet."

"I'll provide her a personal security guard," Cat stated. "If you decide to let her stay. She would be safe."

"But . . ."

"You know you're going to say yes." Annabelle turned imploring eyes on her mother. "You know what this means to me. And it'll be okay, Mom. I promise. It won't change me at all."

A soft sigh eased from between Patricia's lips, and she shook her head as if she'd known she was fighting a losing battle. "Okay. Fine. But be careful. You can stay until next weekend."

"The new park opens on Saturday," Cat said. "Brody's play will be held there that night. Maybe she can stay through that."

Patricia studied her daughter, and Cat could see all the things she was thinking herself. This week could be a life changer. For all of them. "I'll come back and see it with you," she told Annabelle. "Maybe I can meet your father that day myself."

"I don't know why you wouldn't just go with white," Brody's mother argued.

They were both on his cleared-off deck, standing side by side, looking down at the slats. He was trying to figure out which color to paint it. "Because white is boring. It's what I've always had."

"White matches. Plus, the deck doesn't need painting. Why the sudden determination that it has to be done today?"

Because he was trying not to think about what he wasn't doing instead. Cat and his daughter were in Portland at that very minute, and he hadn't gone.

And he was trying to figure out how to tell his mother that he had a child.

That she had a granddaughter.

"It needs painting," he argued instead of spilling the truth. She made a face at him.

"This is about Cat, isn't it? What happened between you two? You've been hard to be around for days."

What happened was, he'd told Cat he loved her, and she'd dropped the bomb that they had a daughter. "We're over. That's what happened."

"Did you make her cry?"

She was talking about the photos from Wednesday night. "I did not make her cry."

"Then tell me what happened."

"It's simple. We weren't meant to be." He walked to the other side of the deck, studying it as he went, as if by seeing it from a different angle, the best color choice would suddenly be made clear. But what he was thinking about was Annabelle. When he stopped moving, he pulled his phone from his pocket.

He had a picture on there. The one Cat had sent to him Thursday morning. He hadn't acknowledged receiving it, but had it been a printed copy, it would have been worn thin by the number of times he'd pulled it out over the last few days.

"What's going on?" His mom followed him across the deck. "You know that's crap. I've never seen two people more meant to be."

He brought up his pictures and loaded the one of his daughter.

"Brody?" his mom prodded when he remained silent.

His answer was to hand over his phone. Then he stood there, arms crossed, as fear threatened to cut off his oxygen.

He hadn't told his mother about Annabelle because he knew he was wrong for not being in Portland today. He desperately wanted to see her. To meet his child. But Cat had crushed him. He'd planned to suggest forever Wednesday night. He'd fallen for her kids, he was head over heels for her, and he'd thought they were on the cusp of where they should have been nineteen years ago.

Only, she'd surprised him. And he couldn't forgive her for that.

Thus, he was here. About to paint his deck that didn't need painting. And not meeting his daughter. Who had his eyes.

"Brody," his mom whispered at his side. She touched one finger to Annabelle's face. "Who is this?"

"Her name is Annabelle," he said. The words barely made it out of his throat.

His mother closed her eyes. She stood there unspeaking, and unmoving, for several minutes, and he watched a thin stream of tears leak from beneath her eyelids. He did not want to make his mother cry. Yet one more thing to be mad at Cat about.

"The phone calls," his mother finally said. She lifted damp eyelashes. "That's why she called so many months later?"

He suspected so.

"Oh my God, Brody. I didn't give you the message."

"It is not your fault, Mother. And we don't even know for sure that's why she called."

"But why else would she?" She stared at the photo once again. "The poor child, she had to be what, seven, eight months pregnant?"

He swallowed. "From my calculations, it would have been seven."

"Where was she? How did they keep this secret?"

"She was hidden away in California. The woman who took care of her adopted the baby. Apparently she's a close friend of Emma Davenport's."

His mother didn't take her eyes off the picture. She didn't even seem to care that Cat's mother had done this. Or maybe she simply wasn't surprised.

"She looks like you," she said.

She did. Except for the blonde hair. That was all Cat.

"She never told me," he pointed out. "She and her mother did this, made this decision themselves, and I never heard a word. That wasn't right."

More tears trickled over his mother's cheeks. "She was there alone. About to give her baby away. Probably scared out of her mind."

"Mom, stop. You can't feel guilty over this. You had no idea."

"But you need to think about these things."

"Why?" All he could see that he needed to think about was the fact that Emma and Cat Davenport had conspired to keep his child from him.

"Because nothing is ever black or white, Brody." She looked up at him, and he saw years of wisdom in her eyes. "Yes, she didn't tell you. That was wrong. On many levels. But she leads a unique life. And a sixteen-year-old, no matter who he or she is, is going to make mistakes. Are you going to tell me you're pleased with everything you did at sixteen?"

He glared at her.

"I know what you could have done," she said, and he sensed from her sarcastic tone that he was not going to like what came next. "Maybe you should have showed up on Arthur's doorstep with a baby on your hip. That might have gone over better."

"Really?" he asked. "You're going to go there?"

She shook her head. "I'm sorry. That was cruel. I shouldn't be cruel to my son, I know. But I'm asking an important question here."

"I don't hear a question."

"What would you have done if she had told you?"

He'd asked himself that a hundred times today.

"Did you want to raise a child? How would that have happened? Give up college? Work all the time to support yourself and a kid, while also taking college courses?"

"I could have." His tone was belligerent. "At least I'd have had the choice."

"Sure, you could have. Cat could have, too. I'm not doubting that from either of you. And I would have helped you as much as possible. But you weren't ready for that. You went off, all hot-headed the next summer, drove four states to confront a man who didn't want to be around you, in a car that barely made it down there. And you thought it was a good idea not to tell anyone you were going."

"I survived it. I made it back. I'm here now, aren't I?"

"But what if you'd had a baby? What if you hadn't survived it? It could have easily gone another way."

"If I'd had a baby, I clearly wouldn't have run off like I did."

"Are you sure?"

"Mom. Cat should have told me about the pregnancy. I should have had options."

"Yes." His mother nodded. "I agree. That was a huge mistake. But look at this child." She held the phone up for him to see. "Would you have been able to give her everything she needed? At sixteen?"

He stared at his daughter. He'd asked himself that, too. "That's not the issue right now," he growled out.

"So what is the issue? Whether you'll forgive Cat or not?"

"I won't," he said. "I can't."

"Okay, then what next? Fly to California and try to meet your daughter? What if she doesn't want to meet you?"

His jaw clenched.

"What?" his mother asked carefully.

"Cat's meeting with her in Portland right now. She asked me to be there. Annabelle wanted to meet me, too."

"And you didn't go?" she yelled. "What's wrong with you?"

"I don't want to talk to her."

"To Annabelle?"

"To Cat."

"But isn't this meeting about Annabelle?"

He fumed.

"Brody." Her tone implied she wasn't impressed. "You're smarter than this."

"You're not being helpful."

"Because you know I'm right."

"Yeah." He threw his hands in the air. "I know you're right. I should be there. What if this is it? She might be gone and I've lost my chance."

"Then you'll make another one. But hopefully you won't be so stupid about it the next time."

He growled under his breath. "I love the support, Mom."

"That's what I'm here for. Now let's talk about the fact that this young lady has my name."

"I know." He actually smiled at that. He'd yelled at Cat about it, but once he'd calmed down he'd realized how special it was. How much he loved being able to give that to his mother. "How awesome is that?"

The phone beeped in her hand, and she looked up, her lips pursed. "It's a text from Cat."

He took the phone from his mother.

Just met Annabelle. She's amazing. She'd still like to meet you. We're going away for the rest of the weekend, but please work some time in for Monday.

He looked at his mom. "She wants to meet me Monday."

"Don't make me hurt you, Brody. You say yes immediately."

At the college? Can you give her directions? There's no need for you to come.

He may have changed his mind about meeting his daughter, but he hadn't changed it about Cat.

"I have a daughter, Mom." Joy filled him then. It had tried to several times over the last few days, but he'd kept it tamped down. He couldn't do that any longer. He had a daughter, and he would be meeting her on Monday.

The sliding door opened to his house, and he and his mother both looked over. Thomas stood there, a strange expression on his face. He'd been with Brody the whole week, and though Brody felt as if they'd given it a good try, conversations mostly remained stiff. Of course, Thomas *had* spent the largest portion of his time while there either on the phone working or out of the house mugging for the cameras.

But still, at least they were trying. It was kind of progress.

"Something wrong?" Brody asked.

Thomas glanced at Brody's phone for a second before holding up a newspaper. Anger blanketed his features. "Someone leaked a picture. Proof that I knew you before."

Which did not go with the picture Thomas had been painting all week.

Brody wanted to feel bad for him. It was his brother, after all. Instead, he thought about what he'd told Cat a week ago concerning her family. Thomas had also made his bed. Maybe it was time he lay in it.

That did not get Emma Davenport off the hook for leaking it, though.

But again, Brody couldn't muster the energy to care. He took the paper from Thomas. It was a national paper, and it had a very prominent headline.

Harrisons knew about illegitimate son.

Nope. That would not go over well at all. He scanned the story. Then he studied the picture that went along with it, shocked to realize he recognized it. And that he knew exactly who it had come from. It hadn't been Emma Davenport.

Devan had stuck this very picture to their refrigerator the night after the fund-raiser that had ended their relationship. It was of him, Thomas, and Arthur Harrison.

His brother had been caught red-handed.

CHAPTER TWENTY-NINE

"Mr. Hollister." Amy's high-pitched voice caught Brody from somewhere around his waist. He looked down to find her sweet face smiling up at him. She'd lost a tooth since he'd seen her at the park last week.

Which made him wonder what his own daughter would have looked like at the same age.

"Yes, Amy." He schooled his face. It was the last Monday of class, and he would miss these kids, but it had been a rough few weeks. He would be glad when it was over. He was also looking forward to getting out to the college. He would meet Annabelle today.

"Where's the special lady?"

He forced himself not to clench his teeth. "She's not here, Amy."

"She's only at the park?"

"Yes." And in Portland with his daughter. And away for the weekend.

Over the last two days, Brody had found himself becoming increasingly jealous over the time Cat was getting with their daughter. Even though it was his own fault he wasn't a part of it.

"Mr. Hollister." It was Amy. Again. He really would be glad for this class to be over. "Yes, Amy?"

One small arm protruded toward the door. "Miss Louisa is here."

He glanced over to find Miss Louisa indeed standing in the doorway. Only, she wasn't wearing her usual charming smile.

She was trying. But she was falling very flat.

Brody glanced at Thomas, who was at the museum with him for the second Monday in a row. Thomas was in the back of the room, preening for the parents of the kids. It was a madhouse there today. It had been a madhouse since Thomas had rolled into town.

Even more so since he'd been trying to cover his tracks about knowing Brody in the past.

Brody should have sent him packing already. After all, their efforts at being brothers had failed, and he didn't care anything about helping Thomas cover his ass now that the truth was out. But there *had* been a few good moments between them over the last couple of days. They'd grilled out on his deck the night before. They'd laughed together. Thomas had even asked about Brody's relationship with Cat.

Brody hadn't told him what was going on with her, of course. He wasn't an idiot.

But he did appreciate the attempt at discussing something other than politics.

He looked back at the door, and Louisa subtly nudged her head, pulling Brody over to her.

"What's wrong?" he asked when he reached her side.

Lines pulled the sides of her mouth down. "You should be watching the news, Dr. Hollister."

"Why?"

"You're on it."

Which wasn't exactly a new thing. But the seriousness in Louisa's expression made him pause.

"They're saying . . ." She stalled, and her eyes shifted away from his.

"What are they saying?" Brody asked carefully.

After a breath, Louisa brought her gaze back to his. It burned into him. Gone was the fun the woman showed for every patron who walked into the building. In its place was worry. She leaned in and whispered, "There's a girl. She has your eyes."

Anger exploded in him.

The Davenports had leaked news of his daughter before he'd even gotten the chance to meet her? They had no shame. It was only one more reason to stay the hell away from Cat. He'd known they couldn't be together. He would never tolerate her lifestyle.

"I'll watch the kids," Louisa added. "The television is on in the break room. You'll have some privacy there."

Without another word, Brody headed to the back room while Louisa slipped past him to replace him at the front of his class. Then he stood there taking it in. Cat and her kids had been photographed running into the Davenport house . . . with Annabelle. In the top corner was the same picture he had on his phone, along with the shot of him and Cat as teenagers.

There was no mistaking her parentage.

Anger ate at him. He didn't want her to have to deal with this. She was just a kid. The sound of footsteps grew closer to the room, and he glanced back, only then realizing he'd sunk to one of the chairs around the small table. Thomas came into the room. He took in Brody before shifting his gaze to the small screen on the wall. He didn't say anything, only watched with fascination.

"This is such bullshit," Brody choked out. "That's my daughter they're plastering all over the news."

Thomas nodded. "I can see that."

Brody hadn't told anyone but his mother about Annabelle, but Thomas didn't seem all that surprised to learn of her. But then, maybe Thomas was used to it. He did have Arthur for a father. It made Brody wonder if he had more brothers out there. More illegitimate Harrisons.

If so, he didn't want to meet them. One was enough.

"They've gone too far."

Thomas nodded in agreement, but he wasn't paying attention to Brody, he was watching the news. Additionally, the hardness of his jaw turned a nasty shade of smug. The sight gave Brody pause. Then it made him ill, as an entirely different scenario entered his mind. One he did not want to believe.

He grabbed the remote and turned up the volume.

The story wasn't just about Annabelle's existence. They were harping on the fact that Emma Davenport had been the driving factor behind keeping it quiet. They mentioned Annabelle's adoptive mother, then showed a picture of Patricia Weathers and Emma in college together. They were blasting Emma.

This had not come from the Davenports.

Brody turned once again to look at his brother, knowing that he finally had his answer as to whether Thomas was exactly like his father. He most definitely was.

"You did this." The calmness of Brody's voice was worrisome, even to himself. Maybe Louisa should call the cops before he got thrown in jail for killing Thomas with his bare hands.

Thomas didn't reply. He just kept watching the TV.

Brody stood, his chair tipping over backward. He clicked off the television and got in Thomas's face. Then he put a finger to the man's chest. "You fucking did this," Brody growled. "*Knowing* she was my daughter."

"You have to understand," Thomas began. He sounded exactly like Arthur. "I took a big hit this weekend. Emma Davenport hid this child. From you, from the world. It was news. It had to come out."

"Maybe hiding her from the world had been the best thing for her." At least Annabelle hadn't had to grow up in the public light.

"Please. Emma Davenport was looking out for herself. This wasn't about the girl. She even told Cat the girl was dead."

How did Thomas even know that?

"The girl's name is Annabelle." Brody's words were low. His brother had just used his daughter. Brody had never wanted to hurt someone so badly in his life. "And you need to leave."

Thomas's brows went up. "Are you kidding me? This doesn't hurt you. This is about them."

"*You* hurt me, asshole."

"I didn't do anything to you. I've been here, trying to be your brother. If anything, that's helped you."

What a pig. And suddenly the clouds cleared. Thomas hadn't been here for Brody, which Brody had suspected all along. He hadn't even been here to show his greatness as a brother—though it had been a side benefit until he'd been caught. No. Thomas Harrison had been here purely to dig up dirt.

"You came here to keep an eye on the Davenports," Brody accused. "You haven't tried to build a thing with me. It's all been about the potential votes. And you used me to get them."

Thomas took a step back as Brody came toward him. "You might as well get used to the way things run," Thomas threw back at him. "You're a Harrison now. And I'm your brother. This is your life."

"I'm a Hollister," Brody spat out. He noticed the crowd of parents watching from the hallway, but didn't let that stop him. He turned back to Thomas. "And you will never be my brother. We're done." He pointed to the door. "Do not ever show up at my house again."

——————— ———————

Brody closed the book on medieval history that he'd been reading and shoved it out of his way. He'd been in his office for the last hour but had been unable to concentrate on anything except the fact that he would be meeting Annabelle that day.

And the fact that every time he checked the news stations, his daughter had been on them.

He picked up the remote and tried again. It took a few minutes, but yes, there she was. Blonde head ducked to avoid the cameras, rushing into the Davenport house in front of Cat.

All thanks to his brother.

Brody had escorted Thomas back to his house that morning, remaining at the front door until he'd left. Then he'd stood in the middle of his kitchen and fumed. He didn't know Annabelle yet, hadn't even met her, and already he was protective. He'd wanted to get in his car and drive over to Cat's.

And the real kicker was, it hadn't purely been Annabelle he'd wanted to protect.

Thus, he'd gotten even angrier.

Cat had looked fine in the footage that had been captured. And clearly she'd made it back into her home. Her kids were with her; they'd made it back in, too. But all of them had been running. As if the blasted paparazzi had been chasing them. It made his blood pressure soar. And it pissed him off that he cared.

A soft rap sounded on his door, and he looked sharply around. It was still too early for Annabelle, only . . .

She stood in his doorway.

He rose, and they stared across the small space at each other. He wasn't angry now. He was terrified. When his eyeballs began to burn from not blinking, he broke contact and cleared his throat.

"Annabelle." He stepped out from behind his desk.

She was so beautiful.

And she looked like Cat. She was built the same, had the same silky hair, and he could see a similar tilt of her chin that Cat got when she was unsure about something. It put a lump in his throat and he suddenly imagined Cat at sixteen. Scared, alone, having just given birth, and handing over her daughter.

Cat was too giving a woman for that not to have destroyed her.

"Come in," he said. He put Cat out of mind as he motioned with his hands. "Please."

Annabelle nodded and stepped into the room. Her eyes were immediately drawn to the shelves lining his wall, and he wished he'd learned a thing or two from Cat. He should have cleaned up his books. Put some order to things. His daughter would think he was a slob.

"This is awesome," she finally said. She moved to the shelves and pulled down one of his favorites. A manual on sixteenth-century European politics.

"You like history?" he asked.

A crooked smile flitted across her mouth. "I plan to get a doctorate."

Her words excited his heart. She was a part of him. She had his likes.

When she faced him again, she kept the book in her hands, and he could see the intelligence behind her eyes. Patricia Weathers had done okay for his daughter. That was a huge relief of a worry he hadn't even known he'd had.

"So you're my dad," she deduced.

He held his hands out to his sides. "Looks like."

"It's the eyes."

"What?"

"My eyes. They look like your eyes. I got Cat's hair and short stature, and your eyes. I'd always wondered. My adoptive mother is a six-foot brunette. We are clearly not blood related."

He didn't know anything about her mother, but her other words stuck in his head. She had wondered about him. Wow. He would have wondered about her, too. If he'd known she existed.

Which immediately brought him back to anger toward Cat.

Annabelle put the book down on a chair and reached for another. The first one fell to the floor. She didn't seem to notice. This made Brody smile.

"*Ohmygod*. I've been looking for this book for years." She picked up a rare illustrated study of the Mississippi Valley. He'd found it on one of his and his mom's antiquing expeditions a few years back.

"You collect books?" he asked. He was still standing in the middle of his office, as if unsure what to do next. Because he was unsure.

"Only history books. I found this in the Library of Congress when my mom took me there in junior high. I've been looking for my own copy since."

"You can have it."

She looked up at him. "You'd give it to me?"

He'd give her anything. And how was it that that was the case? He'd just met her.

Yet the wealth of emotion he felt for her was real. It was over-powering. It made him wonder again how Cat had managed to hand her over.

And it made him think about all that he'd missed out on.

"How long are you staying?" he asked. His mother had begged him to let her be here for this, but he'd wanted to meet Annabelle on his own first. He had promised to call, though, if today was it. He didn't want his mother missing out on the chance to meet her only granddaughter.

"Through Saturday. My mom is coming back and we'll be attending your play."

"Terrific." He finally made himself move. He went to the shelves and pulled down several other books that rated as his favorites. Her eyes lit up with each one.

Damn, she was fantastic.

"Thank you for wanting to meet me," he stammered like a teenager.

She shot him a rolled-eye look and he laughed.

"That sounded lame, didn't it?"

"Totally." She grinned, and he was a goner. He fell completely in love with his daughter on the spot.

As she continued walking the length of his shelves, reading the title of each book, she stroked a hand over the spine of a two-hundred-year-old tome. That particular book never hit his floors. There were some that got special treatment.

She glanced over at him. "How could I not want to meet you, though? You do realize that you're now a part of our country's political history? An illegitimate Harrison? You can bet that'll make the books."

"Then I suppose that means you'll be in there, too."

"I'm counting on it." She turned to him. The book he'd given her was held solidly against her chest. "But I'll *also* be in there for my part in the changes that will someday take place in Washington."

The air went out of his chest. "Really? You want to go into politics?"

"I'll have my name on a ballot the first year I'm eligible."

Of course she would. She was a Davenport, after all.

If this wasn't his life and his daughter, he'd laugh. Whether he wanted it or not, he would be a part of politics for the rest of his life. Because unless this young lady kicked him to the curb, he was in her life for good. He supposed he might as well get used to smiling and shaking hands.

Three bright, sunny New England days left and Cat would have the park donation in the bag. She shook hands with a local business owner who'd been helping all day, the two of them chatting about mundane things as he drank from a cold bottle of water and Cat scanned the kid zone for Becca and Tyler. She found them playing in the sand pit with several other children they'd met over the last week. JP and Vega were helping man the children's area. Annabelle was over there, too, though it was more as an older sibling watching over her brother and sister.

It was a sight Cat would have never imagined seeing. And it flooded her with love.

Her oldest daughter would go back to California Sunday morning, and Cat would return to Atlanta, her vacation over. The kids' lives would return to normal, and she had no idea what would come next for her.

She did know one thing, though. It was looking very much as if all of it would happen without another word from Brody. Which hurt her more than she would have guessed. It had been a week since she'd seen him, and four days since he'd grudgingly replied to her last text.

That had been way too long.

She had *heard* about him, of course. Since Annabelle had met him on Monday, she'd split her time between Brody and Cat. It was strangely similar to sharing custody. Only, their child was old enough to transport herself, so neither parent had to actually see or talk to the other.

It was depressing, and made Cat wonder if this was what her life would have been like for the last eighteen years if she'd kept her daughter. Because love or not, making a relationship last at the age of sixteen rarely worked. The odds would have been stacked against them.

Toss in the logistics, the fact that the world would have forever been watching, and the lack of maturity on both their parts, and she remained convinced that Annabelle being raised by Patricia had been the best thing for her. It shamed Cat to admit it, but at the same time, she felt like such a grown-up for recognizing it for what it was.

Annabelle ambled her way over then, shaking hands and talking with a couple of locals on the way. The paparazzi that remained soaked it up, yet Cat didn't believe for a second that Annabelle was doing it for the attention. She was doing it because it came naturally. Annabelle Weathers would someday become a public figure; Cat would bet on it. She could recognize the signs anywhere. She wondered if Brody was aware of that.

"Did I tell you I met Brody's mother today?" she asked Cat when she reached her side. Annabelle grabbed a yard-size trash bag from the supply pile, and the two of them moved to one of the last areas to be cleaned of construction trash. "I had lunch with them."

"Yeah?" Cat took one end of the bag.

"She's great. Entertained us the whole time with stories of the security guy you hired for her. I think she called him Tank."

"Stone." Cat chuckled as she pictured Annabelle Hollister and Stone together. Cat had heard rumors that there was a bit more than security going on at Annabelle's New Hampshire home. "But Tank fits him better."

"Yeah, he was a big guy. And she seemed like a great mom. Brody was protective of her. It was cute."

Cat could imagine how protective Brody would have been of a daughter growing up.

"It's a shame not everyone can have a mom like that," Annabelle mused.

"Tell me about it." They moved together, Cat tossing a piece of scrap wood into the bag.

"It's pretty cool that I was named after her."

Cat peeked over at her daughter. "It's pretty cool that Patricia kept the name. It means a lot to me that she did."

They both grew silent, each in her own thoughts as they worked to clean up the area. The building of the playground would wrap up in the morning, and landscapers would descend on the area on Friday.

"What was your childhood like?" Annabelle suddenly asked.

"Mine? It was . . ." Cat gave it some thought. It had been normal. At least, she'd thought it was at the time. "I thought it was good. We were prominent in the news, of course, and I understood that from an early age. We always had to be careful about where we went and what we did, but I have two brothers I love to death. I was a total daddy's girl, and until this last week, I had thought my mother wasn't so bad. Driven, yes. I think she might have been the one to sustain our dad's career during periods of his life—whether he wanted her to or not. But she loved us. In her way. I had a good childhood."

She rattled on. As if trying to convince herself that it had been good. When she glanced over, Annabelle said, "I had the best childhood and the best mother in the world."

Cat chuckled. "I'm glad."

"I'm not saying that to rub it in or anything. But just to let you know that it was really good. And also . . ." Annabelle paused, and Cat stopped what she was doing to wait. She didn't want to miss what her daughter had to say. She sensed it was important. Finally, Annabelle shrugged and added, "To say that I understand you giving me up. I thought I was pregnant last year."

Annabelle paused and Cat's eyes went wide.

"God, Mom doesn't know," Annabelle said quickly, throwing up a protective hand toward Cat. "Please don't tell her that."

"Okay," Cat said gently. "I won't. You're a big girl, I'm not going to run to your mom."

Annabelle blew out a breath. "Good. Because she *hated* the guy. She would kill me. But yeah, I had a scare."

They stopped walking to stand face-to-face. The wind blew around them, ruffling both their hair at the ends. Cat found it almost funny how similar they looked standing there together.

"I didn't want my whole life changed because of a baby, you know?" Annabelle added. "I have plans. Things I need to do. To fix. Things I want to accomplish." She gave an apologetic grimace. "I had no idea what I was going to do."

Cat could understand what Annabelle was trying to do for her, and she appreciated it. "My future wasn't my only deciding factor in giving you up, I'm afraid." That guilt hadn't left her—knowing that it hadn't just been about Annabelle—no matter that it had been the right decision. "My family name played into it way more than it should. In fact, it shouldn't have at all."

"So what?"

Cat gave her a pointed look. "What do you mean, so what?" Wasn't it clear?

"I mean, move on." Her daughter looked at her. "Forgive yourself, Cat. Don't feel bad for me. I like you and all, but I wouldn't have chosen you over my mom. Ever."

"Ouch." The truth hurt. "But okay, that's good to know. So Patricia really did do good, then?" Not that Cat had doubted it. Annabelle was amazing.

"She's the best. She's older than my friends' moms, yeah, but I think that gave her something they don't have. She has a better perspective on the world. Not to mention, more money and the patience to actually focus on *me*." Annabelle gave a wide grin. "I realize I'm lucky—though I'd probably deny all of this if you ever tell her I said it."

Cat smiled. "It's our secret. But what would you have done?" she asked. "If you'd been pregnant?"

Annabelle shook her head as a sadness Cat hadn't seen with her before crossed over her face. "I have no idea. I'm just thankful I didn't have to find out."

Cat was, too.

"Are you more careful now?" Cat asked. "You're about to go away to college. The boys are different there, you know? They're older. More—"

"Stop," Annabelle groaned. "Don't even start on me. I don't need another mom. Not one like that." She reached over and gave Cat a warm hug. "You can be my mom, too," she whispered. "I'd like that. Only, we'll just be kind of friends instead of mom and daughter."

"That would be nice," Cat said. She had to fight to get the words around the lump in her throat. She'd hugged her daughter a couple of times over the week, but this one had been different. It had healed something inside her. "I'm glad you stuck around this week." She squeezed Annabelle's hand but did not let herself get teary. Annabelle would be embarrassed. "Think you might visit me again?"

"Do you mean here or in Atlanta?"

"Well, I live in Atlanta." Though she would move if she had a reason. Not that that reason was speaking to her anymore.

"You could move here," Annabelle suggested. "It's a great place."

It was a great place. She'd fallen in love with it as well as Brody. "I don't know. It might be too hard for me."

"I get it. That's part of why I don't want to go to Brown. The guy from last year, we ended rough. We didn't make it through the pregnancy scare like I thought we would." Annabelle made a face. "He's going to Brown."

"Don't let a guy dictate your choices, Annabelle. If Brown is where you want to go, then go. He's just a guy."

"The thing is, I had kind of chosen it to begin with *because* of him."

"I see. Then the slate is clean." She gave her daughter a wink as they went back to picking up scraps. "Only, you'd better choose soon. Your time is running out."

"Tell me about it. Mom's going to lose her shit if I screw up and miss out on going to school in the fall."

"I can understand that. I would probably lose my shit if Becca or Tyler did the same."

"But there are other things I could do." Annabelle cut her a sideways glance. "I hear the peace corps is always looking."

Cat smiled and reached over to hug Annabelle once again. She would be proud if her daughter did *anything* Cat had done. It was nice to hear that the thought even entered her mind. "I may not have raised you, kid, but I sure made a good one."

Annabelle laughed out loud. "That you did, Cat. I'm pretty darned good. And yes, I'll come visit you. Wherever you are. Maybe you can come visit me, too."

"You can count on it."

CHAPTER THIRTY

"K NOCK, KNOCK."
Brody looked up from the papers he was grading to find his daughter standing at his office door. It brightened his day.

"Hey, AnnieB." He'd given her a nickname. It suited her.

"Hey, Dr. H." She'd followed suit. It had been a good week for them. They had so much in common. Their interests, their insights.

He shook his head with pride as she moved into the room and shoved books to the floor before plopping down in the chair in front of him. She'd made time for him every day this week, as if he meant something. Which was good, because if she hadn't, he would have driven over to Cat's place and sought her out himself. Because she *did* mean something to him. He'd met her three days ago, and already he was dreading her departure on Sunday. He had no idea when he might see her again.

"What are you doing here?" he asked. They'd made plans to meet for an early dinner before he would take her to the play. She'd been trying to wait until Saturday to see it in the new amphitheater, but he'd worn her down. He wanted to introduce her to the cast and to Clyde. He wanted to show her off.

"Just hanging out. You heard back from that producer yet?" she asked conversationally.

"No." Which was annoying. It had been over a week. He'd told Annabelle about his dreams, but his hopes were once again plummeting.

"Hmmm." She looked around the room, casual-like, but he could sense a purpose for her visit. He just didn't know what it was.

"You decide on a school yet?" he asked.

"No."

He narrowed his eyes on her. The girl was way too nonchalant about her education. "Tick tock," he said. "Time is running out."

She held up her phone. "I already heard from my mom this morning. She's on it. You can let it go."

He laughed. She was such an independent young woman. And though he never meant to, he found that he was a bit of a father when she was around. He worried about her, wanted to help her make decisions, and generally wanted to impart what wisdom he'd picked up over the years.

She wanted to hear none of it.

Every time he tried, she let him know she was fine, and that he didn't have to try so hard. But he wasn't trying. It simply came naturally.

"So . . ." She perused his shelves from her seat as if she hadn't already gone through his books twice this week. "Talked to Cat lately?"

"Oh." He frowned at her. This was about Cat. "What?"

She shrugged. "What do you mean, what? Just having conversation."

"Right."

She grinned. Every time she smiled like that, it made him think of Cat.

"Okay, fine," she huffed out. "I'll just say it. I think you're making a mistake."

"A mistake about what? I haven't even talked to her in a week."

"Exactly." She shot him a frustrated look. "A mistake. Don't you love her?"

"I'm not sure where you got *that* idea." He had *not* talked to her about Cat. Other than to hear about their time spent together this week.

She rolled her eyes. "I'm not blind. Last week you guys were plastered all over the news."

"Being together doesn't mean love." And why he was talking about love to his eighteen-year-old daughter, he didn't know. It was strange.

"I know that." She made a face. "But you guys weren't just together. I mean, you fell in love a long time ago, right? Before I was born?"

He watched her. Did it matter to her to know that they'd been in love? He had no idea if something like that would mean anything to her or not. But the fact she was asking about it . . .

"Yeah." He nodded. "We were in love. Before."

"And you're in love now," she pushed.

"Drop it, Annabelle."

"She's a good person."

"I know she's a good person." When she wasn't around her mother.

"She quit her job, did you know that?" His daughter was also persistent. "She won't even speak to her mother."

He had not known that. He knew that Emma had gone back to Atlanta, but he'd made no assumptions about anything else.

"She has no idea what she's going to do with her life now," Annabelle said. "I think she would even consider moving up here."

"No, she wouldn't."

"Ask her."

He let out a tiny laugh. "Actually, I did."

"When?" She sat up with anticipation, leaning forward. "What did she say?"

"It was before you showed up."

She sighed. "So what did she say?"

"She didn't. We got interrupted before she could answer."

"And you never brought it back up?"

"The next time we talked, it was about you."

"Oh." The animation left her face.

"Right. So stop. It isn't happening."

She crossed her arms over her chest as she once again leaned back in the chair. "You are stubborn," she observed. "Just like she said."

"Cat has been talking about me?" The damned jump in his heart rate annoyed him.

"I don't know." Annabelle shrugged and went back to studying his books.

"You can be a pain in the butt, did you know that?"

She smiled. "Yeah, I know. But I'm already set in my ways, so don't worry about trying to change it."

He could see the hope in her eyes at the thought of him and Cat getting back together, though he didn't know why it mattered to her. Maybe the romance of thinking her biological parents were meant to be would mean something to her? But he couldn't do that. Not even for her. So he'd make her understand, instead.

He leaned his elbows on his desk and turned serious. "She lied to me, AnnieB. And she shouldn't have. Not about you."

"I get that. But isn't that the past?"

"Well, you're here now. That's pretty present to me."

"I mean your relationship. Her not telling you about me. Isn't that the past? You two *had* gotten back together. Clearly there's still something there. Even before I knew you were my dad, I saw you two in the news. I could see it was more than casual. You have a storybook romance."

He knew she hadn't just called him Dad, but the word had caught him in the chest. It made him hurt more. Because she could have been calling him Dad her whole life. "You're letting the whole Romeo and Juliet thing go to your head," he told her. "That was just a headline."

"And you're letting mistakes that happened almost nineteen years ago determine the rest of your life."

God, she was stubborn. She probably *would* make a good politician.

"I could have raised you." His voice rose slightly. "It's that simple. I could have been your dad. Cat didn't give me the opportunity to choose, and I could have raised you. Especially now that I've met you, and I see what I've missed. It rips me apart. She didn't have the right to do that to me."

"But I love my mom. I'm glad she's my mom. And there's no guarantee I would have turned out the same with you."

"Didn't you want a dad growing up?" He knew he had.

"Yeah. And I often wondered who he—you—were. But I wouldn't change my life if given the opportunity. At all. I'm sorry if that hurts you."

"I should have had the choice."

"Sure," she agreed. "And Cat shouldn't have been manipulated by her own mother. She should have been able to trust her. Depend on her to help her do the right thing. But she *was* manipulated, and you *didn't* get the choice. Cat also thought I was dead."

Her last words were harsh. And Brody agreed with her point. Now that he knew about Annabelle, he understood how rough it must have been for Cat, thinking she had died. But it did not change the facts.

"You don't get it, Annabelle. You're too young. You don't understand."

"Okay," she agreed. "Sure. But I'm two years older than you were when I was born, and you think you were old enough to raise me." She shot him a look. "If you were old enough for that, why can't I be old enough to understand love?"

Damn, she was smart, too. "You're a bit of a smart-ass, you know that?"

She shrugged unapologetically. "I know. It sucks for other people."

He chuckled. She was so amazing. And she was right. There was no guarantee she would have turned out the same if she'd been raised by him. In fact, the guarantee was probably that she would not. But that didn't lessen his anger. Or his confusion.

Because she was right. He loved Cat.

He hadn't seen or talked to her in over a week, and it was killing him. Seriously, he thought pieces of his heart might be breaking off and dying. He loved her. He had wanted to be with her forever.

He did want to be with her forever.

But he didn't know what to do anymore. He was sick without her, yet he couldn't figure out how to forgive her.

Cat stood off to the side of the crowd as she watched Brody step onstage at the end of the play. The applause he received was deafening. The entire community had come out for the opening of the park, and most of them had stuck around for the play.

Clyde had just introduced him and shared the phone call Brody had gotten earlier that day. The play had been sold. It was going to Broadway. Cat's heart was overjoyed for him. She hoped she got the opportunity to tell him face-to-face.

And she had reason to believe that she would.

For the first time since their argument, he'd contacted her today. Sort of. She'd received a brown-paper-wrapped package that morning, addressed to her, Becca, and Tyler. Inside she'd found three huge boxes of crayons, along with three coloring books. The one for her had been entitled *Outside the Lines*. Attached to it had been a handwritten note.

Can we talk tonight?

Yes. They could talk. She very much wanted to talk.

She didn't know what the gift or the talking meant, but she couldn't help but be hopeful. Because without hope, she feared she'd fall apart.

The crowd cheered again as Brody finished talking, and Cat couldn't help but picture her life with him. That's what she wanted. Though she and the kids would be getting on the plane with JP and Vega in the morning, she didn't want to go home. Ever.

She might still be in the Davenport family—and her mother had been right about that to one extent. She couldn't walk away from her name. That would mean turning her back on her brothers, and she wouldn't do that to them or to herself. And there was still the whole issue with Bennett's paternity. She would be there to support him when he learned the truth. But she would live exactly the way she wanted to from now on.

Which meant, with Brody or not, she would be coming back to Dyersport to house hunt. Annabelle had told her that morning that she planned to attend St. Mary's. She was hopeful she'd get accepted as a late applicant for the fall term.

Cat looked across the lawn at her daughter then. At all of her kids. They were standing with Annabelle's mother, Brody's mother, JP, and Vega. And Tank—Stone. The man had become a fixture in Annabelle Hollister's life. Cat suspected that wouldn't be changing anytime soon. She'd talked to both of them earlier in the day, and the guy had a serious crush. Annabelle was eating it up.

"You still in love with the guy?" a male voice said from directly behind her.

Cat whirled. "Bennett!" she shouted.

He stood tall and proud, his posture showcasing his many years in the army, though he'd long ago lost his buzz cut.

She threw herself into his arms. "I've missed you, you big lug."

"I've missed you too, Squirt."

He may not have been around a lot over the years, but he'd never changed. He was a bit distant, he was his own man, and he was also her brother.

After finally turning him loose, she leaned back and peered up at him. Geez, he was tall. She'd forgotten how much.

"So?" he asked.

"So what?"

He nodded toward the stage where Brody remained, talking individually with people who'd come up to congratulate him. "Love?" he asked. "It still there?"

She looked at Brody. "What makes you think I love him?"

"Oh, I don't know. Making goo-goo faces at each other in the tabloids. Having a kid with the guy."

"Ohmygod, Bennett. You have to meet Annabelle, she's the best."

"I will. I promise. But first I need to know about Hollister."

She wasn't sure why, but he seemed intent on talking about Brody. So, fine. She'd talk. She crossed her arms over herself and shook her head. "I don't know if what I feel matters that much. I messed up. A lot."

"Yeah, I picked up on that. Good to know you aren't perfect. Dad always acted as though you could do no wrong."

Her expression dropped. He'd just brought up what she had to tell him about their dad. She slipped her arm through his and edged them both farther away from the crowd.

"There's something you should know," she began.

"Let me go first. I might have an even bigger surprise in store than you do."

"I doubt it." But then she thought about what he was implying. She narrowed her eyes on him. "Are you saying you know what I want to tell you?"

"That your father isn't my father?" he asked. At her gasp, he nodded. "Yeah. I knew that."

"How?"

"Right before I turned eighteen, Dad let it *slip*. We were arguing. He was pissed off because—" He abruptly cut off his words, and his eyes darted briefly away. When they returned, he shook his head before continuing. "We didn't see eye-to-eye on a couple of things."

She studied him, wishing he would tell her more, but knowing he wouldn't. He'd made a lifetime of keeping his distance. "So he just told you?" she asked.

"He just told me. He acted like it came out accidentally, but it didn't. He wanted me to know. He hated me for that."

She couldn't imagine getting such a shock, especially as a kid. Maybe she'd had blinders on toward her dad her whole life, too. But then, he had gotten a teenage girl pregnant. Clearly she hadn't seen all that he was.

"Does that play into why you don't come home much?" she asked.

He eyed her before answering. "You know it does."

She nodded. How could it not? "What's *your* secret, then?"

He looked over her head for a moment, as if looking for the quickest path out of there. But he didn't leave. He once again brought his gaze back to hers. His eyes weren't like hers and JP's. They'd gotten the blue that had been passed down through generations of Davenports. That should have given it away years ago. Bennett's were a sea-green.

"I know who my father is," he said.

Her eyes went wide.

Then he nodded toward the stage. Toward Brody.

"You know how he didn't want anyone to know he's a Harrison?"

Cat turned toward Brody. It was as if the world slowed down. "Yes," she said carefully.

"Neither do I."

Oh. Fuck.

She turned back to Bennett. "Your father is—"

"Arthur Harrison." He gave a little nod with the words. "I personally think you should *marry* Hollister. Keep it all in the family."

"Oh, my God," she whispered. What was wrong with her family?

Bennett smiled then, and suddenly she saw it. He had Brody's eyes. Annabelle's eyes.

She shook her head in disbelief. "He and Mom?" She swallowed. "Arthur Harrison and our mother?"

"That's the story I hear. She cheated on our father right before they got married and didn't tell him she was pregnant until after the *I do*s."

"She slept with his family's biggest enemy?" Cat stood in amazement at yet one more secret her mother had closely guarded. "No wonder she and Dad hated the name so much."

"Makes sense. Dad did not sound like a fan when he told me." He nodded behind her. "Here comes your guy. I'm going to go say hi to the others. Meet this long-lost daughter of yours." He glanced over her shoulder once again, then winked at her. "Good luck."

He left, and Cat slowly turned to find Brody. He looked so good. And he was her brother's . . . *oh, God*.

"I'm glad you came," Brody said. Hearing his voice calmed her instantly.

"I sort of had to be here," she said. "It's my project."

He stared at her as if drinking her in. "That the only reason you're here?"

"I don't know. I also heard there was this Broadway play being performed tonight. Wanted to see what that was all about." She lost the ability to act unconcerned and broke loose in a wide smile. "Congratulations, Brody." She did not hug him like she wanted to do. "I'm so happy for you."

"Thanks." He glanced away from her then, looking toward her family—who stood with his family and Patricia.

"How's your week been?" she asked. She wanted to hear him talk, if nothing else. "Annabelle says she's had a great time with you."

"It's been good." He looked back at her. "I have a kid. That's mind-blowing."

"She looks so much like you."

"And you. She's gorgeous."

Cat nodded. Her nerves had ratcheted up and she'd noticed that her hands were now shaking. She shoved them behind her back. "And Thomas?" she asked. "How's that going?"

She knew Thomas had left town, but she wasn't aware of the circumstances. Other than that his cover had been blown. He'd tried to fake his way beyond it, but no one had bought it. Brody gave her a look now, as if to say that she should know how it was going.

"He's gone for good. And between him and your mom, I'm not sure if anyone in your great state of Georgia would elect either one of them."

"I know. I think the governor is scrounging around, trying to line up a replacement in case the voters try to get Mom out before election day. It's my understanding she's not having an easy time of it lately."

"You're really not talking to her?"

"Haven't since JP kicked her out of the house. I found out about"—she nodded toward their families—"Annabelle, and my brother made her leave before I could."

They both grew silent then as they stood together and watched the others. Everyone was animatedly talking except his mother. She stood slightly apart from the others, in front of Stone, her shoulder leaned back into his chest. It was a comfortable kind of stance.

"You do know I quit paying him a week ago, right?"

Brody turned his head to her. "No," he said slowly. "I did *not* know that."

"Apparently he's taking some time off this week."

"But he's here."

Cat nodded. "With your mother."

"He's been staying out at her house." The horrified expression on his face was hilarious.

"It's not all bad. Maybe you'll get a new dad soon. You could use that."

His smirk was even funnier than his horror. "That's not funny."

"I thought it was," she said drily.

They went back to watching, and Cat smiled now as Bennett lifted Tyler to his shoulders. Annabelle was dancing around with Becca, and the adults looked on with fondness.

"Our daughter is pretty amazing," Brody said.

"She is."

"Smart, too."

Cat smiled at Brody. "She got that from her dad."

He didn't smile back. "How bad do you think we would have messed her up?"

Pressure built in her chest. "I'm almost afraid to imagine."

"Yeah."

They grew silent again. It was a more comfortable silence now. This was a weird conversation, but at the same time, it felt like just the thing that they needed.

"The kids say thanks for their coloring books," she told him.

"They're welcome. And their mom?" He peeked at her. "What does she say?"

"She said that she doesn't do a lot of coloring these days, but when she does, she does try to stick outside the lines."

He suddenly reached for her, turned her to him. His eyes were imploring. "I want to color outside the lines, too, Cat. I do. We both kept things from each other. We both messed up. But Annabelle pointed something out to me the other day. Something that hurt, actually."

"What?"

"She said she wouldn't have wanted us for parents."

Cat hung her head. "She told me that, too."

"I think she might be right."

"I'm so sorry, Brody." Cat couldn't stand it any longer. She had to touch him. She put a hand on his arm. "If I could go back . . ."

"I know. I've thought about that all week. If we could go back. If only you would have told me. If we could have stayed together."

She shook her head. "I don't think *we* would have worked."

"Why not?"

"It took me thirty-five years to see who my mother was. Don't you think she would have played a large part in things? In us?"

They stared at each other, both thinking about the past. Both thinking about mistakes.

"I don't want to do this without you, Cat. I don't want to do *anything* without you."

Cat's eyes rounded in shock. Was he going to forgive her?

"Mistakes or not," Brody continued, "and we've both made them—I want you with me. I can't get past that. I've always wanted you with me."

He paused and she sucked in a breath. "Brody—"

"Marry me, Cat? I can't see anything else to do. I love you."

Their daughter glanced over at them, then, as if she could sense what was going on.

"Are you doing this because of her?" Cat asked, afraid to believe it was real. She knew Annabelle wanted to see their romance as the Romeo and Juliet story the media had made it out to be—minus the poison and death ending, of course. But that wasn't real. It wasn't who they were.

"She wants me to marry you, yes. We talked about it. In fact, she pestered me to death about it. But she's not the one who showed up here tonight with a ring."

"You have a ring?" Cat gasped. She flicked her gaze over him. "On you now?"

"In my pocket."

Her eyes zeroed in on his pants pockets. "Do I get to see it?"

"Not unless you say yes."

She sighed. It was so scary. All of it. And she was terrified to hope. "Look around, Brody," she begged. "Is this really what you want? I'm a mother. I have two kids."

"You have three kids."

She gave an agreeing nod. "I have three kids."

"I want to make it at least four," he told her.

Her heart dropped to her stomach. "You want a baby?"

"With you, I do. I want everything with you."

"Oh, God," she moaned. "You're killing me here."

"Then let me kill you for the rest of your life, Kitty Cat. We've wasted too much time already." He leaned in close. "And I'm not just talking about wasting time not being together. I've missed you this week." He took her hand and squeezed it hard. "My *body* has missed you this week."

She shivered from his words. "Be careful. People are watching."

"Then let them watch." He glanced at the small shed where she knew the newly purchased lawn equipment was stored. "I wouldn't mind if they watched us disappear in there for a bit."

She glanced at the shed herself and felt her cheeks heat. Then she grew serious. She stared up at him. At the stubble she found so sexy. At the nerdy little glasses. She loved him so much.

"Do you really think we could make this work after all this time?"

He took her hand. "I think we have to. We're meant for each other. I'm not sure we could survive another twenty years apart."

She tended to agree. But there was one tiny matter she would need to share with him first.

"Before I answer," she stalled, "there's a teeny-tiny secret I have to fill you in on. It could change your mind."

His eyes narrowed on her. "Another secret?"

"I know," she moaned out. "You'd think we'd have them all out by now."

"Why am I somehow not surprised?" Brody asked. He took

a small step back and widened his stance as if steeling himself, then nodded. "Hit me with it."

She couldn't believe she even had to say this out loud.

"Apparently . . ." she began. She glanced at Bennett, then cringed. "Bennett. My *half* brother . . ."

Brody's brows went up at the phrase.

Cat gulped. "Is also. . ." She dropped her face to her hands and mumbled, "I can't even say it. It's too much. Even for my family."

Brody pulled her fingers from her eyes and peeked in. "What?" He looked concerned. "There's nothing that could possibly be that bad. Unless you're going to tell me something crazy like Bennett's father is also Arthur Harrison."

She stared at him unblinking, and he finally got it. His jaw came unhinged.

"You are kidding me," he said.

"I'm afraid not."

"That's fantastic," he shot out. And he even looked happy about it. "Your mother . . . all her complaining. Her keeping us apart."

Cat nodded. "She takes the definition of hypocrite to a new level."

He chuckled. "I would say that she does." Then his laugh dropped, and he took both her hands in his. "See? We have to be together. We're going to be in the news together forever anyway. Especially when that kid of ours finishes growing up. I think she's going to be a politician."

"Oh, she's definitely going to be a politician. She might already be running for a position here."

"Here?"

Cat's smile bloomed on her face. Annabelle might get mad for spoiling her surprise, but Cat couldn't help it. "Didn't she tell you? She plans to attend St. Mary's."

"But she has a full ride at Brown."

"She never wanted Brown. She talked to her mother about it, and Patricia is fine with it. Annabelle wants to get to know us better, too. And apparently she wants to take classes with you."

"That's incredible." He laughed then, the sound rich and exciting, and pulling the attention of every member of their families. "And pretty damned perfect. Except for one thing." He dropped to one knee. "Say yes, Kitty Cat." He kissed the back of her hand and his eyes shone up at hers. "Marry me."

She nodded then, smiling, and sniffed back a sob. She could see their families practically bouncing with excitement in her peripheral vision. "On one condition," she declared.

"Really? You're going to give me conditions? I should have the upper hand here."

"Sweetheart, you'll never have the upper hand."

"Don't I know it?" He winked and rose to his feet. "Okay, what's the condition?"

"Take me for a ride in your red car again. I seem to remember it has this great backseat."

He roared with another laugh, then pulled her in for a kiss. Flashes went off all around them, which only made him kiss her longer.

EPILOGUE

SEPTEMBER FIRST ARRIVED, AND CAT ONCE AGAIN SAT OUT on the same deck she'd rented three months earlier, sipping yet another yogurt-and-flaxseed smoothie.

And watching her fiancé through her binoculars.

"Do you see dolphins again this morning, Mommy?" Tyler asked from the other side of the deck. He sat amid the pile of toys he dragged outside every morning.

"I wanna see!" Becca raced up the deck stairs, shaking sand from her hands as she did. She'd been working on yet another sand castle. If the ocean didn't wash them away every day, Cat wasn't sure there would be any sand left for Becca to play in.

"It wasn't dolphins this morning," Cat informed them. Though, most mornings it wasn't dolphins. It was usually Brody. And their daughter. "Brody and your sister are heading this way," she told them.

Both kids scrambled over to her, insisting they wanted to look, too, so Cat let them take turns looking through the high-powered lenses. It had become the morning ritual since Cat had bought the house and moved in next door.

Annabelle had decided to live with Brody while she was in Maine and would ride into the college with him once classes started—which would be in only a couple of days. But for the three weeks she'd been there, she'd quickly adapted to her father's schedule. They'd start the mornings with coffee, then a jog, while Cat got in her yoga and her non-doughnut breakfast—and feasted her gaze on her fiancé's powerful strides running up the beach.

The kids played alongside her, and often the three of them built sand castles together or stuck their toes in the water while they waited for Brody and Annabelle's return. The jog would finish with the two of them climbing the back steps of Cat's deck, where Cat would finally get her good-morning kiss.

It was a fantastic way to start the day. The only thing better would be if they were all in the same house together, but until a wedding ring was in place, Cat and Brody had decided this was best. The kids had needed time to get to know Brody, and the same for him. And Cat had needed time to adjust to all the changes in her own family's life.

Her mother had not been booted out of office, nor had she withdrawn her name from the upcoming ballet. She was charging full steam ahead, as stubborn as she'd always been, though Cat couldn't yet tell if it would matter. The family name had been tarnished, and that was not an easy thing to overcome.

The money her mother had paid to Lexi had *not* been discovered and leaked, however, nor had Lexi and Daniel come out of hiding. Cat still hoped to meet her half brother someday, but until his mother was ready to deal with her son being a Davenport, that wouldn't happen.

Bennett's paternity also remained a secret. For now.

He hadn't even confronted their mother with the truth yet, but Cat knew that was only a matter of time. A person could only sit on that kind of information for so long without needing answers.

Additionally, Cat and her mother still were not speaking.

JP and Vega had been to visit, though. As had Bennett.

Cat had watched an interesting connection happen between Brody and her oldest brother as they'd spent a few days together.

Nothing about their relationship was sloppy and huggy, not like it might be with two half sisters just finding each other, but they did seem to accept the other for the man that he was, as well as hold a fair amount of respect.

Bennett, Brody, and Annabelle had even spent a couple of days together hiking in Acadia National Park. It was a bit weird looking at them side by side because they all had the same eyes. But however it had happened, and however strange and weird the whole situation was, it all seemed to fit.

Cat was getting her oldest brother back in her life.

And Brody had his own brother now. One who might actually stand a chance of getting to know him.

Oh, and Vega was pregnant. There would be another Davenport around soon. Cat had already made them promise to visit Maine every summer so the cousins could have those shared memories together.

What would become of Cat and her mother's relationship she didn't yet know. She'd take that one step at a time, and worry about it later. Because for now, she had far more important things on her mind.

"Here they come!" Becca bounced up and down on her toes with excitement as Brody and Annabelle took the final few strides to the deck.

Cat's heart thudded hard. She loved this man more than her life.

And she was ready to marry him. Now.

She wanted to wake by his side every morning. To kiss his scruffy face before he ever stepped a foot out of bed.

But they'd agreed to take it slow. He and the kids needed time.

"Morning, gorgeous," Brody said. Becca giggled at the words directed toward her.

"I made you another sand castle," she said sweetly. She scrunched her shoulders up in the innocent-little-girl way she had that Cat knew always tugged at Brody's heart.

"I see that," he said. He leaned down and put a kiss to her cheek. "Thank you very much." Becca giggled again.

Annabelle had crossed to Tyler's side and ruffled his hair, and he'd wrapped an arm tightly around her leg. They stood together as if they'd been doing so all their lives. It made Cat happier than she'd known was possible.

Then Brody zeroed in on Cat. "The kids and I have been talking," he said.

Cat took in all three kids. Each suddenly looked as if they held a secret just behind their lips. "And?" Cat asked.

Annabelle's mouth curved into a wide grin, but she didn't say anything. She and Tyler moved to stand beside Brody, joining Becca, and Brody dropped a hand to Tyler's shoulder. All four of them looked one hundred percent like a happy family unit. Cat's heart sang at the sight.

"This two-house thing," he started. He tilted his head back and took in her two-story, much larger home, then glanced over at his own before his gaze landed back on Cat. "Annabelle thinks she should live here. She says you have an unused bedroom that's bigger than the one at my house, *and* that it has the perfect spot for her book collection."

Cat nodded quickly. "Of course." She took in Annabelle. "You can live here if you want. Of course. I'd love that. But I thought you wanted to stay with Brody?"

Brody stepped away from the kids then and crossed to Cat. He pulled her to her feet and gave her the good-morning kiss she'd been waiting on since she'd risen with the sun. It was long and slow, and way inappropriate to have in front of any of the kids.

She couldn't make herself care.

"I want to move in, too," Brody whispered when he pulled back. All three kids snickered behind him. "Let's set a wedding date," he urged. "We know we're good. The kids and I, we fit. *You* and I fit. Let's do this, Kitty Cat. I'll wait as long as you want, but the kids and I"—the kids suddenly flanked him on either side—"we're ready. We want to be a family."

"And I want a sister," Becca whispered. Tyler made a gagging noise, and Annabelle shushed them both.

Cat took in her family, the love shining from all of them, and she knew there was no more reason to wait. She had everything she'd ever wanted standing right in front of her. She had the *more* she'd been searching for.

She nodded and shared her own smile. "I think we should do it."

All three kids let out an excited whoop as Brody's arms closed tightly around her once again. After another kiss, he leaned back and peered down at her. "When?" he asked anxiously.

Cat laughed at his hurry, but she was anxious, too. She wanted this.

And she wanted it now.

After all their secrets, after their past. After dealing with the drama that was her family and his. The only thing that fit was them being together. And she did not want to waste one more second of her life waiting to be sure.

She couldn't be more sure of anything.

Pulling his head back to hers, she whispered as she kissed him, "How about this weekend?"

ACKNOWLEDGMENTS

NOT THAT ANY BOOK IS EASY TO WRITE, BUT THIS ONE WAS especially difficult. Loads of secrets and scandals and different people knowing different things all at the same time. It makes a writer crazy. At least, it made me crazy. But even with all the juicy secrets I was putting in the book, I knew something was missing, and I couldn't quite put my finger on what it was. Until someone else pointed it out to me.

Huge thanks go out to the ever-wonderful Cherry Adair, for both her amazing plotting workshop and for her selfless giving, taking the time to provide one-on-one chats with each participant afterward. While working with Cherry, and explaining to her that my books tend to take on a soap-opera-like drama, she got a fun gleam in her eye and suggested the final piece of the puzzle. That Annabelle Weathers had *not*, in fact, died as Cat (and I) had always believed. She was very much alive, and she simply *had* to show up in this book!

I loved it, and I immediately knew that I could finally finish this book.

Annabelle came to life on the page for me, and something tells me that a few years down the road she just might get her own book. I love her that much. And that would all be thanks to the wonderful and talented Cherry Adair.

ABOUT THE AUTHOR

As a child, Kim Law cultivated a love for chocolate, anything purple, and creative writing. She penned her debut work, "The Gigantic Talking Raisin," in the sixth grade and got hooked on the delights of creating stories. Before settling into the writing life, however, she earned a college degree in mathematics, then worked as a computer programmer while raising her son. Now she's pursuing her lifelong dream of writing romance novels—none of which include talking raisins. She has won the Romance Writers of America's Golden Heart Award, has been a finalist for the prestigious RWA RITA Award, and has served in many volunteer positions for her local RWA chapter. A native of Kentucky, she lives with her husband and an assortment of animals in Middle Tennessee.